When
　　Alice
　　　　Lay
　　　　　Down
　　　　　　With
　　　　　　　Peter

MARGARET SWEATMAN

WHEN
ALICE
LAY
A NOVEL
DOWN
WITH
PETER

ALFRED A. KNOPF CANADA

An excerpt from this novel, in slightly altered form, has
been published in *Fresh Tracks: Writing the Western Landscape,* ed.
Pamela Banting (Victoria, B.C.: Polestar, 1998).

National Library of Canada Cataloguing in Publication Data

Sweatman, Margaret
When Alice lay down with Peter

ISBN 0-676-97315-9

I. Title.

PS8587.W36W43 2001   C813.'54   C2001-930581-8
PR9199.3.S93W43 2001

First Edition

www.randomhouse.ca

Text design: CS Richardson

Printed and bound in the United States of America

10 9 8 7 6 5 4 3 2 1

The wolf also shall dwell with the lamb, and the leopard shall lie down with the kid; and the calf and the young lion and the fatling together; and a little child shall lead them.

And the cow and the bear shall feed; their young ones shall lie down together; and the lion shall eat straw like the ox.

They shall not hurt nor destroy in all my holy mountain; for the earth shall be full of the knowledge of the Lord, as the waters cover the sea.

—Isaiah 11:6-7, 9

THIS IS A WORK OF FICTION based on the history of St. Norbert, in Manitoba. Though it draws on historical research, the storyteller, Blondie McCormack, and her family are born of the imagination, and of the landscape, an oxbow in the Red River.

The story begins with what is called the Métis resistance, in 1869–1870, in the largely rural area of St. Norbert, in the province of Manitoba, Canada, on the beautiful land where my family and I lived until our yard finally floated away with the Red River floods in the 1990s. The Métis were reacting to the powerful influx of Protestant white settlers, to the loss of their language rights and the ownership of their land. Their leader, Louis Riel, still provokes either passionate loyalty or bitterness in many Canadians. Some people argue that he was mad, or a liquor trader. I think those versions of Riel are highly implausible, though he did have a visionary temperament, much out of vogue. At any rate, Riel was held responsible for the death of the Orangeman Thomas Scott, who was shot by a firing squad in 1870, so they hanged him and later called him a founding father of Manitoba. Manitobans have a history of electing the same people we put in jail.

This book is written in loving memory of a particular piece of land by the Red River.

And it is dedicated to my daughters, Bailey and Hillery, and to Glenn Buhr.

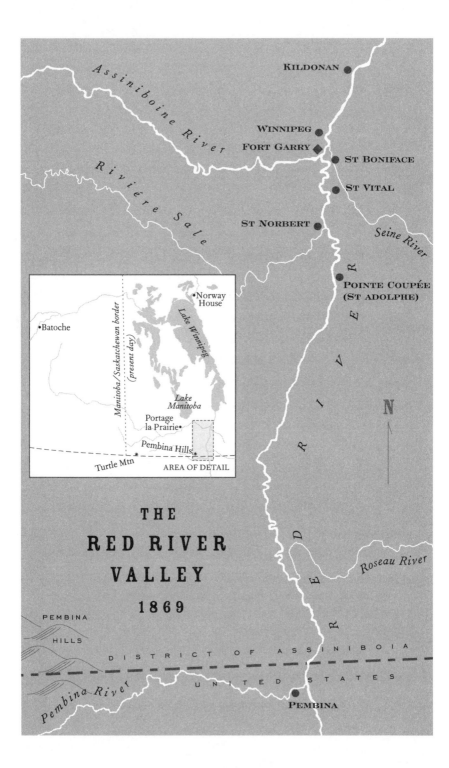

KILDONAN

WINNIPEG
FORT GARRY
ST BONIFACE

ST VITAL

ST NORBERT

POINTE COUPÉE
(ST ADOLPHE)

Assiniboine River

Rivière Sale

Seine River

Batoche

Norway
House

Lake Winnipeg

Manitoba/Saskatchewan border
(present day)

*Lake
Manitoba*

Portage
la Prairie

Pembina Hills

Turtle Mtn

AREA OF DETAIL

**THE
RED RIVER
VALLEY
1869**

N

R I V E R

R E D   R I V E R

Roseau River

PEMBINA

HILLS

D I S T R I C T   O F   A S S I N I B O I A

U N I T E D   S T A T E S

Pembina River

PEMBINA

I'M DIPPING MY PEN into the Red River, always at the same spot, and like they say, all the time into a different river. I have hauled this story out of the fish-smelling muck of the Red, where the willows have fallen, twisted from the spring flood. On the river-bank, thistle pricks your legs and wild cucumber pops underfoot and it all smells like cooked mud.

Right here, there was a fence of willow posts and chicken wire but it fell down thirty-five years ago, and even then I was too damn old to fix it, so the crazy cucumber grew over it. It's too early and too dry for mosquitoes. The only sound is the highway in the distance, and the cooing of the mourning doves.

The heat smells of cut grass, damp clumps of it, an extreme green. It's the end of May. The honeysuckle, cherry, crabapple and plum blossoms are full of bees, like pink-and-white hives in the sun. The scene is entirely benign. No dog on a chain, no malice in the shade, no fear and no ache in your veins. From this lucid perspective, you see me. I am laid out beside my vegetable garden.

When I was seventy-two, I grew a watermelon the size of a tractor tire. You wouldn't think a garden could sense the age of its gardener, but now everything grows stunted, even the carrots, spindly as a baby's finger. Beside me on the grass are a green plastic watering can, leaking its rainwater into my ear, and my hoe, which I must have struck when I fell because there appears to be a small cut on my forehead just beneath my curls. I am wearing my Adidas, the only sensible shoes since moccasins, with knee-high stockings, my old kilt and blouse, and a blue cardigan sweater. My hat is lying upturned in the grass.

I didn't put on a brassiere this morning. I was simply going to do the corn rows before breakfast. I couldn't predict that I'd be seen by anybody outside the family. Since Eli passed on, I have relished my solitude. So it was that I put on yesterday's skirt and blouse, and in the innocence of routine, I went to the garden with my hoe. Softened and kneaded by the loving hands of morning, I did up only the three pearl buttons between my collarbone and my wishbone. I was play-acting, pretending I was young. To my delight, I felt a flush of sexual desire, tender as rain.

I am not a big-chested woman, especially now, of course. My arms sag and my armpits have jowls. The buttons tore off when I fell, and so it is that you see an old woman's breasts, which are like very overripe peaches. I have always had lovely breasts, small as they are. And that devil's kiss, my birthmark, brown as an acorn, at the cusp of rib and breast. It is certainly provocative in its own way. And if you stretch the word a million miles, sexy. Though I am old. I am 109 years of age, since the twelfth of this month. Born on a hot day in 1870. I would have to admit, I am ancient. And today, which happens to be a Tuesday, I am dead as a stick.

PART ONE

1869

CHAPTER ONE

THESE ARE MY BEGINNINGS.

Imagine heat. In the coupled loins of Alice (wearing wool pants and a heavy flannel shirt and, strangest of all, leather chaps, for he'd taken her while they chased a herd of thirsty cattle east from Turtle Mountain to the Pembina hills) and her skinny, ardent husband, Peter. Hot as liquor, the juice that made me, on the night of August's showering meteors in a warm wind sweet with sage. They were alone under cowboy stars beside the embers of a campfire, laughing in their lovemaking. The most successful practical jokers in all the colony. Their britches whispered as leaves in the breeze when they rustled and rubbed together. He thrust inside her and she wrapped her chaps around him and drew her knees up to his shoulders while the seed ran down, itching and hot. A woman in her precarious circumstance must interrupt at all costs and they were careful to spill, laughing. My mum and dad, in God's House of Lords, members of the opposition.

They'd been travelling with a half-dozen men, a sad bunch of Métis buffalo hunters reduced to driving cattle for a retired Hudson's Bay Company officer. It had been a long month for them, feigning manly indifference to each other's earthy scent under the duress of my mother's disguise. It made them hot. And a little silly. And when the men had left them alone that night with instructions to return for the stragglers, a cow and her calf that had been separated from the herd, they both shrugged and spat and threw down their bedrolls, grunting acquiescence.

A lovely night, the stars above. Hunger from a long fast, constant temptation and the arousal, perhaps you know of it, that comes from watching a lover's freedom or solitude, the aphrodisiac of the lover's face averted, the part that leaves you out.

She thought he'd come. Their catechism had reached that stage of exchange where one becomes another, pulse and tide for tide and pulse. Her own juice she mistook for his. She thought he'd spilled; she was safely playing on the shores of pleasure. She was attuned to her rhythms and knew she was ripe. So when she looked above his pounding shoulder and saw the lurid purple of the thunderhead ink the half-moon, cover it, while Dad fought for an end to his need, pounding the walls of his beloved, seeking an end, when she saw the leader stroke of lightning, a brilliant ionized path stark white against the deep purple sky and after a split second another stroke and it was the great intake of breath, dry as rage and bright as a path of quicksilver, she knew, she knew. The next stroke made their hair stand on end, my father's hair longer and scruffier than my mother's theatrical boy's bob. Twenty-five thousand volts.

My father was a compassionate man who would never deliberately inflict his needs upon his beloved wife, but I can't say for certain that he would have had the discipline necessary to stop himself before the fact that magic night. Anyone with the imagination to put themselves in his boots at that moment will forgive him the indiscretion of the fiercest ejaculation by a

white man in the brief history of Rupert's Land. And though my
mother was receptive, the voltage and the heat fired the seed,
knocked her unconscious. She didn't stand a chance. They woke
up fourteen hours later, still coupled, surrounded by hailstones
the size of turtle eggs, black and blue but happy. They smiled
roguishly, knowing, and with muddy fingers combed each
other's sizzled hair. It was two o'clock on the first afternoon of
my life as an embryo. My father withdrew from my mother slowly,
very slowly, flesh welded to flesh, raw.

They would be satisfied for nearly a month. They helped
each other stand and looked out at the trees, the leaves pounded by the hail. The light was white as the inside of an oxygen
tent. They buttoned their trousers. Horses gone. Cow and calf
vanished. They hobbled and sucked hailstones along the old
trail marked by the wooden wheels of Red River carts. They held
hands. They were glad I'd been tipped into the world, off a
thundercloud like a huge tarnished tray, tipped like caviar into
my mother's womb. And scorched there, the seed of a jack pine.
The catalyst, a stroke of lightning.

THEY HAD MET BY ACCIDENT in the stark sun of the Orkney
island of Hoy, where she sat reading and he sat darning his
socks. My mother had been the only female theology student at
the University of Glasgow, establishing what was to become a
family tradition of studying passionately all things extraneous to
survival. Alice had been raised a Wesleyan, and had bred her faith
on a meagre diet of duty and intellect. She'd been preparing for

an examination on the methods of salvation when a sudden sneeze filled her with a need to smell the most northern sea. Telling her astonished family and her sceptical theologians that she was in a struggle with spiritual dryness, she put her books in a carpet bag, promised everyone that she would heal herself and return, and left for Orkney, the most northern place she could then imagine.

My father-to-be was a tenant farmer from Hoy. Sick of mud and poverty, he was yearning to join up with the Hudson's Bay Company and jump aboard a ship headed for the New World. *Sailing west sailing west, to prairie lands sunkissed and blest, the crofter's trail to happiness.* He and Alice sat down beside one another, total strangers, on a hill with a view of the sea. They'd arrived there at the same moment, obviously expecting to be alone, and had hesitated before shyly nodding hello and settling on the warm rock side by each, as if they'd planned it. He reached into his pocket and brought forth a darning needle and a pair of woollen socks, and began to sew. Strangely embarrassed, Alice quickly drew St. Augustine's *Confessions* from her bag and pretended to read. She was wearing a black Methodist gown. Her black-laced boots were spread pigeon-toed, careless and ready. She noticed that he had a freckled complexion, her favourite kind of skin. Then he began to talk in a voice like the wind on the water, his words arriving as if out of nowhere. His Adam's apple floated on his freckled throat. He said there was a land without landlords just across the ocean, a green and verdant place where a man could be free from tyranny, free from history itself. Rivers, he said, long and wild rivers run through the forests, into the great Hudson Bay, in a country where nobody can own you. I'm joining up, he said. The Hudson's Bay

Company can take me there, but then I'm going out on my own and never work for any man, never be owned by anybody, not ever again. Fish, hunt, live free, he said, vigorously stitching his socks.

The effect upon my mother was a heart-stopping reversal of the far and the near. She thought about the university, which had long represented for her the keyhole to freedom, and she saw it as the funnel through which freedom poured itself into obedience. She looked again at the hands of the man beside her. He neither bit his nails nor cut them; they were worn down naturally through the effects of water, wind and soil. She saw a fly walk across his ear, unheeded. She saw the spinning possibilities for adventure, and always the lady, she chose to call it love.

She let St. Augustine fall closed, squeezing the book between her thighs as she leaned towards this stranger and kissed him on his lips, which, she discovered, tasted salty, for the air was full of sea. He kissed her back, respectful and glad, for he considered this a blessing on his voyage rather than any particular attention to his transitory self. Boldly, Alice kissed his raw neck and smelled the grass in his hair, and on the pretense of kissing his hands, she gnawed upon his calluses as if long denied some vital nutrient.

She said, "I have looked for God in all the wrong places."

He replied with a simple and modest declaration of his unworthy nature.

Then he stood, tucked his mended socks and darning needle into his baggy trousers, thanked her for the company, and disappeared over the hill down towards Hoy Sound and the harbour at Stromness.

Alone, Alice saw the perfection of the sunlight on rock, grass, sea. *Perfection.* She studied it all afternoon, until the light grew diffuse, became a green membrane over the world. She gathered herself and stumbled through the dusk to her room at the isolated home of the schoolmaster's widow, got into bed fully dressed and lay awake till dawn. The following morning, she went down to Stromness and searched the harbour and the town. He was nowhere to be found.

ALICE CUT OFF HER HAIR. She put on a pair of trousers and got a job on a boat sailing out of Stromness for York Factory, on the shores of Hudson Bay. She proved useful aboard ship, and arrived with the reputation of a popular young lad capable of work that demanded more finesse than muscle. The chief factor at York Factory was accustomed to boys arriving from Orkney, and he hired her to work on the forty-foot York boats travelling the Hayes River south more than 150 miles from Hudson Bay to the series of lakes midway to Lake Winnipeg, to trade with the Indians who would come north in their canoes laden with furs. Alice worked with all the optimism of a wolf pup on her first hunt, believing she was looking for her underfed crofter. It would be unseemly for a woman to be looking for liberty.

But a year and a half went by, and she knew in her bones that her particular Orkneyman wouldn't be among the industrious Company men loyal to a fur kingdom ruled by London merchants. She began to grow desperate. So when the ice set, early in 1869, Alice quit the Company, pocketed her wages and asked a trader with a dog team if he'd take her on, and in that way she travelled south over frozen lakes to Norway House at the northern tip of Lake Winnipeg, and then south to Lower Fort Garry on the banks of the Red River, almost a thousand miles below Hudson Bay.

Spring thaw. The Red River Colony was a wretched sea of mud. Where was the perfection she had witnessed at Orkney? A vision of sun upon ocean waves breaking perfectly on the rocks, it had fostered her manhood and stirred her desire. She sniffed the air, caught a fresh breeze from the west and hitched a ride with a cart brigade that travelled about seventy-five miles west, over the Pembina hills to the valley where the Métis buffalo hunters would go for the spring hunt, and she slipped into that company and tried to make herself useful.

She found him at last, at the hunters' encampment in the Pembina valley. She saw his freckled throat, leaned in cautiously to sniff his grassy hair, hitched up her pants and suggested they team up. They hunted for buffalo together for a month without Alice making known her true identity. He was greatly relieved, then, to learn she was "the female from the university." He'd been compelled by the slope of her shoulders, her sway-back and double-jointed knees that made him think of a little girl. She was a comely, artless boy with a hoarse voice and brown eyes like a fallow deer. Such was my father's courage and tenderness that even when he thought she was a boy, he'd never let his desire twist itself into hostility. He had been, however, the only one willing to work with her; all the other men had lusted too, and thought there must be something deviant in a lad who could inspire such passion.

They were better than lovers; they were conspirators. When the buffalo hunt failed, they signed up with a crew of Métis hunters driving cattle. There had been only a few buffalo near the Red River valley for several years, but a retired Hudson's Bay Company officer was collecting a herd for private sport, and he hired some Métis, my mother and dad hidden among them, to drive the buffalo over his vast tracts of land along with his domestic cattle. The hunters were tormented by the unnatural curtailment of their instincts. Forced to herd the animals they would traditionally slaughter, thwarted and confined in the New World, they watched with growing consternation the arrival of antipapist anglophiles from the east. True, their outward circumstances had been altered but a little: they still rode horses over unfenced land, had no money, owned nothing and slept on the ground. But the cursorial Métis had lost their true function. They weren't permitted to shoot. Like the old ruminants they herded, the disarmed hunters chewed the cud of rebellion, squinting into the dust stirred up by advancing civilization.

My father was philosophical. Even here, in the brand-new Dominion, he had an overseer in the person of an aristocratic Scot. The retired Hudson's Bay Company officer would arrive with a gaggle of flatulent lords, three servants to a man, and they would bed the occasional Ojibwa, whom they said they found quite frisky if caught young. Buffalo proved better game than partridge or fox. The muzzled Métis hunters herded the buffalo within easy range, and before long, Lord Hardy and Lord Finlayson and Lord Simpson would be sent back to Scotland sated, carrying hairy buffalo heads aboard ship and wearing elegant robes and hats. The New World was certainly wild. Returned from their excursion, they wrote poetry in the vein of William Wordsworth. They had known, in a biblical sense, Nature. And she was sublime.

But for my mother and dad it was truly paradise to work hard and be paid a man's wage, and still—for they were both of an extraordinary intellect and easily bored—enjoy the fact that the expression of their lives was one extended double entendre. They found themselves so amusing that everyone laughed with them, and they developed a reputation as a sort of travelling vaudeville in the camps.

Then, as they say, lightning struck.

CHAPTER TWO

THEY LEFT THE EMPLOY of the retired Company officer.

My dad had long since been depressed over his boss's spec-
ulations in real estate. He felt compromised. Walking gingerly
towards the settlement at the Red, he confided to my mother
that he felt the ground shift beneath them; the black-eyed Susan
and dusty stalks of prairie orchid, the air full of sparrows and
breezes like invisible thumbprints, the bountiful gifts of the
Great Spirit were changing shape as if to hide themselves from
fate. He said he felt like someone witnessing a murder, and the
victim was the land they looked on, there, in the innocent sun.
The Garden of Eden had been sold to Eastern millionaires, and
its beautiful limbs would soon be clothed in pinstripe and
fences. And with tears in his eyes, my father said he was afraid.

Besides, not since the lightning had struck had they seen
hide or hair of their crew of domesticated Métis buffalo hunters.

They walked most of the way over the Pembina hills to the
junction of the Red and the Rivière Sale without seeing a soul.
But for twenty miles of that trek, they hitched a ride in a cart
pulled by an ox.

It was a hot afternoon, and my mother and father had been
walking for two days. They were still pretty tender here and there,
and they walked like a pair of hounds, sniffing at the blossoms of
Great Plains lady's tresses. The air smelled sweetly of skunk, an

aroma they both enjoyed. They told the urgent autobiography of paramours, needing to re-create themselves now, with the lover arrived to heal the story into shapeliness, to make graceful the erratic gestures of a life. Occasionally one of them would drop out of earshot, distracted by the shriek of a falcon, ambling to catch up and beg for a recap, a clarification. "Your mother had a nice singing voice?" "You saw me in a dream?"

My father was terrible for mumbling into the breeze, turning his long, skinny back, his voice nested in the hair of his chest. But my mother, still an earnest Methodist, would tell her life all in a breath, fighting for air, stalling the laughter. She was in the midst of a description of her family back in Glasgow, a long, loving history lasting at least an hour and a half—with her heart pressing her larynx and her eyes blind to the aspen stands and swift fox, her memory so full of the particulars of her lost family that she was hyperventilating—when my dad put his hand over her mouth and pulled her down into a low-lying stand of cattails. An inadequate hiding place, more a starting line if they found they had to dash.

Two Red River carts, noisy as stuck pigs, rolled into view. Two oxen walked peaceably in an atmosphere of panic, seeming to exist in uncanny quiet while the carts shrieked and tin cups rattled in the breeze. They were stacked with gear; a lantern swung, tipping coal oil into a basket of onions and potatoes set upon a serpent's coil of hundred-link chains.

My mother and father hid while the first cart screamed past. In it there appeared to be five soldiers, though their uniforms were filthy and my mother had the impression they'd been lifted from dead bodies, perhaps somewhere in the south, where American soldiers were battling the Blackfoot. But when the second cart rolled by, my mother moaned deeply, an old hunger suddenly recalled. There, seated between a red-haired man with mutton chops and a shining brass sextant, was a woman. Blinded by a sudden and irrational grief for woman-hood, my mother stumbled out to the middle of the trail and stood helpless, her hands forgotten at her sides, her mouth open, a drop of spittle upon her lip. The driver was given no option. The cart came to a halt, dust floating in sunlight and silence thick as honey, out of which recommenced the singing of birds. With her eyes fixed upon the skinny dress-up boy, the woman motioned them to climb aboard and indicated they could settle into the bale of straw.

They rode all afternoon in deafening noise, reluctant to speak above the din. The only words the young woman pronounced were in a language so foreign it sounded counter-clockwise. The driver didn't appear to understand a word she said, and he didn't appear to care, but he nodded affably, saying, "Yep," or "I don't imagine." Three times the woman touched his shirt sleeve, and when the cart stopped she waved to my mother to follow, gathered her numerous skirts and disappeared into the bush. My mum was terribly anxious when this happened the first time. Alice was, you will remember, disguised as a man. But somehow the woman knew. She led my boyish mum into the bush. They were facing each other in green shade alive with the buzzing of mosquitoes. The woman put her hand under her skirts and withdrew a leather-bound volume of the Bible. It was in English. It was unlikely she realized that it was sacred text from which she tore two pages, both from the Song of Songs, and handed one page to my mother. The paper was very fine, high quality. The woman squatted and suddenly her face was lit by a smile, her perfect white teeth and full red lips against a tanned face and blonde hair. She smiled as if the common fact of bladders was a source of amusement infinite and humane. My mother unbuttoned and squatted too. They began to laugh while the fragrant pee ran in golden creeks between their feet, and they walked back to the wagon breathless and happy. The young woman took her seat. She was, once again, solemn as an old photograph and just as gnomic. Thus they resumed their creaking journey.

My mother was a shameless voyeur. All afternoon, she focused her gaze upon the woman, my dad occasionally poking her ribs to make her stop. My mum would look away, embarrassed, but drawn like a dog to a buried bone, she would be back at it before long, fixing to understand how a woman with no English could be seated between a hawk-nosed Loyalist with mutton chops and a shiningly elegant sextant. At last she could not deny her curiosity a minute longer. Shaking off my dad's restraining hand, she crawled up to their seat and crouched there, a kid between two grown-ups. Dad couldn't hear the words she spoke into the man's ear (which was full of curly red hairs, as if the mutton chops grew from that source). Without batting an eye, the fellow pulled a ledger from inside his shirt. Mum crawled back to Dad, clutching her prize.

It was a surveyor's notebook. The land was sketched in pencil, artfully, bulrushes to indicate marshland, and stands of maple, poplar, pencilled as if the words themselves were drawings of trees. He'd traced the meandering of the Assiniboine River, and identified each oxbow, the shifts in vegetation: "Oak, Elm & Ash" on the south side, "Elm, Maple, Willow" to the north, "Principally Poplar & Thick Brush" in the bend. And within the margins his splendid sketches, a pair of mallards, a peregrine falcon, imma-ture/mature, in flight/at rest, a burrowing owl with young (they looked like monkeys, but my mother didn't know that, having never seen a monkey; thus, the young owls resembled young owls). My mother could not have been more moved by the sight of a painting at a museum. It was the first time she'd seen her unkempt new country represented in artistic form.

She tried to share her enthusiasm with Dad. But my father's face was seamed with sorrow and he ran his worn fingers over the grid that lay upon the topography like a net, like a snare. My mother saw the land loved by an artist, but Dad saw the surveyor's scribbles as scars inflicted on his weary freedom. He pointed to the surveyor's remarks and watched my mother's lips move as she read, "Little of the land has been cultivated, though the soil is rich black loam. The people who wander through it know noth-ing of agriculture and will not prove to be desirable landowners. It is my considered opinion that they will never give up their roving habits, unless, perhaps, faced with starvation."

My parents descended for the last time at the first encounter with the Rivière Sale. The men nodded as impassively as a pair of duellists, and then the surveyor squinted at my dad and said, "I don't believe I recall your name."

"The name's Peter McCormack," said Dad. "This here's my wife, Alice."

The surveyor took a look at muddy little Alice and burst out laughing. Alice ignored him and reached longingly to touch the woman's skirts. "Are you *his* wife?" she asked her.

"No! She ain't my wife," said the surveyor. "A bohunk. Belongs to the bohunk on the wagon on ahead some."

The woman shrugged and met my mother's eye, and revealed a reservoir of mirth vast as a decade of rain. As the wagon rolled out of sight, my parents heard the untamed wheezing of a hurdy-gurdy and then the woman's lush voice singing in her mirror-imaged tongue.

THEY REACHED THE RED. Already, my mother was starting to feel the nausea that would plague her through the course of my gestation. She was that kind of woman. Within hours of fertilization. There was for her no gradual acceleration or nuance of trimester. Maybe they hadn't heard of trimesters in those days. Pregnant equalled pregnant. Full stop.

She tried to find a way to express to my father the radical change taking place within her. It was a mixture of joy and deep melancholy. She removed her hat and rubbed her head. She scratched her invisible balls. The freedom granted by her disguise was abruptly precious, now she was fated to lose it. She would never in her future life earn as much as she had earned as a boy. She would never enjoy a woman's labours as she had thrilled to the work offered a scrawny seaman, a novice trapper or an unseasoned cowboy. The silver maples bore yellow seeds whose blades floated down on the early autumn wind. She scooped up a twig of seeds, hurrying to keep up with my dad, and with her nail she peeled seed after seed and put them in her mouth.

She searched her pockets as if looking for words, but found instead a spoon she'd brought from Scotland. It was the first in a collection of spoons she would harbour till her death. A worthless spoon, mostly nickel and crooked from riding in her pants, it was a king's pattern with an obscure family crest upon its stem.

The riverbank sloped like a woman's lap in a green-checkered apron bleached by a dry summer. They walked through cutgrass and blossoming thistle towards the muddy shore. There was a wide clay shoreline of baked, fishy mud, for the water was low. In the fissures between the clay tiles ran red long-legged spiders. They stood holding hands (in my mother's other hand, the spoon like something growing, urgent), looking at the pale waves on the wide river, a broad view of the Red's bend. Sweat formed on my mother's upper lip. Fish smell and smoke. There, only fifty feet away, a bonfire. Tending it, a young Cree. He wore a wool coat in the heat, handsome clothing, a tall hat. He looked at my parents over his shoulder as if they were insectivores, maybe a couple of plovers eating spiders. They heard a screen door slam shut. From a wood shack, across the grassy slope, walked a woman carrying a baby in a papoose. Even from a distance, you could see she was beautiful. She, too, was dressed finely. She, too, threw my parents a brief, diffident glance before joining her partner by the fire.

From her molars, my mother tasted a bilious acid, the flavour of rotten apples. She was throwing up, projectile vomiting, before my father had time to turn around. It was a miracle because she hadn't had any food in four days. Copious amounts. Things she'd never eaten, food not available in the Red River valley in

1869. Oranges and mango, artichokes and lichee nuts. The future cuisine of the Dominion. I say again, my father was the most compassionate man in the history of *Homo sapiens,* and he leaned towards my mother and held his hand to her forehead, supporting her head while she emptied her extrinsic puke. The acid made her voice as high-pitched as a whistle. "I need," she said.

And Dad said, "Anything. Anything at all."

"I need a home," said my mother. And at once the nausea was gone. She stood, clear-headed, wiping her mouth, ecstatic.

Dad was already walking towards the campfire. He had the wisdom to stop halfway and sit down on a storm-fallen tree. My mum joined him. They stared at the water for three hours. The two couples ignored one another all afternoon and into the evening, when a waning moon climbed out of the forest in the south. Then my dad, looking at the old moon, said, "This is good land."

The Cree nodded. The beautiful woman rocked to an unheard song.

"My woman is carrying a child," said my dad.

The Cree gave him a scathing look. It was in bad taste to speak of one's good fortune to a stranger.

"We need a home, see?" Dad persisted. "You've got—what?—I bet you've got 160 acres, am I right?"

No answer.

"We'll pay a dollar an acre," said Dad.

The Cree's head went up. He motioned to the woman, who produced a bag with a beaded string and handed it to him. The Cree opened it, withdrew a piece of paper. "One hundred and sixty dollars," he said. My parents were startled by his voice, startled to hear a French timbre on the syllables.

My mother had the money she'd earned in her two years as a man. She'd kept it in her hat. She handed it to my father who handed it to the Cree who handed it to his beautiful woman. The two men shook hands. Thinking she might enjoy the privileges of manhood for a few more months, my mother also offered the Cree her hand, but he looked at her with gentle ridicule. He said, "Your baby will have a long life." His voice was as soft as hide. Then he removed his hat and filled it with river water and doused the fire, and soon my mother and father were alone in the dusk on 160 acres of bush by the Red.

CHAPTER THREE

MY MOTHER WORSHIPPED WORDS. Spoken, written, words of love, fibs, prayers, sung or shouted—she respected them all—jokes, bragging, any myth involving theft and the names of things that make the world vivid. She learned the local name for every growing thing on her new property. She had an ear for foreign words but hadn't quite got them organized; she learned countless words of Cree and Ojibwa, French and German, but she was not yet tempted to assemble a sentence. Sometimes at the riverside, while she stroked her growing belly and watched the reflection of trees and sky upon the water, Alice would make up songs with words from whatever language came to mind, long melodic phrases strung together like exotic shish kebabs. She sang high-pitched and childishly, and my dad liked to stand in the grass near by and listen.

When the Cree couple had departed, leaving the two incipient parents to celebrate their acquisition, my mother held the title up against the dim moonlight and sang a little song in Finnish, Gaelic, Dutch, with a word or two of the mysterious tongue spoken by the round woman in the cart. Her accent was impeccable. Then she carefully folded the ostensible land title and put it in her hat, where she had once hidden her money. She didn't look at it again.

Anyone who has borne children will know: the embryo will express its character right off the bat. That very night while they

slept (shy to take ownership of the shack just yet, they slept outside, on precisely the spot where I would finally lay down my old
bones and die), I began to declare myself in the form of
exhausting dreams. Tired as my mother was, we had a good time
together, she and I, and she would corroborate, if only she
could, that my presence made her feel beautiful, passionate and
alive. My mother's laughter, those nine months, came from the
place where happiness and a nearly intolerable ache live together.
My father loved her, awestruck and confident because her tenderness for him was utterly trusting and unrestrained.

They bought a plough and a pair of horses, and began to
prove to the surveyor that they could live in the future; they
would take on this agricultural revolution with their bare hands.
My dad adapted to the farmer's life as if he were still chasing
buffalo: urgent, quick-witted and inventive. But though a mild-
mannered man, he kept an iron core of anger in the form of an
interior argument with the mutton-chopped surveyor. It fed his
determination while he fought with tree stumps and blackflies.
He wondered at himself, and hoped his new wife wouldn't catch
him when he talked out loud in the bush, maligning that brass
sextant, the trespass of a pencil over the prairie. My father was
haunted by the vision of red hair crawling out of the surveyor's
ears. But spurred by indignation, they made good progress, and
by early October they had cleared five acres and packed sod
around the shack in preparation for winter. The weather was
turning cold—not all at once, but like a conqueror in paradise
the north wind occupied more and more of the darkening days.

October 11 was my dad's birthday, and they were going to
quit work early and celebrate by heating up the icy river water

for a bath. My mother had made a few friends in the parish of St. Norbert, which at that time was a vast area running about ninety miles south to the American border, though like us, most people homesteaded close to the junction of the Red and the Rivière Sale or ten miles north, where the Red met the Assiniboine River at the village of Winnipeg. There weren't many people anywhere in those days, and Alice was hoping to store up on some companionship before the snow arrived to pen them in. A Ukrainian woman from the adjacent homestead, with whom my mother shared many bewildering "conversations," had given them a rain barrel, and it was this that they would use for a special birthday bath.

They preferred to be naked, even on a chilly day, as a way of celebrating their isolation and as a means of memorizing, without access to paper or pen, my mother's burgeoning physique. Though it was early in my gestation, my mother had a belly like something carved of blue marble, and her breasts were full, pink, warm to touch. So there they were, unimpaired, parading about their fresh-cut homestead, when a broad-shouldered man upon a roan mare appeared out of the blue.

The wind was from the south that day and carried the sound of his approach away from the river. Such was the man's stature, his dignity, his command, that my parents stood surprised but unabashed before him, naked as the day. The stranger was of gentlemanly demeanour and, as they would soon learn, of such a visionary temperament that he looked down at my father and mother each in turn, full into their eyes, and they knew beyond doubt that this great man was looking directly into their souls. He never even realized they were unclothed.

Quickened by the wind, the mare backed away a four-step and he kicked her into a march on the spot, though she drifted sideways and my naked parents followed, unknowing. Mum yearned to touch the red folds of the mare's neck, where sweat clustered the hair, oily and sweet-smelling. He was a handsome man with a wonderful complexion. He looked about their shaggy clearing, the blond sap in the tree stumps, fresh-cut logs stacked beside the shack. He read the age and extent of their homestead in that quick glance. When he again regarded my parents, it was with optimism, the expectation of goodwill. His voice carried easily on the wind. "You have newly come to this place," he announced. "Yet we make you welcome."

"Well, thank you," said my father, holding up his hand. "Peter McCormack."

"I am Louis Riel," said the man. He was looking again at the land, as if that was where he located human rhetoric, in fences and sod shacks. He winced in pain, thinking. "The Canadians have come with their chains, to steal our land from us."

"Well, we paid, you see," Peter began, and drifted off, uncertain. This fellow, so appealing, so obviously in charge. Peter hoped to find himself on his side, which would appear to be in opposition to these *Canadians*. Until that very moment, my parents had entirely forgotten the political aspects of their own desires.

"They do not respect the laws of our tradition," said Louis Riel. "They do not even honour our right to live here peacefully, as we have for so many years. This is our native land."

"Yes, well, see, we're entirely committed—"

Riel turned his brown eyes upon my parents. "You are not Métis. Yet you have sympathy."

"Well, see," said Peter, "we liked the hunt."

"Ah." Riel nodded sadly. "You liked the hunt." Their pact was firm and real. "But we will farm okay too," he added, with that wilful optimism. "*Mais mes amis,* these Canadians, they do not follow the contour of the land with their bizarre maps. It is a madness to place their lines so. Such stupid lines make no way for our cattle to get the water. And the fat size of their claims. One hundred and eighty acres, why? That is too large to farm such. It is of no sense. Very clumsy, these new people."

"One-eighty acres. That's a big parcel." Peter looked guiltily at Alice. "Awful big."

"Why do they?" asked Riel, his boyish perplexity mixed with that brilliant intellect, and my mother and father leaned towards him, my mum's belly pulling her towards the heat of the mare.

"Well, if there's anything we can do—"

"Even now"—Riel nodded gravely—"now, the Canadian emissary is laying the chains of our subjugation."

"Red hair, curly, seems to grow out of his . . ." My father indicated with his hands the source of the surveyor's mutton chops.

Riel nodded, and for a moment the two men shared a mutual revulsion of man, mutton chops, sextant, chains, pencil. Then Riel drew himself up as if to knight my chilly, naked parents. "We invite you to join our struggles, today, this moment," he said.

They followed him. They dressed quickly and followed him. My mother hadn't given up the privileges of trousers, and so it was assumed that Louis Riel had acquired the help of two

more men, one rather effeminate. For it truly was him. The
revolutionary, soon to be the prophet Louis David Riel. And
they would not spend that first winter in the shack upon their
own land. They would find themselves (my mother hiding my
globe-like presence beneath a buffalo robe) in an army. And before
the vernal equinox, they would betray each other. And before my
birth, they would forgive each other. And in that way, my mother
and father brought me into a world of hope, of largesse. An
environment thriving on its differences, on a lovingly nurtured
variety that would expire so gradually I never noticed its dimin-
ishment—not until I was forced to see how small, how uniform,
the world had become, not until I was ancient, reluctant, under
the uncompromising tutelage of hawk-eyed Dianna, the great-
granddaughter of my soldier-mum.

CHAPTER FOUR

SOMETHING WAS HAPPENING TO DAD. Perhaps the cause was too pure, the moment too precipitous. The Hudson's Bay Company was tired of trying to govern that huge territory called Rupert's Land, 1.5 million square miles—the entire drainage system of Hudson Bay—granted by King Charles II back in 1670 to those true lords and proprietors, "the Company of Adventurers of England Trading into Hudson's Bay." Rupert's Land, the Hudson's Bay Company freehold, was 40 per cent of what would eventually become Canada. And in 1869, all that land was sold to an Eastern, Protestant, Anglo-Saxon powerhouse for £300,000. Cash. No one living in the old freehold could guess the future. My dad, Peter, got so nervous he developed a tic in his left eye.

The Hudson's Bay Company and the Crown struck the deal in March. But no one thought to mention it to the twelve thousand people living in the Red River Colony. They read about the sale a month later, in the newspaper.

It's always off-putting to be sold. The folks living south of Winnipeg, the French and the Métis and anyone else who, like my parents, had yearned for freedom, were sick at heart. Their new government, they were informed, would be run by a lieutenant-governor, an Orangeman, William McDougall, and his "appointed" council. But if this *Canada* wanted to buy their land, why couldn't they buy it from the people who were living here? Indian, Métis, French. Is there an original owner of such land? This is what comes from settling down, my dad thought sadly, guiltily, his left eye twitching. You become simultaneously self-righteous and hypocritical. Where did he and Alice belong if not here, on the banks of the Red, the land bought from the Cree? And now bought again from under them by this *thing*, this *Canada*. And there was me to consider, the rubber ball in Alice's belly, growing, making my innocent demands to colonize a raw and beautiful place, St. Norbert, the land he had begun to love.

Early in November, Riel's soldiers, the Committee of Safety, slipped inside the Hudson's Bay Company's stone head-quarters, Fort Garry, what they called the Upper Fort, and took control. And when they controlled Fort Garry, they effectively controlled Rupert's Land. It was a coup. Louis Riel established what he called a provisional government.

The Red River Colony fell into the grips of a standoff: annexationists (largely English-speaking Protestants, some of them more eager to join the United States than Canada) on one side; the Métis, Catholic, French on the other. (The Indians—Saulteaux and Sioux—truly parenthetical, were out in the cold, unimpressed by the Métis coup, which must have struck them as little more than another colonization.)

Alice and Peter preferred the company of "rebels," and were duly assigned to the dormitory called Bachelor's Hall at Upper Fort Garry. At the fort, my dad, finding himself in a gap between governments, in the cleavage of the old fur-trade monopoly and the new Eastern cartel, began cautiously to cheer up. "A provisional government," Peter said, rolling the words on his tongue. "Provisional." The fresh snow rippled around him. So it was at Bachelor's Hall, in the cold stone fort, that my gestation would take place. This was where Alice and Peter would winter, in isolate paranoia, disguise and the grievous error of violence.

It was not easy. They were sentries, my father on day shift, my mother working nights. My mother's disguise forced her to suppress her instinct for cleanliness (they would never take that birthday bath), and in the cold nights, she would climb the bastions of the fort to look south down the Red, where her homestead lay like a sleeping giant, and imagine the rain barrel full of hot river water.

Fort Garry, occupied by Riel's Committee of Safety and comprising voyageurs and buffalo hunters armed with muskets and revolvers and hunting knives, was an opera house of male fellowship, and while the men were generous with their fraternal affections, my mother's condition was leading her inexorably down the path towards maternity, and in the midst of their chivalry, she felt alienated, chippy, small-minded and sad. And the men were just a little offended by this rotund and fastidious man who would not take a bath. For my own part, I feel that my congenital affection for male companionship and my tolerance for all forms of bacteria were fostered in utero.

It must be said: my father fell in love. They were the same age, my dad and Louis Riel, only twenty-five. Dad was impressionable; it was part of his lifelong charm, a curious empathy for endangered species. He loved the smells of wet wool and sweat, the manly, casual scent of Bachelor's Hall. From Riel's provisional government, a consummate state would emerge, alive to the possibilities of—imagine!—the chance for betterment, simply that; a fair shake. In the rebel leader with the comely moustache, my father had found a champion. In the company of Métis soldiers, a feral home. When Riel raised the Métis flag, a fleur-de-lis and a shamrock against a pure white background, my father shouted with joy. Being neither Métis nor French, nor Irish, my exiled Orkney dad at last could pledge allegiance to the flag of impossibilities, of digression on the narrow path to motherland. He was like someone enthralled by Passion music, singing with his optimistic tenor the Passion of St. Riel.

His zeal was chaste. He loved the company of men. He was imaginative. My mother was a man. Step one on the road to revolution. He had uncanny intuition. When he listened to Riel, my dad would stand with his head at an angle, his entire body listening with an intensity that locked his jaw shut, curled his toes inside his boots. He listened like an osprey listens to fish at the bottom of a lake. But like a bird, fish, buffalo, he was overwhelmed by external forms. He forgot that the corpulent night sentry with the crabby mouth was his parturient wife. It slipped his mind.

Winter was a sullen season. In the valley of the Red River, a bitter blanket of snow smothered the settlers' hopes. The future was dark as night, short as day. It was twenty below. Wind blew down from Hudson Bay, snow around the log houses hardened like some terrible parking lot of the future, and the grey sky sucked the light from the miserly sun. Christmas came and New Year's passed. My father slapped Mum once on the back and gave her a bear hug that lifted her from the ground.

Then he laughed and rode away, for he had again become a scout, and he spent his days roving the fields with the other scouts, stopping for a pipe in the windbelt by the Red, warming himself with tea and sugar because booze was forbidden by the pious Riel.

Wrapped in a great white capote, her womb hardened in a sustained contraction, stumbling through the drifts, my mother went out one afternoon to study her own misery. The brittle crust broke underfoot, plunging her up to her thighs in granular snow; the crust cut her flesh, and around her, like dust or nebulae, eddies of snow swirled in the lustreless light. She had never been so lonely. If it wasn't for me, if it wasn't for my thumb-sized feet under her rib cage and our murmuring prenatal dialogue, Mum herself might have turned to dust in the sinus-stinging dryness of that cruel winter of 1870.

She was at the end of her rope. Her nose ran, her tears froze like sleepydust upon her eyelids, and she called my father's name into the mean winter air. She wore a toque over her ears, and snow is a great baffle, so she didn't hear the approach of a man on horseback until she saw the mare's legs, oxblood red against the numb blue snow, and heard the warm breath through the creature's nostrils and looked up past the shaggy head into the ruddy face of Louis Riel. Riel couldn't bear to think that one of his men would indulge in the sin of self-pity, and so he preferred to think that my mother was praying. "Pardon my intrusion upon your spiritual exercise," he said to her. My mother smiled. "If a horse you would find," he said, "a messenger I need."

He sent her ten miles north, to Kildonan. She was to spy on the militant party of Canadian annexationists who were holed

33

up at the old stone fort there. It was said they'd taken a prisoner. She hooked her capote over the saddle horn to hide the fact that she rode sidesaddle, hoping to delay my birth. We were cantering over the frozen river, a foolhardy act but exhilarating for both of us. The horse voiced its breath, lungs drumming, and its body warmed her legs, reminding her of how desperately she needed to be touched, and she hid her face from the wind, so she didn't see the rider overtaking her from the east or the frantic man running towards us. He spread-eagled across the packed drifts and steadied his rifle with his elbows and fired, vaguely in our direction. Our horse went down, starboard side to, but my mother skipped off unhurt and made a beeline for our assailant. She assumed our horse had been shot. She didn't look behind her, or she would have seen the other rider lying bleeding in the snow. She ran towards the rifle; she wanted to warn the man, his bright red Assomption sash indicating that he was one of us, that the Canadians were after him. But the fellow panicked. He figured my mum was one of his captors come to carry him back to jail, and he closed his eyes and fired again. Mum was close enough to see his terrified face. It was poor Parisien, the slow-witted woodcutter. Just as she reached him, there came a flurry of horses carrying ragged, underdressed Canadians. Parisien wept and begged in French for mercy, but they chased him and swung from their horses with great oak clubs like primitive polo mallets, sporty and larking.

Mum stumbled underfoot, and when one of the Canadians jumped down, she grabbed his arm, beseeching him to show mercy, but the fellow (a tall young man with skim-milk skin and a peevish, twisted face) shook my mother off with such strength that she flew back and struck her head against Parisien's rifle. When she became aware of the warm blood between her legs, it produced her first spasm of maternal vigilance. She lay where she fell, afraid to move, horrified by what she witnessed.

"You goddamn son of a bitch," the skinny man wheezed through his nose and upper palate, the words steamed upwards by the heat of his rage. He staggered on the thin soles of leather riding boots like he'd just stepped out of a saloon, wearing a light jacket, and in bare hands whitened with frostbite, he gripped an axe. The back of Parisien's head was flattened by oversleeping and a cowlick sprung up at the top. "You goddamn half-breed fool. You ugly son of a bitch. You depraved idiot, you half-breed Indian Catholic bitch dog. You Pap, you Papist pap pap pop popery." He slowed to take aim. Simple Parisien sat up, licked his finger and tried to calm his cowlick. The skinny Orangeman smirked and swung, and a broad gash opened the skull of Norbert Parisien. "Gotcha, you son of a bitch half-breed!"

Parisien sat still, his eyes drawn upwards, as if to look at the back of his own skull, and his face was transported, tranquil. His assailant stopped for a split second, the freezing air abruptly full of fear. Then, as if to overcome his own fright, the fellow yanked the red Assomption sash from Parisien's waist, tied it to the pommel, fastened the other end about Parisien's neck and, jumping into the saddle, kicked his horse into a trot, dragging the limp bundle over the snow. The sash and the blood from the wound left a watery red stain on the ice. The horse stumbled, confused by the uneven weight it pulled, and my mother lay back and looked up at the blank white sky, feeling the urgency of my coming between her legs, thinking of our mutual blood, how it would melt with spring and confirm for the river its English name.

CHAPTER FIVE

HUGH SUTHERLAND WAS DEAD.

He had been on a mission from his father to deliver a message to the Canadians at the other fort when he'd overtaken my mother, his horse racing behind her, over the waves of snow upon the river. Shot in the chest by Norbert Parisien the woodcutter. Parisien would stubbornly manage to stay alive for another few weeks.

It knocked the wind out of the Canadians. They wanted to go home, back to the Protestant town of Portage la Prairie, sixty miles to the west, a long walk in the middle of February. They were worn out. For nearly a month they'd eaten nothing but bacon and bannock, and the skinny Orangeman would not eat bannock; he said it would cause him to speak French gibberish, and then he laughed with his mouth full of raw smoked fat, emitting an odour of wood and whisky and the first sulphurous indications of dysentery. His name was Thomas Scott. He was afraid of nearly everything, but mostly he was afraid of courage, so he called everybody a coward and became addicted to alcohol and rage. He hated Louis Riel like he'd hate a successful and neglectful father. Métis, Catholic, sober, solitary, authoritative, worthy of a frightened man's hatred.

And my mother hated Thomas Scott. She was a virgin to such ardour. He was her first true hate. The incident with

Parisien the woodcutter had changed her in ways at once subtle and profound. Scott's sneer had diminished the world she loved; his twisted smile as he struck Parisien with the axe had eviscerated her faith in human goodness. She wanted him flayed. Her introduction to evil had occurred at the moment of her initiation into the guardian role of motherhood. She'd been bleeding a little each day, a frightening secret she kept to herself. In her loneliness and anxiety, with an anger against my father that she dared not acknowledge (thinking such petulance would make her a lesser man), Mum configured Thomas Scott as the source of evil and danger to her unborn, and with logic understandable only to a pregnant, slighted woman disguised as a soldier in a drafty fort, she wanted to kill Thomas Scott and remove him from an otherwise blameless world.

She found him, sneering, in the line of cold and hungry men stumbling home to Portage la Prairie as the winter dusk froze the gristle at the end of a bitterly cold afternoon. She spotted him in a ragged line of forty-eight men, dragging their Canadian tails across the white windy plain beyond the fort. My mother was on guard duty. She hollered and leaped on her horse and raced right up to that band of miserable federalists. She stuck her rifle under his chin, and she might have fired then and there but for the voice of Ambroise Lepine calling her back to line. One of the Canadians, old Mr. Pocha, asked what the Métis wanted of them. Ambroise Lepine removed his beaver hat and answered, "Louis Riel asks you to come inside."

The men looked longingly at the smoke rising from the chimneys, the huddled warmth. Ambroise Lepine smiled. "You are in time for dinner," he said. It was magical: the bloom of

camaraderie, the delicacy with which the Métis demanded sur-
render, the graciousness with which the Canadians accepted
defeat. Thomas Scott said, "You're bloody cowards, the whole
lot of you, you shit-for-brains, priest-buggering . . ." And so
the prisoners went in to dine.

My mother followed, a vulture in a flock of good-natured
prairie chicken.

How she longed for Scott's death. When the dysentery got
worse, it was her job to take the man from his cell to the outhouse. It was constant. She was always a little late, and he cursed her
for being a coward when the smell would bring bile to her mouth,
her eyes stinging and the other prisoners regarding her with
compassion, glad to be relieved of his company, if only for the
little while Scott sat on the latrine drawing analogies between
what passed through the swamp of his intestines and Mum's
forebears. She wanted to hurt him badly. She had never in her
life raised a hand against a single soul. Swallowing vomit, holding her breath till I thought I too would expire, she dreamed she
would gouge out his liver. She prayed that he would expel every
organ in his rangy body—intestines, gut, heart, eyeballs—
through the vacuum of his filthy sphincter. Please, God, prayed
my mother while the nausea turned my home into a bilge, take
not only his excrement but the whole man. Lord, take him
inside out through his vile bum.

At last the Métis council could stand him no longer.
Everyone, my father and mother included, sat in the gallery of
the council chamber watching the court martial. One man after
another testified under oath: Thomas Scott had threatened to
assassinate *le président* Riel; he'd attacked a guard; he'd struck

down simple Parisien; he was a murderous rebel, a stinking threat to our provisional government. My mother ignored her husband, who sat beside her judiciously smoking his pipe. Mum was blinkered, harnessed to her new hate. Then Riel stood and asked the tribunal to show mercy to the prisoner.

Scott didn't understand French. He had a hangover, a miracle in a dry fort. His tongue was a dead fish in his mouth. The shaggy tribunal was an unreal joke, and he was a martyr in a land of barbarians. He sneered. My mother stood with my father's restraining hand upon her arm. Without looking at him, she took Dad's pipe and smoked it herself. Janvier Ritchot moved to invoke the death sentence. My mother bit down on Dad's pipe. The tribunal voted four to two in favour of Scott's death. My mother cried, "Praise God!" Scott looked from her to Riel, and Riel, who had no vote, spoke gently in English from a great distance. "You will face a firing squad tomorrow at noon."

My mother looked down at my dad, pipe in teeth. "I will be among his executioners," she said, exalted. Dad could only look. She had won greater liberty than either had imagined. The pregnancy had lengthened her face and coarsened the cartilage of her nostrils, deepened the trough running from nose to lips, caused the peach fuzz there to darken. She left my father sitting in the empty council chamber.

She took guard duty that night, and watched the foolish parade of petitioners come and go. She knew that grace is not granted retrospectively. She was a raven at the door. If she could, she would have knit black wool. We sat, she and I, and watched the condemned man. We watched him without pity. We were very strong.

Without sleep, she ate her noon meal and went with the firing squad to the snowy yard. There were six of them, squinting into the low winter sun. Scott was led out, a white scarf about his eyes. The smell of snow, creamy light behind his blindfold, the impatient breathing of his executioners. His legs gave way and the minister helped haul him forward and then let him fall to his knees. His hands, secured behind him, hung limp at the end of a ridge of spine, and as was always the way with him, he was underdressed. My mother's ears were full of ocean. She raised her rifle. She moved smoothly. She had almost reached her destination. From the corner of her eye, she saw a white handkerchief fall. She fired into the sobbing chest of Thomas Scott.

Maybe she missed. Six shots had been fired, and there was a lot of blood. Scott curled on his right side, and a moan, deeply uttered, of no voice, of all voices, reached my mother like repentance, like eternal purgatory. With an everlasting groan, he tried to rise to his knees. Someone stepped forward and put a revolver to Scott's head.

She went to a corner of the yard to wait for Dad. The burden of her guilt was a fat gout she would ask him to heal. She sat cross-legged on the cold ground, expecting him, her chest in a vise. Her heart had run away. And I curled comatose, as if I too had abandoned her. She stayed there all afternoon, into the night, when she felt an atavistic care for her unborn and took herself to bed. She lay awake till the fort woke up and lit the morning fires, and she carried out her duties the next day, crouched inside herself, unable to come out. Still my father didn't approach. She saw his back as he walked out with other sentries. She heard he was sent to St. Boniface. It wasn't known when he would return.

It was a week or more. I hadn't moved and even the bleeding had stopped and she thought I would be stillborn. The sound of Thomas Scott's agony filled the cavern of her soul. Her own life was bankrupt. She hadn't known that Scott would carry within himself the song of all voices, an unfathomable chorus of human voices, beyond justice, beyond blame.

She had killed a man. She had killed a man. She had killed a man. The breath entered her lungs while she chanted, "I have killed a man." It was her liturgy. A folk song. Slowly she unfolded and lifted her head and breathed deeply. I took my cue and shifted in my dark cradle. And my mum looked out with gentle eyes, with her newly won compassion, on the catastrophe of human nature. The limestone of the walls of the fort was made of pressed bones, the colour of ash. An entire wall of bones, of forms extinct, remembered in stone. How beautiful it was in the winter sun.

CHAPTER SIX

CROCUSES LITTERED THE YELLOW GRASS like painted eggs. Everyone had grown dependent on the emptiness of winter when spring intruded on their spare rhythms, restless as a traveller come home.

Alice and Peter came to the land by the Red, late one night, early April. In the pitch black, they threw buffalo robes upon a bit of high ground, the hides soaking up the icy mud beneath them. For the first time in months, they approached each other male to female, and maybe my father was shy to find himself sleeping with the mountains and valleys of a woman in the dark.

My mother awoke first and propped herself up, chilling the space between her bare chest and Dad's. She thought she heard someone breathing. It was the great lungs of the river, breathing like a god on the run. The lid of ice had broken overnight. Field snow from the Dakotas was pouring into the northern delta. It flooded the willow banks and rose up beside them, rushing by. She watched an ice floe smash into the full-grown elm below them, clipping it like the stalk of a sunflower, the tree crashing against the brush, and before Peter had woken up, the current had clawed the elm into its ragged passage. My father awoke and saw and heard and gathered the bedding and carried her up to higher ground all in one motion.

Their shack was washed away to Lord Selkirk's stunted farms up north. But they were lucky. The weather stayed dry, crisply clear. The river rose another four feet and then stopped. For weeks it was a stranger, stopping just short of real violence, racing through the willow paths. My parents listened to it breaking the branches, gnawing at the banks, while around them the cleared land lay mute, white grass at dawn, warming to a muddy gold. My father dreamed that the seasons would relent and make this the last winter the earth would ever endure.

My mother loved the flood. She couldn't fence in her gratitude. She shucked off her fat man's trousers for a full bright red cotton dress and a thousand knitted shawls. "Glory," my mother said. "God praise the motion of melted ice. Glory for fingers of heat, and a man's body to nest me. Lord, grant me fast, awesome events, and oh please Lord, protect me from tiny things and boredom."

She'd grown accustomed to crude amniotic energy, and she spent her mornings seated on the stinking buffalo robes in a heathen's communion with the Red. With her innate genius for polyglossia, she was speaking to the fast, mucky river-flow and it was teaching her the terrible imperatives of water, flood, birth. She went into a trance, breathing so slowly that Dad wondered if she'd died, though he didn't disturb her, so mesmerizing was her sympathy for the fearsome meters, its deep, fast currents and an intermittent piccolo or childish sirens, and the icebergs like tiles torn off the Coliseum.

They learned their lesson well. They built the second house high behind the crescent of wood that made a natural dike. The new house was made of logs plastered with clay, a nice little place with a kitchen. Later, when Prime Minister Sir John A. Macdonald realized that the "impulsive Half-breeds" would need to be "kept down by a strong hand until they are swamped by the influx of settlers"—that is, Protestant Anglo settlers—and allowed the right kind of settlers to stake vacant land wherever they found it, Dad put up sheds and fences and a stable. If you didn't build a lot of "improvements" on your land, you couldn't prove you owned it— weird and probably illegal manoeuvrings, but effective because no Métis hunter would have the time or the money to build that kind of thing. So while all around us Métis and half-breeds were being kicked off their land, my dad was busy putting up fences and sheds. And a barn, because even though he was nestling into the farming parish of St. Norbert, he would always be more nat- urally a buffalo hunter than a farmer, and while he rarely kept many cows, he at one time boasted six horses. The fire has long since taken all that away, but the high wooded riverbank lasted for years, and many springs we crouched behind it.

My father never did tell my mother his fears: how he didn't really believe things would ever grow back, how the execution of Thomas Scott had changed the world. He didn't want to hurt her feelings. He had forgiven her. He knew she was guilt-stricken; that was enough punishment for anybody. But the deaths he'd known were healthy, as full of vitality as procreation. He'd seen many friends die—on the hunt, in the neighbourhood—and while he wept for the dead, somewhere in sorrow there slept the sugar and starch for new growth, a hibernation underground, for life gnarled in the roots.

But such was not the case in the death of Thomas Scott.

THE FINAL MONTH OF MY GESTATION was spent in meditation, a dance, a joke and unreasonable hope. They stopped talking out loud, my mum and dad. They built the house and tilled a tiny garden. An animal-quiet hummed between them, a dumb contentment. *Le président* had announced the return of civil rule. Near our homestead, the great barricade was dismantled, and Peter joined the men for several blissful days of camaraderie while they tore down the obstacles to peace. Their Métis comrades-in-arms were astonished to learn that Alice was a woman, and they were delighted by the ruse (though they might have looked at her funny, this woman who had insisted upon executing Thomas Scott). The geese had returned, proud and plump and yelling, and on Sunday mornings the great bells at the St. Norbert Convent clamoured for miles and miles down the river, rising through warm, blue air.

Everything was new. Mail moved freely and uncensored. There was a general amnesty. Amnesty for geese, for gardens, for the Métis; amnesty for husbands who enjoy the company of other men; amnesty for remorseful wives who do not care to speak. A dawning happiness. Amnesty for Catholics; the promise of grace, even unto the Catholic Métis, even unto the rebel, the too eloquent, too charismatic, too bold Louis Riel. Lengthening days ripe with time for planting, time to plan for my arrival, time to make a province out of squatters' territory. And it shall (on orders from Ottawa) be called Manitoba, and hereafter no one will remember whether it was, in the language of the Assiniboine, "the lake of the prairies," or if it was Cree, "the god who speaks." So they'll say it in English, call it real estate and swear it has always been so.

She went into labour like a jackrabbit, so fast they were stunned. Even her Ukrainian neighbour and best friend, round as a fresh loaf, who had borne nine children, told my dazed, sweating, rapturous dad (a blistering hot day in May, mosquitoes had hatched the night before in a cyclonic night storm in a heat wave, fast baby mosquitoes, but my father liked mosquito bites, he liked to slide his hand down the back of his shirt for a good scratch, and his own nicely muscled back kept the heat of the day in it like soil and over new harrow trails the rich black mud stayed warm through the short nights), her Ukrainian tongue filling him with happiness and visions of pure water running across a creek bed, and Dad understood more than her information, he read her nuance, that his wife was giving birth within the hour, that his wife was singing an anguished love-chant, and though her voice was as guttural as a pig's, deeper than lowing cattle, his name was embedded in it, the current of her devotion beneath her agony, her birth song, the awful tearing of life into life. Mum squatting, even in hysteria, a zealous anti-colonialist, a pure squatter, gripping red-knuckled the limb of a willow tree, for her friend had prepared a birthing bed at the edge of their clearing, she'd made a great fire over which the river water boiled in a vat like an upturned clarion bell, and she skimmed away the twigs and bark and brewed fresh cedar branches and washed my mother's hot flesh with tepid cedar tea and smoked away the edge of pain till my birthing wasn't painful or sharp but blurred and earnest and Mum committed herself to giving me life, liberty and happiness.

It was the twelfth of May when my mother clutched the willow tree and wailed her birth-chant and Dad's Christian name. Downriver to St. Boniface, Riel listened to the saints singing in clouds full of lightning, and way beyond to the East, where colonies are conceived, ran the great machinery of Canadian territorial claims, playing a trick upon the upstarts of the Red River. Yes, a province was being born, yes, of two languages (and our Ukrainian friend, invaluable midwife, the enchanting linguist lending her persuasion to Mum's ear, *Give over, my beloved, give over to the violent sea, give over to the inevitable death of birth, give over to the new, my round old moon, give away your life for life*). Oh yes, a province, with an elected body of good men and true and even French, united with the landlords in the East, and near by our neighbours looking with some anxiety at pencilled scrawl upon a land title, a fading, incomprehensible claim of ownership for land they'd shaped and carved for two years or for fifteen years or for a generation, and worse for those who had not penetrated the mysteries of the Land Office, those whose names had not been scrawled upon a dog-eared surveyor's field book.

Suddenly my father remembered Mum's hat and the scrip that she'd tucked into the hatband, its tea stains of sweat. With the sound of Mum's thunder in his ears, he left the fireside and the midwife and went into the house. A doubt, sharp as broken glass, had presented itself. He searched the house till he discovered the hat, which had fallen under their bed, and he got down on his knees and withdrew it from amidst the dustballs and sat in a mote-river of

sunlight and took the ostensible land title from her sweat-
band, sniffed it affectionately and opened it with care. It was
not, of course, a deed, a scrip or a title. He already knew.
What Dad unfolded was a charcoal drawing of a buffalo.

Even with a heart of dry ice, my father admired the refinement of the lost Cree's art. He quietly folded it and put it in the
leaves of his favourite book, Henry David Thoreau's *On the
Duty of Civil Disobedience,* and later, when my mother had
regained her strength, he would show her this proof of their
fragile claim to a home, and she would be so thrilled by the
artist's depiction of the lost creature, *Bison bison* (otherwise
the buffalo), she would fight Dad to the ground, holding him
between her knees, pinning him down as if she would plant
them both, and she would say, "Here is our land; let them dig
us under if they want a better claim!"

But they were squatters, and their rights to the land to
which I was at that very moment descending through a narrow,
urgent passage were naught, less than naught, for they'd worked
it for only a few weeks and had less claim to it than the neighbours who had raised the roof on five or six buildings, barns,
sheds, who had cleared roads through bush and tilled their
ever-growing gardens.

And the strange death of Thomas Scott hung in the air like
the as yet unimaginable mustard gas.

⚓

I WAS BREACH. Born so bruised, so swollen, bum first, the first
sight of me a bowel movement, that Mum thought I was a boy

and Dad cheered, "He's well-hung!" and she was a little disappointed, but she rallied when she recognized me, swollen, bulging and blue. In every other aspect, perfect. A daughter. They washed me by the light of the fire, for in the strange ways of birth, seven hours had passed like a divine ellipsis. The three of them, my father, my mother, our midwife, stared at my calm sleep. I wasn't yet human and I slept the sleep of angels, nothing in my soul but sky. They gazed in wonder undiminished by their irrepressible laughter. I am a modest woman, but I say with uncharacteristic pride that without uttering a sound, without thinking a human thought, at the first ass-backwards sight of me, I made people laugh. When the skull became obvious in my later years, seeing the rictus smile under my transparent skin, I would recall my family's laughter in the first moments of my life. My father, my mother, our butter-smelling midwife running their warm, roughened hands all over my new body, exclaiming over the unearthly softness of my skin, the revelation of five toes, my long white fingers, each with long sharp nails (my mother chewed them, owning me however briefly), laughing tearfully over the black hair on my ears (which my mother began to lick away), laughing over my blatant genius when my lips suckled in sleep. My mother lay glowing like a rose window, the thick robes opened and she heedless, naked, innocent while they washed the blood from her thighs, and I slept at my mother's breast, my left hand upon her right breast. My father, leaning on his heels, tugged at his pipe, joy flooding his throat.

So it was that all three of my admirers were witness to the strange occurrence just an hour past my birth.

It began as a dust funnel at the centre of Mum's mind. Birth is an ecstatic, all-consuming, pure line of action on the Euclidean plain far above sea level, where our messy homestead lay. But there is an end, there is an end to ecstasy, an end to flight, and the landing is difficult, the dread deep in the gut when angels become glider planes repaired with tape and clothespins.

Through the visible darkness, a figure rose from the river and walked towards our firelit manger, past it and into the woods. Mum alone saw his passing, saw the white face, his scanty rounder's jacket, his thin-soled boots soaked with icy runoff and his six wounds, five to the scrawny body and one to the side of his face, right ear dangling. But worse, he would not meet her eyes. And the humiliation in the gait of Thomas Scott was beyond endurance. She had not only killed the body; much worse, she'd murdered the pride of the arrogant Orangeman. His broken spirit skunked by.

My father and our midwife saw the pallor on Mum's cheeks and thought she was going to hemorrhage. They hurried to her aid, and in that second, all three looked down to see the ivory spoon of my sternum, suddenly marked. Call it a birthmark an hour after birth, but Thomas Scott's ghost tattooed me, bright red, though it would fade to ochre, then dun, over my many years, become beautiful as pain becomes beautiful when it's past. The brand that appeared on my infant skin so suddenly, like a devil's kiss, marked my mother worse than it marked me. She cried out. And then she passed out. "The ghost of Thomas Scott," she would tell me as soon as I learned that it was words she was speaking, "the ghost of

Thomas Scott has left his mark on you." Running her dry hand over the spot, an unhealable blister, "You've been touched," she would say, "by the death of an Orangeman, a drunken rogue, Thomas Scott."

CHAPTER SEVEN

THERE WAS A BOBCAT in our woods that summer. My mother saw the print of its big soft pads pressed into the gumbo at the river, where it had gone to drink. The nights were loud. I grew dependent on the voices of wood frogs from the marsh behind the forest and wouldn't sleep without their ululating drone, and forever after that sound would slow the pace of my heart and I'd fall into peace as if returned to harmony with my mother's heartbeat. Then our sleep would be broken by the scream of a rabbit when the bobcat got it.

My parents never really named me. The dark newborn's hair had given way to a white cloud of curls floating about my head. So they called me Blondie, a purely descriptive designation, really not a name at all.

My mother carried me in a sling stuffed with clean cotton. Her hair had grown very long, and she wound it into braids that lay like soft ropes around me. When my mother was a man, her driving energy had been situated in her cerebrum, rather like a propeller on the nose of a plane. But returned to womanhood, she decelerated, became as low-pitched as the diesel throb of the frogs, as if she were driven from a source low in her belly. She wore skirts and aprons. The only articles of a man's clothing that she would not relinquish were my father's woollen socks, because they fit with her beaded moccasins, and her hat, rain or shine.

With the moccasins, the papoose-sling, the cotton skirts, the shambling hat, she looked like a Métisse. She had a narrow beak. Her strong Methodist jaw, her muscular upper lip, her big-knuckled hands and long arms were attached to a short, wiry frame.

She was having a bit of trouble relaxing into civilian life. It wasn't very interesting being an ordinary woman in the province of Manitoba. The land was wonderful, but the politics were, quite frankly, ugly and deceitful. Thanks to Riel, Sir John A. had indeed granted us bilingual schools, given us a few seats in the Canadian Parliament, promised treaties to settle the Indians. Everybody got excited at the prospect of being railroaded. He had a genius for economy of scale. He could have been a brilliant ecologist, with his grasp of tautologies, of recycled manure. Every Christmas in our meagre household, as I unpacked my tiny Christmas stocking, I'd have Sir John A. Macdonald on my mind. He would have made a brilliant housewife, the way he could stretch a morsel of liberty, a tidbit of dignity. Sir John A., the Mother of Confederation.

Macdonald packed the hundred square miles surrounding our homestead with all the provincial status we could eat. It got hot in here, steamed up with our new responsibilities, nerved up with the shock of our brand-new identity. And around us like a wine-dark sea lay the vast holdings of the Canadian government, the sable empire of what was still called the North-West Territories. Administered from Ottawa. Hawks and eagles, owls and rabbits, bear and wolf, Cree and Ojibwa. Latent, veiled in royal rhetoric. Real estate. Millions of acres of real estate. Make sure it's Protestant, British and white. And keep it out of the hands of the Americans. The quick old boys in Ontario planned to run it for themselves.

It began to rain. It rained for four days. We went out (my white head protected by a wild rhubarb leaf) to pick the end of the corn, knee-deep in mud. A warm rain and no wind, but hard, hard rain. It began to resemble punishment. My mother had a spacious soul, and she accommodated the ulcer of guilt from Thomas Scott's death sentence. Thomas Scott lived with us, so to speak, in the dark corners, but we still lit the lamps, remained loyal to day's light and love's warmth. We let him stay on, a deranged boarder. We owed him that.

But the rain fell so hard and for so long it seemed unnatural. It was dark inside our little house. My father had gone to Winnipeg two days before. Sir John A. Macdonald had sent Col. Garnet Wolseley and twelve hundred soldiers out here to *save* us from "the Half-breeds." It was a *friendly* expedition, with some British regulars and a whole lot of Orangemen aiming to avenge the death of Brother Thomas Scott. The troops had stormed Lower Fort Garry, hoping to wipe out Riel and his men, but were disappointed to find the front door open and the fort abandoned. A short distance away, Riel stood watching them awhile before he turned to the south and walked into exile (and in exile he would be elected to the House of Commons). It was open season on the Métis. The soldiers set up the Loyal Order of the Orange in Winnipeg, and that grand organization began to rule us all. Inspired by booze, the soldiers beat up Métis men and raped the women. With all the brawling, Dad told Alice she had to stay home with me. My mother was feeling a certain ambivalence towards being a woman.

I had an earache and told her so the only way I could. She paced, patient, singing old Wesleyan hymns that depressed her. But the downpour drowned out her singing and my crying drowned out the downpour and she began to hold my wailing little body just a bit too tight. At last, when she heard me sharply cry out and understood it was from the tiny, secret pinch she'd given my thigh beneath the shawl, she stopped. She put me down. Very carefully, she wrapped me in fresh moss and put me in the sling and covered it all with her old capote. She left my dad a note. She took a bit of dried moose meat, a few cold pancakes and—selfish thing—a small bag of sugar, for she was becoming secretive and liked to wet her finger and suck on sweets. A coal lamp burned over the wash basin. She blew it out. We headed for Winnipeg, a ten-mile walk.

My father hurt like a virgin at an orgy. A weaker idealist would have lived at O'Lone's saloon. But pain never scared Dad. He held the hurt bundle of his idealism like it was a puppy in a blanket. He had visceral humility, a thorough fidelity to being alive, even when it hurt. He felt such gratitude for the privilege of taking part in life's adventure that the tears would bite his eyes and his laughter was a cry with joy in it, and my mother would touch him, struck by awe for the spirit she saw there.

Idealism made him suffer. And his pain, on the raining afternoon my mother tried to walk to town, was an astonishing hot red thing. Dad had been on his way back home, worried about Alice and me, when he first saw Col. Garnet Wolseley trot by wearing bright red trousers and a tunic adorned with loops of gold thread and brass buttons and medals for heroic deeds for the British army in China and India and Crimea. Wolseley's cherry-red gallantry glowed like embers, receding as he rode wetly north, back to the Lower Fort, downriver from Fort Garry, to dinner and a fire. If you followed Colonel Wolseley down the muddy road towards his comfort and his cognac, it would have been a peaceful little scene deserving of our nostalgia for British soldiers come to save the English-speaking pioneers from impulsive half-breeds who had, without provocation, *dyed their hands in the diabolical butchery of the brave, young Orangeman Thomas Scott.* If you were deaf, if you kept your sentimental eyes upon the heroic colonel's blue-blooded slog home to his toddy and his bath.

My father began to hurry home. Just south of the St. Norbert church, in Métis country, the soldiers were hunting for Riel. They had tracked a man they thought might be him right onto our property. Dad could hear the whooping and shouting in the bush quite near our house, and he ran towards the sound with his heart in his mouth. He stumbled into a clearing, and there he found the Métisse; she lay with her face in a puddle. A russet skirt with a pumpkin-coloured apron, torn, had been lifted to expose her bare legs and buttocks. Her long black hair had been pressed into the mud by somebody's boot. Dad gently turned her over, wiped the dirt from her nose and mouth. She stirred.

Everyone was dangerously subdued. A boy of perhaps four years of age sat near by. Dad smoothed the womans skirt over her legs, but he was stopped by a hand with red hair sprouting between the knuckles, and he looked up directly into the hairy ears of the mutton-chopped surveyor. The fellow grinned a grin conspiratorial and obsequious. My father stood, straightening his hat. The child stood, mimicking. The surveyor said, "Looks like you've picked up a stray."

Someone began to giggle. The haggard collection of soldiers were staggering drunk. A fat man laughed so hard he doubled over and then sat down, aiming for a fallen tree trunk, which he missed, and floundered in the mud with a bad fit of hiccups. Mutton chops winked at Dad.

The very drunk have flight patterns like swifts or swallows, abrupt and veering. Suddenly, the fat soldier stopped laughing and spoke to my father with elaborate care. "Are you a murderer?" he asked my dad. All the soldiers fell silent. The speaker rose and, with an injured expression, wiped his trousers. Two hiccups in succession, and then he said, louder, "Are you the one put the bullet to Brother Scott's head?" Through the willows, Dad could see the wide, grey river. The Métis named Goulet had drowned not far from shore, a stone's throw. Both my parents knew Goulet well. He'd been a member of the court martial that had condemned Thomas Scott to death. The soldiers had killed Goulet by throwing rocks at his head while he tried to swim across the river.

The little boy spotted a frog in the grass and began to chase it into the woods. He was only as tall as the milkweed. When he came to a fallen tree, he crept under it and disappeared into the bush. Dad made a move to go after him, but the soldiers cut him off.

My father knew we make the world by looking; we're always making it up. So he wasn't surprised to see my mother emerge from the woods with me in my sling and the boy's hand in hers. He'd conjured her, wife and murderer. Mum was looking refreshed, wearing her capote and her wet hat, and looking for all the world like the boy's aunt.

They saw my father's inspiring glance and turned their attention to us. My mother, always happy to chat with strangers, gave them a winning smile. This was the final insult. These brave men had walked over fifteen hundred miles of bog carrying barrels of salt pork, expecting to free the Anglo pioneers from the rebel breeds, only to find themselves before a cheerful squaw flirting like she was their equal. The most coherent of the drunken soldiers shifted his weight, rubbed his nose with his hand and said, "And who the bloody hell might you be?"

"She is my wife," my father said.

The soldier turned back to my father. "I picked you for a breed soon as I laid eyes on you." Then he squinted, wiping rain from his brow.

"I know who you are." It was mutton chops. He pointed at Dad. "You shot Thomas Scott."

My mother and father looked across the drizzle directly at one another, a mated glance, serious and resolute. My mother's hand calmly stroked my back. Dad yelled, "Run!" In opposite directions. My mother back to the woods, dragging the little boy, while Dad made for the river. "Lynch the bastard!" we heard the soldiers shouting. My mother looked behind and saw that they'd gone after Dad. She stopped, panting. In the quiet woods she crouched to catch her breath, studying the soaked red bark of a spruce and a moth, grey and dusty, closed up. Nobody was coming after her. It felt like hide-and-seek. She could hear the soldiers yelling near the river.

She went to the riverbank. Dad was swimming across. He was a pretty good swimmer. Mum saw this with a sharp pang of love; there really was nothing the man couldn't do. The soldiers threw stones into the water until at last one struck him. He sank, came up once with blood on his scalp, and then went under. My mother called his name. But he didn't reappear. The rain fell so hard it made splashes on the surface.

They turned and circled my mother. No one said anything. Mum bolted, but a soldier pinned her to the ground, surprised to find her so bulky, and I was squashed by his weight. Just then, my earache got terrible, and the soldier, though underfed, was tall and the pressure of his weight made a funnel for rainwater from Mum's hat brim into my ear, and I began a howl that inspired my mother to sing, "Come, let us to the Lord our God with contrite hearts return . . ." The soldier pulled back, my mother bellowed, ". . . and though his arm be strong to smite, 'tis also strong to save." The soldier knew the song; he heard the brogue somewhere in her multicultural repertoire, for though she seldom spoke one dialect in particular, when she was scared the Scot in her came out. He backed off and scrambled to his feet. Mum stood up, holding her song like a gun.

The poor soldiers were perilously close to sobriety (they'd be nearly two days without relief, for the saloons in Winnipeg had been cleaned right out and they'd have to wait till Monday for a wagon from Pembina). Everybody had a hangover. Mum stepped on the soldiers' toes, jiggled me with sharp pats to the backside. "All people that on earth do dwell"—her brogue a tonic of sulphur and molasses—"sing to the Lord with cheerful voice!" The soldiers, headache-shriven, picked themselves out of the mud and began to file by. You'd expect them to drop a penny in her hat. Mum pursued them, holding me before her as if I were a votive candle, bawling, "Him to serve with mirth, his praises forth to tell!"

At the fallen body of the Métisse the men stopped and gave a little bow, and the woman seemed to be waking up, as if their departure were lifting a spell. The sobering soldiers took the same road their brave leader had taken just an hour before. They walked with the indifference of people too ill to care. My mother hummed her hymn and patted my bum nervously, watching them go. Dad was dead. And the Métisse . . . she turned to the woman. A beauty, the mix of French and Cree, dark bony features, older than my mother by about ten years, standing up in pain. There was a matter-of-fact quality to her movements, and my mother, who could not survive my father's death, was swamped by dread. It was raining again. Everything had to move forward, was already on its way to the impossible future.

"Okay," the woman said with the lilt of French. She looked at Mum with tolerant distaste. She shook off my mother's hand. "Don't. I'll be okay." She looked around. "What have you done with the little boy?"

In her mind's eye, my mother saw the grey moth upon the red spruce. "I'm positive," she said. Always stubborn, she reached again for the woman. She hoped to rid herself of awe. She pulled her to the bush. "He's here. Somewhere."

The Métisse said, "Shut up." But she kept my mother's hand in hers. "Listen." It took a minute to hear anything, but then gradually the sound of rain. And the voice of the child near by. "There," he said to a couple of frogs in his pocket. The women were rather shy, watching him. The Métisse touched his hair, lifted her eyebrows when he showed off his catch.

"He's not really mine," she said. "I found him. He got left."

He smiled, self-conscious, coy.

"What is your name?" my mother asked him.

"Eli," he said. He looked out the corner of his eye. My mother felt afraid for him. He seemed to feel he was fibbing about his own name. But the Métisse brushed the hair from his forehead and murmured, "*D'accord.* It's okay. Eli is your name."

HER NAME WAS MARIE. My mother was soon speaking discontinuous words of Cree and French. Despite her own injuries, Marie cared for my mother that night, and she collected a few drops of my mother's pee and let it into my ear and cured the ache, and my mother said it must be an Indian cure, and the woman said, no, not Indian, she'd learned it from Baptists in South Dakota.

Marie had stayed away since the June hunt, travelling south down the Missouri River, farther than she'd ever gone before. Then she'd heard about the trouble with the soldiers and had come home.

"Where is that?" my mother asked.

"Home?" Marie looked out from under the steaming branches they'd cut to form a shelter. She smiled calmly. "I'm home now," she said. "This is our land."

"Yours? This is your land?"

Marie put a rosehip in her mouth. "Ours," she said.

"Oh. Well. Yours." My mother bit her lip. "We have a lot in common."

Marie tipped her head. "No," she said, "not much. But you're going to hang around anyway."

Then my mother did something that she would not have done before shooting Thomas Scott. She said, "I'm not leaving." She flinched when Marie turned to her. But stayed. Wavering. "We could share . . ." But stopped. A look of sardonic pity passed over Marie's face.

My mother needed to fall asleep, and she felt this as an urgency to lie down beside my dad. The rain fell, though it was warm again that night. She asked Marie to watch me and left their little shelter, calling my father's name, her guttural chant. She went down to the river. There was a fire burning on the other shore.

Through waves of rain, she saw his fire burning. She thought, It's too big. Too big and not safe; a fire as big as a house, with wet rocks around it. Like a breast, my mother thought, and she saw him leaning, thoughtfully, my philosophical dad drying himself. Mum wasn't sure he was real. When she called out to him, he didn't respond. It was a windy night. She stood beneath the willow bower, the itchy grass waist-high, and called him. How could he have got such a fire going? He was so familiar, his elbows on his knees, but the image flickered. She watched him till she was sure she'd made him up. And returned to our shelter seized by jealousy against death.

The next morning at dawn, while the rain continued to fall, my mother returned to the shore in a fury. If he was a ghost, then he'd damn well better turn back into a man. In the ordinary morning light, it could be his body or a piece of wood there at Vermette's Point, that land across the river. She waved at him, shouting. Dad woke up, and he stood and removed his hat and waved back. She could see even at this distance that his body was

subdued, as if he'd emigrated, left home for good. He was con-
sistent; each time she whistled and waved, he stood up and waved
his hat at her. And then he put his hat back on his head and sat
down. He stoked the ashes and stayed there all afternoon.

It occurred to my mother that they would need a boat to bring
him across. She conferred with Marie, who brought her brother
from Pointe Coupée, just upriver from St. Norbert. Marie's
brother, the small and handsome François, gazed sagely across the
water. The two men waved their hats politely. Then François
shrugged and looked at my mother. "He looks okay," he said.

"But you have to bring him home," Mum said.

François sighed. "I'll get my cousin's boat," he said. And
went away.

My mother stood on the riverbank, staring longingly at
Peter, who looked back at her, almost like a stranger. François
appeared at last, rowing upstream from around the bend, and
crossed the river. Alice could see Peter kneel down, the two men
conferring, François taking up his oars again and rowing back.
He tied the boat to a willow and climbed up to stand before
Alice. "He asks me to look after you. I say to him okay. Marie
and me, we will look after you for now."

"But," said Alice, "I have to see him. You have to bring
him back."

François picked up Eli and held the boy upside down and
said, "Maybe he need some time to think."

My mother looked across the rainy Red. Her beloved
Orkney, standing on the other shore, strangely calm, and she
knew that François was right. Peter would come back when he
was ready.

He would remain on the other shore for forty days and forty nights.

The rain cleared, and fall graced us with shining, smoky light. My mother became friends with Marie. Mum managed this through a youthfully bland acceptance of Marie's generosity. She couldn't afford to look at it too carefully. Sometimes when she was with Marie, she felt dizzy and afraid, as if she were patting a deer or sailing a big boat, that sense of tricking power with a fragile gesture.

And though I couldn't yet sit up without drooling, I fell in love with Eli.

WHEN WE REALIZED THAT MY DAD, Peter, wasn't going to join us right away, Marie took us to her house near by. We'd never seen this place before on our walks through the land we wanted for our own. The house wasn't visible from the road, and was connected only by deer trails. A squat construction of mudded logs, it was camouflaged against a stand of black spruce, a rare, nearly impossible tree in these parts, though it's common farther north. Inside, the walls were plastered with buffalo hair mixed with clay. The single room smelled of hide, and the sunlight glazed through windows of buffalo-parchment skin. I never cried again, but lay quietly, blinking in the room's albuminous light, cooing in its animal fragrance.

While we waited for Peter, the two women travelled back and forth between the two houses. With the help of Marie's brother, François, and their countless cousins, they stacked wood for winter, and Marie showed my mother where the Seneca grew, the wild licorice and bedstraw. She knew the land, an oxbow surrounded by the Red, inch by inch. Sometimes we slept at Marie's cabin, almost without noticing. Marie must have noticed.

Waiting was a task my mother knew well. She'd waited to go to university where she'd waited for God—an expectation she hadn't quite relinquished on that Orkney coast where she'd met her future husband. She'd packed St. Augustine, along with her

own father's socks, for the long voyage overseas, where she waited
to find him and then waited for the right time to reveal herself.
She didn't need to wait for him to fall in love with her. The wait
at Fort Garry was hard; in fact, had proved beyond her. Shooting
Thomas Scott had given her a new lease on life, and prepared
her for another fifty years of more or less patient waiting. But it
was hard.

Why is a woman's love supposed to be expressed by patience?
Such an unpredictable expression of strength.

And while Peter stayed in the wilderness, he saw change shed-
ding its own skin. The Orkney buffalo hunter who had spent his
youth travelling the surface of life had stopped, homesteaded.

He felt enormous grief for his future. A farmer. How had
this come to be? Concurrent with that was his unease over "our
property," his desire to make our claim to it invincible. Our
false claim. He was still rocked by his loyalty to Riel, by the joy
that had come from the companionship of an army of idealists.
Wolseley's drunken soldiers had mistaken him for a breed. But
Peter knew that he could never truly belong to such company.
And hell, he hated belonging to *anything,* didn't he? Didn't he?
So why was he driven to build so many fences? Why did he find
himself loving this place, if not through a sense of belonging?
The marks of his ownership filled him with pride and a com-
pulsion to do more, to *improve* the land. Was he completely
cracked? Or could it be his having a child now? Was that what
had caused this weird burrowing activity? He was driven by a fate
larger than himself. The fate of paternity. Fatherhood. A truly ter-
rifying concept. He stayed forty days and forty nights on Vermette's

Point, across the Red from his wife and child, because of ambivalence towards his new fate. The torment of ambivalence kept him there.

He saw his significant insignificance bleed into the earth, and at last he grew devoted to its benign reception. A parasite huddled in the earth's rank fur, he nestled into the miniature fact of his own existence. He was nothing, yet he was also crucial to the scheme of things. It was true. And what is true is also false. The world is spinning a yarn. And he was grateful. He aged into permanent youth.

On four separate nights, he dreamed that he was an insect. Not in any extreme empathetic sense; he was also himself. The insect varied. But invariably, he ate himself, popping his own vile body into his mouth. Chewing. The bitter taste, the poisonous secretions. The necessity.

He thought not about rain but about the spaces between the raindrops. His idealism would flourish, but it wouldn't hurt, not quite so much. When the dreary light of compromise lit upon Dad's idealism, it would thereafter rise up, leap elsewhere, quick as a flea.

This is what I know of my father's sojourn in the wilderness.

On the forty-first morning, my mother and I went as usual to wave at Dad. It was nearly the end of October, and the day was dull with coming winter, starved of light. When we arrived at the river's banks, Peter was already there. He waved once and disappeared, and Alice and I turned away, despondent. Alice felt too sad to make the walk home, so we sat down where the willows made a bony hammock. All warmth had slid out of our world, and we were left in the stark, declining day leading inexorably to solstice. An ugly bit of weather. Even the geese early departed.

Then the sound of Peter's shout from upriver, clear enough in the absence of geese and wind and other life. Through the cavity of afternoon, Peter's voice, calling, "*Alice. Alice!*" A hundred yards upstream, a stick man walking on water, yelling for Alice. Then we made out the raft that carried him and the pole he used to push his way. He'd waited until the river fell low enough, and took his chances, gauging where we'd seen the steamboats grasshopper over the shallow parts. Midstream his pole couldn't touch bottom, and then the current was carrying him down the centre of the Red. He wasn't going to make it. As his raft passed by, he dove in, the current carrying him downstream. Alice and I leaned out over the muddy water, and she held on to a wild rose bush, not noticing the thorns in her palm, trying to see if Peter had made it to land. The raft was a bump on the broad brown river. Quiet. Mum called out; the air felt thick as lard. She called a third time. And then Peter answered. "Yo!" he said. Alice looked at my fat face in the papoose and asked me, "Did he say yo?" She scuttled through the brush, protecting me from scratches and branches, in a dead heat, until she reached him at last.

PART TWO

1885

CHAPTER ONE

When they have crowded their country because they had no
room to stay any more at home, it does not give them the right
to come and take the share of all the tribes besides them. . . .

This is the principle. God cannot create a tribe without
locating it. We are not birds. We have to walk on the ground. . . .
—Louis Riel, at his trial in Regina in the summer of 1885

IN THE SUMMER OF MY FIFTEENTH year, my mother went tem-
porarily insane. It was an urgent season, tormented by
grasshoppers, the locusts of doom. The previous fall, my father
had built my new bedroom at the back of the house, and it was
there that I would dispense with my virginity. We'd just had two
bad years with no money anywhere: poor crops, failed gardens,
dissatisfaction on the faces of the grown-ups, hungering want in
the children's eyes. The great boom in Winnipeg would soon be
over and the speculators had migrated west into Saskatchewan.
The buffalo were gone for good and the Indians were dying of
scurvy. Soon, they would hang Riel in Regina and send his adju-
tant general, Gabriel Dumont, into the American circus, and
the great Cree chief Big Bear would be chained up in Stony
Mountain Penitentiary. As I look back on it now, I marvel over
how bad things were, how we can tread water even when it's full
of leeches and toads.

I was a good shot and loved to hunt. It was off-season, so I was just shooting squirrels. The fields of Red Fife wheat were evil with the clatter of the grasshoppers, their weird skeletons sawing and leaping up like the devil's fiddlers. So I took my Winchester into the bush at the north edge of what we liked to call "our property." I was talking to myself, a habit I'd inherited from my dad (whom I now called Peter, and my mum was now Alice to me because I had to discourage them from thinking they could lord over me just because they were old). I still lived at home because I figured Peter and Alice would shrivel up if I went away. They were not exactly deficient, but middle-aged people are unstable and need constant reassurance.

The day Alice went mad the weather was beautiful: not too hot, with a slight breeze. I was having an imaginary conversation with Big Bear. It took the form of an apology. I was in love with the Cree chief; he was my version of a beat poet. I'd seen the photographs of him in the *Free Press* and loved his dusty black suit, his modest felt hat upon shaggy, silvering hair. I'd scanned the articles, threshing the narrow lines of print to seek the seeds of quotation marks, listening for his stubborn, mild-mannered and sundry ways of saying no.

"Big Bear," I said (a squirrel, motionless, upside down), "my parents are idiots who know not what they do. My whole dumb tribe is greedy and blind and we can't see what's beautiful." Because my dad had borrowed money and he looked pinched and anxious and I hated my mother's forgetful face when they were busy building fences and more fences and I wanted Peter to chuck it all for freedom (I mean I wanted him to take a day off). I was never going to be like them, Alice and Peter—predatory, avaricious, foul-smelling, pillow-faced, laughing to themselves in the morning and too damn busy for me.

I took aim.

"Big Bear. You are the bird flying over the land. We are the axe, the saw, the railway, the school, the money, the stupid church, the ugly guy who's a judge; we are the Anglo, the golfer, forgive us, the merchant, the thief in the top hat, that goddam guy who loaned my dad money. Forgive us, Big Bear, because we're scavenging dogs in the land of the Great Spirit. Help us to understand, O great chief in Saskatchewan, for you are the bird, and I guess that makes us the forest."

I squeezed the trigger. Squirrel everywhere.

You are the bird and we the forest. Not too sure what I meant by that, but Big Bear was angelic, proud even in defeat, and the bird and the forest became my litany, quivering with poetic uncertainty, feeding my sullen protest at the supper table. The Canadian soldiers had chased Big Bear and his soldiers through the bush from Battleford and lost him. He doubled back east a ways, to his birthplace near Fort Carlton. And there he surrendered. My alternative rock star, my rock of ages. Charged with treason for protecting his own land. He was going to jail. But then, the Canadians made the whole country a jail. Fences everywhere. The Indians couldn't leave their reserves without somebody counting heads, checking up on them. Just like me, I thought. Just like poor little white me.

I WENT TO MARIE'S LOG HOUSE on my outings almost every day. Marie had gone away with the little boy, Eli, after Wolseley's soldiers had buttoned their trousers, and after she and François and their numerous cousins had helped Alice survive Peter's sojourn in the woods across the river. Marie loaded her things onto her brother's wagon. Alice stood by fretfully, and finally blurted out, "Come home, or back . . . yes, come back whenever you like." Marie and François stopped and looked at Alice, blank-faced. Alice blundered on, "I mean, after all, it's your . . . that is, it's our . . . or I . . ." She stopped. François kindly nodded and resumed his work, avoiding Alice's eyes, but Marie gathered up her tolerance and distaste and gently withered Mum, who looked away in shame.

We lost a lot of Métis after the 1870 troubles. They couldn't stomach the government. They moved west to Saskatchewan and Alberta, or south to Montana and the Dakotas, where they could hunt just a while longer, preserving a migratory life, shepherded by their Catholic priests.

Abandonment enhanced the magic that surrounded the place. There still remained Marie's small knife on the crooked table and a green copper box with a lid, which I liked to remove to sniff at the remains of the dusky Seneca root. On one wall hung a pair of snowshoes with painted frames. There was a mud oven which I never dared light, and a mud floor over a stone foundation. The rafters were lined with skins—buffalo, fox, bear, rabbit. The surprising cluster of black spruce that grew up around the cabin made it humus-coloured and nearly buried the low walls in sprouting roots. In the intervening years, the land seemed to have sunk farther into bog. It was connected to our house by a nearly invisible path, and no one guessed my secret grotto. I was like a philanderer with an apartment.

And so I learned to enjoy the gift of solitude. I talked to myself. I was a soul misunderstood, perched in the pungent dust on the ground of Marie's grotto, speaking thus when I sensed the presence of a foreign creature. A good hunter, I lifted my nose to the wind and went completely still. The shadow of a man fell across the slant of sun through the doorway. And then I heard him breathing. My heart pounded through the tips of my fingers. I leapt up and grabbed my gun and was at the door to see his first blink of consternation. There stood a young man looking at me.

He was ugly in a wonderful kind of way. His hair was brown by default and as erratic as the fur on a feral cat. He had a short back with thick thighs, oversized hands on muscled arms. His eyes were an uncertain mix of green and brown, but clear, clear-sighted. I took special interest in the arms where he'd rolled up his sleeves: muscled flesh on the lower part of the forearms where the skin is soft, with light hair on the upper part, just to the wrists joining to the huge hands wrapped around his rifle, which he cocked across his barrel-sized chest.

"Scare you?" he asked, grinning.

"No," I said. "You should be careful. You'll get yourself shot one day."

"Yes, I guess I will."

I lowered my weapon. I liked him strongly and I thought he should know. I held out my hand. "I'm Blondie."

He laughed, but it was nice. "That's for sure," he said. "That's your name, yep. Blondie. For certain."

"Kind of stupid. My parents did that to me." This was a sore point. My hair grew in dense and difficult blonde curls, and my name only drew people's attention to it.

"They've got eyes in their head anyway. Yes. Blondie."

We stood like that, smiling at each other. Then he said, "I'm Eli."

It shook me. I'd loved Eli the boy all those years; the name was one of my sacred names, like the bird-and-forest song I carried with me. "You're full of goddamn horseshit," I told him.

"I may be full of horseshit, but my name is Eli."

"How old are you?"

"I'm twenty years of age. Give or take."

"Then you're a different Eli because he'd only be about seventeen or so by now. Anyway, you're white."

"Didn't mean to upset you."

"It's okay."

He was looking at Marie's grotto. I was desperate to get him to stay.

"This is where I live," I told him. He was distracted, listening to something, but it wasn't me. "Part of the time anyway. On my own. But I have to look after my mum and dad. Alice and Peter. At their place."

I asked him home. Asked him if he would be hungry and lied my face off all the way there. I did all the cooking, I told him. I broke the horses for Peter and kept the place going. I told him—this was my biggest fabrication—I told him I was a friend of Big Bear's. But after that I shut up, because a shadow rippled across his face and I had an idea he knew something. I was dying to touch him. I made us walk side by each where the path was just wide enough for one. We were laughing and I was lying and it was just a great day. In sight of home, he grabbed my arm to stop me and he kissed me. I moaned from my feet up. We looked close at each other and that was when I saw the green part of his eyes.

But right away, things went straight downhill.

Eli and I arrived at the gate to the road that led to the yard. The place was riddled with fences and gates. Peter thought fences made the land his. A brand on it, his signature. He never lost his anxiety over the false scrip he'd paid for. He was like a sailor who couldn't quite get over the fact that his ship would sail upon so changeable an element as the sea.

I was leading Eli home through the gate. I'd forgotten all about Peter and Alice. I was going to get Eli into the kitchen and then through the door into my bedroom. That was as far as I'd planned. I wanted all his attention. I was an empire for him to discover. He was the luckiest guy alive. My wisdom was as clear and urgent as a broken mirror. I'd teach him everything I knew, the whole package: politics and a real understanding of nature. We'd go live at Marie's cabin, and hunt and roam and never settle. But first I'd get him into my bedroom and show him my copy of *Walden*. He was in for a wonderful time.

And then my mother, Alice, showed up. Seeing her was not just a letdown—it scared me half to death.

Alice had been growing smaller ever since she'd hit forty. Dad told her it became her, and he called her his little boy, which struck me as a bit distasteful. But in a single day in July 1885, Alice seemed to lose thirty pounds and, I swear, at least a foot of height. She intercepted Eli and me at the gate, coming at us from the side and forcing us out of her way. She didn't look up, huddled over as small as a crone. She wore a thin white nightgown, so threadbare you could see the shape of her legs through it, and I thought I could make out the dark hair of her sex through the fabric, something that would make the devil himself cry out. Over her head and shoulders she'd thrown a ragged diaper, for in her grief she imagined herself a virgin on the verge of annunciation. Tears funnelled over the dry lines of her face and I saw that the skin on her throat had come away from its binding, and I thought, Her flesh is abandoning her bones. In her hands, she fumbled with a string of garlic as if it was a rosary. Whenever Alice was over-whelmed, her Methodist guilt gave way to Catholic ecstasy. As she passed, we heard a supplicant's gibberish, a Gregorian mix of many tongues, for by then Alice spoke at least thirteen languages, and at that point in my life, it seemed to me she spoke them all at the same time.

Alice walked the perimeter of "our property" the way a well-trained German shepherd will piss on its own frontiers. She walked so close to the fence her nightgown snagged on its rough wood. My dad, Peter, followed close behind. When he saw us, he winked, as if to say it was just a game. Peter was gristly, permanently fifty, with a quick, porous soul and a nervous system as transparent as the veins of wild vetch, as nimble as a winter-ing finch. He walked near his wife with his hands gliding in the air behind her, and when her idiotic shawl fell, he gently replaced it. I considered my options. I chose to ignore them completely and took Eli's hand to pull him towards the house.

"Who are those people?" he asked.

"Nobody," I said. "Just two people walking."

I got him inside. The sun showed the narrow strips of polished maple in the new floor and lit up the fresh whitewash and the new cupboard with its willow dishes and her collection of spoons, and for the moment I was glad my parents were philistines.

"Are you hungry?" I asked him, steering him through the kitchen.

"Of course," he said, glancing through the new glass windows to see Alice and Peter on their weird tour.

I grabbed a fresh loaf and the honey jar, and gently pushed him through the doorway and onto my iron-post bed.

"Here." I handed the food to him. Then I got down on my knees and shuffled under the bed. I kept my best things under there. I had to show Eli my pictures of Big Bear and Chief Poundmaker with the gorgeous braids like sweetgrass. The best thing I owned was a tusk of what I thought then was an elephant that Peter had dug up when he was clearing land. I got all this stuff out, and Eli sat with the honey pot and bread in his hands, looking at me, and at that moment I knew everything.

He looked at me with clear-eyed humour. He was mine. I quickly shoved all my stuff off the bed and took the food from his hands and lay down. Looking up at Eli, I felt for the first time what it is to be a woman. He looked, really, like a man. Muscled. I could see his nose hairs. He was strong and bushy. Behind him, the sun was striking through the west window to light up the sprouts of green leaves still growing out of the thatched ceiling. Everything around us was sunny and green, and the quilt we'd float upon was sky blue, egg blue, God blue.

But that was not to be the occasion of my virginal divestment.

I'm sure Eli would have lain down with me; even a young man as honourable as he could not have resisted such temptation. But just then, the sun was enveloped by a thin cloud that turned the sky bright ochre and three ravens flew by, their M-shapes becoming for my excitable mother a signal of demonic intervention. It was a good thing. With the approach of evening the mosquitoes were getting terrible, and Dad was prepared to follow her all night. Eli and I heard my mother scream, scared as a rabbit, carnivorous as an owl, one high, wild shriek. We sat bolt upright and could see her through the window, collapsed on the ground sobbing, Dad trying to comfort her, crouched there, both of them weeping. I nearly felt sorry for them then, though they'd spoiled my chances with Eli.

Outside, the air was like the underside of a mushroom, milky pale lavender and musk, the scent of fire from miles away, likely as far as the Pembina hills. The sunset was exaggerated, though at the time I thought it was the effect of love. My mother in her white gown looked like a snow goose shot from the sky. When my dad lifted her in his arms, she went limp as if unconscious, but it was a long sob that had taken the wind from her until, with her lungs nearly collapsed, she gave such a gasp, a mournful, wheezing cry that made me run from her, bawling, embarrassed, as if she'd struck me. Dad followed and hugged me and said, "It's the ghost come back."

"He's never gone," I said, pulling away from him. "Why's she acting up now? The bloody hell with Thomas Scott. The bloody hell with that cow called Mama."

Between us, though the evening was warm, flakes of snow

were falling, catching on my dad's eyelashes. I stuck out my tongue and tasted smoke. It was more than sun burning in the red sky. Yet it felt unreal because we could not hear a fire. The evening birds were sharply singing.

ALICE, AT LAST, RESTED. My resentment of her was a charley horse in the solar plexus where love lives. She was my mother. She had no right to get emotional, not in front of Eli, not even in front of me. I was so embarrassed, I got tight with mother-hate.

Eli cooked supper that night. Odd to remember this now because it was his first introduction to the family, but we were too tied up to thank him for it. The prairie fire to the west was listing up in bright yellow waves with red margins and then the impossible black sky. Quiet, though, and the wind eastwards. It lit the house, and we kept vigil in this throbbing illumination. Alice was a white thing on the couch, Peter and I in chairs beside her, while Eli paced between us and the stove, except when he went to sit in the doorway for a pipe. Every time he did this, I thought he'd go. But he didn't. He stayed.

And then, from the dark corner by the woodbox, there came the sound of a chair scraping over kindling and high-pitched ghostly, triumphant laughter. The corpse of Thomas Scott was corpulent with a diet of victory. He wore new shoes and chewed on a cigar. He laughed so loud he woke up Alice, who pushed herself up on an elbow and looked at him through strands of greasy hair.

"I've just dropped in to say hi," he said.

Alice nodded. "I knew you were coming. It's about the trial in Regina, isn't it. Riel is going to be convicted. I knew it," she said. "I knew it even before I saw the crows."

"Perceptive," he said, cleaning the nails of his right hand with the nails of the left. "And such a nice hostess. It's been—" he searched his empty bottle of a brain for the word—"fun. I feel . . . fed."

"Like fungus, like rot on a young tree, you miserable dead bastard," said my dad.

"Uh-huh. Yeah! Or as the Frenchies say, 'Wyoi! ExactAmAnt!' Tsk. A sym-pathetic man." Thomas Scott stood. His new shoes had already been soaked and curled in rain. He stretched, yawning. "Want to hear what the judge will say to Riel?"

"No!" cried Alice.

But before her protest was spoken, the ghost grew till he was eight feet tall or more (though the ceiling of our house was not more than six), and his spare frame filled out and a great white beard grew on his face with the snow white eyebrows, and the thin jacket of Thomas Scott became a flowing robe of black velvet and his cigar grew long until it was a gold sceptre inlaid with rubies emitting a red light. His voice, which had been reedy, now came from the depths of the hallowed halls of judgment, resounding the words "Louis David Riel! I hereby pass sentence upon you!" And the wall behind his shaggy white head flared as if by fire, and upon it we saw the great stark shadow of a gallows. His terrible voice bellowed at us with the force of a cannon. "You will be taken to the place appointed for your execution, and there be hanged by the neck until you are dead!" The apparition began to evaporate into a smoky dew, floating as transparent as a day moon, but still the voice came, solid and huge and mordant. "May God have mercy on your soul!" it shouted through air that was suddenly saturated with the smell of burnt fat.

It was very hard to get to sleep after that. My mother sat on the couch, pensive, with her hands tucked under her thighs, staring at her toes beneath her nightgown, transfixed but less gloomy than I'd expected, as if chewing the cud of her fresh guilt. It is beyond nature to doubt the word of a ghost. Riel was surely to be hanged for a murder in which she herself had taken part. He hadn't had a vote in that tribunal back in 1870. My father would argue with her, rather tentatively, that Riel had assumed leadership in our so-called rebellion, but Alice knew that Peter too felt uncertain and uneasy. And she knew the power of her own bloodthirst. I saw her heart growing, painfully, to accommodate the new cargo, the prophesizing spirit of Louis Riel.

By the light of the western prairie fire, I put Eli to bed in the stable. I carried a straw tick out for him and tossed it into the loft. He was distracted, standing silent in the yard, looking to the west. I went and stood beside him. "It's just like '79," he said. "When everything burnt up." His face was strained. He looked at me. "They did it on purpose. That was the end of the hunt. The buffalo couldn't come up because everything was on fire."

"Who's 'they'?" I asked. The notion of conspiracy, with its by-product of paranoia, is bred most easily in the minds of adolescents and other rednecks.

But Eli put a name to them, and again I suspected that he knew more than I. "The Americans," he said. "They set fire to the whole border and burned the buffalo back down south."

"Why?"

"It starved the Indians," he said. "Sitting Bull was waiting for the buffalo. They didn't show. And the Indians starved. So they'd take treaty."

"Well," I said, "maybe."

And Eli shrugged. A devastating gesture.

I left him in the yard, looking at the fire. I think in the night he removed himself to Marie's grotto, but of this I can't be sure. I felt a surge of health and wakefulness despite the sombre atmosphere at home, and went often from my room that night to stand at the door looking out. My mother remained, a wax figure upon the couch. Her patient suffering soothed my resentment, relaxed the hate-knot in my belly. A dark, sleepless night walled by the western fire, and my mother glowing with pain and patience. She was no longer an embarrassment. While I swung between her and the inspiring absence of Eli, the charley horse inside me was released, soothed with fresh respect for the size of this diminutive woman. How she could house her torments so generously.

<hr/>

ELI WAS ALWAYS ANCIENT. It was in part a question of style. He was shabby and debonair, vain and disinterested. He was short, but he seemed tall. The most learned person I've ever known. Knowledge clung to him like burrs to a buffalo. But his was the wisdom of an older world, the one burnt out by the American agents who would set fire to an entire border to starve out the Sioux.

It was apparent he was illiterate the first time we spoke. His ear was too good for a literate man, his memory too clear, and he knew many names for things—the name that told its purpose, its local use; the new colonial name; and sometimes the old Native names. Seneca or cattle herb or rattlesnake root. Wild rice, river rice. Big bluestem, turkey foot, muskooseeya.

One afternoon, I was hurrying through the house to fetch something for my mother. We'd been busy outside all morning, building a corral for Dad's three new horses. My arms ached and my hands burned pleasantly from the stone hammer, and I rushed in, distracted and light with the thoughtless pleasures of work, in a hurry to get back outside. Shocked, I saw how still, how graciously abandoned, was our sun-dusted house. Out of place at the centre of the room was a spoon-back chair of bent maple, reddish wood upon the waxy floor, horsehair adrift. Upon this chair were Eli's shambling hat and his gloves, his fingerprints pressed in horse oil, the shape of his hand. I was unnerved by how worn they were, how ragged and how dispossessed. Pale green, faded grass colours, vulnerable and ready. I heard his voice outside, laughing at some joke of my father's. He had inhabited us and let himself be inhabited, which seemed terrible at that moment. Intimacy itself was terrible, and I felt sick. Later, when the day cooled, Eli donned his hat and gloves for the last hour of work before sleep. I watched him put them on, and was relieved that the hat acquired dignity on his shaggy head, his gloves when filled with his big hands gained authority. I was glad to see him walk away that night. Separate from me. Not my responsibility.

He stayed in Marie's cabin. My father was pleased to have some help while Alice recovered (she was simply inclined to be healthy, partly, I think, because she liked herself better that way). We worked all day and told stories through the night. Love, even my erratic love, made the shortest sleep sufficient.

We had a couple of acres of wheat, four acres of oats, half an acre of potatoes and half an acre of peas. If that doesn't sound like much, why don't you go for a long walk in the heat behind a pair of oxen while you push at a plough knee-deep in mud? We'd soaked the wheat in barrels with a fistful of lime before we sowed, so it came up very fine, no smut, no rust, and we hauled water all the way from the river in pails we slung from yokes over our shoulders. It was worth it. We got three and a half dollars a bushel selling it for seed wheat. Add to that two-fifty a bushel for the potatoes and two dollars a bushel for the oats, and we'd do okay. The peas mostly went to the raccoons and birds, but we had a good feed all the same.

I knew we were boarding a stray. Eli wouldn't be around for harvest. But for now, it was green summer. At night, my parents told stories about the hunting days. And you could tell by the way he listened, and sometimes, when they'd pause, he'd finish their sentences, that Eli knew the hunting life, even though he must have been about ten years old when the buffalo, and the life that went with the buffalo, disappeared.

It was a dark night without a moon. Once night settled, the mosquitoes left us in peace. We stoked a big fire down by the river. Kept some new potatoes cooking in embers at the fire's edge. Peter had just delivered a long, boasting tale of a hunt back in '68, when he'd shot fifty buffalo, fourteen of them at one run, over a butte in the Northwest, letting go the reins and lying back on his horse's rump as they fell downhill, straight through the middle of an animal sea. He emptied his cartridges and reloaded without thinking, and only when he stopped at the bottom, with all these buffalo wheezing or dead around him, did he figure out that he'd had to load his rifle while his horse fell down that hill. When he'd stripped them and loaded up the tripe and fat and hides, it took ten carts to carry everything back to Cypress Hills. Could have used a boy to help him. He winked at my mother, speared a potato, blew away the ash and bit gingerly, blowing. "Seventy-eight was the last time I ever saw a good-sized herd. Seemed they dried up in a day."

We sat quietly, listening to the wood burn. Nobody wanted to go inside.

At last Eli spoke. "I made my way here travelling south from Batoche through the Qu'Appelle valley." He stopped and sighed. A little potato burst its skin, and its white flesh crackled in the fire. Eli sat with the weight of his own reluctance heavy upon him.

"I rode through the reserve at Indian Head," he said. "They were starving to death; some of Piapot's band, others. They hung their dead in the trees. That was their way. It was getting dark. They looked like . . ." He rubbed his face. We didn't look at him, in case he couldn't say any more. "They looked like caterpillars or something. And the families—just walking around, you know, real sick. I got down off my horse and went into the camp. This little girl comes up to me, and she takes a hold of my hand and she shows me where to put my horse. A young girl, maybe seven years of age. She takes me to her family's tent and tells me, 'You sleep here.' There was two more kids inside. Everybody else is dead. Her parents, they died, both. I, course, have a few things I give them. But she had a cough. I stay two days and she died.

"She didn't even weigh a feather. I give her to an old man there. He says he's her grandfather. Then I ride directly back up to Batoche and join up with Riel."

My mother, Alice, moaned involuntarily, but she was perfectly still. She didn't look at him; she stared at the fire.

You could see that Eli had left many parts of himself behind. His face was sad, but he laughed a little. "A lot of Indians didn't even like Riel," he said.

Peter said gently, "Riel." He looked uneasily at my mother, who was still struggling painfully with the worry over Riel's upcoming trial. But Alice pursed her lips, poker-faced. Dad almost whispered, "It's music to hear the name."

Eli nodded. "A fellow with pure intentions," he said. "Excitable intentions. But a highly decent man."

"Very highly decent," whispered Dad. "I loved that man. I admit I did, and I do. He's a rare man."

Eli politely ventured, "He might've altered a little since the '69 trouble. His rope frayed somewhat."

My dad hesitated. He'd heard the rumours: a lunatic asylum in Quebec, back in the 1870s. But surely that was just a ruse. Still, it pained my father severely to know that Riel's way, his Catholic . . . yes, his Catholic imagination, all clouds and voices—that way of inventing a future so far from the cowardly discipline of the bankers' Confederation—could be ground down under the heel of this cunning new mercantile world. A vision sneezed up the great Protestant nose of Canada. "He's the last of his kind," Dad said. "The air around here, it doesn't foster poets and such. Not any more."

"Well, perhaps we did the necessary. I guess I'm glad. It's past now anyway." Eli's sadness seemed to float him up and away from the fire.

Alice twitched. "You fought with the Métis?" she asked. "You joined that crew?"

Eli and Alice looked each other in the eye.

"You're him, aren't you?" she said. "You're Marie's little boy."

He barely nodded. "Well, I wasn't," he said. "You know I don't know where I come from. But yes. Marie took me in."

"Where is she?" You could feel Alice sending her own roots down where she sat. Contrarily, she added, "Is she coming home?"

Eli shook his head. "She got the TB. A year ago now she's died."

My parents exchanged a quick, furtive glance. Eli noticed. He smiled, sadly teasing. "I think I brung her with me, however." Impish, charming. "Yes, I believe Marie followed me home and took up residence in the old cabin. She's on the premises, I'm sure she is. Or something's nagging me to eat right and get more sleep." He laughed. We laughed. Nervously. "Beautiful lady," he said. "Terrible nag."

Peter poked a potato, offered it to Alice.

<hr />

ELI DECIDED TO RIDE BACK west to Batoche and then head north to Regina to witness the trial of Riel.

I was heartbroken but Peter was devastated. He expressed an ardent, anguished loyalty to Eli, pretty much love at first sight. For my dad, the great Canadian Confederation marked his initiation into sedentary adulthood, and so it seemed a matter of course. But he saw that Eli had been given one of the most difficult handicaps: the curse of being born into the wrong century. Eli was a hunter. And the New World was a farm.

Eli rode the Carlton Trail to Batoche like a man reading the lines of his own hand. He was never lost, and as a nomad he was always home. Up the steppes of prairie, leaving the basin of the glacial lake where its old shores rise to the Pembina hills, and up, northwest, through the Touchwood hills to Gabriel's Crossing and Batoche. Blues pale and tender, blowing acres of bluestem, hilly as a woman's shoulder blades, and the scent of animal and the oiled-leather creaking of the saddle and Eli's boot in the stirrup and under them, tall prairie, swaying and distant.

With Eli gone, life was a bore. It was harvest. I hated the way daylight exposed things in our yard: the bush, Marie's grotto, my bedroom. Things sat up, matter-of-fact, perhaps useful if one had the strength and purpose to do anything. I worked to defy the flat fact of loneliness.

Alice regained her strength to the point that it seemed quite safe to let her read the newspapers, and we were able to speak the name of Riel while we ate; the name came out a normal size and volume and we could properly pronounce him and we waited for his execution to be stayed.

But I was fifteen. I was connected to the world through sympathetic magic. If I slept on my left side, Riel would hang. If I succumbed to a third piece of my mother's flax bread, Eli would be killed in a fight. Hat on backwards, the moneylenders would cancel Dad's loan. Boots placed right to left—or worse, if one fell over in the night—Riel would hang, Eli would die, Peter would lose the farm. Alice alone was safe from the quick trigger of my influence. Our future was littered with hidden mines.

Fall soured summer. The crop was okay. We persisted. We worked hard. We hired a guy to help out awhile and I loaned him a pillow and he complained later that I'd given him head lice and it took endless washings with Mama's bleach to rid me of the scratching and my hair turned white and dry and stood up frizz-full of static and nobody would touch me because I gave off such a shock, worse if you'd just licked your lips before a goodnight kiss.

It began to snow in October, but not enough to stay on the ground. I wished it would. Without snow, the cold gnawed on the deepest roots, ate light and life till it was all zero. Freezing cold. Sound of our shoes on frozen mud, horses slipping, and I was there just yearning, praying for the bafflement of snow.

It got sunny. Really cold. Waking up to a silver skin of frost, I looked over the edge of my bed and saw my left boot pointing east. And I knew. My prayers and complaints, my appetite for fresh bread, my carelessness with my hat, all had led to this: Riel would hang and the world would lose, lose, and it would mark the beginning of an evil era where the good guys die because they're good and the bad guys win because they're good at being bad.

And Riel did hang. November 16, in the morning. He asked for three eggs and a glass of milk. Then he walked alone onto the scaffold, and they put a noose around his neck and dropped him through the floor of the gallows. And Eli would tell me later (not realizing it was an accusation, and confused when I responded to his story by getting down on my hands and knees and begging forgiveness) that Riel had stood with his head high and tried to calm the frightened priest.

"Courage, Father," Riel had said.

Courage.

CHAPTER TWO

DAD RESPECTED MY FONDNESS for Marie's cabin, though he never went there himself. Whenever he saw me heading in that direction, he got quiet and pious, like somebody coming into church. I never asked him why. He and my mother framed the drawing of the buffalo and hung it over the kitchen table. And they built fences around the fences. "Our property," he called it, spitting. "Our p-property," twitchy and defensive.

"Our property" had begun as a place to lie down, no bigger than the space of a dream. The disbursement of $160 hadn't defined it much. The land they'd supposedly bought was a shadow at the outskirts of firelight, yielding as far as the tall, dead white oak, its bark peeled away; there, where the land lies low and then rises a little, and to the east somewhere, the lightning-struck elm, a great hump of roots that looks like a bear.

When I was born, Peter turned into a wood-gnawing creature. His early patriarchal impulses were suburban. Tools of fatherhood: axe and harrow. He cut down five, ten, fifteen, twenty acres of bush, harnessed horses to their roots and hauled them into great pyres and set fire to them. All day, the slender branches of silver-leafed aspen smoked beneath the flaming roots of elm and oak, slowly smouldering while my dad returned to the house and lifted his blonde infant in his smoky hands to his smoky chest.

They slept with fine black soil in their hair, littering the bedding with grasses and ash; they dreamed thick green dreams of fire and seed.

And Marie hovered over our lives. Her cabin grew out of the strange stand of black spruce on land we wished to be ours. Marie was fixed. She arrived, as soft as the dust on a moth's wing, and left a permanent dye upon our fingertips. She would linger.

And Peter had borrowed money from somewhere.

The moth will stir at the back of the mind.

<hr />

Cher père du Manitoba. Sorry you hung.

THERE NEVER WAS AN AMNESTY, but in the first week of December 1885, it snowed overnight and the next day, a thaw loosened the ground, and then they brought Riel's body to his family land in a wood coffin. The Riel farm was northeast of "our property." Eli was in the party bringing home the discarded saviour, the migrant statesman. A tousled prophet with self-doubting eyes (the photo-reproduced icon on our tourist pamphlets—moustache, chubby cheeks, wavy black hair).

What might've happened if the lawyers for his defence hadn't pinned their case entirely on the question of Riel's sanity? What if they'd said, "He's sane as most of us, just not as foxy. The man's got a point." Of course he was nuts; he wasn't a landlord! Native and Métis land rights? Self-government? The right to edu-cate your children in your own tradition? What was the history that we lost over the lawyers' crummy judgment? Is it ghosting down the Saskatchewan River, rising with the morning dew? How good we are at losing our own glorious options.

The thaw was accompanied by drizzle, all afternoon, making pockmarks on the new snow, so within twenty-four hours winter was shrunken and aged. The fine sleet fell without a sound, hanging in the air, and it didn't smell like rain, but the stink of manure in the barn got strong and the wet gold hay glowed as if you could see its decay.

I went with my parents in the wagon to pay our respects at the Riel farm. I knew Eli would be there. Still, it shocked me to see him sitting at the kitchen table, his legs crossed, messy and dignified and so accomplished in the task of wearing his own skin. It made me miserable with love.

The body was in the parlour, Riel's widow lying on a chaise near by. She was frail with tuberculosis, and overcome with the trauma from the fighting at Batoche and all the years of struggle and exile. Her name was Marguerite. She would be dead by spring. We walked into the wood-warmed house with rain dripping from our chins and noses. The wake had just begun, and it was shapeless in our hands and unrefined. We were outsiders, our grief unreconciled with the community of mourners, and I was envious of their calm distress.

The women cooked, the priest prayed. I sat at the table, in the leaking boat of my self-respect. The room was an ark, the unkosher mix of the women's relentless fixings and the flesh-horror of the muttering priest. Peter stood shy and uneasy at the edge of conversations in French. And my mother, Alice, chameleon, rolled the dough for *de croxegnols* and listened, a brown-eyed boy-hag. To my eyes, she alone in the room could find her way through French and Latin; through the prognostics of cooks planning the next hour of consumption; through the unredemptive politics of the Métis, their slow inventory of loss. The snow-melting rain continued all afternoon.

Eli was included in the conversations of the men. I was given a doll and a five-year-old girl to entertain. She was a dull little thing who wanted to play house. Me, stuck with this dumb kid in ringlets. Humiliated and so bored at one point that my eyes actually rolled back in my head, revealing the vein-riddled eyeball, the only time in my whole life that ever happened to me, weird, and I know it happened only because I awoke sitting upright and looking at this snotty girl's scared face.

"Your eyes just went completely white," she told me, revolted.

"No kidding!" I said.

"You snorted too. You snored. You make me sick!" she said and started to cry, so I took her by the throat (we were beneath a table, the doilies of the tablecloth draped about our ears) and told her that if she didn't shut up, I would chew off her fingers, and I put one in my mouth, tasting pork fat and nearly throwing up. I scratched the feeble veins in her feeble wrist.

It was the longest afternoon in Canadian history. When at last my parents released me, I gasped and said goodbye (my voice had gone high, something of nerves and embarrassment, the contagion of this stupid little girl's voice). Eli turned in his chair and nodded, watching us with that clear-eyed comprehension.

Peter and Alice and I opened the door and stepped out into a changed world.

The earth was washed in a transparent film of amber, four inches of ice beneath which we could see mice run and frogs paddle and the oxblood of dead leaves. Ice coated the trunks of trees, the walls of the barn, and on the big gate, a magpie with a long wicked tail was frozen by its feet to the rail. We walked holding hands. Dad's legs slipped out from under him, and we all fell on top of each other, scrambled to our feet, scuffled along at a snail's pace. Upon the petrified land, snow fell in flakes the size of saucers coasting through the air, and even as we readied the wagon, snow covered the ice and our glimpse of a glass world was lost behind a blanket of white. It was a sticky coating that fell so fast it provided a decent passage for our horses, and so we made our way slowly home.

The wind picked up. Snow clung to the branches, six inches of it on the north side of the trees. Stuck to the hides of the horses, to fences (there were no electrical wires, no telephone wires, only grey-white sky between blue-white branches), eight inches of snow, upside down, defying gravity. My parents pulled up the wagon at the outer gate and stopped, looking at me with snow battening their eyelashes. They just sat there blinking. They looked like baby animals. I blinked back, waiting for them to proceed to the barn so we could shake down the horses.

"You go on in," said Alice. She wore Peter's old beaver hat, piled high with snow, and thick white epaulets of snow lay on their shoulders as they sat batting their white eyelashes like docile guards in the Gulag. I climbed down and stood beside the wagon, looking up. Peter gathered the reins and clicked at the horses, and they rode off, disappearing from view into the hypnosis of a gathering blizzard.

Deafened by white, I stood a minute, feeling the collar of my shirt get soaked. Then I walked to the house and went inside. Calcium light, bone blue. I stood around awhile. Stoked the stove. Sort of hungry. Still hypoglycemic from boredom. God knows where my parents had got to. So I went to bed.

I was looking at *Walden,* eating Mum's earnest bran cookies, wearing Dad's socks, when I thought I heard them come in. Sound of breath, of boots on a wood floor, and I realized it wasn't my parents. I had been curled on my side. Listening, I rolled onto my back, looking up at the thatched ceiling, Vandyke brown, and the vanilla daylight. Eli walked across the kitchen and stood at the door to my room. I turned my head on the pillow to see him. He was staring out the window at the wings of snow. He glanced at me and smiled, then looked back at the window and said, "It looks just like feathers on an owl. Something strange flying by. Strong, you know."

It smelled good with him coming in. I put my hands behind my head and breathed with that shudder of happiness you usually earn only after hard crying. After some time, Eli came over and sat on the bed, leaning over me, brushing the hair from my forehead. His hand felt dry and rough and smelled of horse. I lifted my chin and he put his hand on my cheek, and I rubbed against the rough callus on his palm and thumb. He looked me in the eye and nodded. He unbuttoned his jacket and let it fall on the floor. The quilt was wet. He unbuttoned his shirt and took off the undershirt, a faded red. His chest was thick, covered in hair; it looked like a piece of granite, moon blue with points of pink like feldspar, a chunk of flesh. He unbuttoned his pants and, his eyes on mine, raised himself just enough to pull them off with his long johns. Cold, he lifted the covers to climb in beside me, and I saw his chest and stomach as a wedge upon the narrowing pelvis, slightly misfit so the flesh bulged above the hips and groin, like two bodies stacked upon each other and covered in coarse black, curly hair. I longed to put my tongue against the black hair. His skin was cold and soft, and I especially liked the chill skin on his thick arms. On his elbows, he leaned over me and I breathed in his good sweat, the kind from working, not nerves, his smell, woolish, horse, winter, melted butter. I kissed his shoulder, putting my tongue to his skin.

Eli's face rarely lost its laughter, but a seriousness made me put both hands on his face and down to his shoulders, pulling him and shifting flat beneath him and moving under his hairy legs. I could feel him chilly on the inside of my warm legs where my nightgown rode up. It was way too much. I bent my knees so my dad's socks were at the back of his knees and lifted myself up to him, and he was hard and cold even there, so it was a chilled hard thing that entered me then, and Eli pushed his face against my shoulder and entered me like a man thrusting into a blizzard. I was dry and had never known the walls of myself before and hadn't thought about my interior skin before that moment, so it was my own flesh Eli introduced me to as well as his. I was determined to know more of this and pushed his shoulders hard down on me and my hands ran over his back, which was soft and muscled, and then the privacy of his bum, which I had never before considered either, a wild contradiction of a shape I'd thought only children to own, a twin round bum, and I pulled him up into me. The pain was certainly manageable, nothing

more than a sliver or pain we might impose to heal ourselves,
belonging to the flesh, not inflicted. Then that was gone and I
got drunk on him. Faint with it. Cried out. Bringing my knees
up under his armpits and amazed for the pull in him and how
we could get so far, mixed with him if only I could pull him farther. If I could just make him move in that hungry wall he'd
unearthed inside me and make him touch it. All of a sudden Eli
goes rigid and he's suddenly on his knees on the bed and I'm with
my legs around him breathing with him and I look down and what
was cold and hard is shining like an egg in the nest of damp hair.

Eli put his hands on the bed and moaned. His muscled,
hairy chest folded over his stomach, making waves of flesh with
whorls of hair. I made out the shape of a face on Eli's chest, like
seeing a man on the moon. I tried to make him smile, but he
only moaned again. "I'm sorry," Eli said. "I'm so sorry."

Nothing could have hurt me more than did Eli's contrition.
It was a hot knife in me. He pulled his legs over the bed, snagged
on the blankets, and then sat thick and sad on the edge. The goose-
bumps lifted up like whitecaps on faraway water. It was about four
o'clock. My room had been yellow, brown, pale orange, warm and
hopeful, but with twilight all this left us rigor mortis blue. Eli's
silence when he arrived had been full of wit and friendship; now
we were quiet because we were different from each other, different from the day and what had just transpired between us.
The glorious hunger of that, Eli made into an ugly, misshapen
mistake twisted by guilt. I was too hurt to cry.

Moaning, Eli put his clothes back on. He was cold. "Why
don't you warm up under the blankets?" I asked him. "Just keep
everything on and get warm first."

But no. He said it again, "I'm so sorry, Blondie. Please forgive me."

But he didn't understand. I sat up. I didn't know what to say. I was so insulted by his guilt. It made me ashamed. Later I could get mad about it, but just then, with my flannel nightgown and my socks and my frazzled white hair and chapped lips and a hangnail I'd chewed off, I was just an ugly little girl. He shamed me.

"You're not to blame," said Eli.

My nose suddenly ran; I could taste the salty snot, and I quickly wiped it across my cheek and sat trying to dry off my face. Eli picked up his coat and put it on. He was bulky and he still looked chilled. He put his boots on like a boy would, sitting right down on the floor to put his feet in them. We had nothing to say to each other. He stood up and dusted off his hands. As he was leaving he leaned over to kiss the top of my head, but I lifted up my face and when he kissed my mouth he got a fierce electric shock, and when I pulled away my nightgown lit up with static, you could see it in the darkening room. And then he walked out.

CHAPTER THREE

THE CHIEF JUSTICE WAS DRUNK. After my parents dropped me off, they went directly to his home in Winnipeg, a journey of maybe six hours in the snowstorm. His house was an oak log structure built in the 1840s and so considered "established." He answered the door wearing a burgundy velvet dressing gown tied loosely with a gold-tasselled rope about his middle. He had an enormous girth and a narrow chest, so he was shaped like a drop of water. When he was drunk, he was mean. He had given up sobriety years ago, though he wasn't always so obviously drunk, and he retained a powerful influence over the old Red River Colony. The storm was at its peak. Peter and Alice stood frozen at his doorstep, inhuman figures caked in snow.

"Yes?" said the chief justice. He had a powdery face pinched with ill will. "What is it?" A genius in a land of bumpkins.

"I am Peter McCormack," said my father. "And this here is Alice McCormack, my wife."

"It is an absolute delight to meet you," said the chief justice, and closed the door.

After a moment, Peter lifted the brass knocker and pounded again. The door opened immediately, and the chief justice stood there with a cigar, smiling grimly. "I know very well who you are," he said, letting them in. "You owe me a lot of money."

"Which I'm paying back." Peter shook himself like a wet dog, flinging snow on the wainscotting. Alice just stood there, melting quietly.

"Don't bother," said the judge. "Why don't you borrow more? I've got oodles of cash." Sticking the cigar between his contentious teeth, he shuffled towards a pair of French doors and pried them open. Looking back at my parents, he said, "Do come in."

Peter entered the judge's library on his toes, obstinate and thinly dignified. Alice trailed after him, shapeless, damp as protoplasm.

"Drink?" The chief justice offered port.

"No," said Peter.

"Yes," said Alice.

The chief justice poured three from an ugly decanter. Alice, looking at it, thought, Grown children who are larcenous just like him, rheumatic wife who hates him. There was that baking-soda smell of false teeth in the judge's library, though the fire burned as it should in an appropriate hearth and the leather-bound books stood uncut in a glass cabinet. On one wall there hung a huge map of the new Manitoba, a grid upon the topography and the sections in faint red. Alice, the idolatress, was mesmerized. On a wood pedestal stood a snowy owl stuffed in flight, a wingspan of three feet, its wild concentric eyes alien and turned towards the room at an angle impossible even for such a bird, as if its neck had been broken.

The judge sat down at a rolltop desk and dipped his pen in ink. "You have repaid me exactly one-third of what you owe. At 8 per cent. Never missed a payment. Why should you pay me back now? Borrow more."

"I don't like owing," said my dad.

The chief justice shook his pen, flung ink at the map. "You are desirable," he pronounced. "I mean that in a monetary sense," he added, directing his attention to Alice, who removed the beaver hat and freed her hair from her damp collar. "Put on weight," the judge intoned. "Fatten your wife," he told my dad.

"I don't like owing," said my dad, never aware of repetition.

"I'll tell you what," said the chief justice. "If you refuse my offer, I will investigate the propriety of your claim. Latour Road. That's funny. I thought that was Métis land."

Alice and Peter stiffened. The moth wings stirred at the back of their minds.

Guilt-stricken, Peter made a clean breast of it. "That's right, Métis. We paid for it, but then again, we never did. It's confusing. I don't want to think I stole it. I'm trying to prove up."

"Good man. It will take more. Put up some fences. You'll need a loan."

"It's very good of you, sir," said Alice, her accent of choice north England, flat and nasal.

"Think nothing of it." The chief justice stood and walked unsteadily towards her, holding out a promissory note. He leaned over her, his low girth touching her and she looking up into his wet mouth. "The money comes from infant estates, you see."

"Oh, God," said Alice.

Real-estate speculation on the land supposedly allocated to Métis "children" was a sordid sewer running under and feeding the recent economic boom. Nearly one and a half million acres had been promised to those with a mix of English or French and Indian ancestry, but the Manitoba government pretended that "children" meant little kids, not Métis offspring. In the wink of an eye, four thousand people lost their entitlements, and packages of 140 acres were given to the English settlers. The rest of the land was bought from the Métis for peanuts and resold at "true" value. The Métis lost their river lots to us, and people like us. Alice and Peter moved heavily towards the door, the taste of the judge's sweet port in their mouths.

"We have lightened their burden. The half-breeds cannot *farm*," the judge was saying, and he waved the note before them. "We have relieved them of an improvident responsibility. Have no worry. Good legislation, good laws, and we'll quiet their claims. Of course, there's a slim chance your ownership is legal and binding. But we can't be too sure. Put up a new barn. Build fences. It's all on the up and up."

"Up and up," said Alice, longing. "We must go home." And took the loan.

<hr/>

AFTER ELI LEFT, I got up to take a pee and bled into the chamber pot. Even in my devastation, I was forming a fresh resolve. I had a plan that would save us all. It needed only my parents' arrival home to confirm its necessity.

I was sleeping when they walked in. Six o'clock in the morning and still dark. I was reconciled to my own power. My eyes retained the vision of Eli's shining egg in its nest. When my parents stamped into the house, they looked like Lord and Lady Macbeth. And I thought, That's enough, I see the light. But I said nothing.

I rose to make them cocoa. Alice noticed my bloodstained nightgown, but she was so exhausted I think she took responsibility for it, as if it were her own or otherwise communal. Mothers are strange. My parents were getting older by the minute. I put them to bed, and then lit a candle at the little desk in my room and wrote out my plan to save the world from extinction.

Because I had learned a terrible lesson. It was only too clear. Everything I looked at shrank away into nothing, like Eli's desirable egg. Marie was nothing but the whisper of a moth. Riel was forever extinguished, along with the rights of more than four thousand Métis children. Eli had told me once, when we were out looking for the vanishing lady's slippers, that my eyes were focused too far away. He said my eyes made everything close up disappear. I was so in love I thought he was paying a compliment. But it was merely descriptive, raw information. Whatever I looked at disappeared: Marie, the Métis, Peter's freedom, and now Eli. I sat up till noon.

What I devised was a plan for my own education. A woman with my power had to be cautious. Thereafter, I would focus my potent attention only on what was truly irrelevant. Latin, naturally. A bit of history of the slave trade in the Congo, followed by the navigation routes of fifteenth-century Portugal. The tragedies, Greek. I would spend six months reading this fellow Pliny, because he'd died in Pompeii (I'd already learned that in Spelling). Then Luther, Wesley and Augustine (in honour of my mother). By mid-summer (when Eli was likely hired out in Alberta, never mind), I'd be working on a history of Mesopotamian law, subdivided: culinary, marital, inheritance, military. I would memorize the names of every Roman senator, every British king, and learn the difference between a Plantagenet and a Tudor. I vowed never to look directly at anything ever again, never to learn anything that was not *extremely* foreign to St. Norbert, Manitoba.

Glance aslant at everything I loved, learn the foreign names for things familiar. Not common wood nymph, but *Cercyonis pegala*. Not monarch butterfly, but *Danaus plexippus*. Not Us, but Them. Not St. Norbert, but Canada. Not love. Intelligence. By this means, I would protect all that I loved. By learning. Through an exotic translation from touch to intellect, from knowledge to book-fed ignorance. Not the Red River in spring runoff full of debris from North Dakota, but the Nile and its delta, and all the mummified kings, pyramids, slave labour too ancient to matter. Not Protestant land swindles, but the Norman invasion. Chaucer (surely irrelevant). Boethius. Okay! *On the Consolation of Philosophy.* That's a good one.

Irrelevance. My allegiance thereafter, my calling, my devotion. Irrelevance. Saviour of all that would remain secret, of my heart. An education in irrelevant information. So my home and loved ones (yes, and those departed in error, made crazy by the foreign god of guilt) may survive in blindness, in colonial disregard may we thrive.

PART THREE

1900

CHAPTER ONE

OVER THE NEXT FIFTEEN YEARS, Eli would get so bow-legged he'd eventually walk like a crab, sideways, see-sawing on a bad knee. Dust and cattle bristle had baked into his strangely handsome hide, so he was camouflaged against the sun-burnt grass as he sidled over the fair face of the district of Saskatchewan, near Batoche, at a place called Duck Lake.

A hot wind blew hard from the west, ripe with the smell of blood. Shaggy blond grass, indifferent to thirst, made waves on the mild bulges in the land by the South Saskatchewan River. Eli couldn't read a watch, but he always knew the hour. It was noon. Vernal equinox. Broad daylight. The wind's fingers pushed at the grasses, drew faces, erased them; the wind whispered names, phrases trailed off painful as accusations. Eli always treated daytime hauntings with respect. He tried not to be afraid.

The only other white man at the Duck Lake camp was an eager sergeant major sent West to oversee the slaughter of nearly a hundred head of cattle. The government of Canada intended to feed pemmican to the North West Mounted Police quartered up north, in the mining district of the Yukon. Pemmican, once the staple for fur traders, is sun-dried buffalo meat pounded into a powder and mixed with fat. Since the buffalo were gone, they'd have to make do with domestic cattle and a few fat horses. The Mounted Police hired Cree Indians from the nearby reserves to do the killing and manufacture, in exchange for the heads and offal of the slaughtered animals. And the police sent the sergeant major to make sure that no tainted ingredients went into the pemmican. A man by the name of Clark. A boyish man who was forever falling in love.

Sergeant Major Clark didn't know a bull from a cow, so he in turn had hired Eli from Batoche to run the show. Eli was the man people looked to when they wanted a job done. Clark always spoke to Eli as if they were at the fringes of a marvellous ballroom. Eli strained to hear Clark's voice above the constant wind. "It's going awfully well, isn't it?" Clark asked, nibbling at a thick moustache.

Clark looked wall-eyed towards the pole frames. Splashed like poppies across the dry prairie wool were countless tents made of thin slices of flesh. The Crees were loading horse's guts and the heads of cattle onto wagons, preparing to go home for a few days while the sheets of meat splayed across the frames were cooked by the sun and wind. About fifty Indians would stay at the camp to boil down the fat and marrow, and sew up the hides with sinew for the great sacks of pemmican.

Eli looked at Clark's seal-like face, smooth and fulsome, and shrugged.

"It must bring back a lot of memories for you," said Clark, bobbing his shiny head.

Eli twitched, suspicious. "Why? What've they told you?"

"Uhh, well, they . . . I mean to say, the great buffalo slaughters! Killing for tongues and all that, skinning the wild beasts, et cetera. Right here! On the open prairie! Oh, yes! I know all about that. A lifetime ago, mind you. You were . . . why, I bet you were just a boy!"

Eli relaxed. "Oh," he said, "that." He stared over Clark's optimistic shoulder. In the blowing grass appeared the face of the old blind warrior, Assiyiwin, who seemed to nod sadly, and then the wind again, taking him away. Eli tried a polite smile for the young soldier. Must be about twenty-three years old. Wouldn't know anything.

"Nothing much to do now," said Eli. "You going to hang around?" His jaw was aching, *Please go.*

Clark tipped his head, considering. He ran a bright tongue along his teeth, gathering a little ball of dust, and spat. Wiped his mouth on his sleeve. "Love to stay. Let's pray to God this heat holds," he said.

It did. All night. Heat rank with rendered fat and bone marrow. The smoke made everyone nostalgic. Some of the stories were told in English for the benefit of the rather sympathetic Clark, whose Cree was limited to *meegwetch*, "thank you." By firelight, stories of the great hunts in the 1860s. *A thousand buffalo, like thunder, black air, so many!* Long, warped fingers held up, trembling before an old face like a stone on the prairie, the noise of ten thousand buffalo cupped in his broken hands.

The old men made fun of the young men. "So serious," the old men said, laughing. "I am working!" They mimicked the young men, who swaggered under the weight of a hind of beef and ordered the women around. "Butcher this!" said the serious young men. A job with the white police, some pay and the chance to slaughter domestic animals. "Real hunters," the old men teased. The young men tried to smile. But one young guy with a twisted face got mad at the teasing, this lesson handed him by the elders. And the elders looked at him with the compassion of the healthy for the ill, compassion mixed with fear. The young would need to develop an appetite for the bland taste of counterfeit. Pemmican, oh sure, made of cow.

The twisted face turned on Clark and asked, "You like hanging around with Indians?"

Clark nodded eagerly. The elders laughed, but the young men grew sullen.

Twisted face went on. "You like us? You come home with us. You like eatin' dirt? You like poor? You like Indian dog shit?"

"Thank you," said Clark. "Uh, *meeg*—uh—*wetch*. I have to join my regiment farther north. But thank . . . *meegwetch*. Most kind."

Twisted face sneered. "Eli stayed with us. When he was hiding. My grandmother was hiding too, in the woods. When everybody was in trouble in '85." Slyly, to Eli: "You came to our reserve to stay out of jail. My father hid the white guys from police." He shoved Eli's shoulder. The elders sat still. "Eli was hiding from the whites, his own people; he buried his white face in Indian skirts. We always pay for your fear. And for the fuckin' Riel. Shit. You want to hear an Indian story?" He stood up. The man beside him tried to pull him back, but he shook him off. He pointed at Eli. "I'm telling a story this Eli, this . . . friend of Indians is scared shitless you'll find out, your Royal Highness soldier."

An elder interrupted. "Sit down. Your feet stink."

The younger man sat.

For a moment, it seemed the story would die with the fire. Then the elder said, "Tell. Tell what you tell." But he looked through narrow eyes, a warning. *There are limits to what can be told to the white policeman.*

Twisted face shrugged. "Ahhhh, it was an asshole half-breed working for the police—that's who shot Assiyiwin. Assiyiwin came in kindness, an old man, nearly blind. Métis and the police, they want to fight on our land. Our chief, he says, 'No, we don't want Riel's fight.' Assiyiwin is a warrior when he is young. He's not afraid to fight. But he goes with the chief. The half-breed traitor, that McKay, he points his gun. Assiyiwin says, 'Why have you so many guns, grandson?' Fucking McKay shoots Assiyiwin in the stomach. A good man, an old man." His body seemed to shrink, a certain helpless smirk. "What is a warrior now anyways?"

Clark went pale. "I'm so sorry, dear chap." The young men finally broke up laughing, rolling back, mimicked "dear chap." Clark blinked and smiled. He enunciated carefully. "But could you," he said, trying to be heard, "tell me what is going on? Please. If your . . . if your *people* did not want to fight, then why was your man shot?"

The older men were silent. Too many secrets and no one to trust.

Eli rose and walked away from the fire. Clark was acutely aware of being white. The silence was so prolonged that even the Indians, who weren't normally anxious to fill space with speech, began to sniff and twitch. Clark cocked his head to one side, ears perked hopefully. Finally, an elder smiled kindly at Clark and said, "*Itineesit atim.*" This broke everybody up. Twisted face pointed and laughed. "*Itineesit atim!*" Patted Clark's head. "Smart dog!"

The elder pulled himself wearily to his feet. Passing, he too gently patted Clark's head. "Good night, Smart Dog." As he disappeared from the light, the old man said, "Maybe Eli will tell you why our land is now our prison."

THE HEAT HELD and the meat dried. Eli was a favourite with the women, and they'd let him take the willow flails from their hands, flirtatiously, as if they were handing him their last remnant of clothing, and they'd walk a little behind to get a better look at the muscle on his thick brown arms when he drummed at the hide-threshing basin. The wing-beat of air when Eli hit the shingles of meat was an intimate sound, and the women watching him found a warm rock to sit on, distracted, daydreaming as the dried meat gave way beneath Eli's flail and broke into a pigeon-grey powder. He held the pot of hot, melted fat for them, tipped it into the basin while they stirred. Such affinity is reserved for men in the kitchen. That's where you find the men who love women. The gossipy side of men is a great aphrodisiac. I forgive Eli. Really.

The pemmican was ladled into the hide sacks, pounded tight, sewn up into big boulders cooling in the evening of the last day of Eli's bachelor life at Duck Lake.

Eli had abandoned me fifteen years before, the heroic fool. For fifteen years after the rebellion, he'd worked at the ferry at Gabriel's Crossing. A decade and a half spent looking after a dozen horses. He didn't marry. Clark, enviously watching the women watch Eli, asked him about this. Clark himself was badly smitten in several places, admiring this woman for her grace, that girl for her ankles. I don't know what Eli said. It doesn't bear thinking about. Maybe the occasional visit, maybe some degree of intimacy. Never mind.

Despite himself, Eli got involved in local politics. He fought every speculator, every railway official, every local commissioner working for Ottawa's "Indian Affairs." He didn't know how to read. He used his voice, and his sadness. Eli's sadness hurt the world into laughter. He filled the wintering kitchens of his neighbours with intoxicating nostalgia.

Five years earlier, Eli had acted for Riel, worked like a missionary to make the Northwest Rebellion a real Indian–Métis movement. At the Cut Knife camp, Eli and Riel's Métis agents had tried to persuade the Indians to join them, singing the praises of the future, which was a return to the past—the police evicted, their land returned to them. Almost all the Indians were disinclined to go Riel's way, but a few of the young men went out and murdered some whites, a selective revenge upon local enemies.

By way of a response, the Canadians hanged eight Indians—six Cree and two Assiniboines. On November 27, 1885. Wandering Spirit, Miserable Man, Little Bear, Bad Arrow, Round the Sky, Iron Body, Itka and Man Without Blood. Hanged them all from a massive scaffold, in unison, at the barracks at Battleford, on the North Saskatchewan River. They were not buried on their own reserves; the government did not wish to foster ghosts. The hangings were witnessed by families from the reserves surrounding Battleford. Our beloved prime minister, Sir John A., had written to the Indian commissioner,

Edgar Dewdney, that the executions "ought to convince the Red Man that the White Man governs." Very subtle. Miserable Man had asked for a pair of thick-soled shoes for "the long walk between this world and the Other Side." I wonder if this wish, too, was denied. Likely. They didn't want Indians going far. Even dead ones.

The rebellion in '85 had left the Indians with nothing but a death chant in their bellies. Sir John suspended the annuity payments to those "rebel" bands. He starved them out, all the way to Montana.

People mistook Eli's regret for idealism, and voted for him in elections he never even ran in. He gained himself a campaign manager, Randy, a racy little fellow with a typesetting machine who dreamed up Eli's campaigns while the candidate himself was in the barn or on the ferry, unaware there was an election. "BETTER DAYS!" was Eli's campaign manager's slogan. And Eli always thought it referred to the lost past, and it always made him wonder why people insisted on voting for what was missing, expurgated, extinct. The politics of regret made him sadder and sadder, and the people adored his sorrow and elected him to municipal council.

They were loading the pemmican, the whole crew, chatting, a lot of teasing, especially for Clark, who was by now so full of gentlemanly desire he seemed always on the verge of tears. Clark got all misty-eyed and pulled Eli to the side and said, "I'm thinking of staying." The two men looked at the scenery. "I love it here," said Clark. There was a nuptial quality to this confession, a sense of commitment mixed with virginal ardour. "I'm thinking I should leave the police. These people know something. I can't explain. I want what they've got." His earnest seal-face blinking. "I hear you're the man I should talk to."

Just then, the sound of a horse. Eli and Clark watched the stranger ride towards them. It was obvious from the way the man sat in his saddle, like a mechanized gopher, that he was military. Clark actually whimpered, he was so excited to see one of his own kind. And yes, on the brink of betrayal, he wiggled and wagged and finally collected himself to raise a stiff salute as the officer rode towards them.

"Good Lord! It's Roberts!" The puppy tail wagging as if it would come off. "Roberts! Good Lord!"

"Hello, Clark," said Roberts. The Indians stopped work. Stood quietly, wary as a chain gang at head count. Roberts had a silk-lined voice in a steely body. Great military bearing, the puffery of the second son, Ontario-bred, British by choice. Wore a moustache similar to Clark's, but bigger and loopier and top-lofty. He looked down upon the Indians from his horse. Clark, underfoot, barking as pleasantly as a golden retriever, tried to introduce Roberts to his new Indian friends. Without even a glance around him, Roberts announced, "I'm on my way to Winnipeg. Then to Paardeberg. South Africa, you know. I suggest you join me." He turned his horse, as if setting off at once.

"I say," said Clark. He followed Roberts a short distance and then hesitated, looked back longingly at his new friends, who suddenly seemed very shabby. Roberts dismounted. Brought Clark close, spoke in his ear, but his voice carried on the wind. "See here, Clark. A great many of our men are going," Roberts said. "Buller's on top. And a lot of the lads from Cut Knife have gone over. In fact, it's Otter's command."

Eli walked towards them. "Otter," he said.

"Oh!" Clark nibbled. "Eli, I'd like you meet my good friend Roberts."

Standing in the piddle pool of Clark's enthusiasm, Eli drew in a breath. "Otter's the fool who attacked Poundmaker's camp," he said.

"Fought the Indians in '85," said Roberts. "Five hundred Indians."

Eli turned back to the wagon. Everyone there was watching quietly. The fun had gone out. The grasses blew, each blade divulged by yellow daylight. "Was no five hundred—" He stopped. Where was he to go? He looked back helplessly at the people loading pemmican—not real pemmican, not really five hundred men, no real soldiers, no true story, no home here for such a man as Eli. He tried again: "Poundmaker . . ." A very tall, very handsome man, dead, like Marie, with tuberculosis, soon after his release from prison. Eli turned back to Roberts, who looked at him somewhat more openly, quizzical, and Eli saw that even Roberts was not a bad man. "Chief Poundmaker saved Otter's life," Eli said.

Roberts winced. He did not like debate. The Indians read the futility in his face and were poisoned by a terrible fatigue. They abandoned their work then and there, leaving the rest of the pemmican on the ground. Clark said, "Oh." The kindly elder turned to him and smiled a little and joined his people in their modest protest, walking off the job. That left Clark and Roberts and Eli sitting on five tons of pemmican destined for the Yukon.

Roberts wanted to be happy. He poked Clark's arm. "Are you with me?" he asked him. "We'll join Strathcona Horse and go to South Africa."

Eli said, "You're going to Winnipeg to join, are you?"

Otter was fighting the colonials in South Africa. Eli had let himself assist with a bit of bureaucracy, exacting slave labour from regretful Indians. He realized that if he himself wasn't extinct, perhaps he should be. He smiled. He smiled and decided to die.

The best way for a hero to die is to challenge the element most dangerous to his soul. For Eli, that would be a British cavalry fighting a colonial war.

"Do you think this Strathcona Horse outfit could use some pemmican?" he asked.

Roberts and Clark suddenly looked roguish and young. Boy, this was real frontier stuff! Clark and Roberts and Eli sat down on five tons of pemmican no longer destined for the Yukon. They crossed their legs. Roberts offered them cigars. They sat and smoked, the three men, and looked to the west. All they got was sun in their eyes.

I KNEW ELI WAS COMING, in a blind and deaf way. The soles of my feet knew it, skin dry and flaking and cracked so badly I had a recurring nightmare about baby spiders living in my feet. My only exercise, the few steps from bed to desk. The back of my knees knew it because the eczema got hot and itchy, a rash that splashed across the back of my legs, dry and festering. My crusty hands knew it, and my sore pink eyes blindly discerned when I looked up from my desk by the window and imagined three scruffy wise men approaching. The sunlight seared like a flash-light in the eyes of a caged rat.

Except for distracted visits to the backhouse, I hadn't been outside in fifteen years. My father brought my books home from the post office. The last batch was delivered on May 1, in spring rain on a day greyer than an old woman's whiskers, and I'd shuffled out in Dad's socks (the same) to fetch them from the porch. I had a quick look around. The world was messy. I took the books inside my cave to maul them.

I had not been eczematous for all of the fifteen years of Eli's abandonment. It was a gradual thing. At first, I'd flourished on my diet of ideas. Back in '85, I'd started out with Coleridge and his gang, and it was great for a while because I'd concurrently developed a taste for dandelion wine and I made my way through De Quincey's hallucinations on friendly terms, eye to dilating eye. Even Tennyson, though sober, lured me down leafy paths of learning. I always felt like I was nearly There (so long as There was not Here; I kept my oath of allegiance to the Imperial Empire of Irrelevance). Just one more book, one more month at my desk, yet one more season eating paper. I was the teacher's pet, the most obedient student in the Commonwealth. I ploughed through Longinus's *On the Sublime,* plodded through Plotinus's "On the Intellectual Beauty." Burped through Edmund Burke's "The Sublime and Beautiful Compared." Stolid, stubborn, strict in my categories. Under my bed remained hidden my treasure box: *Walden,* the photographs of Big Bear, the petrified tusk. But I never once touched them during my long tenure as gullible student. As the eggs would never touch the jam on my plate, Thoreau's *Walden* would never touch Aristotle's *Metaphysics.* The tusk would never touch Sir Francis Bacon. And Blondie McCormack would never touch another man.

I was a retroactive virgin. There was no map for a farm girl in St. Norbert, Manitoba, at the end of nineteenth century. History was a whiteout, a tomb full of wig powder and scurf. I nearly cauterized the hunger in me for green things, for belly laughs. After a while, I forgot why I was pursuing the gaunt bums of geniuses. Lost in the blizzard blanketing the real estate of the Commonwealth, I'd aim for any grey shape looming up from the pages of the bug-eaten books.

The problem with static electricity grew so acute that I could touch no one, even in summer, for fear of an electric shock of sufficient magnitude to inadvertently erase their memories. It was a living hell, but I remained dedicated to my own cloister, my prison of split ends and paginated dreams, a starving person convinced that everyone else is a glutton, that joy is a bad joke, that we live alone and die alone. I was a teenager until my fourth decade, a pathetic figure in a flannel nightgown and my father's socks in June 1900, when Eli returned to me.

I was reading Descartes that afternoon, the twenty-fifth of June 1900. Learning the principles of radical doubt. When I dared look out my window into the chaos of real life, I simply practised my lessons on Eli, doubting with a novice's talent the possibility of his existence. But when I saw him dismount and stand in the yard on his wishbone legs, holding his hat with his attitude of perplexity that is both courageous and shy, I held my hand against the light and looked through the skin to the red blood inside and I could see the white stems of my fingers under my own marsh water, and then I looked between my fingers at the dazzle of sun and Eli, still there, persistently fleshed, holding the end of the reins, his long arms at his sides.

I stood, tipping over my chair, and walked on scabby feet away from my desk and through the kitchen, a room that seemed glaringly loud, and out the front door and noticed for the first time that Alice had brought foxglove to grow in the mud by the porch. A meanness rose in me, the meanness of a war vet who returns to find there are no jobs. I walked towards Eli like a martyr, like a liberator. I reached to touch his dusty blue shirt, holding its thick grainy blue between my fingers. His shirt was warm in my hand, and it felt clean to touch, sandblasted. We stood like that in the dust, with sweet tufts of quack grass sawing the air of the fenced yard, my hand on Eli's shirtsleeve. I looked at Eli's short brown eyelashes; he glanced at me and looked away.

It was confirmed. I had saved him. All those years of toil had preserved his life, though he'd certainly aged. But age became Eli. How a face like an abandoned barn could be so handsome is beyond me. I said, "You must be forty years old."

He said, "You must be Blondie."

It was only then I noticed the other two men, Clark and Roberts. How do you do, Ontario types but nice enough. I asked them in. Said I'd feed them. And the soldier boys removed their hats. Their boots made a nice mallet sound on the kitchen floor. They were tall and fine-looking. Their long ride in fair weather had tanned them; their eyes were bright, their lips were red, and their moustaches were waxed into two points, blunt and kind as butter knives. The kitchen filled with the fragrance of sun-washed manhood. I excused myself and went to my bedroom, closing the door.

I stood looking through the crack between the oak slats of my door. I could make out a long masculine leg here, a muscular neck there, where it ran broadly into a collar. Strains of their chesty voices drifted on beams of light through the rough wood door. I was breathing hard. My flannel nightgown gave my chest, my ribcage, my backside keen pleasure. Oh, to be touched. I wanted to get dressed. No. I wanted to take a bath. I reopened the door. Eli was sitting in the same corner where the ghost of Thomas Scott had drooled protoplasm so many years before. He saw my uncertain haste. And stood to say, "Why don't I find something to feed these gentlemen."

"Good," I said. "You do that. I'm going for a swim." I stopped on the porch and said loudly, "You have to stay here."

Down to the river I went, and out to the dock that Peter had constructed out of whisky kegs and fence posts. Precarious affair. I sat naked on the edge. To my right, at the river's edge, silent as the water itself, stood a whooping crane on stick legs the colour of driftwood, its huge tufted body with long white feathers that curled down over the black tips of its wings. My dad had told me the cranes were all gone, turfed out since the time of Marie and her grotto. This one seemed forgotten. I pushed myself away from the dock, wondering if it would fly off. The water was cold and full of tiny living things. I swam as close to the fast current as possible, just till I could sense its muscle wrenching my arms, then I skimmed back off it like a swimmer at the end of the pool and raced back. With each stroke, the scales were falling from my body. Water was a palm or a tongue or a paw, and when I stood on the floating dock, my rash had been cured and my skin purified by its gentle abrasion.

Rubbed myself dry with my nightdress. Somehow my limbs were still round and muscled despite the years of vegetative reading. My thighs were ample and strong, and my belly was firm with just enough fat on it; as round and white as the petals of anemone were my breasts, and the bright devil's kiss my sole jewellery. I was thus occupied with a reunion with my flesh when I felt myself watched.

Standing to the groin in a thicket of wild cucumber, the blushing Clark. His pink cheeks glowed. His eyes held mine. I dropped my gown. Considered catching a handful of Red River to throw into his sweetly beaded face. He was solemn. If he'd smiled, I would have transformed him into a stag and sicked the dogs on him. If I'd had any dogs. It was a lovely moment, but I couldn't hold the nymph pose a second longer.

Suddenly, Eli was running down the riverbank carrying his gun. He ran like a stalking cat, low to the ground, blood on the tip of his tongue. He crouched to the river's edge without once looking at me and raised his gun. The crane lifted, revealing angel-white feathers beneath its wings, with a span that took my breath away. It straightened its stick legs and seemed to think itself into the air, for it was airborne before its vast wings swept down. I heard the explosion and smelled the blue sulphur and charcoal of Eli's rifle. And then the bird fell, falling as heavy as a man's body; I heard the air shoved from its lungs and an eggshell sound when it crashed on the riverbank.

Clark leapt down to join his brother-in-arms while I threw the damp nightgown over my head. When my head emerged, I saw the two bold hunters holding the crane by its wing tips while they marvelled boisterously over the colossal prize. "Wonderful shot!" exclaimed the blushing Clark. "Very clean! Very bold move!"

They carried on this way for hours, obviously trying to prolong a perfect communion. Homopathological. With passionate care, they carried the dead thing to the house, where its wingspan was measured and its beauty properly appreciated. "Eight feet, three inches!" cried Clark, as if he would lay down his gauntlet, Childe Clark to Sir Eli. Who was quickly saturated in shame.

I stood in a sea of testosterone like the maidenhead on a battleship. Roberts and Clark strode over the corpse of the bird, crushing its white feathers into the dust and straddling its brilliant red head, its ochrous eye. "Good Lord! Will you look at that eye!"

"A cruel eye!"

"A damn cruel eye! I've heard of a crane just like this one attacking a child once. Good Lord! A right hostile bird!"

Clark began to babble. "It was a whooping crane exactly like the specimen before us! Wounded it, a poor shot"—an admiring glance at Eli—"maimed by an inferior marksman. An Indian, as I recall. In a snit because he hadn't shot a buffalo, lifted his gun and"—staggering, lifted an imaginary rifle—"BLAM! Thing dropped, all right. But then it began to run around. Dripping blood. Held up its wings, just like this one. These creatures have beaks, look at it now." And he poked at the bird's head with his toe. "See that beak? It's for digging roots. That's what they eat. Monstrous beak. I saw one such specimen drive its beak right through an oak paddle. Ferocious birds. And once enraged, extremely vicious." He quivered. "This bird wanted revenge. It went right for the children, screaming a sound like a drunken reveille. I only wish I could forget it, the most vicious sight I've ever seen, war or peace. It could outrun a horse once it got its speed up. Imagine the poor little child, without a prayer, a little Indian child who had tripped and fallen down on its knees, with this terrible bird standing over it and just about to disembowel the child then and there."

"But you killed it," I suggested.

Clark looked at me. Confident. He'd pretty well married me and had five children by me with that one voyeuristic glance. "Right," he said. "Quite right."

Eli swayed and lifted the crane in his arms. The bird was so heavy that Eli carried it as he would carry a dead man, the cloud white wings tumbled over his chest, and I swear the crane clasped Eli in its arms. He staggered under the weight of his angelic prey and stood before me with his offering.

"God save thee, ancient Mariner!" said I.

Eli's hazel eyes divined my need for him. But he winced and said, "I'm going to South Africa."

"Well, take the goddamn bird with you."

He backed away, the white bird around his neck, and turned and fled into the bush. Recrimination had made him blind. And fixed to the past, he crashed through the overgrown path to Marie's grotto. Clark and Roberts and I watched him go. "That's bush!" cried out the faithful Clark. "He's walking into bush!" He glared at my chest beneath the flannel nightgown, as if the cause for Eli's sudden lunacy lay there.

"Why South Africa?" I asked Clark.

"Why? For queen and country!"

In socks, in damp nightgown, I followed Eli. His rigorous grief and the bulk of their bodies had bulldozed a fresh trail. I found him in the clearing by Marie's cabin. He stood, rotating slowly with his face lifted to the sky, in his arms the radiant bird. I took the crane from him and laid it on the ground. With his rough fingers, Eli plucked at its flight feathers.

We buried it in the shade of black spruce, the crane as large as a man. All was still. We breathed together. The ground was made of decayed things, roots and needles and blown maple leaves rotting like the pages of a book.

❦

ELI MADE A NECKLACE of leather and attached to it three white feathers. He stood upon the mound of rust-coloured earth and slipped the necklace over his head, tucking it under his shirt. And this from an illiterate man.

I followed him back to the house, where we rejoined Clark and Roberts. Eli was as calm as a ship in the doldrums, mesmerized by his own jealous folly. But there was a heat about him. I felt it when I handed him a glass of water. When his hand touched mine with the inevitable electric spark, the water in the glass clouded over and bubbled slightly. He kept glancing over his shoulder, as if hearing a footstep behind him. Other than that, he looked great. And I yearned for him till I thought I'd fall down.

They'd left their wagon at the gate by Lord Selkirk Road, and Clark and Roberts were suddenly convinced it would be stolen. Roberts was eager to retrieve it, but Clark stopped him and said, "Blondie will give me a hand." He looked at me. "I'll bet you're good with horses," he said. Eli laughed sadly. I pulled a pair of Peter's trousers over my nightgown, snapping the suspenders, and plugged my feet into my boots. To Roberts, I said, "Help Eli with supper. Make enough for six." Roberts looked peeved.

Up the road, Clark swaggered, each of us leading a horse, for they'd left the traces on the wagon. My father's fences extended like Chinese boxes around our whitewashed homestead. At the edge of "our property," Clark halted and pulled me to him in ardent desperation. His moustache was auburn. He grabbed a fistful of my frizzled hair and touched his lips to mine. Up close, I got a view of the effect of heat on wax: his moustache drooped abruptly about the corners of his smirking mouth, and a bit of melted wax stung there and made an instant blister. The shock was a bright one, blue in colour, with flashes of yellow at its edges. The bolt entered Clark's mouth and travelled down his windpipe, showering him with intestinal gases. For good measure, I kissed him again. His head scrolled back on his spine; it drew his eyelids back over his eyeballs weirdly, all red veins, and I was instantly cured of any illusions about his good looks. He smelled funny too. Like bad blood sausage.

Being an Ontario man, Clark looked for an external source for the terrible odour. We were standing close to the wagon full of pemmican. "Goddamn Blackfoot," said Clark.

"Cree," I corrected him, anxious that the electricity had indeed altered his memory.

"Cree," said Clark, recovering. "Quite right. Childlike people. That meat, by God, has gone bad."

Of course it hadn't. The pemmican was dry and hard. Clark sat down at the side of the trail. He pretended to be judging my ability to harness the horses. He was like a drunk woken up after passing out, trying to recall last night's lust, to measure the remorse. I let him off the hook, carried on as if nothing had happened, although I did take advantage of his forgetfulness by acting the part of young male hick. I had a plan.

<hr/>

THE HOUSE WAS REDOLENT with Eli's stew. He put wild parsley in his stews. Anyone would love a man like that. I was working Clark over in my delicate way: by suddenly walking more bow-legged than Eli; by speaking with a jaw taut with male energy, droppin' my g's. Eli stirred some turnip into the stew. Then he fished out the feather necklace and stared at it, disconsolate. He looked as if he'd already married his own death. I put Peter's pipe between my teeth and lit a match on the seat of my pants. If Eli was going to South Africa, then so bloody well would I.

Clark and Roberts and I were just settling down to a bit of poker when Alice and Peter came home. Eli was sitting on the front steps when they appeared. It was nearly ten o'clock. The sound of their horses and then the wagon emerging in the purple night, and the silhouettes of my parents' hatted heads. They spied Eli by the lamplight. Peter stopped the wagon fifty feet away. They looked at each other in silence. From inside the house, I sensed a gladdening of the air and went out to the porch. I couldn't see my parents' faces, but I knew they were smiling.

"Hello, Eli," said Peter, calm and warm.

Eli stood dusting his rump, and walked to them. He held his head high, as if he was leaving room for the lump in his throat. He opened the barn door and then led their horses in. No one said another word.

It was normal for Alice and Peter to get home so late. Alice was teaching school in North Kildonan. Peter, after he'd done as little as possible towards keeping our farm running, would take her to school and then travel back to Winnipeg, where he'd spend the day in conversation. Peter had dutifully cleared enough land for planting and adopted the role of unsuccessful farmer. But by 1900, he was beginning a new career, as philosopher of Impossibilism.

Impossibilism had travelled to St. Norbert from the West Coast, from British Columbian mining towns, from Vancouver's disaffected Marxists, who saw nothing but an ugly twin in the socialists' reforms of capitalism. The Impossibilists rejected any compromise and every conciliation with organized bureaucracy.

The all-means-nothing crowd, I guess. An anti-crowd, a restless bunch, quite wonderfully allergic to any kind of salt-to-pepper relationships: union to industry, now to when. Impossibilism was the left hand refusing to shake hands with the right. It just didn't go in for twos.

Peter and Alice were probably happier than they'd been in their whole lives. Alice's school was full of new immigrants fetched by that great importer of manpower, Clifford Sifton. Sifton figured he'd outsmarted the British radicals by refusing the applications of Londoners and other urban machinists. Hungarians, Romanians, Bulgarians, Russians, Ukrainians, Jews, Italians, Germans, Dutch, Swedes, Finns, Poles and orphaned British children from the English countryside—all were invited to provide cheap and servile homage to Her Majesty's Dominion. It was Alice's heyday. She was teaching in all her thirteen languages. At sixty, she looked ageless, with a muscled face, lithe as a gymnast.

Alice had a keen sense of smell. About two years earlier, she had sniffed on Peter's urgent body the briny scent of radicalism. Peter's passion for Impossibilism smelled of the sea, of fishy breezes and oily salt water, and of logs, fresh-cut timber, corduroy roads, sawdust and pine. It took her back to her first freedom aboard the ship out of Orkney. Since Peter had fallen in love with revolution, Alice had fallen ever more in love with Peter. Of course, they completely neglected me.

Peter and Alice were introduced to Clark and Roberts, with whom they were polite but uninterested. My mother couldn't take her eyes off Eli. She looked suspicious. She leaned on her heels as if she were fat, and opened her arms to Eli like a brood hen, totally out of character. Eli gave her an awkward hug. With her arms around his barrel chest, she slyly nuzzled his armpit. Something in this investigation made her jump. She held Eli in stiff arms, then squeezed his face between her hands. "SNAP OUT OF IT!" she yelled. Her voice was strange, sharp, nerve-racking.

Eli, stunned. But already, the blush of hope on his cheek. Alice spotted the necklace and tugged the white feathers out from Eli's shirt. "Whooping crane," said Alice. "You shot the crane. Who would make you act like such a damn idiot?"

She turned and nailed me with the hot iron of her accusing eye. I forgive my mother for this. She was of an older generation. They blamed women for everything in the old days. A lucky thing, too, because Eli needed all the help he could get just then. He looked arthritic. She released him. Passing me, feigning to hang up her hat, she whispered in my ear, "Sulphur and ash. And hydrocarbons, whatever the hell they are. That man wants to die. What'd you do to him?"

"Nothing," I hissed back at her, fifteen again. Bitch.

"That'd be it, then," said Alice. And hung her hat, grimly disappointed.

Dawn came like a girl in a yellow crinoline, crisp and bright with dew. Clark and Roberts and me, the three gamblers, had played all night. I saw the fingertips of sunrise touch the trees across the river through blue pipe smoke and the farts and belches of my slack-sphinctered buddies. I lost badly. Out of practice. Won me the confidence of the boys. I was the perfect mix: kind of a woman, but not very pretty; kind of a man, but she plays cards like she feels obliged to lose. Says sorry every time she bets on a pair of jacks. I did. Sorry. It was four o'clock in the morning. For the first time in fifteen years, I hadn't had anything to read for eighteen hours.

Playing cards is different from reading. At first, you think a card game is just a stupid little story. Then the stupid little story turns into a parable, a life battle; it turns into your autobiography. And when the sun comes up, the game turns into a letter from the bank—a hangover, worse than the dry heaves.

Cross-dressing is not what it used to be. Clark was a nice enough fellow, but he was not Flaubert and this was not the nineteenth century. I became aware of a quality of purposeful mediocrity in our conversation. It was suddenly a big gaffe to be passionate; significance itself was in bad taste. It was the beginning, the embryonic coagulations, of the twentieth century.

But me and Eli, we were going to South Africa with Clark and Roberts.

SOON ALICE AWOKE and stumbled from their bedroom to stoke the stove for coffee. She lit a fire so big the flames ran up her arm when she slammed the lid into place. Without really thinking, she licked at the singed hair and walked past our card game and out the front door, I presume on her way to the outhouse. It was a bright morning. The stove made it unbearably hot. Clark and Roberts and I, suddenly dying of the heat, put our cards down and crowded out to the front porch. "Whew!" said Clark. Roberts said nothing. "Hot!" said the articulate Clark. Roberts sat on Alice's porch swing, working his brain for something to say. Being upper crust, he would make only summary statements, so he couldn't enter a conversation till it had stuttered into speculation.

"No rain," said I.

"Yep," said Clark.

"River's low," said I.

"Worse out West," said Clark.

"Dry year," said I.

"Not a cloud in the sky," said Clark.

"Some feathery ones," I said, pointing. "In the east."

"No rain in that," said Clark.

"Sure could use rain," said I.

"Very dry out West," said Clark. "Drier than here."

"Yep," said I. "Looks like a hot one."

"Yep," said Clark, and sighed and stretched like a man after hard work. "Gonna be a scorcher."

Roberts ran his fingers through his hair and it miraculously fell back glossy and neat. "That is a mare's tail," he said, pointing to the eastern sky. He looked freshly bathed. "It portends a change of weather. You're quite right," he said to Clark. "It will be a very warm day, with temperatures as high as ninety-two degrees. The weather this afternoon will be enervating. And then," he said, rising and walking away from us, "it will rain. Very hard. Very, very hard."

"Well," I said, scratching my head. My hair crackled. "Coffee?"

"Yes," said Clark. He had suddenly remembered his British accent. "Though I prefer tea."

Dad was in the kitchen when I went in. He tucked my head under his arm and knuckled my skull, immune to the static, though my clothes clung to him. He smelled of brine. "Hot in here," he said, releasing me.

"Gonna be a scorcher."

Dad poured coffee. "How many?"

"Me and Clark," I told him. Dad looked up, alarmed. "Not me and Clark like that," I said. "Me and Clark coffee."

"Nice enough man," Dad said, pouring a cup. "His friend is a bit of a stick."

"They're both okay," I said. "Going to South Africa."

My father looked at me shrewdly over the fog he'd raised on his coffee, took a sip, said, "So?"

"So?"

"So what's up?"

"You tell me."

"Blondie, lass," he said, "since when did you invite comment on your life?"

The screen door opened and Eli walked in, my mother close behind him. That was our reunion. Our Upper Canadian Loyalists were down taking a swim; we could hear their shouts: "The water's splendid, old boy!"

"Righto," said Alice, making a face. "When are the queen's representatives taking their leave?"

"We're going to South Africa," I said.

"Hot day," said Alice, blithe and deaf. "Gonna be a scorcher." She looked at Eli. On her strong, tanned collie-dog face, a look of concern. "What's eating at you?" she asked him.

"I'm all right," said Eli. He was shy.

"He's going to fight the Boers. And I'm going too."

My mother waved at me as if I were a mosquito. She had a hard time thinking of two things at once. That's why I'm an only child.

"Why would you do that?" she asked Eli. "What have the Boers ever done to you?"

"It's either that or join the circus," said Eli. He smiled and looked up at us to make sure we wouldn't take his despair to heart. Lightly, "No place left to go. Should have been hung with Riel." Sipped his coffee. He pretended it was funny. It was pathetic.

"Come on, Eli," said Alice. "Have something to eat."

I moaned when I saw she meant to stoke the stove.

"The man doesn't need to eat, Alice." It was my dad. Harsh. I was uncomfortable. My parents often disagreed, but it was always from the inside of their conspiracy. We were all four standing in the hot slabs of sun. The open-screened door exaggerated Dad's freckles. He seemed to twist himself up. "Eli's absolutely right!" he cried. "God help us! He's right! He may as well fight the Boers as join the circus."

"That's pure bunkum," said Alice.

I was sweating head to toe. I kicked off my boots and stripped down to my undershirt.

"It's true," said Peter. "There's no place for a man like Eli. He's not a banker, and he doesn't sell farm implements. Who wants a buffalo hunter with a talent for breaking horses? He speaks four languages. Who cares? Cree? Ojibwa? French, for God's sake! Can he play golf? Does he row? Is his father a Methodist?"

This last one was a possibility. We all looked at Eli, who shrugged without an ounce of self-pity.

"He can't cheat the land office because he can't read or write!"

Eli winced. Peter put his arm around him and started to walk him out the door. "He's the last one," said Peter. "We've got to preserve him." Out the door into the sun. From the porch, Peter's voice: "The last of an extinct species." Together the two men walked out, towards the raw path to Marie's grotto. "The new situation is impossible."

"Impossible?" asked Eli.

"It's impossible." And then they disappeared from our view. Alice and I were left in the kitchen. "Damn!" said Alice. She stopped. "Do you smell the sea?"

I did. An ocean wind, there in our kitchen at six hundred

feet above sea level, on our unsuccessful farm by the Red River, almost a thousand miles inland from the ocean water of Hudson Bay. The salty scent of Impossibilism, that restless left-handed ideal with its alloy of anarchism. Pungent, fishy and fresh, with a whiff of bilge. I looked at Alice. Alice smiled. "Eli stays here," she said. "Go to South Africa yourself, why don't you?"

⚜

IN THE RAINY NIGHT, I sat in Peter's undershirt and boxer shorts on a chair in the middle of the kitchen, where a breeze blew through the screen. There is no relief when one's sweat rises to meet the humidity in summer air, the fresh rain falling on one's own salt. Skin meets skin or wood or hide or cotton, so to move is to evaporate. Sitting on a wooden chair in the rainy breeze, golden skin a salt lick. Badly wanting Eli. Who was not present at my climatic annunciation, did not witness my skin, my flesh-petalled hue, or taste me. He was near, Eli, but he was not present.

I could hear Eli's voice, Adeimantus to Plato, disembodied, boyish. Peter's catechisms, my father's treachery. Training Eli in the impossible theories of Impossibilism. The lessons were taking place on the porch on my mother's swing, with the rain running madly from the roof, a ledge of rain, for we had no eaves. Green rain. It kept Clark and Roberts in the barn. This was an advantage. For I had chosen to take my mother's challenge. I'd go with them to Cape Town. By ship from Halifax. And I was listening, as a prisoner will listen to a sneeze from his juror. A pleasant sneeze? A kindly cough? Will he like me? I ran my hands over the blonde hair on my legs as I waited to learn.

Will I go to war alone? Or in the company of my brilliant friend, my beloved Eli?

The rain let up and the trees were dripping. All the years of studying were nothing compared with this. I was badly bruised by longing. After fifteen years of fasting, I wanted to speak and kiss and make demands.

Alice fretted about "the boys," as she called Clark and Roberts. She walked out barefoot through the mud to fetch them. As it turned out, Roberts was asleep. My mother crept in through the barn door and whispered to poor Clark, who lay wide-eyed in the straw and was glad to be offered more simple entertainment than lightning and thunder. He even held her hand as they walked back to the house.

Alice brought Clark up the porch steps, interrupting the Republic. Peter finally shut up, and he and Eli came inside with Clark and Alice. I sat stolid in my wooden chair. Eli's hair had curled, and he looked baffled and honest and good. Evil Alice wiped her feet on a potato sack and asked us all to be seated.

"Now," she said, "we will hear from Sergeant major Clark." She leaned towards him. "I'm sorry. What is your Christian name?"

"Christian?"

"Yes. What did your mother call you?"

The ears of Smart Dog perked at the sound of the word "mother," like "cookie." "Mother? *My* mother?" He chewed the moustache. "Clark," he said.

"Clark," said Alice. "My daughter is already old. But a mother, as perhaps you know, will always nurse her young."

Clark, a city boy, blushed.

"She will nurture her young, even when her young, even when her ungrateful young, is merely a specimen of immobilized energy. She reads, you see," said Alice to Clark. "That's all she does."

"She's . . ." Clark began. "She's . . ." He rocked to and fro in his seat, nibbling, trying to recall why he was beached on the female pronoun. "She's not much of a card-player." He smiled at me cheerfully. "Good thing we were just in for matches," he said. And gave my knee a shove.

"Sergant Clark!" said Alice, with a glimmer of Count Otto von Bismarck. "My daughter is considering joining your regiment. Please inform me who is your commanding officer!"

Clark answered brightly, "A man you may well know!"

When people leave home, they lose much of their understanding. They just can't know what words mean; they don't know the stories behind the nouns and when the verbs did what to whom. Take Clark. Poor, dumb soldier.

"Blondie," he said, "will be under the command of a great soldier. General Buller proved himself as a young man right here! Right here at Red River!"

"*General* Buller!" said Alice.

"Of course, he was only a captain then. Under General Wolseley. Think of that! Thirty years ago. And Wolseley a colonel."

"Wolseley," said Alice, and looked at Peter. "A general."

"Ohhh, he was only, maybe, say, thirty-five years of age when he came out here to put down the rebellion. They say it was a terrible fight. Wild half-breeds. It made Wolseley's career."

"Career." Alice looked jaundiced. "It made his career."

"Yes! Quite! Voyageurs, they say—the same ones brought him out here—took him to the Nile to help Gordon. Of course," Clark confessed manfully, "Khartoum had fallen and Gordon was dead by the time Wolseley arrived." He brightened. "But Buller was right here! I suppose he might have walked on *this very property!* They say he came *this close* to hanging Riel over breakfast. So the story goes."

The room was quiet. Clark, still confident, groomed his moustache with his fingers and gave a little click with his heels as a show of respect. "Did you meet the man? General Buller, I mean."

Alice flexed every muscle in her body, head to toes; she pulled her lips back from her long, yellowing teeth and spat on the floor like a camel.

"I met him," she said. "He was singing 'God Save the Queen.'"

"That . . . that would be . . . him. . . ." Clark's enthusiasm was spent. He looked at the bright spot of spit on the floor with polite disgust.

Alice changed mood and shape. She softly came beside me and wrapped her arm around mine. "You must go to South Africa, Blondie, darling girl of mine."

"What?" said Peter.

"She goes. That's my final decision." It was just like Alice. She changed character as easily as she shifted tongue. Peter and I looked at each other, confused, trying to remember when we'd had a matriarch. Alice adopted new roles so fully that she brought a history with her, and within minutes our family was led by Alice, had always been led by Alice.

"What about Eli?" asked my dad, tentative in his supporting role.

"We'll need someone here to help with the farm. We're
losing a valuable farmhand," said Alice, squeezing my shoulder.

"Pardon?" This was just slightly over the top.

"And Eli can stay on till Blondie gets back from the war."
Having spoken, Alice sat at the kitchen table and dealt herself a
hand of solitaire. We were, it appeared, dismissed.

We shuffled outside. It was impossible to talk in front of
my mother. We held a sub-rosa council in the yard.

"She's out of her mind," I whispered.

Dad stood straight, weighed his judgment carefully. "She's
never been wrong before," he said. "Sometimes she seems
wrong, but later it turns out she was right."

"What the hell are you talking about?" I asked him.
"You're cracked too."

"You'll be fighting for the glory of the Empire," offered
Clark.

I was trying to talk to Dad. "Thomas Scott!" I hissed.
"Don't forget Thomas Scott!"

Clark shouted, "You knew Brother Scott? The great
Orange martyr!"

"My mother shot him," I said.

"Oh," said Clark. "Good heavens."

Dad calmly asked, "Blondie, do you want to go to war?"

I looked at Eli. I wanted to go to bed with Eli, and if I had
to go to war first, that's the price I'd pay. I thought I
could get it right this time. Besides, the war was quintessentially
irrelevant, and I hadn't lost the habits of a student.

Eli had pulled the necklace from under his shirt and was counting the feathers over and over, onetwothreeonetwothree-onetwothreeonetwothreeonetwothreeonetwo, and my love for him endured one of those devastating growth spurts, became a new wild mix with the fresh additive of sympathy, something protective, akin to friendship, but it hurt.

My father was waiting for my response. "Blondie?"

Like a kid scared to dive, I gripped the edge with my toes and said, "I guess so."

"Are you sure? Because you know you don't have to."

"Yeah," I said, "I'll go."

Clark slapped my back. "Good fellow!" Then he stopped, looking ill and bewildered.

"What are you going to do, Eli?" I asked.

onetwothreeonetwothreeonetwo

Eli looked up. He had tears in his eyes. He was smiling. His voice was low, from that warm, thick chest. "I came here wanting to die," he said. "Losing the hunt, working for fake Brits forcing their railways on us, and their roads and their sewers and their artesian wells and their foundries and their mills and their meat-processing plants. Their community halls, their churches, their schools, their municipal governments, their district governments, their provincial governments, their Dominion governments. It was all too much to bear. I wanted to die." He looked at Peter, son to adoptive father. "But Peter's given me hope. I want to live. I want to see the day when this entire nightmare is over and the world is a fair and free place again."

"That's impossible," said Clark.

"Yes," said Eli, his face lit with optimism. "Exactly!" He

kissed me on the mouth. Slight spark. "I respect your decision, Blondie," he said.

That night, sleeping beside my packed bags, I dreamed that the moon was Eli, but Eli had become a beautiful bull, white with a muscular back and polished white horns, and he played in the surf and lay down and let me touch his breast and caress the soft folds of his flesh, and then he let me mount him and he swam out from shore, far across the wide ocean, and I felt frightened in my sleep and looked back to my little room far behind me, but I held onto that white horn and it took me out to the green and windy sea.

CHAPTER FOUR

ALICE CUT MY HAIR with quick, determined scissors while Peter wept and plucked away at a borrowed guitar. My mum and I made moustaches of my blonde curls and swept the rest into the compost heap, like thin, white wood shavings. She hadn't wavered from her decision to send me off to war. But I know she was living in some confusion. She and I would look at each other in surprise, waiting for the other to speak. Here she was, pretty well kicking me out, yet she seemed hurt by her own decision, and she was always mad. Once, after yelling at me for leaving a dish in the sink, she suddenly gathered me in her arms and said, "This is your chance to grow up. You will become a woman by first becoming a man." She let go. There were tears in her eyes. Then she shrugged and said, "I can only say it worked for me."

We fixed up the barn with some bedding and furniture, and Roberts and Clark lived there all summer. Clark loved "our property" and the land around it. He loved the sweet scent of clover, the summer storms, the first tincture of yellow in August. He loved the Red River, he said, and spent many hours fishing from its banks.

Eli took up quarters in Marie's grotto. Peter planted as little as possible, but Eli proved to be such a good farmer that "our property" suddenly took on a look of prosperity. It seemed that harvest came very quickly. Eli's latent talent for growing things flourished and his bandy legs seemed straighter and he looked happy, winking at me when he donned his old hat before going out to the fields. At night, he and Peter would resume their perpetual conversation about that unanswerable ideal called Impossibilism. I was busy pretending to learn Dutch and German under the tutelage of my distracted mother and so I ignored their apocalyptic mission statements.

"The capitalists are digging their own graves," Eli said to me while he passed the young corn across the table.

"This is the first year we haven't had to dig the worms out of the corn before we could eat it," I told him, rolling a cob in butter. "How'd you do that?"

And Eli responded, "Their downfall is the inevitable outcome of a system based on the exploitation of the workers."

"It really is a miracle," I said to Eli. "Best corn I've ever tasted."

Eli looked at the corn as a Zen Buddhist would examine a screwdriver. "The ruling class will crumble," he said. "It's just a question of time." His confidence was a youth serum, his cheeks were as rosy as little crabapples.

"Best chicken too; best I've ever had," I told him. "Best beets. Best bread. Best butter. Best company."

And Alice, in German, "*You have no self-respect.*" To Eli, in English with a Japanese accent, she said, "Man has only begun to develop his enormous talents for large-scale destruction."

THEY TOOK US to the train station, Roberts and Clark and me, in the wagon full of pemmican. The place was nearly deserted because everybody was harvesting. Back in '99, hundreds of people had come down to the station to stare with doubt or envy at the A Company, off to fight the Boers. But when Pretoria fell, the British brass told everyone the war was finished, and in England people believed them just long enough for Lord Salisbury to stage a highly successful election. So we were considered an afterthought, tourists, scavengers flocking to nibble at war's cold remains. I didn't even get to wear one of those funny white hats. Roberts and Clark sported very compelling North West Mounted Police uniforms. But I was forced to wear mufti.

When it was time to say goodbye, Roberts was pure ambition, clicking and shining like a thoroughbred at the gate. Eli shook his hand with a sort of rueful affection. We all treated poor Roberts this way; he was a professional soldier, that was his fate. But with Clark, it was somewhat different. Clark blinked and wagged happily; he hugged everyone, lifting Alice right off the ground in his enthusiasm. Eli uneasily embraced him for a moment, then gave him a manly tap on the jaw. When it was my turn, Eli pulled me into his big chest for a fraternal hug. We couldn't kiss because I was dressed as a man. Mum and Dad stood watching. Dad was quite frankly a wreck. And while my mother appeared to be determined and decisive, you could see that she was in a lot of pain. When it came time for us to say goodbye, she kissed my cheek tenderly and I told her that I loved her. She nearly broke down, but she said, "If you get too homesick, Blondie, just . . . come home." It really was terrible to say goodbye. Transvestitism had become a family tradition. And so, at the end, we all felt very close.

CHAPTER FIVE

CLARK TALKED MY EAR off all the way to Cape Town. His monologue began as soon as we had found our seats aboard the train in Winnipeg, and it carried on without stop all the way to Quebec City. Over the entire Canadian Shield, he sang his autobiography, an extended poem filled with minutiae, for Clark took astonished pleasure in variety. On his life's path, he would remember every pebble. He seemed to have fallen in love with every place his duties had taken him, as if he would seek to attach those locales to himself, to form himself out of extraneous landscapes and the duties of a colonial soldier. I began to think that Clark did not fully fit his role in the Canadian militia serving under the British army; he seemed to be straining to subdue a sense of loss even through the aggrandizement of his many affections. Still, he was a sweet and tender man.

Once, as we sat together—me at the window, watching the Dominion roll away, and Clark turning in his seat so he could see my face, as he always did when he talked, study your face intently—he suddenly stopped and, suffering a mild spark, flicked my earlobe with his finger. He began to laugh, a lazy giggle, and again flicked at the soft white lobe of my small and perfect ear. "Look!" he said. "It flaps a little! Ha, ha! If you flick it. Ha! It wiggles on its own!"

Even aboard ship, while I wormed my way through three days

of seasickness, Clark's voice leashed me to the world, gabbing and gabbing on and on. By this means, he saved my life. I had known the smell of the sea in small doses from my father, just a whiff when he would walk in from impossible conversations with his radical pals. But nothing could have prepared me for the huge lungs of the breathing ocean. Nothing could have prepared me for the strangeness of our voyage, or for the sorrows that would befall us.

We arrived in Cape Town and immediately took the train over the Great Karroo desert towards the town of Kimberley, where Roberts was to wait for further orders. Roberts had ascended military echelons to the position of colonel, some say because of a lucky misconception that he was a blood connection to *the* Field Marshal Frederick Lord Roberts, the commander-in-chief of this "white man's war." (*Our* Roberts went on to join the South African Constabulary in the Orange River country, and he would stay on after the war ended. The military was his life. He would re-enlist in 1914 and die in France, his lungs blistered by mustard gas.)

Roberts looked very fine that day in the hot winter of 1901. He and Clark and I had played poker all the way from Cape Town to Kimberley, a journey of about four days because the train kept breaking down, leaving us to bake whether we stayed within the shade of the suffocating compartments or sat out on the coarse, grassy sand. When we finally arrived in Kimberley, Clark and I looked like old socks, but Roberts descended onto the station platform glossy, clear-eyed and wearing a new uniform. The South African inland heat was yellow and dusty and strange. Roberts sailed away like a yacht into a fresh breeze, though the air was rank and still.

Clark and I stumbled after the other men in our battalion. We began to walk. The British army still did not have sufficient access to horses. We marched east, towards Natal, on a meandering path by the Modder River. The mention of a river made my heart ache (a wide artery through our land, small waves raised against the current in an east wind, flooding with broken ice, or in mid-summer, low on the mud bank flanked by willow, wild cucumber and rose). I didn't know the name of anything around me. Already, I was almost delusional with homesickness. I asked Clark to tell me my name. He combed his moustache with his hand and said, "Your name is Trooper McCormack." It was no help at all.

We walked for three days, with a thirst that dried us till we looked and smelled like smoked fish, through thorn patches and stunted bush, choking on dust kicked up by the cattle and the wagons. Clark spoke his constant monologue, his cracked mouth chewing on salt beef washed down with the last spit from his water bottle. He was already in love with South Africa. His words kept me pinned to the glassy mirage of that inexplicable land. Such heat in January, such yellow heat, was beyond understanding. Clark told me that it looked just like the desert near home at Carberry. He knew a lot about the hilly country to the west of "our property." He fondly renamed things with our familiar names. Wild sunflower and Indian grass, wild rye and juniper.

"See?" he said, pulling me up by the elbow. "Yellow evening primrose. Only it's red. Just like home, Blondie. If winter were hot as Hades in a dry year, it'd be just like home."

"Smart Dog," I said to him, gasping for air, "you're from Ontario."

"I'm a servant of the Crown, Blondie. I am loyal to Her Majesty."

"That's who you're fighting for?"

"Empire. Yes. Her Imperial Majesty."

"You're a good man, Clark," I said.

"You're a good man too, Blondie."

"But you're an idiot. A fawning, sycophantic, boot-licking lackey of the ruling class."

"I miss Eli too," said Clark.

I forced him to stop. Exhausted soldiers flowed around us. A wagon rolled by, driven by a black man, the first black man I'd seen since leaving the docks at Cape Town. "I've made a mistake," I told Clark. He tipped his head. The army crawled over the earth. "Please," I said, "I don't love the queen."

Clark put his hand over my mouth and hauled me to the edge of the column. I saw more blacks, mostly driving carts, unarmed. "What are we doing here?" I was panicking.

With surprise, I realized that Clark was angry. "We are fighting for the British Empire," he said. "It's that simple. It's what we do."

"It's not our country," I pleaded.

"Of course it is! South Africa belongs to Britain!"

"No!" I said. "We're not at home! We have no right to be here!"

"We have as much right to be here as anywhere," Clark said. "Anywhere!" A cart passed: a black man, his eyes on us. Clark laughed bitterly. "It is the same here as at *home!* What makes you feel at *home* on your farm? Don't you dare get self-righteous on me. I'm a colonial soldier. Everything else is a lot of hypocritical sh— sugar. I may be . . . naive in some ways, Blondie. But I'm not stupid."

"I want to go home," I cried, clutching his arm.

Clark looked at me with a bit of fear in his eyes. "Our home is the British Empire." He shook off my hand. "And now it's time to defend that empire. We are nothing," he said. "We are nothing! Without loyalty."

He began to walk away from me, and I dragged on him. "I could be loyal, Clark! Wait! What am I loyal to?"

"You know very well," he murmured so quietly he could scarcely be heard above the clatter of the carts.

"Can't we just go back to St. Norbert? You said you loved it there! The smell of clover and all, our own river!"

Clark suddenly turned to face me. To my horror, I saw that he was crying. He waved his arms at the parade of foot soldiers, at the blacks driving carts pulled by the precious horses. "This," he said helplessly, "is my home. Now! Do you see who I am? I am this!" He turned his back on me and fought his way to the middle of the thirsty column. The last look Clark gave me was one of humiliation.

I stood at the edge of the river of white soldiers and black servants. Clark disappeared from sight.

<hr />

I COULD NOT GO after him. I was exhausted, pulled by an under-tow west to Kimberley. My flesh was a foreign weed twisted right out of the soil, withering. Because I was travelling against the current, I was cut off from any companionship, and it took me perhaps five days to find my way back. I was never lost, because I could feel in my bones the direction that would eventually lead me home. But I had no supplies, and was forced to beg for water and a bit of food. By the time I got there, I think I was nearly dead. My fight with Clark cut away the shreds of my resolve. I didn't know what to do next. I wanted to go home. But home, now, was in abeyance, a state of suspension. Another colony. Yes. But mine.

Kimberley was in mourning. Queen Victoria had died. Everyone seemed genuinely grief-stricken. I needed to talk to Roberts; he alone was my link with Clark. I found him at the company headquarters. Roberts looked up from some paperwork when I walked in. I was too exhausted to speak. There was a jug of water on his desk. I reached for it, but Roberts forced me to wait while he poured it into a glass. His secretary looked at us oddly. Roberts closed the door.

He turned to me, I saw, with genuine concern. He, of course, knew that I was a woman. I suddenly realized that for such a stuffy man, he'd shown remarkable tolerance. He waited while I drank my fill of water and had calmed down somewhat. Then he poured a glass of whisky, gave it to me, stood back with a fatherly manner and said, "Do you know about the fighting at the Modder?"

"No," I said. "I turned back." I threw back the whisky and held out my glass for more. I would get drunk; such are the rules for cowards like me.

"It looks very bad," he said. He walked to the window, looking out, one hand tucked behind his back. "Very bad," he said quietly. "We have suffered many losses."

"Oh, God. Clark."

"We don't know yet. We'll be transporting the casualties here."

"When?"

"Very soon." Roberts turned to me. "Let's get out of here," he said.

He took me to the officers' club. The place was crowded, everyone wearing black armbands, in honour of the queen, I guess, though there were so many dead to mourn. We found a small table, and Roberts ordered a bottle of brandy. He was bitter and sad. "These Boers," he said, "they fight like . . . almost like children, vicious children. They don't obey the rules of war. They sneak up on horseback; you can't tell who is going to shoot you. They dodge and sneak."

"Like Indians," I said.

Roberts looked up sharply. "Yes. I suppose so." He nodded to himself. "I hate losing." He took a healthy drink.

"Roberts," I said hesitantly. "Have you ever wondered whether we should be here at all?"

Roberts laughed unhappily. "It should never have come to this," he said. "And the Boers know it. We *own* South Africa."

"That's what Clark said."

Roberts refilled our glasses, toasted me out of habit and drank quickly. It appeared to clear his head. He looked closely at me. "Why did you come back?"

I hesitated. "I had a fight with Clark. He went on ahead. And I . . . turned back." I looked about at the smoky room full of uniformed men and lowered my voice. "I guess I'm not the right kind of man to be a soldier."

Roberts shrugged. I hadn't understood before that he was generous. I began to hope that he might help me with my dilemma. I took a big drink and plunged ahead. "Roberts, can I ask you something and you promise you won't get mad? You see, Clark, he got mad. And hurt."

Roberts fondly smiled. "Sweet man." He squinted at me. "I mean that philosophically," he added brusquely.

"Oh, yes. Clark is a good man. Do you think he's all right?"

Roberts bit his lip and took another drink.

"Because, see, I feel responsible. For everything. Like, like this war. Could you tell me, and now don't get mad . . . What *are* we doing here?"

"Fighting for queen and country." Roberts peered at me. "Did you hit your head? Do you feel hot?"

"I'm fine. But what I want to know is, How come Britain *owns* South Africa?"

He laughed. "We bloody paid for her! Outrageously! Six million pounds to the stadtholder." He considered. "Of course, that got us some additional South American land."

"Six million pounds. For their diamonds and their fields of gold," I said.

Roberts glared at me. "For the right to defend their ignorant masses from slavery." Again he took a good swig. "The gold too. And the diamond mines. Of course." He combed his glossy hair with his fingers. "You're going to argue that this war is corrupt. Men have been arguing that in the British House of Lords, for God's sake, Blondie. But you just don't understand. Is it corrupt to use the riches of an uncivilized country? To, what say, take that country out of darkness and into the light? The empire *must* civilize the world. It is our destiny. And it is our responsibility. That's what empire does. And I, for one, am proud to be a part of it."

A tiny fly landed on his glass and perished. Roberts removed it and lifted the glass to his lips, and he smiled as he said, "Besides, my friend, Canada is no different. It was a Scot aristocrat first bought the Red River land, correct?"

"Lord Selkirk," I said miserably. I could see where this was going. Roberts was starting to have fun.

"Righto!" he said, pouring us more brandy and winking at me. "The mad Scot. What'd *he* pay?"

"Ten shillings," I said, and drank.

Roberts leaned back in his chair and roared with laughter. "Not so mad after all!" he said. "Course, that was just a lot of land with a lot of Indians on it. No gold. No diamonds." He shook his head in wonder. "What a whim."

"Well, sure!" I said. "But we've got rich land too! Rupert's Land, the old Hudson's Bay Company land? My dad, Peter, says it cost 300,000 pounds. Maybe that's not a lot of money, but that land is rich!"

"Ha! Spoken like a true colonial! Do you get my point? We bought Canada for, what say, furs, of course, and forests, I suppose. We were somewhat misinformed. Bought ourselves a pack of trouble. But look what we have done for the Indians!" He offered me a cigar, which I accepted, lit them both and laughed again. "Y'know what the Americans paid for Alaska?" He leaned in conspiratorially and whispered, "Seven million dollars." He fell backwards, laughing. "Seven million for a block of ice! Oh,

God, why do we worry about them? Oh, oh my. Fools."

I was getting the hang of the cigar. "But, Roberts," I said out the side of my mouth, waving my cigar at the crowded room, "I don't think you've answered my question. This 'darkness into light' rubbish"—I blew out smoke—"how do we get away with it?"

"Y'mean, really?" I nodded. He laughed. "Y'want to know the real God's truth about South Africa, Canada, Australia, India?" I nodded yes, please, sir. He was swelling up with rhetoric and pride. "Why stop with the British Empire? I'll give you more! What's got the French so much of Africa? Even the Boer, damn him, but part of me will admire him despite myself. It's *seed*, Blondie. The Boer is a mix of Dutch and French. Imagine a great hand dipping into a storehouse of French seed—Normans, Huguenots, émigrés—and sprinkling the nations with *la sperme splendide*. It has given the Boer *soul*. Yes," he said, "I will grant the enemy a soul. France may not have founded any countries, but by God, she's made every other country the richer by the emissions of the best seed. Seed!" said Roberts, and leaned back, stoking his cigar cheerfully. "That's what builds empires! That's what makes us welcome in these uncivilized places! Seed! They're crying for it."

Roberts saw my look of disappointment and straightened up. "C'mon, Blondie. Look at Canada! All that land? What were the Indians going to do with it?" He tapped his chest with his fingers. "British seed. The best goes West. Look at you! Your own mother and father came from the Old World!" He pointed at me. "A Scot. You. That's why I like you. Those potato eaters, those Irish, let 'em go to the States. But you. I like a Scot. You're one of ours."

Just then, Roberts's secretary entered the bar and made his way to our table with such obvious anxiety that those he passed stopped chatting and followed his path to our table. He saluted and waited. "What is it, Dwyer?" Roberts asked.

"The casualties, sir. They're at the hospital morgue."

The bar went quiet. Roberts sat up very straight. "The morgue? Are they all dead?"

"They brought us only the dead, sir. The wounded are being treated at the field hospital."

A soldier at a nearby table overheard the news of casualties, and he rose to his feet and began to sing. The sound of chairs pushed back, every man in the room rising, their voices filling the room, and as I fled, they made a pure and ardent male chorus. "God save our gracious king! Long live our noble king!"

The morgue was full. At first I went to the wrong body, a soldier with thick hair and a moustache like Clark's, and I sobbed but knew it wasn't him. I studied the face of the dead soldier till I thought I couldn't be shocked by the impressive nature of a corpse. I turned to walk away. And saw him. His eyes were open, as if his brain had exploded through some kind of impact that forced the eyes out, hemorrhaging, so they were layered in a white, nictating film, with blood seeping from under the lids. His nose was small and blunt, as it hadn't looked in life. I said I was sorry. I am so sorry, Clark. I wanted to hold him. I tried to lift his shoulder, but his arm had come away beneath the shoulder blade, neat and hard, with little blood, carved through to the bone. I peered beneath the blade: Clark's white bone, black blood. I'm so sorry, I said, patting the cloth on his stiff chest.

I sat with him all night. The lights burned brightly in the morgue. I didn't know it was morning when they came to take away the dead for burial. They put his body on a stretcher. I tried to straighten him, but there wasn't much I could do. I followed them to the graves.

Roberts was there. The sun was hidden by cloud. Roberts was again stiff and formal, but that did not disguise his sorrow. He gripped my arm briefly. We stood beside one another and waited for the bodies to be safely bedded. Then everyone went away. But I told Roberts I'd stay awhile, and then be along. Even in grief, Roberts had an invincible shine to him, as if he carried about him his own special atmosphere. He nodded and left me there in the graveyard.

It was peaceful among the dead, their freshly rested bodies put out of sight, and so recent you could feel they were still dreaming, not quite gone. The cloud drifted off, and in the sunlight the colours were bright, brilliant, the grassy air prickly and green. I began to feel myself, the faint papery sound of my hands when I touched them together, the fine pores of my skin. In the grass beside me was one small blue flower that had somehow escaped being trampled. It was the bluest thing I'd ever seen.

And then I left him there. I took the train back to Cape Town and the ship to Halifax, and then a train back West. I left Clark in the dark garden of the dead in South Africa. I left my friend there, and went home.

CHAPTER SIX

THE TRAIN SLOWED DOWN long enough to let me leap off into dried mud stubbled with tufts of grass. The afternoon smelled of honeysuckle, lilac and thunder. They'd been flooded that spring. Driftwood lay on the east side of the road. Towards the Red River (which was still quite high, though it was the end of May, and a white scar ran along its banks, caused by the water's sudden retreat), the land was littered with broken wheels and broken dolls, bicycles, all kinds of private belongings that had been swept away. The flood had plucked an elm tree and laid it in the middle of the field, shining, a gigantic chewing bone.

There was enough water in the ditch to grow green stalks of cattails and common rye grass, cutgrass and a fine onion-like blade that looked something like wild rice, with a small burst of seed at its head, sunlight moving over it all, so the green fused and the blue sky shone between. The thunderhead lay off to the east, behind our homestead. A hot sky, edged cleanly by the plum-coloured cloud with twigs of lightning. I shouldered my pack and started to walk down the road towards our house, towards the stand of ash trees and the storm. I carried the message of Clark's death like a stone under my tongue.

It wasn't any fun being a man, especially with my face wet, as if I'd lost a layer of skin. When women cry it's patriotic, a vote for home. But I was a man in uniform. People were cool. The

Boer War was maybe the last rich man's war. A cavalry war. It belonged to men who cut the pages of their books with silver letter openers, knew how to handle a brolly and a shoehorn, a golf club, a tennis racquet, a tiller and the reins—some of which were useful in South Africa. Strangers were unsympathetic; perhaps they figured I had been cauterized by wealth, crying over my gin.

I think I was crying as I made my way home. It would help to explain why I became such a vivid electrical conductor.

The sun burned with heat as sharp as the cry of the tern tipping its wings in the alluvial field beside me. I counted my steps and counted the dead butterflies, and then began to count the days since I'd last been a woman. I shucked off my knapsack and took off all my clothes. The breeze and sun felt very good. Just then, the cloud spoke out deeply, thunderous. I grew aware of being naked in a cyclone; I heard the great wings, felt a strange, beating heat.

I left my stuff on the road. My skin wrapped in tears and yellow light, I walked home empty-handed and bare-assed on a nimbus of dust, into grape-coloured air, above me a purple lid closing on the daisy eye of sun. It smelled of rain. I wondered if Eli would be there. I would deliver my stone. The road formed a T, at the junction of which was a gate to the overgrown lane to our house. The ash leaves sounded like water. They stood lopsided in a row. Under them, creamy blossoms of saskatoons and tiny buds of rose. I stood naked at the junction, and the thunderhead with its cold lip pressed above the gate.

From the field to my left came the sound of a mouth organ, a corny, folksy tune somewhere in the grass between the ash trees. I went towards the music; each step seemed to send it farther away. I followed like a minnow mouthing the cribbing of a dock, followed where the road ran in sunshine at the iron blue edge of the storm. From a hundred feet away, I knew it was him. The song he played was as sad as a song can be, his elegy for pure intentions.

I drew close. The tune faltered when he drew a breath, as he made a commitment to the next phrase. Sometimes thunder overran him and he played bravely under. It got louder and he played on, bold as a kid stealing from a garden, hesitant, then running hard.

When at last I saw him, he was facing north, seated with his back against a tree. He wore the same battered hat. His hair was long and tied behind. A patient, tranquil man. I walked quietly around to stand before him. Just then, the wind blew the first brush of rain, lifting my short hair from the nape of my neck. Light rain burned and then cooled my naked skin, emitting a sibilant glow. I saw the pleasure in his face when he looked up, startled and glad. He smiled with the harmonica at his lips. Thunder was bowling along behind the flattened sky. "Hey, Zeus," I said. He came towards me.

The storm crashed through, falling in on us like a forest burning, a mine caving in, and there was the strong scent of sea. The rain fell in torrents, Poseidon's backhand slap, ripping the clothes from Eli's back and laying us in the mud. Everything was black with stark strobes of light. We hid our faces from the rain, made ourselves small as one, his muscular back, his cool face. I found I could talk while I kissed, and I poured everything into him and he into me. The lightning struck the ground beside us as I kissed Eli's chest, but the pleasure had pulled Eli's head back just then and he caught it, like a shotgun in his ear; it shattered his eardrum and ran through his loving throat and through him as seed to the calyx of iris and stippled us, a permanent engraving upon the land where we would grow our gardens, and the intolerable delight placed me beside myself and I was looking at the mud, where a tiny blossom of blue-eyed grass stood up in the rain. And then, truly blessed by Bacchus, we both passed out cold.

AND SO IT CAME TO BE: Eli and I were married the following day.

Everyone was there, Alice and Peter and all our friends. The mirror-tongued midwife spoke at length, and we all wept to hear her wisdom and goodwill and we vowed to follow her advice through all our years together. Peter's Impossibilists made an appearance, obviously reluctant, but when they were witness to the ardent joy coming from our feverish lips, how we entwined our blackened fingers, and when they saw how our teeth laughed in our storm-burnt faces and our bare, blistered feet danced on the cool grass (for it turned sunny the following day, which was a Saturday; there was a soothing breeze and it was not too hot), when they saw that we loved each other more than we loved weddings, they focused on our nuptials with intelligence as clear as telescopes, recognizing in Eli and me the happiness, the beautiful coincidence, of lucky love. We ate honey cake and goat's cheese; we drank water imported all the way from Shoal Lake in the east and Alice's dandelion wine. We danced all day and all night, and the Impossibilists stood on chairs tipsy on the grass and made grandiloquent speeches, and everyone felt the day was soon a-coming when we would be glad like this forever. And so we rejoiced into the rosy dawn.

And Eli and I knew, as Alice and Peter had known before us.

It was the seed of the jack pine. The catalyst, a stroke of lightning.

And we knew the child fired this way would be a daughter.

And our daughter would be called Helen.

And Helen would be the most beautiful woman the world had ever known.

PART FOUR

1902

CHAPTER ONE

WE MADE OUR HOME in Marie's grotto, slipping into its shady rooms as into the third hour of sleep. I belonged there, among sheaves of dreams. Yet I was a visitor.

Marie's grotto was a place of happy melancholy. It smelled of parsley and hide. The spruce lumber for the walls had been well oiled when it was first cut, and the old pine floor was waxed with beeswax, the window frames and cupboards with a mixture of pine resin and sunflower oil. The midwife had made curtains, quilts, rag rugs in Galatian dyes—cherry red, blueberry and a hectic pink of unknown origin—and these lay across the muskrat skins, the pelts that had survived the years. Its light was the colour of steeped tea, and everyone in its vicinity looked young and sunny and well. Even my dead mother-in-law, Marie.

I grew, orb-like, and like Alice before me, I refused to wear clothes. As the time of Helen's birth approached, there ran a dark brown line down the centre of my belly and my pelvis opened and my bare feet splayed. I was splitting in two. Winter had delayed nearly till Christmas, the warm weather permitting me naked freedom until December, when it got cold enough to skate over at the Rivière Sale, the Red being too wide and treacherous. The air was just cold enough to freeze the shallow water, ice so smooth you'd swear it moved.

We'd skated for a week, our wet chins chafed by woollen scarves.

On the day it finally snowed, the baby began to tumble and dance. My mother came with the midwife, and they sat on my bed and placed their hands on me and all the while they spoke to each other in God knows what language, nodding and cracking jokes as if I weren't there. I laughed when they laughed.

I was an onion. Within me, skin upon skin peeled back of its own accord. A most pleasant divestment. My outer skin stretched like deerskin on a drum.

She came in a late-winter snowstorm. It was a lovely storm, and we were celebrating quietly with warm milk sweetened with rum and a fire in the stove. Very cold. Eli and I were dancing, his woollen jersey rubbing cleanly on my skin, for I was such an oven I wore nothing but a pair of moccasins and the old red Assomption sash I'd stolen from Alice's memory chest, faded and beautiful, wrapped around my belly. When the waltz came to a close, we kissed one another formally, twice. And then Eli put on his buffalo coat and went to find a horse that had escaped from the pen that morning. "He's probably standing at the gate, waiting to be let in," he said as he shouldered the coat. "That horse is a dog." He filled his pipe and went out.

When he closed the door, he was utterly gone. I could hear nothing outside except the cold crack of air and the gracious music of falling snow. Suddenly, somebody threw a bucket of water on the floor. I yelled, and slipped on a puddle under me. My legs trembled and my feet planted themselves wide apart. I tucked my hands beneath my belly, and my face grew as long as the face of an elephant and then my arms grew till they dragged to the ground and I trailed my claws on Marie's wooden floor and the carvings from my claws would remain for many years to come. I crawled under the big table littered with books and winter cuttings of plants. I think I was singing a song of turtles, and then with my reptilian hands on either side of my shell, the crashing of books and plant-cuttings. When the turtle lifted on her claw legs, she banged into the kitchen cupboard and her shell knocked down the spoons and dishes Alice had bestowed upon our marital home, and in the broken china the turtle cut her ancient paws and the blood came from a breach in her self and I raised myself by putting my hands upon my thighs and with all the strength of time itself I tore myself in two.

Eli returned just in time to receive the waxy infant. He cradled her. We found the blankets fallen off our bed and laid Helen down and pinched the cord and a gust of pain brought out the afterbirth. Eli lifted her lovingly and put the tip of his finger in her mouth, and we heard the sea-born creature breathe. We knew her. We said hello in the shelf of peace. He tied the navel himself, for he'd learned to sew by stitching saddles. We cleaned her with snow heated on the stove and wrapped her. Helen's face was the colour of anemone, and her features, the soft bones, translucent. Even in her first minutes, her beauty was . . . strange. Overwhelming. I didn't sleep for many nights afterwards, not because she fussed, but because I could not take my eyes off her, as if I were waiting for her beauty to subside.

ABOVE THE BLACK SPRUCE it was sunny and gay. At the end of April, the snow at last turned to cornmeal in green grass at the base of the trees. I awoke to the sound of snow tobogganing from the roof and opened my eyes directly into the solemn gaze of my child. Blue-black eyes and, at nearly two months of age, precise black eyebrows and thick black curls. No resemblance to her mother. She'd been watching me sleep with a look of unmistakable pity.

The heat woke up the flies, buzzing against the glass for a final hour before dying on the windowsill. Helen fumbled with dead flies and licked them into her mouth. I was unfamiliar with children and didn't realize how remarkable was her coordination.

The door opened and Eli walked in, behind him the shadow of my mother-in-law. Her voice, that atonal bone sound, a falling note not unlovely to the ear but changeful, a tone of constant fall. "The baby should not eat bugs," she chimed, "especially when the bugs are freshly dead."

I sighed. Eli shrugged hopefully. There was the bright chirrup of melting snow on the wood porch. Helen twisted herself out of my arms like a fish out of a net, and Eli snatched her up just as she was about to fall off the bed. "There now," he said, and turned towards the corner of the room, where Marie occupied a kitchen chair. She was more a collection of dark green light, a gathering into shape. She smiled peacefully and then she said, "It's time you two were properly married."

Now, at the sound of her voice, Helen lay her head on her father's neck and fell asleep.

"But first, would you like tea?" Marie rose and went to the window. The daylight showed her to be quite real, though it seemed to be evening where she was, or raining, or June. Beneath the window was a drawer that I had never been able to open. Marie pulled it easily and withdrew a packet of dried roots and herbs. She set the kettle on the stove and it quickly began to steam, and she offered us tea that smelled of licorice.

We sipped, smiling politely. It was sort of her house. I wondered if I'd get a chance to talk this over with Eli, if we could maybe set down a few rules in the future. Marie, more corporeal than usual, put her cup down and looked at each of us, candid and fond. She smiled at Helen. "Poor little one," she said, "to be the cause of so much suffering."

"But," I protested, "she is a joy!"

Marie nodded, as if there was no contradiction. "Powerful wishes are always innocent." She passed her dusky hand over Helen's face, and Helen dreamed she was falling, flung her arms out. Marie said, "She will need more than forgiveness and mercy. But they will give her only pearls." For a moment, this phantom grandmother looked infinitely grieved, then she brightened, and business-like, she asked us, "Would you like me to hear your vows now?"

Eli seemed to understand. He put the sleeping baby into her cradle and stood, waving me to attention. I joined him at his side. And we became husband and wife. Again. In Marie's jurisdiction.

In a backstage whisper, Marie said, "Remove your gloves!" I realized that Eli and I were wearing ornate riding gloves with beadwork and long leather fringes. We took them off, embarrassed.

"And now," she said, "repeat after me. I take off my glove . . ."

The promise we would make to each other would be a

beautiful misunderstanding, a necessary promise impossible to keep. It was the treaty between Mawedopenais, the leader of the Ojibwas, and the Great Mother, our dead queen, spoken more than thirty years ago, when I was a baby and Marie was the adoptive mother of a little boy precariously named Eli. We gave each other everything, and in exchange we were promised security and peace everlasting. In one hand, we held the right of trespass, and in the other, the privileges of privacy. We promised boundaries; we permitted access. One of us believed we'd won the right to unlimited enjoyment of life's necessities and pleasures. The other understood that we'd placed limits upon ourselves (always in a free and non-compulsory arrangement), that we would thenceforth own a certain share of the land, the water, the air and all the gifts of the Great Spirit therein. We were both committed to this covenant, and spoke from the bottom of our hearts.

> *I take off my glove and give you my hand, and with it*
> *my birthright and my land—*
> *And in taking your hand I hold fast all the promises*
> *you have made . . .*
> *All the promises you have made . . .*
> *As long as the sun rises and the water flows . . .*
> *As long as the sun rises*
> *And the water flows.*

When we'd made our faulty promises, we kissed and thanked Marie, who nodded agreeably and offered us cold duck with chokecherry jam.

And when the time came for us to go, we bowed and saw each other to the door and waved goodbye, Eli and I, hopeful, waving goodbye to Marie, and Marie, with confidence, seeing us out, into our own futures, like tadpoles swimming into the fishy light of our flawless memories.

CHAPTER TWO
1906: HELEN'S EDUCATION

As SOON AS SHE WAS ABLE to walk with some assurance, Helen used her new skill to walk away from me. When I remember her now, it is always the back of her head I'm seeing, her determined shoulders as she toddles out of the yard on some business of her own. She always treated me with dutiful affection. In fact, despite a certain distaste for the corruption of middle-aged flesh, she loved me, in her evasive fashion. I was non-essential. Everyone was. Though she was fond of us, especially when we were near by.

Helen's beauty was an attribute of such magnitude it became an independent creature, a sort of symbiotic organism that attached itself to my daughter. In photographs, she seemed upstaged by her own beauty, which was like a competitive friend sticking her head in front of the camera, obscuring the presence of a shy child who satisfied herself with the vicarious pleasures of living life through another. Helen's beauty robbed Helen of herself.

Her grandmother Alice was no fool. She saw that Helen was in danger. Alice would watch my little girl walking through the cow parsnip with the sun flashing from her raven hair. She called to her, but Helen never came when we called; we would have to fetch her. Helen was listening to her own ticking heart, dazed by the fracture between herself and the resplendent girl the world saw. My mother was a nineteenth-century woman, and she perceived the problem as one of simple vanity. And being an idealist, she thought to correct what seemed like vapid girlishness with a good strong dose of her favourite medicine, that being formal education.

So Alice took Helen to school.

My mother would come for Helen every morning at five o'clock. I would gather Helen up in my arms and walk down the path separating our houses. She would clutch me with cool little hands about my neck while we bounded down the path through the dusky leaves. Her living grandmother greeted us at the clearing, a white figure half lit by a lantern held high, and with an easy shift of her weight, Helen was gone. From one life raft to the next. Always with that same detached gaze. I stopped them and demanded my kiss, and Helen would lean out from the ledge of Grandmother Alice's arms and obediently put her lips anywhere in the vicinity of my face. Then with a trace of a smile, she was gone.

During the long buggy ride, she stared up at the fading stars, listening to Grandmother Alice sing, and when they were drawn into the streets of Winnipeg and the horses drummed on cobblestones and her grandmother fell silent, Helen sat up very straight to stare at people. The city had grown big by then, and there were many people walking and many carts with milk and newspapers and pigs and bread, and at least in the richer south part of the city, there were electric streetcars.

One morning on their way to the school, they saw a horse and wagon collide with a streetcar. The wagon tipped over, dragging the horse down with it. The horse struggled to its feet, twisting the traces till one snapped off and splintered into its neck. It was trapped, speared, gaffed half-backwards, its front legs buckled, then it stood and pulled the wagon on its side over the street, the wood frame breaking up into pieces. Alice tried to cover Helen's eyes, but Helen pulled away. She was keen, alert, interested.

By the time they arrived at the Mission school, there were a dozen children waiting at the door with that forthright insistence of hunger. Those were the ones without food at home. Some members of the church distrusted Alice's method of supplying food and clothing to bribe the children to come to school. Salvation is sufficient unto itself, they argued; such economic meddling will defile the true spirit of the church. My mother agreed and removed the school to its shoddy digs near the CPR station and the Dominion Immigration Hall (which was always overflowing with those "stalwart peasants in sheepskin coats" so desirable to the Minister of the Interior—as long as the shabby Europeans left town quickly to farm, and as long as they did not get the vote).

The first job was to feed the children. Not all the students of Alice's school needed breakfast; in another hour, nearly forty others would arrive, warmly dressed and fed. But the first hour was the loveliest. Mr. Kolchella had lit the stove long before. They sat peaceably at the refectory tables, to sip porridge sweetened with lots of Grandfather Peter's honey. Helen had a couple of friends among the children attending this early communal meal, two silent little boys with handsome, dirty faces who became her companions. Helen unconsciously took the seat at the head of the table. The two boys sat at either side. The friends spooned their porridge with darting efficiency and then sat mute, all three holding hands. These were Helen's first suitors.

The children were let out to the yard to play while Alice and Mr. Kolchella washed the dishes and replaced the porridge bowls with tattered books. My mother hated the school bell, but the kids loved it, as they loved flags and military medals. She had only to stand on the steps, holding it by its clapper like a dead animal, and the kids would stampede inside.

Mr. Kolchella was Austrian-born. He was, like Alice, slight, and strong. He had a very wide mouth with long white teeth, a big, triangular nose and genial brown eyes framed by thick lashes. All of this eloquence was fit into a tiny face, just as his enormous energy was barely squeezed into his diminutive frame. Mr. Kolchella taught in German, Slavic and Bohemian. Alice somehow covered the others, with the help of the children themselves, who had little regard for their mother tongues and preferred bewilderment in English to knowledge in their own language.

Classes proceeded through a relay, in which information was spoken in, perhaps, Polish and transformed into Yiddish by the recipient, who substituted half the words with Russian or Chinese and sent it forward through a cycle of perhaps twenty languages before it was returned, transmuted, to Alice in English. A game of Grandmother's Whisper.

The lessons had an athletic quality. Giddy children leapt up to pluck words out of the air. Knowledge was a fat man; the kids seized him roughly and tossed him around, shrieking with laughter. It was a boot camp for anarchists.

The school day ended at two o'clock. The students had been fed once more, some soup and, on some days, bread. It made them drowsy. "Goodbye, old gentleman," said Alice, shaking the sticky hand of one of Helen's solemn suitors. The boy nodded and bowed to Helen, and then stopped at the door and said, "Here we are tomorrow." "No," said Alice. "Tomorrow is a holiday. We'll see you in three days." The suitor understood the word "no" but was confused by the rest and too proud to ask. Grief rippled through him. Helen went to him and kissed his cheek, murmuring something that seemed to fill him with painful admiration. Before my mother could stop him, the boy reached for a pair of scissors, and with his eyes upon Helen, his motion small and furtive, he stabbed the scissors into the palm of his hand. When Alice reached him, he was holding his bleeding hand up to Helen's face; she wore that intent look again, awake. She drifted while Grandmother Alice bandaged the boy's hand, but before he went off, he shyly came to her. Once more she kissed his cheek, and then she gently nudged him, *Go home.*

When he was gone, my mother kneeled down before her granddaughter and looked at her for a long time, thinking. Then she said, "People—male people—will try to give you strange gifts, Helen. You do not need to accept them all." Helen pulled away. Grandmother Alice held her. "Be careful what gifts you take." But with a quick, resentful glance, Helen was gone.

Every day on the way home from school, my mother and Helen stopped at a shop near by called the Evil Eye. Above the shop, Mr. Kolchella had two small rooms that he shared with his tiny wife.

Mr. Kolchella was Mrs. Kolchella's second husband. Mrs. Kolchella's first husband had been executed in Russia only a year before. "It was a shock," whispered Mr. Kolchella, taking Alice by the arm. "They made her watch." He shook his head and looked back shyly at his wife, who was standing at the window looking down into the street. "There were other things," confided Mr. Kolchella, "which I will not name in front of the child. The soldiers . . ." His eyes filled with tears, and he shrugged bitterly. "We are not far from the animals," he said. Mrs. Kolchella turned from the window and smiled at them. Helen, who had been making pictures at the table near by, fiercely resumed her scribbling.

The Evil Eye smelled of leather and polish. Its windows were full of glass jars piled on waxy furniture. The proprietor was a man named Mr. Cantor. They were good friends, and they always addressed one another as Mr. Cantor, Mrs. McCormack, Mr. and Mrs. Kolchella.

They sat around a table at the back of the store, drinking coffee hot from the stove. The table was littered with newspapers in Russian and Ukrainian and Yiddish. Of the four adults, Mr. Cantor had the biggest lap, and though he often got furious, he never jumped up and down like Mr. Kolchella and Grandmother Alice did, and he wasn't all bones like Mrs. Kolchella, and so Helen would go to Mr. Cantor. She climbed into his chair and put her head against his chest and listened to them argue the way she listened to the trains from her bed at night. Mrs. Kolchella sat beside Mr. Cantor, and when one of the adults would evoke too clearly the cruelty known only among such old people, she would reach her tiny hand to stroke Helen's hair, humming an aimless lullaby to protect the child with a veil of white noise.

They said it was a bad year. Mayor Sharpe (and Helen, hearing his name, thinking of a man with hands like scissors) had cut down a strike by the employees of the Electric Street Railway Company by bringing in the militia from the nearby Fort Osborne barracks. As the mayor read the Riot Act, the soldiers had arrived with bayonets and a loaded Lewis gun. Helen understood a riot as something grown-ups do, something with women and soldiers. She dozed against Mr. Cantor's baritone chest and dreamed of soldiers. The mayor has a machine gun; the government executes old husbands; execute is electrocute, what the government was going to do soon in the city. It is safe only behind danger, inside its ribs, to go to the adults with the mad hearts and soft hands. Helen learned that war is inside people and we must go to the lap of the strongest man with the quietest body, and thus, at the centre of the storm, we will be safe.

There was a marvellous bird at Mr. Cantor's store. Two feet high and bright blue, with a beak the colour of raspberries. With its dragon's claws, it gripped the bars of its cage and rocked back and forth. Helen thought it was an angel from the wilds of heaven.

The bird spoke a language so strange that even Grandmother Alice couldn't respond. Mr. Cantor said it was a parrot and it came from South America. It spoke sentences like the drummings of a partridge, softly percussive, wood on earth. A remarkably gentle voice, coming from the rapacious red beak. The parrot was, Mr. Cantor said, the sole living creature that could speak a word of the language of a lost tribe. All the speaking people were gone, and they'd left behind only this creature. The parrot was older than Mr. Cantor, older than Grandmother

Alice. When it died, it would take with it the last words of the lost people. Helen imagined her own forest growing over the blackened logs of her house, her little bed sinking under the trees and the dark bushes. She laid her ear against the man's chest.

Outside the light thrown by a wood stove, there is a constant riot going on, stirred by the sharp fingers of soldiers. But inside, behind the empty glass bottles at the Evil Eye, was a cadre, a place of peace. Helen listened. With vibrating voices, the adults invented a new medicine. They called it revolution.

Everyone said "revolution" a different way. Mr. Cantor rolled the R in his chest, a low pneumatic rumble rising through the very back of his throat, with the N nicely flattened by his tongue. But Mr. Kolchella opened it up like one of those wooden dolls, and it became a sunny word full of A's and generous U's. But Grandmother Alice winced and spat, and the small-scale Mrs. Kolchella refrained from saying it altogether, and every time the word was spoken she looked anxiously at the door.

When Helen asked what it meant, she received so many answers she came to know only that "revolution" was the last word on the lips of the last angel. Helen saw a blue pinwheel spinning so fast it cut her beautiful face, and the light released from that lit up the world.

ON A COLD, RAINY DAY my mother took Helen to school with her as usual, and when they arrived two things happened.

Waiting for them at the door was an extremely anxious Mr. Kolchella and a stranger, a man in a heavy coat with a notepad sticking from his pocket.

"*Tribune*," said the man, sticking out his hand at Alice. "You don't mind answering some questions."

"Are you really a curious kind of man?" Alice asked him.

The reporter looked at her, balding, as bland as a job application. "You are Alice McCormack," he said.

"*Mrs.* Alice McCormack," said Mr. Kolchella, dancing on his toes.

"Alice," said the man, "do you speak any English at all?"

Alice was delighted. "Only when I'm forced into it by dreary monoglots such as yourself!"

The reporter had four very long grey hairs draped across his head. Helen, who was not feeling well, winced and tugged at Alice's hand. "Grandma!" she cried. "Grandma Alice, please!"

The man focused on Helen. "That kid's sick!" he said.

"She is not!" cried Alice, an indignant grandmother. And then, "My God, child! You're burning up!"

She put her hand on Helen's forehead, and Helen responded to that gesture as will any self-respecting McCormack woman: with a volcanic flow of vomit that splashed over the cob-blestones, missing her new black shoes, for she was always careful with her clothing, but spraying the reporter's trousers generously.

"What's wrong with her?" he asked. He shielded his face with his hand.

"She's throwing up," said Alice.

"Typhoid!" cried the reporter, and then he fled.

My mother bundled up Helen and held tight her hot little body and said, "Mr. Kolchella, please tell me the truth. Am I a destructive hag who imposes upon her offspring ideologies that will only bring them to ruin?"

"He may be right," responded Mr. Kolchella. "It could be typhoid. There's been a fresh rash of the fever again this spring." He turned Alice away. "Go to my home, and I'll close the school. Wait for me there. And Mrs. McCormack . . ." he said. Alice turned to him, sobbing, holding Helen. "You're wise in the ways of destruction. It's what brings us to life."

IT WAS A RARE BIT OF LUCK for the *Winnipeg Tribune* that the news of yet another outbreak of Red River fever coincided with the news of the "seditious teachings of a north-end anarchist." Their readers were greatly relieved to learn that the children dying of typhoid in the north end of town were attending school in thirteen languages, in a manner declared to be "subversive and destructive of Canadian citizenship and nationality." Nobody to blame but themselves.

Helen was too sick to travel back to St. Norbert, and so

she was billeted at the Kolchellas' home, above the Evil Eye. I was frantic for her. Her grandmother had decided that Helen was safer in the city because Eli and I drew our water from the Red.

"It's the Red River fever," she shouted at me from the window of the Kolchellas' flat.

"But, Mama!" I said. "It came from school! It's from the sewage in the city!"

"Nonsense!" said Alice, and closed the window.

When her fever subsided, Helen rested on Mr. Cantor's chest. She was in the first stages of an addiction: forever after, she would hunger for the sound of a man's heartbeat.

And it was in this repose, in the peaceful backroom of the Evil Eye while Grandmother Alice and Mr. Cantor and Mr. and Mrs. Kolchella argued in voices softened for the benefit of the convalescent, that Helen developed one of her terminal contradictions.

Mr. Cantor was reading from that radical rag, the Old Testament, and its incendiary passage, the Book of Isaiah. "And they shall build houses and inhabit them, and they shall plant vineyards, and eat the fruit of them. They shall not build, and another inhabit; they shall not plant and another eat."

Helen asked him again and again for this "story." She soothed herself with the warm rumble of his voice. Mr. Cantor imagined that the child yearned for virtue, that she listened to the story for its frisson of justice. How could he possibly know the sensuous quality of Helen's imagination? How she dreamed of flowering vineyards with iron fences and marble fountains, a walled garden decorated with the engravings of fruits and flowers, a stone house with many windows and a veranda with pillars. And a carriage house. A very grand carriage house. With rooms above. Where all the servants live.

CHAPTER FOUR

BY THE TIME I BROUGHT HER HOME, Helen had a vertical fracture running down the middle of her soul. She was an incendiary conservative, a desperado of luxury.

She overcame the typhoid and the accompanying traces of pneumonia, and became as womanly as some unearthly aristocrat in the Middle Ages, with her thin shoulders, her extremely narrow ankles and her long white feet. I brought milk and marmalade, bouquets of dried corncobs, russet gold; laid them by her pillow and stared at the contrast with her black hair, white skin, in the slanted sunlight. I was her suitor too.

Around us there continued the great debate over the nature of perfection. My father was disgusted by the efforts of the Liberal Party to, as he said, "stick a turkey in the fox den."

"It's wrong!" said Peter. "They're buying us off! Goddamn capitalists! Bunch of foxes! Goddamn SOBs!"

My dad had taken up cursing the goddamn bourgeois bloodsuckers who thought they could buy up a couple of labour candidates and ride a white ass to the legislature. He lived in the eternal state of opposition. Bloody bastard leeches, parasitic buggers—damn them all to hell. His oath of allegiance to Impossibilism. If we reject, resist with all our cussing strength, the seduction of capitalism, damn it, then . . . then.

Utopia. The sun shone full on the innocent face of the millennium.

Nothing had been tried. Nothing had been found wanting. Peter's Impossibilism suggested that nothing was impossible.

There were only the sarcastic burps and spewings of the wretched Thomas Scott to suggest otherwise. A sporadic guest, all the worse because you didn't know when he *wasn't* there. Especially when my parents let themselves be hopeful, I'd wonder if we weren't making him up. Just *anticipating* his detractions would conjure his drooling spirit.

And naturally I had my own problems over at our grotto, preserving some independence from my dead mother-in-law's influence, however soulful and benign. I hadn't mentioned it to Eli, but when Marie heard our vows years before, when we saw each other to the door, I had hoped fervently that that would be our last, fond farewell. Then I could have told my husband that I missed his adoptive mother. It would have been a great non-relationship. But Marie had continued to live with us after all.

The ice crystals were glittering. Eli and I rose before dawn and lit the fire and warmed ourselves standing by the stove, wrapped up in his old robe. I held his hand. Eli had lost the thumb of his right hand just that summer, when he'd pinched it in the steel fittings of the new sulky plough. Now when I touched him, pain ran from the back of my own throat and down to the tip of my spine, though his wound had long since healed. I liked to hold his imbalanced paw. We were quiet. Our few years of marriage had taught us that our lives retained their raw edge, that we could still hurt and bleed. We watched the wood burn through the open door to the stove.

That morning, when dawn showed the blue rain puddles in the yard, Eli went out to get the horses ready. He'd hired out to build houses for a real-estate developer who'd bought up a bunch of river land south of Winnipeg. From the window, I watched him walking with vanishing purpose. Eli was surprised by the sky with its skim milk shine, the crisp manure, his garden of bleached corn stooks and icy green piles of tomato plants. He became quite lost, slowed, stopped, stared at the yellow wood chips that littered the ground. His face rippled with memory or wishfulness or regret. The window was bevelled by a fine line of frost. He felt me looking and looked back. His forest-coloured eyes belonged to no one but him.

Eli needed to be lost. It was cruel to expect him to remember where he was going. He was most at home adrift. His nomadic compass had no true north; his nomadic clock had no midnight. Everywhere was here, and it was always now. I saw him smile and nod his shaggy head at Alice, who was charging across the yard in her rubber boots and flannel nightgown. Alice burst in. "He can't go off and work for that thieving developer!" she said. And then, "Thank God you're here!" and I looked behind me to see that Marie's form occupied the rocking chair. Just then, Helen walked sleepily into the kitchen and stood looking up at her grandmothers. Marie reached and touched Helen's curls. "It is time for her journey to begin," she intoned, and Helen shuddered.

Alice handed me my coat and purse. "What did you marry?" she asked me.

Marie interrupted with a laugh, a most curious, undomesticated laugh. "Eli is a buffalo hunter," she said.

"What buffalo?" I asked. "What buffalo now?"

My mother pursed her lips. "You're not too old to smack, you know!"

"I'm just asking what buffalo."

Mum threw up her hands. "Honestly, girl!" She poured herself some coffee, offered some to Marie and then said, "Of course not." And to Helen, "You're too young." Cranky, she blew steam, muttering, "One dead, one too young. And one too stupid. Who said anything about buffalo? We're talking about Eli! You know? Eli?"

"Daddy!" said Helen, always the opportunist.

"Just look at him!"

All four of us stared out at Eli, whose attention had been drawn to the braided clouds. Three females and a phantom, all of us seized by love. Mum's voice grew tender. "Blondie McCormack," she said, "you go and get yourself a job."

CHAPTER FIVE

JOHN ANDERSON'S SHOES were made for walking on Tyndall stone steps. His square and handsome hands were formed by God Himself to jingle loose change in the pant pocket of his blue wool suit. His clean jaw suspended keenly from his ears; his upper lip (behind a handlebar moustache) was fine and strong, and the lower lip full but not too full. His brow was broad, and a phrenologist would say he had great intellect and a genealogist would say he had good bloodlines and a banker would say he was solid. John Anderson was born *right*. He had a law degree, a low handicap and a high return on his investments.

I went to work for John Anderson just after the New Year. In a way, it was Helen who found the job.

Helen was now so beautiful that people averted their eyes. She was an oriental poppy. Her beauty was scandalous. She would attract a crowd. Passersby stopped dead in their tracks, banging into one another. Generous souls were struck by joy at the sight of her. For Mr. Kolchella and the rest of the quorum at the Evil Eye, Helen's extravagant beauty affirmed something: she gave them reason to believe in the essential plenitude of the material world. The others—women eager to protect their measure of vanity, men convinced that abundance is the Devil's work—stared and withdrew, and stared and withdrew, while Helen watched. She knew. If we were walking, she would let go of my hand. She took no joy from their joy, nor displeasure from their envy. She was fixed to a fate beyond her immediate circumstances.

And so it was Helen who chose John Anderson—that is, she chose John Anderson's house, and John Anderson was part of the package.

We discovered his mansion while out walking through the rich part of town. Helen was wearing little boots trimmed with rabbit fur. I held her hand like a polar bear clutching a teacup. It was very early in the morning, the streets still dark, dawn arriving late and flat and blue. The previous night, fresh snow had fallen in a strong wind. John Anderson's house rose like a sailing ship from the billowing snowdrifts. It was made of stone. Two coal-oil lanterns burned on either side of the grand entrance.

Helen tore away and ran up the circular drive. To my dismay, I heard her utter a cry of pleasure. The front door to this ghastly mausoleum lay within a portico topped by a rampart, for the house was built defensively. I heard Helen take a diver's breath, and then she plunged forward, towards the door.

I cried out, "I will not work here!" All of a sudden, I was grieving for Clark. The mansion took on the look of a soldier's uniform, and I became a biting dog. I realized that my friend's death had left me with an aversion to anything resembling a military officer, and this house looked like a general snoozing after dinner.

My lips curled back and I began to bark furiously. "Helen, if you do not come back here I will spank you! Do you hear me, young lady? I will take away your bunny boots! Helen! Don't you *dare* walk away from me!"

Helen swept towards the yawning portico, a little fish swimming towards the shark's mouth. Just then, the front door opened and a youth of about fifteen years emerged, by appearances the son of the czar. He stopped at the steps and said, "This is my father's house."

I laughed out loud. Helen walked right up to him. He said, "You're trespassing!" Then he saw her face. And stopped dead.

Helen went calm; a lily in a vase would not be as calm as Helen was just then. She lifted her face to him without affectation, impartial and remote. When I drew close, I found them squared off, bee to flower. I stepped into the middle of that awful equation, thrusting my face into the face of this Romanov and saying hi, for I knew that would turn him off.

The devil only knows where Helen got her persistence. The little brat spoke clearly: "My mother is seeking a place in your household."

I turned on her. "Hsst! You are a shocking liar!" I cried. "God will punish you for your sins." This was sheer genius on my part. I knew that no rich Protestant would go for a religious zealot. But Helen's beauty cured men of both blindness and insight.

"We happen to be in need of a cook," said the needle-nosed czarevich. He had big adenoids and an oversized Adam's apple, and he slurred his words, as if his tongue were waiting for the maid to bring him cocoa.

"You will have to speak up," I told him. "We are not accustomed to the corruption of the English language. Are you British?"

"My grandfather was British." This was obviously something he said often. "Though he got up here from the United States."

"So that is a false accent. I thought so. Come, Helen, we cannot stay with people who deceive us with godless rhetoric."

The boy was trying to see around me. This was the reaction to my daughter's beauty that I most feared. Neither generous nor resentful, young Fauntleroy was merely avaricious. He looked greedily for another sip of Helen's charms. "I don't know about red-trick," he said. "All's I know is we need a cook."

"She makes very nice sourdough," said my vixen.

"I'll tell Father you're here."

I could feel the tidal swell of Helen's willpower and took desperate measures. "Stop!" The boy turned towards me, his eyes on Helen. "We haven't been properly introduced. How will you explain that to your British–American merchant father?" I stuck out my hand. "I am Blondie, wife of Eli the buffalo hunter. How do you do?"

The boy seized on the chance to display his nice manners. "I am Richard Anderson, son of John Anderson, KC." And he put his hand in mine. Well, I let him have it with all the electrical energy I could muster. Half that voltage would have singed the eyelashes off an ordinary man. But Richard had the wits of a wooden mallet, and his wealth and prestige acted as the perfect insulation. "I'll get Father," he said. And hurried off.

***

AS IT TURNED OUT, it was not John Anderson who would hire us but his wife. She was a pigeon-breasted matron, warm as a factory clock. I have never met anyone less interested in humanity. She greeted us each morning with renewed vigour, but within seconds her attention flagged, her eyes wandered, almost cross-eyed with boredom, studying the stone floor of the kitchen, resting her eyes. She called me Barbara. I corrected her for a while, and then I just gave up. She did like my bread, though. And I soon became famous for my baking all over what they called Millionaire Row.

Other managerial wives began to ask me for a loaf here and there, and I found I could fit in quite a bit of baking in the mid-afternoon, between lunch and the dinner party. I charged the ladies twenty cents a loaf, much of which went back into the housekeeping money to pay for Mrs. Anderson's flour and milk. But Mrs. Anderson soon learned of my sideline, and she came charging into the kitchen just before cocktails. She looked remarkably alert.

"Barbara," she said to me, "I will have a word with you."

"Yes, ma'am." I winked at Helen and wiped my hands. Helen smiled that half-smile because she knew I was imitating Grandmother Alice's imitation of a black servant.

"Barbara," said Mrs. Anderson in a conspiratorial voice, "this has got to stop."

"My mother does voices," I told her.

"You are my cook," Mrs. Anderson said.

"It's just for fun," I said. "No harm."

"But you're *mine*," she said.

I scratched my ear and looked over at my daughter. This was taking a seedy turn.

"I pay you to cook for *us*." For the first time, Mrs. Anderson looked directly into my eyes, but still she didn't see me. "You get my drift," she said.

"Mama," said Helen.

Mrs. Anderson was in danger of becoming fully conscious. She turned her entire bodice towards Helen and said, "Who is this child?"

"My daughter, Helen. She's here most days with me."

"What is she doing?"

"Polishing silver."

"But who is she? Who is she really?"

I was becoming alarmed. "Helen. My little girl."

Helen sat at the top of a small, apple green stepladder. She was very still. Mrs. Anderson walked towards her till she was at her side. "Helen," she said. "Your daughter." She looked up at me quickly, making a comparison between chicken and egg. "Helen."

Helen yawned widely. Even her tongue was beautiful. Mrs. Anderson looked, wondering, into Helen's mouth. Her own face wore a forgetful expression, slack, nearly innocent.

"Where are you from?"

"We've got a bit of a farm in the St. Norbert area, to the south of here. As I told you."

"Oh, yes." Mrs. Anderson took one last look and closed her eyes. Her hand clutched the ledge of the porcelain sink, the diamond rings captured by her arthritic knuckles. Helen picked up a spoon and her tarnish-blackened rag. She was placid. And full of rage. The household cat leapt up to settle itself on the pastry board, jade eyes, quickly asleep.

"You should not come here," said Mrs. Anderson to Helen.

Everything stopped: cat, faucet, kettle, the fire in the stove.

"What are you saying, my dear?" John Anderson stood at the padded swinging door separating us from the dining room.

"John," she said. "I was just having a word with Barbara." Mrs. Anderson teetered towards her husband.

"How do you do?" he asked me. He had an enormous forehead and a face accustomed to smiling. He was very trimly made and wore his expensive clothes as if he'd just played cricket in them. The handlebar moustache was rather like Clark's, and that made me sad. His eyes were brown and confident. I made a clumsy curtsy. "Actually," I told him, "my name is Blondie."

He brightened and laughed. "Obviously," he said.

His wife tugged at his arm. "You haven't yet met *her*, then. You haven't met this, this Helen."

"My daughter," I said. For some reason, I was unable to go to Helen as I should have. I seemed to be stuck. I think I pointed at her, like a tourist in Eden. "Helen."

Helen turned slowly towards John Anderson, in her hands the rag and spoon.

"Good God!" he said. His ears seemed to pull towards the back of his head. He suddenly looked young. I was confused. He belonged to the camp of the generous. He coughed and looked at me with Clark's bashful eyes and said, "She is truly lovely."

"Yes."

He turned to my little girl and bowed a little. "I am pleased to meet you."

Helen appraised him and decided he could live.

"I must find Richard." Mrs. Anderson backed out of the room. "Goodbye," she said.

John Anderson watched her go. "I see Edith has woken."

"Mr. Anderson, I won't work for you if I can't bring my daughter with me as I need to."

"Is it you who bakes the bread?"

"I bake the bread and roast the pork and fry the bacon and stir the broth."

"Are you Russian?"

"My mother is, a little, sort of, or actually not at all. May I ask you a question?"

"Shoot."

Helen, at her little ladder, polishing like a jeweller, burst out laughing and said, without looking up, "Shoot!"

"Do you love money?" I asked.

"Oh, yes. Indeed."

"Ah."

He shrugged. "Is that all?"

"I suppose so."

"Then I will see to our guests. I assume there will be guests." He turned to go.

"Wait!" He obliged. "You seem like a decent fellow."

He did not respond, but put his hands in his pockets, debonair and lucid. "Do you need money?" he asked.

"No! Lord! No! That's . . . that's disgusting. I'm sorry, I just wondered . . . well, never mind and good evening."

"If you ever do, you know, you could speak with me."

"Mr. Anderson, what I want to know is, Have you ever killed anyone or otherwise cheated to become this rich?"

He smiled, nice smile on a fatless face. "You put too much salt in the gravy," he said. "I do not like much salt. Just enough." He indicated a pinch and then again retired his hands to his pockets and elbowed through the swinging doors to his dining room.

"The doors whisper here," observed Helen.

"I hate red velvet," said I.

"I love it."

And so we resumed our unquiet evening. After some time, I said to her, "I think you should stay home with Daddy."

Helen said, "I have to marry Richard."

"Over my dead body."

She looked up at me, and there was her anger, some peat fire from the bog of ancient history. "Maybe so," said she.

CHAPTER SIX
1911

ELI BRIMMED WITH JOY. It was that last day of winter, when all of winter's sky colours were suddenly bright with spring. Soon, too soon, the blossoms, the weeds and work from dawn till dusk, for while Eli had agreed to be unleashed from the economy, he still worked hard on our small farm. But today, for now, Eli was deliciously unemployed.

It called for a celebration. He wished for a moment that he knew how to read and write. Unknown to him, he was wishing for the telephone. He needed to announce the rodeo.

It was a strange day for a rodeo. The horses would slip in the mud, and the calves were too small for roping. It was nice out, but the roads were nearly impassable. Eli had risen at three a.m., when the ground was still frozen, and he travelled to four of the neighbours before they'd had their coffee. And it is a true fact that three out of four he interrupted making love before their children had woken up (the fourth were night people). My dead mother-in-law said it was *a sign*. The rodeo would be a success.

Eli was the only buffalo hunter farming in St. Norbert at that time. Most others had been cleared out west to Saskatchewan, like songbirds from a forest on prime land. But the neighbours had many talents, and 90 per cent of the time, their energies were devoted to turning those talents into labour. The rodeo was Eli's way of switching things around: turning labour back into talent, where it belongs.

People came from all over, and mud seemed immaterial and the sun shone. Eli baked bannock over an open fire. The midwife sang a song while my dad, Peter, played the fiddle. Dad hadn't realized till just then that he knew how to play the fiddle. There was saddle bronc-riding and bareback bronc-riding, but not too much of it because we had only one stallion who was mean enough. By the time we finished with the bareback riding, the stallion was so exhausted he was gentle enough to serve in the barrel racing, where he won first prize for the young neighbour boy who needed just such a victory.

The boy belonged to a dour Methodist family whose appearance at the rodeo shook Alice's faith in atheism. She'd been bolstering her shaky rejection of God with a sort of paint-by-number version of fundamentalists, but when MacDonald and his scrawny kids showed up prepared for a party, she had to recognize the strange mix of things. For his part, MacDonald tried to justify his secular pleasure by turning Eli's rodeo into an agricultural fair, progressive and earnest.

Old MacDonald hauled with him the ten miles between our homes his latest farming implement: a deep-cutting blade. He'd fashioned it in his own barn, for he was a pretty good blacksmith. This plough could cut through sod like a hatchet, turning the soil a good two feet deep, "where the real fecundity of mother earth is hidden from view," said MacDonald ("*veuuuw*," he said). And while people squinted at him and shrugged, as if to say, "Who cares about deep blades on a plough," you could see that the seeds of competition had been sewn. A bit of envy and a bit of fear. By fall, there would be many new blacksmiths in the neighbourhood. The soil would never be the same; mother earth would soon be aging fast in the prairie wind.

But farm implements do not belong at a real rodeo, and Eli gently discouraged any further references to tilling and such. When the races were over and everyone was wondering what to do next, we heard a gunshot and the crows scattered up from the compost. And there was Eli, dressed in his buckskin and beads, wearing his fancy moccasins and the Assomption sash and an eagle feather in his hat. He rode the newly broken stallion, a fine black creature of great dignity and intelligence, marching backwards, cutting tight circles and changing leads. Eli reined in quickly, and the black horse rose on its hind legs and Eli yelled, "Throw!" and my mother tossed something into the air. The blue glass bottles fell in sunlight and exploded into a bright, sparkling shower when Eli shot them out of the sky.

Helen had been perched uneasily on the outskirts of the party, sulky with the grown-ups, rude to the kids. She would not wear her farm clothes, and the hand-me-down shoes from Grandmother Alice made walking difficult in our yard, so she got stranded on the bench near the firepit. We'd been forced to ignore her. Eli and Alice didn't notice her when they began their game with the gun and the blue glass. I was watching from the tall corral fence. Alice laughed and tossed a bottle high over the firepit; we watched it spin through the air, and my heart stopped when I saw Helen's face raised towards it. Eli didn't see her there. He fired, and the glass rained down upon her. Helen watched till the last moment, when she covered her face with her hands.

The blue glass rained down. Miraculously, there was just one sliver stabbed in her left hand. I took it out with tweezers. I was curiously grief-stricken over the possibility of the smallest scar on my daughter. Her perfection had become a liability, yet I was unwilling to relinquish even a fraction, as if it would let her loose. And I so wanted to keep her.

The rodeo changed Eli. He hung back that day while I tweezered the glass from Helen's hand. She and I were on the porch with a bowl of water and the bandages. Eli hesitated at the steps as if he would say something. Then he walked by and went into the house. I could hear him walking inside; his boots were louder, his body less contained.

When I'd finished with Helen, she went into the house. I listened, but they didn't talk. I tossed out the water and took my things to the kitchen. Eli was releasing Helen from a hug, and as he did so, he placed his wounded paw against her face and looked at her with a strange, intense objectivity. She smiled, shy, almost apologetic, and slipped out of reach. Eli went back outside without speaking to either of us. Next thing I knew, he was in the corral, working with his horse, hour by hour.

That was a Friday. By Saturday, Eli was a gun-slinging, cow-punching, bronc-breaking rodeo cowboy. Suddenly he could yodel and spit, and his legs grew more bent than ever and his eyes, which had widened into a farmer's guileless gaze, narrowed with perpetual mirth and his voice, which had got higher, a breathy tenor as high-pitched as the wind in grass, burrowed deep into his barrel chest like he'd swallowed his own larynx. He suddenly knew the words to more than five hundred songs. By

Sunday, Eli was stewing coffee over an open fire, and that night he took me to bed outside on a bedroll smelling of cow dung, and he leaned over me and looked down with those brand-new wrinkles and sang a sad ballad about his mother. Not Marie, but some old white kind of Ma. It was just a song.

He grew reckless, restless, solitary, but I loved this version of my husband too. Eli could turn into a blue-eyed bat; love is permanent.

We let the farm go that spring, much of it fallow, just a few acres of rye. For my part, I got hold of some cabbage seeds and radish, onion and garlic and turnip, anything that tasted hot or grew underground. Potatoes, carrots, a half-acre of gladioli. With the money I was making as John Anderson's cook, I bought a trailer and hitched Peter's black stallion to it, and we kicked and cantered back and forth from the river to my garden with water, for all the days of May and June were dry. Eli continued to sleep outside, so I did too, though it wasn't my first choice. I found an old jib sail in the basement of the Andersons' house and rigged up a tent to keep off the dew.

I rose with Venus and rode to town in time to cook the Andersons' breakfast. Helen was always with me. On one hand, she was indifferent to me, favouring the company of her cowboy dad. But she insisted on coming to the Andersons', and I was very glad to have her. She was bewildering. She didn't really like me much, and we were stilted in conversation. I was always stunned by her beauty. Maybe that's what made her standoffish. I was forever staring at her, backing up for a better look, then zooming in on her flawless skin, the curve of her shoulders, the slim bone of the clavicle, her dark blue eyes, lush black eyelashes and brows.

Helen liked to polish the silver, and she knew every serving spoon and ladle. She loved the mother-of-pearl fish cutlery, she said, palming them, the weight of them and how cool to touch. She liked to polish everything, glass chimneys, crystal, to oil the oak and walnut wainscotting of the Andersons' dining room, though there were other servants for that. But Helen did not polish or oil like a servant. Hers was an act of ownership and intimacy and defence. She loved the swinging door between kitchen and dining room. Through it she passed to a richer world.

She wandered freely through their house. She would be gone for hours, and then come back to the kitchen smelling of candle wax and gardenias and stand mystified beside me at the sink, watching potato peelings fall from my hands, their odour of earth, their mud eyes. I let her be. When she'd been quiet awhile, she would sigh and then talk in a desultory way. She said there were coloured balls of clay in the billiard room upstairs. She pinched a bit of raw pastry from a bowl that sat in a larger bowl full of cracked ice and put it in her mouth. Then she dipped into the pocket of her apron and produced a grey stone, holding it out to me, a petrified egg. "What is it?" she asked.

"A piece of moon," I said.

"What's it for?"

"Where'd you find it?"

"At Mrs. Anderson's bath. She's got her own bathroom, Mama. Even Mr. Anderson doesn't go in there."

I held the moon full of holes, a rough, hard product of Mrs. Anderson's bath. "Throw it out, child," I said. "Poor thing. No wonder she's daft."

"Did she make it with her body?" Helen began to laugh.

"She is a turtle, Helen. At night, she turns into a turtle and sleeps in the bath."

THEY GAVE HER CLOTHES. At first I thought it was patronizing and therefore quite safe. As long as they felt that Helen was beneath them, they couldn't harm her, their weapons would be misdirected. Shawls and such, lace collars, a nearly new pair of shoes. Then she found a way of wearing them that was entirely her own. She would costume herself and walk from our back-room with her consciously distracted attitude, like a dragonfly clicking its wings in the kitchen, strangely exotic and purposeful. She didn't sit; she hovered. She was still a child. A faint mauve vein ran over the petal flesh of her eyelid.

CHAPTER SEVEN

MR. AND MRS. JOHN ANDERSON, KC, and son were throwing a
party: one hundred guests in the ballroom, an eight-piece
orchestra, music so sentimental it made your teeth hurt, people
dancing with their collective heart on their sleeve and their
respective noses in the air.

A respectable lady is led by her nose, neither too much
nose nor too little. Her father's, her husband's, fortune will be
the moat about her womanhood, should she be properly governed
by her proboscis. Wearing silk with lambswool and horsehair brocade, the women seemed to sail on their slippers to the bathroom,
as if their destination was a silly detour en route to a real throne.

I'd spent three days preparing for that party. Helen and
I stayed in town, rather than making the journey to and fro so
early and so late. We slept in the little room off the kitchen. I
missed Eli, but it was pleasant there, with only the work in the
warmth from the stove and the dewy breath of my daughter
asleep beside me.

The night before, I'd woken up to an empty bed. Her pillow was cool. This was new. I had risen countless times in cold
winter nights to care for her as a baby, but I'd never been forced
out to search for a delinquent.

The house was sleeping, snowlit. I walked a path of Persian
wool through panelled walls and walnut beams and cornices.

There was a fire burning in the west room. By its light I saw them sitting: Richard in a chair, Helen on a couch. I was struck by the complete absence of tension between them. Richard was draped catlike across the chair, his gold hair rather long, wavy, shining around his narrow face, his nearly feminine beauty. Helen leaned against pillows with her knees curled beneath a mohair throw, her head supported by her hand. By the fireglow, something gleamed on her throat. They were undistressed by my appearance; Richard hardly glanced at me while he completed some inane commentary. I walked close to my daughter and reached down to touch a string of pearls around her neck, a double strand, cream with pink shadows, cool as a breeze.

"Who gave you this?" I asked her.

Helen's half-smile, a nod towards Richard, who remained blandly sitting, a hint of pride. "They're pretty," he said. "Father found them at Panama."

"They come from oysters, Mama."

Richard put his small hand over his mouth and smiled. He crossed his knees over the side of his chair. "We're having oysters tonight," he said. "Maybe you'll find one inside. Put another log on, will you, Barbara?"

"You realize Helen can't accept your gift."

He didn't miss a beat. "No, of course not," he said. "But I would like you to keep them for her until you feel she is old enough to accept them."

"If you hurt my daughter, I will kill you. You do know that."

He smiled again. A large mobile mouth with full lips. "I wouldn't hurt Helen in a thousand years."

The effect upon Helen was palpable, though she barely moved. He felt it, and looked at her over his handsome little fingers. "I wouldn't, honest to God."

He began and ended with pearls. Good taste was Richard's only virtue. It is terrifying that style should wield such power.

I was too busy to worry any more that day. Blue oysters lay in crates of shaved ice. The local knife-sharpener spent hours shucking them, and the kitchen smelled of the sea and the icy air made me light-headed. We did find one small baroque pearl, as grey-blue as snow in the clouds. I told no one but gave it to the knife-sharpener, who said he had a little girl at home and it would make her very happy.

John Anderson liked the kitchen. He'd bring one or two cronies in for a conversation without party noise. He always said, "Hello, Blondie," and then leaned against the counter with his arms crossed while his guests stood uneasily looking into the servants' territory, trying to keep clean. One thing about hanging out with rich people: you'll always know what's going to happen in the future. Rich people know more than others about what's coming because they're the ones pulling the strings.

Thrice, he arrived through the red velvet, padded door: once with a thin gentleman wearing a monocle; once with a chubby gentleman smoking a cigar; once with a fat gentleman drinking a martini. From the thin man, I learned that the biggest, most unsinkable ship ever made was soon to be afloat off the coast of England. From the chubby man, I learned that the biggest canal ever dreamed of was being dug in the muck between North and South America and it would bring prosperity to all. And from the red-faced fat man, I learned that Germany was ambitious but she would never be foolhardy. All in all, it looked like the world was growing more glamorous, more powerful and much, much safer than ever before, and I was glad I'd brought a child into *the cradle of humanity.*

⟨ornament⟩

THE ANDERSONS ENTERTAINED perpetually, though not on such a large scale. Mrs. Anderson's errand of the day was to find her way to my kitchen. She did not stint in her duty but came right in, nearly to the stove. She looked directly at the top of my curly head and said, "Twelve for dinner, Barbara." I made friends with the grocer, Buchanan, and told him to send the freshest and the best and make us first before anybody could even know about the sturgeon caviar or the Mediterranean artichokes.

The maid fell in love with the delivery boy, a terrible cliché but she was kind of dumb. I knew that it was an infatuation, and that she'd need to keep her job, so I served dinner on the nights she was hiding in the garage kissing him in the back seat of John Anderson's Model T. Thus I furthered my education. Those dinners were the equivalent of the evening news.

Offering the Andersons' guests a deceptively simple meal of asparagus and lamb with mint jelly, I learned that Austria would fend off the attack from Russia with just a little help from Germany (and at the edge of this discussion, the women dipped in and out like Labradors at a beach, "*Sophia Phillips had a German butcher. . .*"), and that the French wouldn't get involved at all because the Morocco thing was a red herring and

Lord knows it will go no further. ("*Phillips? The kaiser had a cousin called Phillips, but a German way of saying it. Phillipmunster or like that, I think; Phillipvagner, something, I'm sure.*") Because the Germans wouldn't touch Belgium when they knew the whole world would be at their throats ("*Is Germany a real country? I mean, it was Napoleon, wasn't it? Bismarck? My father always said, but I can't quite recall . . .*"), and the new king would never let Great Britain get involved in a continental argument, but if they did, by Jeezus, we had the navy, and that fellow Churchill had created a first rate Admiralty.

"There's going to be a war," I said. I hadn't realized that I was speaking my thoughts out loud. Everyone stopped talking. John Anderson leaned back, eased his trim belly and gracefully adjusted his trousers. "Well, we certainly hope that you are mistaken, Blondie," he said.

I was carrying two silver chafing dishes, the edges of which I rested upon the buffet. I was overcome. I somehow just *knew* there would be a war. You get a different idea of things when you're the invisible cook in the kitchen, listening in from the edges. I had been filled with a reawakened grief for my friend Clark. I heard John Anderson's voice as a swimmer will hear a call from shore. He was speaking with his guests. "Blondie is quite the political philosopher," he said. Everyone laughed.

His tone was not unkind, but I felt powerless and utterly sad. I did not let them see my face. Punishing myself, I looked under the rock of memory, where black beetles secrete puffy white eggs, and there I saw the severed shoulder, bulged eye of my friend, my lost Clark. Another war was coming. I felt it in my bones.

"You are a very indulgent employer," said one of the younger women at the table, putting her hand on John Anderson's arm.

I took up my dishes and made for the kitchen. John Anderson's voice followed me. "I would like a word with you, Blondie, when our guests have gone."

My back to them so they would not see my pain. The velvet puckers of that stupid door like wounds on obesity. Clark had been dead for ten years. At the dinner table, the company laughed again. I turned towards the foolish guests, bumped open the swinging door with my backside and entered my domain.

John Anderson did come to speak with me while I was cleaning up the last dishes, but it was not to reprimand me for speaking out before his guests. He wanted to talk about the possibility of war. We talked for a long time that night, and many times afterwards, in a rich season of friendship. He approached me always as a possibility distinct but unverifiable. Perhaps he treated everyone that way. He was a speculator, a habit of mind that found him friends in all walks of life, though he was thoroughly upper class, like a character actor or a lark in a glass cage. His place in the city's establishment was both his strength and his weakness; it gave him the innate power to go wherever he chose while it denied him relevance. He was himself a luxury.

His law practice had become for him a genteel hobby. He was preoccupied with real estate and racehorses. Outside the phlegmatic decorum of his shady mansion, and quite distinct from his dutiful friendship with Mrs. Anderson, John Anderson was chrome before the invention of chrome, a jet engine, a fax machine. Hearing the news of the great canal at

Panama (and with his characteristic aerial view, he recognized at once that Winnipeg would no longer be the Chicago of the North, no longer the hub for transcontinental rail traffic), he travelled south in person to see it. He didn't understand distance; he thought everywhere was here. He was never on time for business meetings because he never did figure out that everything in Winnipeg is and always has been twenty minutes away.

Yes, he was a capitalist, and yes, he loaned me money (no interest, and I paid him back faithfully, for Eli's new love of rodeo did not yet feed the farm), and yes, I was and will remain fond of him even when he appalls me, and it is a documented (by a photograph) fact that when he drove out to St. Norbert on speculation that the south bend of the Red might be worth development, and I introduced him to my mother and father, Peter turned his back and Alice raised her hands before her in the shape of a cross. Eli would have nothing to do with him. In fact, I guess Eli really hated him. But he didn't say anything because it would have looked like he resented my liberty as a *working woman.*

I was distracted by my friendship with John. Together we watched the gathering clouds of war. There was a thoroughness in Winston Churchill's naval administration that put the lie to diplomacy. "Boys like to fight," said John. And then he sobered. I knew he was thinking of his leonine son, Richard. "Surely there won't be conscription." He looked to me for confirmation.

"Kitchener has no faith in Territorials," I said slowly, for I was loath to make him anxious. "If Germany has 250,000 men, Britain will need a third more. There are surely that many in the reserves."

"Is he a strong general? Kitchener?" John Anderson looked like a boy when he asked questions like this. I felt like

Rudyard Kipling, O best beloved. John Anderson did not treat me as an equal, but he approached me as a storyteller. He heard stories as parable, and understood that they are as false as they are true, in equal proportions, in equal tension; this is the nature of suspension.

I could only shrug. "He is well-meaning," I said. We laughed sadly. "He'll kill as many of the enemy as he can. He'll offer up the faithful British Islanders, and then he'll come looking in the colonies for more young men and offer them up too."

"I hear he's awfully excited about the new rifle."

I nodded. "In the Boer War, more people died of disease than got shot."

We both sighed.

Gently, I offered, "Maybe Richard would enjoy the navy."

John Anderson stood up nervously. "There won't be a war."

"Maybe you'd better try him on the water. See if he's got sea legs. He sailed that little wood boat when he was a boy, didn't he? I'll bet he's a natural sea dog."

Mr. Anderson stopped. "Put Richard on a boat?"

"Sure. Just a fun boat. For fun."

And so it was decided. And John Anderson knew just the boat.

RICHARD ACCEPTED HIS FATHER'S PLANS to see England and France as his right, scarcely nodding. "That would be nice," he said, giving his father one quick look. "A very nice thing." The cast-iron Mrs. Anderson granted permission to make the preparations on her behalf, and stood patient as a fence post while the dressmaker and the milliner stitched a new wardrobe.

They would be gone six months. When he heard the news, Eli nodded, took his guitar outside for his own private celebration. At first, I was relieved too. We needed a sabbatical from the John Anderson family. We both wanted Helen out of Richard's languorous reach.

I planned to begin Helen's education in earnest. My own scholarly pursuit of irrelevance had persuaded me of the absolute relevance of all things. My nerves were worn; I'd been working too hard, and that might account for the preternatural vividity of all things.

Cabbage butterflies, for instance. I had to stop to think about it. Does their flight have a purpose? They eat. Do they have teeth? I didn't have time to look. I was anxious to know. Are we sure they eat? White wings in updrafts of sunlight.

On such a path I intended to take Helen. Our curriculum of improvisation required courage, alertness to the trembling motivations of the cabbage butterfly. Between one fact and its sibling, gossamer wings, veins and arteries and chromosomes, information leaks and pulses, forever altering.

I wanted her to read what I'd read, especially the boring stuff, because that would strengthen her resolve. She would read Edmund Burke's "Of Beauty." It was my maternal contribution, more important than bread-making (which she scorned). She would read; further, she would stay awake while reading "The Sublime and the Beautiful Compared."

I would update her studies to suit the modern age. Hydroelectrical engineering. Automobile mechanics. And all kinds of political theory. Her grandfather Peter could help there. Thorstein Veblen, *The Theory of the Leisure Class*—a necessity for every young woman. Dad thought it soft. Gave her Engels and Marx. Helen resisted. Good, I thought. Give her rein. She could study the history of art, sure, if that's what she wanted. Biographies. I suppose so. Biographies of great courtesans. Well, okay. Sure. Long as she's reading. We were divergent, Helen and I. I thought history, she thought gossip. I believed in my method of lateral shift, but I also believed in the importance of the follow-through. Helen took my method ten steps to the side. She would remain mistress of her own republic. If something bored her (and everything did), the fault lay beyond her control, in the thing itself. The world, however relevant, proved unworthy.

Yet she was avid for Richard. She only pretended otherwise. He knew it. She betrayed herself by the way she hurried up the Andersons' walk in the morning. Once, I looked up and saw Richard watching us from an upstairs window, his posture of amused arrogance, a sniper biding his time.

At home, she found all contact exceedingly painful. I bored her so badly, I took pity and stayed out of her way. With her father, she was as yet instinctively confident. Eli's spurs woke her up early, ringing like tambourines on the floor. She opened her bedroom door and came out smelling of cookie dough, with her wild black hair waving on her cheek. Eli was spreading three-inch slices of bread with jam. She sat beside him and did likewise. Neither spoke. They solemnly chewed, and with her jam-sticky hand, she plucked at the silver buckle on his hatband.

I came in from the garden to rinse the carrots in her old baby bath on the porch. When Helen saw me she climbed from her chair, went back to her room and closed the door. Emerged twenty minutes later dressed in the second-hand clothes from the Anderson house, tucked in, transformed, an evening dress with a cotton shawl about her waist, three ivory bracelets at her elbow, black leather shoes with a buckle, sort of an Egyptian quality, suddenly tall, her hair in a rouleau, which I took down, standing over her, both of us in a rage, so quiet I heard the dripping at the new kitchen faucet, braiding her thick hair. Wrathful silence. She went to the wagon and waited there, bored with royal boredom, haute boredom, Aphrodite-at-a-flea-market boredom. Waiting for her mother-servant to hobble up, smelling of a cowboy-lover, of lye soap, of anxiety; an obsequious hag, her nag, her old mum.

Beside the wood stove at the Andersons', she made herself a couch of pillows covered with some discarded drapes, plush velvet, royal purple. She curled up, chewed a strand of her hair and read the biography of Mrs. Vanderbilt. I worked and tried to ignore her. I have felt like a servant only in my daughter's presence. If I hummed, she sniffed at me. If I murmured to myself, she would stop and look. I had neither solitude nor company. I had an adolescent daughter. A daughter more beautiful and more dangerous than Circe, more captivating than Calypso. The kitchen became a prison.

She began to make her demands.

She wore a garland in her hair, coneflowers, of all things, wild sunflower, small sprays of aster. It was September and Indian summer. The flowers were bearing fruit; their florets drew away from their receptacles, revealed stamen, pistil. Yellow with dark brown discs, set in her coiled braids. Still very young, she had the potency of an older girl, as if Richard's presence had created a hothouse.

She appeared at the swinging door with flushed cheeks, looking like a girl who has recently been kissed. In her distraction, she held the door open, her gaze unfocused, and I saw Richard in the dining room behind her, his small hands in his pockets, his look of excited satisfaction. The air was full of broken constraints. Through the open door, I caught Richard's eye. His slight smile, his pride. He then dismissed us both and disappeared.

"Come in or go home," I told her. Our eyes met for one horrible, naked moment. We began to bustle. She dropped her shawl, rolled up her sleeves, and for once actually proved useful at the sink.

"Good drying weather," said she.

"Yep," said I, "sun and wind, wind and sun, that's what it takes."

"How are the turnips coming?" she asked.

I stopped and turned to her. "Who wants to know?"

She blushed. "Just trying to be nice. Why bother?"

Acrid silence.

Never give up on your kids. I tried again. "Peter's happy with the rye this year."

No response. A coal mine caved in. Tap, tap. Tap, tap. Signs of life.

Vipers hatch and breed in the silence of an adolescent, quickening in our children's righteousness. The kitchen filled with them, asps and snakes. Helen's set jaw. A lovely frown, crisp habit with the vegetables, scrubbing with a brown bristle brush, suddenly tall. "Are you taller than I am?" I feigned surprise. Helen, given the chance to top me, stopped and stood and let me stand proximate while we measured shoulders. Hers an inch below. "Not just yet." The scraping of vegetable skin resumed. "But soon," I said, yearning to give her something, a pint of blood, both aortas. "Give you another winter, and you'll out-grow your mum. You're becoming a woman, Helen."

"Then let me be."

"Don't I? I think I do. You do as you need."

"Not what I really need."

"And what is that?"

"Travel," said she.

"Certainly, my darling. I'll sell some gold and you shall travel."

"What if you didn't need to?" Then, "What gold?"

"I was joking, dear. Mother was being funny, ha, ha."

She speared me with a look. "You'd say no."

"Don't be so sure. Don't be so hard on me, please, Helen. I'm not your enemy."

"You just want to make me work in the kitchen. You want to keep me home so I can be just like you, a bitter old lady with dried-up skin. Your hands are wrinkled. Your face is wrinkled. I'm never going to be like you."

"No, that's true. You'll be rich and beautiful and feel no pain and do no work and have many children who never cry, and you will never grow old because you'll live in a glass casket and God help you."

"Bitch," said Helen clear as ice.

I swung round and slapped her before the word had quite left her lips.

"Well," said Helen, "that's that."

"Get your things. I'm taking you home to your father."

"Go to hell." Then she fled, of course, and I thought, Jeezus, children are vaudevillian.

"Helen!" I shouted. My shout was a formal resignation from the employ of the house of John Anderson. "You will come here at once! You will do as I say!" Of course she didn't, and wouldn't, and Edith Anderson was in the bath and didn't hear a thing, and Richard was playing pool on the third floor and stopped, just as he'd aligned his final shot and lifted his head, the light falling on his golden curls, and he looked up through the lead-paned window and smiled and aimed down the length of the cue and banked the eight ball into the corner pocket, winning yet again against himself.

But John Anderson heard my cry, and he stepped across the carpet and pushed through the swinging door, knocking gently on the kitchen wall. "Hello?" he said. "I thought I heard you sneeze." He smiled.

"I was just about to murder my child."

"Ahhhh. But she murdered you first."

"She is evil." I untied my apron. "John Anderson, KC, it's been very nice knowing you. But I am finished here, and will forthwith take my deceitful bitch-goddess back to her father."

"She could come with us, Blondie."

I stopped.

He said, "Richard has asked me about it. They're very young but—"

"She's a little girl!"

He shrugged. "The world is changing."

"Don't give me that 'world is changing' crap!" I was going to touch him, let him feel the cattle prod of my electric touch. "You disappoint me, John Anderson. You disappoint me more than I can say. You turn out to be the same as all your fat pals. *Fin de siècle,* my eyeball! The world's been faint and sick for eons, and you're just as decadent as the rest of your butt-lazy cronies."

"Yes, but it really is." That ineffable generosity. What an ass of a class specimen; what a class act as a simple human being.

I couldn't tell him I distrusted his son. He saw me hesitate and pressed his advantage, running off to get the illustrations, the map of the *Titanic.* We stood at the pastry table, and he showed me the four smokestacks, told me the proportion and weight of the hull. He had the drawings from the shipwright. Typical of the man. Biting his pipe with excitement, pointing with its stem at the six air compartments that made the *Titanic* unsinkable.

Richard walked in, leaned back and watched me as I squirmed.

"Think about it," said John. "What an education! She'll see London. We'll go to Paris, and I promise to stay away from Belgium. She'll be in no danger."

"She's too young."

"We'll look after her. Won't we, Richard."

Richard's slight smile.

"What will she go as?" I asked.

John didn't understand me. "As? Well . . . As?"

"What will she go as?" I couldn't find other words for it.

"As . . . as Helen. She'll go as Helen."

John Anderson was innocent. He clapped his hands. "There! It's done!" He softly punched Richard's shoulder. John Anderson's innocence always won him vast returns.

CHAPTER NINE

ELI BECAME A BIG RODEO STAR, making saddlebags of money. Not only bronc riding, but playing his guitar and singing those homeless cowboy songs in front of hundreds of fans, dressed with a black string tie and a silver knot at his throat, a silver buckle at his waist, long and lean, for he'd got taller in his black cowboy boots, and his black ten-gallon hat with the silver hatband set with turquoise added another six inches. Broncobusting kept him mellow, his voice burrowed into his leathery soul and his whole body said, I'm lonesome and I want it that way, ain't no home for a cowboy. Helen and I were two gold pieces he kept in his chest pocket, right next to his homesick heart. I enjoyed the moonglow of Eli's reflected fame, being the good woman in all those aching songs—my gal, rose of my heart.

The money that came to Eli from the rodeo seemed like the kind of money to throw at a new wardrobe for Helen: easy money, glamour cash. She had to have travel clothes, walking shoes, a good wool coat with a cape because the ship would pass close to Newfoundland on its way to New York. She needed evening dresses with matching bags and stockings and dancing shoes. They were travelling first class. Two other families from town were going too, but they were only going second class. Hats and kid gloves, a shawl, and of course, the pearls. Seeing his money spent this way, Eli grew ever more reckless in the rodeos, which served only to make him richer.

Richard watched us attire his prize. He brought her more gifts. Fastening drops of amber to her ears, he touched her face as if his fingers would leave an imprint on the soft surface. She blushed, modestly raised her eyes and kissed his cheek.

My distaste for the young man grew more acute. He bought her a short lamb coat, breathtaking with her hair, her ivory complexion. We were pinning a dress when he carried it in. Surprised, I too exclaimed over it, "How lovely!" She danced about the room, smiling at us both and said, "Oh, thank you!" He looked at her with neither fondness nor friendship, but a custodial regard. His voice was smooth, having changed without becoming raspy, a manly tenor. He wore a coal grey wool jacket with a white collar.

They were stylish. Their style was an end in itself, an activity, like racing.

Eli took a gulp of cold coffee and put his mug on the porch step. He'd just come off the fall circuit, and he was stiff and sore all over. "Walk with me, Blondie," he said and took my hand, and we went walking through the golden woods. It was a warm fall day. The leaves smelled of apples. We walked down to the riverside, the water brown and still. Dad had fixed up the dock last spring. Eli began by loosening his string tie and unbuttoning his pearl buttons. He wrenched off his boots and pulled off his pants, and wearing only his hat, he unbuttoned my dress and stripped me down. We held hands and jumped into the river. The freezing water ripped the air right out of our lungs.

ALICE EYED HER GRANDDAUGHTER'S COSTUME. "You look like a girl," she said sadly. "I never thought I'd see the day when a McCormack woman would go off wearing women's clothing." Young girls mimic women even better than women mimic women. The white kid gloves, the rouleau, tendrils on her throat. She'd brushed her eyebrows and fainted them with brown shadow.

The moment of their departure. Raining. Grandmother Alice refused to come with us to the train station. Grandfather Peter had a bad back. He walked out painfully and stood beside the carriage that would take his granddaughter into the arms of the enemies of the revolution. He stared straight ahead. Helen's desire to be off too urgent, she patted her grandfather's crustaceous white hand. Dad nodded and hobbled back to the house, tears running down either side of his long nose.

With my heart in my father's shirt pocket, my conscience up my mother's sleeve and my first loyalty wrapped around my daughter's little finger, I climbed up beside my husband and we rode off, a rodeo champion, beautiful Helen and me.

John Anderson greeted us at the station, to the merriment of loose pocket change, and took Eli's hand in both of his. John Anderson found friends where Eli heard coyotes. Eli shook John's hand. I'm not sure whether, in his innocence, John understood Eli's subtle generosity. Then our strange Aphrodite sweeping past.

There were twenty minutes before the train's departure. Helen, hearing this, panicked, not at leaving her mother and father, but at the delay, for she did not want to be our child a minute longer. Eli and I gazed at her, ashamed for her, in love with her. Took pity on her and said we had errands to run, we must go. Everyone but John Anderson felt relieved. He had tears in his eyes and said he'd take care of her for us, that was a promise.

We went back to the house. I stood in Helen's room, looking. A messy child. I let things stay where they'd fallen. If tomorrow came, it would not come to her empty little room.

"Does she know we are abandoned?" I asked Eli.

He considered, then pretended he hadn't heard me. Marie's dirge, the clock, the rain.

<hr />

I MISSED HELEN while she was on her travels, but I didn't envy her. I like it here. Inland, where the river flows up the middle of the continent. The sun will skin you alive. And in winter, we are so thoroughly bereft of heat and light, we can know cold for what it is: the end of ourselves. A message from dead stars: There's nothing out here, lucky for you, so cheer yourselves with one another. The days are as broad and free as the wings on the heron swinging over the slough. And come winter, the days will be as crisp and short and dark as an eighth note.

Eli and I received her belated postcards, which I would read to him, inconclusive things rather like the effusions of a lover who has already left you for somebody else. She began to use the word "dashing."

"What?" asked Eli, peering at her script.

"She says Dover is dashing."

In dismay, he looked again at the yellow photograph: boats, a castle. We received postcards from cafés on the Continent (she had learned to say "the Continent"), and from coffeehouses in London. From these scraps, we learned that it was really nice overseas. And she mentioned a lot of shoes. She was, it would appear, buying many pairs of shoes.

I wrote her back, c/o a postbox in London. The anonymity of her address was a kind of sanction for intimacy. It was awkward at first, when she'd recently left and I still hadn't hung up the clothes in her room and I still adopted the mother's postponement, the politely maternal attitude of waiting, my first letters to her full of questions (which she never answered) and bits of information that had been carefully chewed till everything came out all grey. "Is your coat warm enough?" "Do you like overcooked beef?"

Eli and I were parents in waiting, standing in a triangle with one side missing. For a time. And then, after several weeks, something shifted and we began to face each other. We had a marital affair. We ate at funny hours. Winter was as imperative as sleep. We were living off the remains of last year's rodeo money.

From this romantic cocoon, I wrote letters that gradually grew more reflective, chronicles of hibernation, snoozing notes about love and life, very effective emetics, I'm sure. Helen became a steady white porch light on the other side of an impassable field. Our correspondence never corresponded, my confessions to her deflections. During the cold months, our worry over her was numbed by our snowed-in helplessness, the pleasing darkness. Which, of course, must come to an end.

We woke up in March. Helen was to board the *Titanic* in April. She'd walked a beach at Brighton, had luncheon in Piccadilly, shot ptarmigan at Dundee. It was her fate that her body would exceed her, like a social class, like an addiction or a disease.

I blamed her for enjoying the banality of the age, the blond, blue-eyed world in evening dress, nibbling canapés behind the trelliswork of the Parisian Café, my raven-haired daughter presiding from the birdcage of the gilded age. From England to Newfoundland, from one island to another, fragment of the Old World to a rocky piece of the New.

We thought she was merely boarding a floating restaurant. What can we do with the occasion of our child's pain?

CHAPTER TEN

ON ENTERING THE DINING ROOM at night aboard ship, it is the men's white collars that you will see first, their black tuxedos invisible, the candles blown out by sea breezes. It's dark. The pale flesh of their hands and faces, cigar smoke, and eventually, the nacreous glow upon the women's tall necks, and dinner in the main salon may be observed.

Richard has never been so handsome. His is the most fashionable attire. While the older men may have something interesting to say, Richard's amused silence, like a secret enforced by his own small hand at his lips, holds for Helen all potency.

American gentlemen, a senator named Remington and a banking something. The Remington senator reaches for an ashtray, touches Helen's arm, turns with gruff Bourbon civility to apologize and really looks at her for the first time. He says nothing to Helen, but he draws on his cigar and then tips it at John Anderson. "Pretty girl," he says, without much of the drawl of the second-class passengers, but with a boldness sufficient to cause John Anderson to lean privately to his ward's beautiful ear and suggest it is time to say good night.

She retires unwillingly. Does not undress or remove her strand of pearls. Does not scribble or read or fully think, but runs her hands down her satin gown. Up and down.

Richard lingers with the men. He has, at the end of his line, a beautiful fish.

In the chaos that follows, Helen retains several images. One of Richard climbing into a lifeboat with the women and children. Is it the terror of the night that has reduced him to childhood?

Then the black, heaving back of the sea. Thirty-five people in the lifeboat. With the exception of the bosun and Richard, all of them are women with their children. Helen is colder than she has ever been. So cold when her small group of survivors pulls alongside the *Carpathian,* where ropes descend and arms reach to pull them up to safety, so cold that her hand has frozen to the gunnel and the sailor sent down to get her thinks she's in shock. Her isolate calm spooks him, and he pries off each finger with a fearful viciousness disguised by the dark. He breaks three of Helen's fingers. They haul her up by her arms because she can't hold on to anything. Standing on the *Carpathian,* she looks at her hand. It is a dead bird; the pain shrills when she thaws and the swelling starts.

Richard, as one of a collection of women and children. His handsome tuxedo a costume. Helen comes to know counterfeit.

They disembark at New York, and at last we learn that she is alive. She is sent home to us, Richard too, with Mrs. Anderson, who does not walk, and they are collected by John Anderson's lawyers while we take Helen away, and no one speaks. No baggage. No bodies in caskets, no corpses at all. Fifteen hundred people are drowned, their bodies consumed by tiny organisms, leaving behind jewels and many pairs of shoes. The ocean makes a clean sweep.

After that there are debutantes. In various pockets around the world, there will always be debutantes and their boys in evening dress. There are always *Titanics*, with lovely people dancing over treacherous seas. Our thirst for glamour remains. It is the innocence that we must, at this juncture in our story, pronounce extinct. Three men and one boy from Winnipeg died when the *Titanic* went down, which tells us more about the bold aspirations of this town in those days than would any figures for grain sales. *The Chicago of the North.* The icy sea swallowed the entire Edwardian era in one gulp.

Helen moved back into her little room. She'd finally grown taller than I was. I think I was afraid of her; I didn't want to make her fly off.

I miss John Anderson. For a long time after, I was careful to be chilly with everyone. Despite their goodwill and imagination, for all their beauty and charm and brilliance and nice suits and plans for the future, people have a tendency to die.

<hr>

I WENT BACK TO WORK for Mrs. Anderson. For several months, I drove to her house early and worked in the kitchen with a brittle sort of clarity. In the profound absence of John Anderson, KC, our relations in the house were altered. With Richard at the head of the family, Helen was no longer a girl. I went alone.

John Anderson's drowning plunged a hole in the painted canvas that once made our world seem absolute. There was a constant buzz in my ear. I proceeded from the premise that there would be a bookend for the encyclopedia of our grief.

It was many weeks before I saw Richard; he was leaving by the summer doors leading from the sunroom. I said hello, and he froze for a few seconds before turning smoothly. He tried some unctuous chat and then dropped it. Looked at me with hurt, furtive eyes.

I suppose people thought Richard had grown up, assumed responsibility. Must look after his mother now, be a better man at business than John, bless him, but a man can't be too soft, and John . . . well, he's gone now, and what an awful way to go, makes me shiver.

Richard firmed up. The vague, casual boy became a series of taut muscles pinned to loose joints, a combination of soldier and ragtime dancer. No longer pensive or bored. Where once the house was calm with a thoughtless inheritance, a long measure without any expectation of change (which is uncanny, that an upper class can be invented out of homesteaders, truly, as if there had been countless generations of John Anderson, KCs, and their sons; in that house, built to emulate the British upper class, it was easily forgotten that the aristocratic lifespan of John Anderson's lineage was about ten minutes), it seemed now to be a queer, chipper place, as if all the rugs had been removed. You couldn't avoid the sound of shoes on the floor. The clocks chimed and the hours still equalled sixty minutes, but the big brass pendulum would surely swing loose on the quarter-hour and kill somebody. Richard was nervous.

Mrs. Anderson would not get out of the bath. She lived in the porcelain tub, in a room white with steam. She called me, her voice like a lamb's or a sea creature's, sounding the foghorn of her fear. "Baarbaaraa!" I would fetch the kettle and go to her. Her skin was pulling away like butter in water, swelling up in the bath. She had a rather pleasant body, but for its gradual disinte- gration, and I was sorry to see her come apart. She was near- sighted and declined to wear her glasses while she "soaked," as she liked to call it. I'd enter, quickly shutting the door behind me to keep the room hot, stunned by the conservatory humidity, and Mrs. Anderson would look up, blinking through the steam with the nocturnal defencelessness peculiar to near-sighted people, her pale, softening face above rather broad shoulders and plump breasts resting upon the folds of her stomach. "Oh, you brought me more hot," she would say. "How kind you are." She would turn her face away while I poured the water by her potato-like feet, and her eyelids would flutter in despair.

So it went, while the real world grew ripe and green and hard and rooted and dried and snowed and froze and then melted and grew ripe again. Richard was somehow too old to go with his chums to the university. But he bought a seat at the Winnipeg Grain Exchange and began to make a lot of money trading futures. His youth and the circumstances of his father's death isolated him from the others of his class, and he was declined a membership in the Manitoba Club, it was said, until he came of age.

He liked to row in summer, and he grew strong. He played a good game of golf. His neck and chest were muscular, but his face remained narrow, a golden face framed by golden hair. As he got very rich, he became as porous as the pumice stone beside his mother's bath. He never frowned, but he never fully smiled either; he always looked as if he'd tricked somebody and they must have liked it. He was pleased. And he was wounded. Living in a small city made it much worse. There was a moratorium on Richard's respectability. He was haunted by an unspoken question; it hung in the air, made him jaunty with loneliness. Everyone needed to know, before fully gripping his hand, before opening their smiles to his eloquent mask: What saved Richard and what sank John? Everyone had liked John. Why was Richard here? A father without a grave. It made Richard an eternal son.

And at home with her dad, Eli, Helen shut herself in her room. Through her closed bedroom door, we heard her voice accompany her dead grandmother's lament. Marie, inspired by our bereavement, had become an almost gladsome dirge, a marimba plunking, yet always with that vertiginous, descending atonality.

CHAPTER ELEVEN

1914

I don't want a hyena in petticoats talking politics at me. I want a
nice gentle creature to bring me my slippers.

—Sir Rodmond Roblin, premier of Manitoba,

to Nellie McClung, suffragist

GERMANY ENTERED BELGIUM the day the United States opened
the Panama Canal. Things had been fairly quiet on the home
front. Mrs. John Anderson had been in the bath for more than
two years. She looked like a parsnip.

With John gone, Richard came downstairs. He worked in
his father's library, which was at the front of the house, in the
northeast corner, lamp-lit even on the sunniest days and cool.
Like his father, Richard worshipped telecommunications. He
spent the day on the phone, and when he went downtown it was
to send telegrams or play with the phones at the Winnipeg Grain
Exchange. He had not made contact with Helen since April
1912, when the train had brought them home empty-handed
from New York. He slipped into adulthood the way a soldier
slips into uniform. His adolescent hideout had been a room
beside the billiard room on the third floor. But now he had no
time for billiards. A bulb had burnt out on the landing and no
one bothered to replace it.

The day the war started, my mother, Alice, got mad at a newcomer just moved in across the road, and she hitched Eli's stallion to the harrow and ran over the man's dog. It was partly an accident, but it upset her so badly she decided to resign from the Political Equality League (a group of social reformers and suffragists), which had been the secondary source of her distress. The League had been her hope and her life till then, but Alice was suffering from jealousy and shame.

Alice had been aiming to destroy the man's lawn. He had bought ten acres of MacDonald's farm. MacDonald (what they called an original settler because we'd lost the record of the grottos beneath his homestead) had grown too old, and with the exception of one son, who was a rancher in Alberta, his offspring had moved to Winnipeg, where they'd bought half a dozen apartment blocks and established a rental agency. Nobody wanted the farm, so old MacDonald was selling it off, piece by piece. My mother was of the opinion that it was degenerate to sell anything less than 160 acres at a time. Then when the newcomer planted a neat tea towel of Kentucky bluegrass and a tiny flowerbed, Mum saw red. A family of burrowing owls had been living in that field, which had never been cultivated, and there were tentative pools of lady's slippers that had bloomed just that spring after an invisible presence of nine years (Alice had counted the years; she thought the invisibility of the pouting blooms signified her own decline, and though Peter continued to be demonstrative and she continued to respond, she felt in her heart that she had lost her allure, that it had in a sense gone underground, forever, unlike the furtive chthonic nourishment in the roots of the lady's slippers).

It was a nice dog, a well-groomed collie dog that kept to his own territory. When Grandmother Alice ran over the dog, Helen was forced to come to her aid, because Grandpa Peter was at an Impossibilists' meeting and Eli was back on the fall circuit, which had started early because everybody was having fairs where they could hoist the Union Jack and show off how British they were, even at Brunkild and Tolstoi.

Helen hadn't spoken since the *Titanic* went down. Not a word for more than two years. I tried sending her to the local school. The teacher came to see us, though, and suggested, looking carefully around our kitchen, that Helen, while a very *pretty* girl, appeared to be . . . um, that is . . . as some girls are . . . please understand, I'm not saying she's dumb, but perhaps *distracted* . . . yes, distracted is the better word. From behind the closed door to Helen's bedroom came a loud whumping.

At Helen's request, Eli had built her a loom. She wove woollen rugs, which remained piled in her little bedroom. Sometimes when she was sleeping, I would steal in and unroll them and admire the pearly tones she favoured, the blood red waves woven through.

Her education was adjourned. Helen rarely left her room. She was *thinking*. But she was not thinking *about*. She inhabited a spot of time as precise as the quarter-inch scar on her hand, and that is where she lived: in the moments of John Anderson's death, when wealth had proved no cure for the terrors of the body's edge, the flesh that freezes, drowns, is cut and broken, and through that rupture Richard had fallen into the pantomime of outer space. Helen wove, and her broken hand ached when she wove. The loom banged, shuttled, interlaced warp with the filling threads of those moments when luxury had betrayed her.

But when Alice harrowed the collie, the dog didn't die right away, and its screams brought out the rather hysterical owner. Alice, who liked dogs and felt an awakening of her old guilt over Thomas Scott, nevertheless found the neighbour's reaction ridiculous, and she climbed down and took the man's hands and placed them on the stallion's bridle and told him, "Hold tight, he's going to rear." Then she raced back to our shack, because she knew Eli kept his buffalo-hunting gun in good condition at all times.

Helen saw her grandmother come in, her skinny old face fierce and determined. She couldn't help following her back to the neighbour's lawn, running to keep up. Things were pretty much as Alice had left them, though the dog had quieted a little because one lung had been punctured. The dog looked up gratefully at Alice. And Alice, tender, dry-eyed, shot him in the head. The pioneer suburbanite cried out, and Alice removed his hands from the bridle and climbed up, motioning to the stunned Helen to join her. Alice shifted over to sit on Helen's lap.

"You crazy woman!" The man wept as he stumbled beside the cart. "You killed my dog!"

"I'm sorry about the dog," said Alice. "I truly am."

Seated beneath her skinny grandmother, Helen sniffed at the scent of blood in the air. When she spoke, her voice had the sweet, oily timbre of pounded walnuts; she whispered, "May your lawn get leaf mould!" She had the reins. Louder, she called out, "May your grass be choked by knotweed, by black medick!" Her lungs full, her heart triggered by rage, galvanized by violence.

"I hope you get dandelions! I hope you get plantains and fungus!" She circled the man, who stood over his dead dog. "May you suffer from creeping charlie, from shepherd's purse! May you spend the days that remain in a war against cutgrass and chickweed and bedstraw!"

"Hush now," said Grandmother Alice. "Take us home, girl."

Helen cut across the lawn and took the ditch up to the road. She was panting when they pulled up at the barn. Grandmother Alice trembled. They were unhitching the horse, either side of the traces, when Alice looked her granddaughter in the eye and stopped. "What is happening to the world?" she asked Helen.

"Shhhh," said Helen. "Hear that?" At the border of the yard, poplar leaves' small slapping. "The outside edges are cracking."

"Wait," said Alice. "Hitch him up again. I'm going into town. I resign from the human race. But first, I'm going to resign from the League."

"I'll go with you," said Helen. "I'm joining up."

And so it came to pass that my mother, my daughter and I were running up the stairs towards the unlit boy's den on the third floor of John Anderson's mansion. Helen was ahead, tucking her skirts, her jaw set the way it had been when she was first learning to walk away from me. I chased after. "He's not up there, you idiot!" I told her. "He's in his father's study! Wake up and smell the coffee! Everything has changed!"

Grandmother Alice came last. She was stuck there because Helen insisted and she had no choice, which was perfect, because she had at last a chance to see the capitalist's domicile against her own wishes. She didn't even try to hide her curiosity, her delighted interest. Transparently happy, she stared at the velvet wallpaper and bevelled glass and voluminous drapery without avarice or disdain.

"I'm just stopping on my way to quit the League," Mum said loudly. "I will not listen to that McClung woman a minute longer!"

"Helen, stop rushing off and talk to me!" I said. "Richard is downstairs in the library!"

But Helen had reached the landing. She stopped. Her hesitation was the first hint of shyness. Mum and I caught up with her. Though it was a sunny day, the landing was dark and smelled of mildewed books. We began to whisper.

"He's here," she hissed. "He's always here."

"Look at that!" Grandmother Alice pointed frantically at the billiard table in its abandoned, dusty room. She was waving her arms and jumping on her little feet. "I'm going to try it!"

"Grandma, no!" With one hand fastened to Alice's arm, Helen pushed open the door to Richard's den. Richard was standing in his father's posture, hands in pockets, in a slant-ceilinged room lit by an unlikely mixture of electricity and pungent afternoon sun. He barely flinched, but his very blood seemed to thicken and ripen in his veins. I wondered how he always came to be so amused.

Helen, the instant lady, entered the room. "Hello, Richard," she said.

My mother stuck out her hand. "Alice McCormack." Richard took it, I thought, gratefully.

"Sorry to barge in," I said.

He seemed pleased, careful but pleased. He found Alice a chair. He would not look at Helen. We glanced about. "I come here now and then," he said to me. "I can't stand the telephone."

This was most likely true, as was his addiction to the instrument.

"I'd hate the telephone too," Alice confided, "given the chance."

"Those were John Anderson's," I said. I walked towards the framed plans for the *Titanic,* hung on the wall. The blueprints looked like a star chart. And beside it, also framed, a replica of the engineers' drawings for the Panama Canal.

"It opens today," Richard said. "Funny coincidence. Funny day."

Helen put her finger on the speculative white line of the *Titanic*'s hull. Richard recoiled as if she'd touched him. You could have lit an entire town with the current that passed between them.

"Hot in here," said Alice. "Reminds me of a judge I once knew. Only it was winter. He never really worked either. Oh! It's a rocker!" She began to rock violently. "Pardon me," she said. "It's an awful affliction, being sensitive the way I am. Yes, this judge and you . . . All on paper, aren't you."

Richard took her literally. He searched for himself on the star chart, the drawings. "I imagine you've heard," he said. He walked to a dark alcove and turned on a small brass lamp with a green shade, very Winston Churchill. There, behind him, a map of Europe with pins stuck into the border between Germany and Belgium. "The war has begun," he said. He went to an old pine toy chest and opened the lid and removed a bottle of Scotch whisky and three glasses. "We'll have to share," he said. Then he stopped suddenly and said to Alice, "You're probably a prohibitionist. I'm sorry. I didn't mean to offend you."

"Lord God, no," said Alice quietly. "What's the world coming to? Prohibitionist. Pour me a drink. This is the saddest day of my life."

We drank to our health. We drank to the dead. We drank to the future. And to the future dead.

Helen sat down on the floor and Richard took a chair opposite. Helen, refreshed by two years' silence, gave herself over to reading the curve of Richard's lip. He looked well. More fully formed, much more formed. As if it had never happened. She felt, briefly, light. To suspend, to lie upon the high pressure of Richard's quick forward motion, never to look to the side, never to look inside. He was ever-more stylish, for the effect of a new subtlety in both his manner and his dress. She swayed. The whisky helped, a luscious passivity, a holiday. Yes, Richard had recovered, and more. He looked at her without embarrassment. Something in Richard's way of laying his eyes on you, a blue looking that displaced you, did not take you in, but knocked you out of way, that he might take your place. But oh, Helen thought, it is an intelligence, as abstract as a hawk's, yet charismatic. She would marry him. And when Richard next looked at her, she masked herself, as if she were fencing.

CHAPTER TWELVE

My MOTHER BEGAN TO QUIT, and once she got the hang of it, there was no stopping her. Quitting left spaces in her life that could be filled only by starting. She quit eating beef and started eating chicken. She quit smoking and started drinking (Scotch in the evening for one hour only; neat, four ounces and no more, quickly). She quit sleeping and started to walk at night.

She remained keen, grew increasingly generous. She said to me when I caught up with her on one of her sleepless jaunts, the two of us walking beside the woods with the sound of broken trees bowing, "The shadows are red. I never knew that before. I mean, they're red in daylight, Blondie. During the night, they're green." She sighed and drew her coat around her, for there was a south wind, rich with fall. "I have reached a conclusion," she said. "Things will go on without me. True. It doesn't matter. Things were going on without me all this time." She chuckled. "I didn't even know. I'm very lucky I stayed alive long enough to find out." My mother took my arm, a rare event between us. I tried not to touch her too strongly in case she disappeared.

Quitting is an act of protest only if the quitter sticks around and reminds the joinees of her quitter status. Alice went through a bad patch when she quit the Political Equality League just when the League was having so much fun. Nellie McClung and that brilliant group of suffragists, black cloaks thrown over their evening gowns, staged a mock Parliament at the Walker Theatre. McClung played the Conservative premier, Rodmond Roblin, a chivalric ass, and of course she stole the show. My mother didn't have a mean bone in her bird-like body. But she had a lot of bones, and a few of them ached youthfully, like green willows divining the underground streams of envy.

The day Alice quit the League, she came home in a foul humour and poured herself a mug of Scotch and sat at the kitchen table with her cape on. My dad, Peter, was making cabbage rolls and singing one of Eli's cowboy songs. When he saw his wife come in like that, he put his spoon down and pulled up a chair, wiping his hands, waiting. "They're going to miss you, Alice," Peter said.

"You're just saying that because it's impossible. It's okay. I'm going to become the first female agricultural journalist and wear a man's suit."

"That'd be good," said Peter thoughtfully. "Been done."

Alice blinked. "I'm getting strange in my old age." She offered him her mug. "Want some?"

Peter took a sip and gave it back. "I hadn't noticed."

"You know what we become when we get old?" she asked. "Ourselves. It gets harder and harder to disguise ourselves."

Peter moved his chair close to hers. He put his hands on her knees and looked into her face. "It would take a hundred years to know you."

"I don't really want to quit the League," she said, wiping her nose on her sleeve. "I just got petulant. Why'd they have to join up with that old fox? Why'd they have to put their cards in with the Liberals? I want the vote as much as anybody. But it's half a cup equality and six cups bigotry. What am I going to do?"

"Stick around and make a lot of noise?"

She winced. "I'm tired, Peter."

"Shhhhh." He put his arms around her.

"They're stuffing the vote in with conscription, did you know? Tobias Norris wants to be premier. Give the ladies the vote if we'll vote for his damn-to-God Liberals. Conscription. The liberty to send young boys to war. I can hardly wait. And prohibition for God's sake! Ha! Ha, ha and ha!"

"It's always a funny mix," said my dad.

Alice pulled away. "Here I am telling *you*," she said. She straightened herself, but then shut her eyes against some fresh pain. "I'm afraid of the future. What if they shut down the school? Everybody's so . . . so Ontario all of a sudden."

"It's not so different."

"But now there's a war."

Peter took the mug and drank from it. "Anyway," he said, "we've got no choice but to drink down the bad with the good."

"McClung is pretty funny," said Alice. "She even does voices. I just wish she'd been born French or something. Jewish. It's the taste of tea gets stuck in my craw."

"That's the taste of power," Peter said. "Very bland, so nobody will notice it's working."

"I like her a lot. That's the honest truth. It's just such a tea biscuit, a fur hat and muff, kid gloves . . . Ohhhh, what's the use? I don't want to quit. But I don't want to *belong*."

ONE MORNING, Alice went downtown to teach school. She had been walking much of the night, travelling like a beetle over a piece of amber. It was like that in her quitting phase, moving towards the border between darkness and light.

My mother had always enjoyed the arbitrary nature of her own opinions. Whatever role she played, she played with gusto and more; she loved the excess of her own characterizations. She was happiest teaching at the school by the CPR station, where the kids understood perfectly that their teacher was a ham.

Humming a fugue tune, Alice trotted up the broken sidewalk to the school wrapped in the wing-cases of her black wool cape, around her neck a red muffler and on her head a red tam-o'-shanter. She swept into the classroom saying, in German, "Brrrrr, it's as cold as Grampa's bare knees!" She removed her cape and scarf, and then realized that the class was standing stock still. She recognized the smell of fear. The children stood rigid beside their desks, staring at her, immobile but for their lips, bird beaks through which came a reedy song.

"Rule Britannia," the children were singing in falsetto, "Britannia rule the waves. Brit-ons never, never, ne-ver shall be slaves." Alice took this in with horror, looking at her joyful mix of wildflowers and learning that only the petunias might be permitted to thrive. Above them, hovering over the teacher's desk and covering the enormous hand-drawn map of the world that had been Mr. Kolchella's great achievement, was a Union Jack the size of a golf green, the biggest, reddest, bluest Union Jack on the face of the earth.

My mother took a look around and saw the victorious figure of a classic marm, a real old biddy in a brown suit, an orphan's nightmare, standing in one corner, keeping time with a ruler to the children's prison song and fixing Alice with the loaded blunderbuss of her righteous eye. The children finished the last verse and waited.

"You sound like escaping gas," Alice said gently to the children.

She removed her things and opened the closet beside her desk, where she'd hung a mirror just a bit too high, and stood on tiptoe to adjust her hair. Out of the blue, she took a lipstick and put it on, something that she'd never done before, and the children were heard to twitter. It was an inside joke. She could make out the reflection of the class behind her. The children met her eye in the mirror. Alice winked. Fifty-nine children did their best to wink back. To the mirror, she spoke, "And where is our good friend Mr. Kolchella?" All eyes went to the stranger lady standing in the corner. Alice closed the cupboard. Then she smiled. "How do you do!" With open vowels, she rushed forward, offering her hand like a hostess on Millionaire Row. "So glad! Welcome! Do sit!" She put the Marm in an empty desk. "We have a visitor! Children!" Alice clapped her hands. The kids were all smiling by then. "We're going to play Who's Got Mr. Kolchella?"

The Marm had a voice as pretty as a blue jay. "Mr. Kolchella is in custody. All enemy aliens are in custody."

"Well, that's a shame because I need him here to teach the children the history of democracy. Class! Let's show Miss . . . uh, Mrs. . . ."

The dried old biddy squinted. "Smith. Mrs. I am from the education department. And I have come to shut down the school."

"Smithstein! Smithski! Let's show Miss Smitzniuk what a good Canadian class we are."

The class tumbled into action. The room was filled with the sound of thirty wooden tables and fifty-nine wooden chairs dragged over a hardwood floor to make an erratic barricade. They worked like patriots preparing for a rebellion, a good thing, too, because that's what they were. The children looked as if they were in a silent film, mouthing words to each other with a rational clarity you see at times of crisis.

Ten of the most underfed kids came downstage and sat on the floor, and then suddenly the play was on in earnest and they clutched their stomachs, moaned and fell over unconscious and woke up and moaned and fell over again. "I'm hungry, I'm so hungry, I'm really, really hungry. No, I am, *I am*." The huge kid, seventeen and smarter than he looked, leapt out from behind the chairs and said, in a bully's voice, "Pay up!" He pulled an old potato out his pocket and pretended to eat it, waving it in front of the starving habitants (because that's what they really were). "I said *pay!*"

"We don't have money for tie-ethes," the hungry kids whined. "We can't pay the church the money, and we don't have wheat because of the early frawest." The big kid was at a loss for words, but with great significance, he waved the potato in their faces and stormed off. Everybody cheered.

"What is going on?" demanded Mrs. Smith.

"It's the 1837 Rebellions. Well, we're mostly doing the

Lower Canada drama, with Louis-Joseph Papineau leading the French against the British colonizers, but next week we'll do William Lyon Mackenzie's tavern brawl against the oligarchy in Upper Canada," said Alice modestly.

The Marm's mouth opened and shut, like a dying cod, and Alice leaned towards her as she would to a slightly dense child. "You remember, dear, the anticlerical, anti-British revolts out East?" prompted Alice. "Papineau? Exiled to the States? Never came back to Canada? Yes? He gets the children excited, you see. There just aren't that many good Canadian revolts, yes? For self-government? Freedom? And the children do like to see a good rebellion, don't you find? How kids like justice?" But Mrs. Smith really looked lost now. In a stage whisper to the kids, Alice said, "Our visitor is confused! Chase the seigneur!"

The kids covered their mouths with embarrassment. "We forgot to chase the seigneur!" And the red-headed boy leapt up and ran right out of the room. "Good riddance," said the starving habitants, who didn't want to leave the stage.

Alice said to Mrs. Smith, "Being from the education department, you do know what the seigneur is. The powerful landowner, yes?" She slapped Mrs. Smith's knee. "Of course you do! How I'd hate to patronize you!"

Twelve handsome boys swaggered out, swinging pretend walking sticks and smoking pretend cigarettes. Every once in a while, one of them would say, "Polo?" through his nose, and his colleague would answer, "Certainly! After we kill the rebels." For clarity's sake, one boy asked, "What are we called again?" and he was answered, "We're the Montreal cavalry!" "And what do we do!" "PROTECT THE RICH!"

Mrs. Smith was making a peculiar movement with her hands, fidgety and weird. Her chalky little body began to shake. Alice wanted to rub lanolin onto the flaky skin, but instead she reached over and handed Mrs. Smith her umbrella, anything to stop that autistic thing with the hands. It worked. Mrs. Smith gavelled the umbrella and shrieked, "Stop it! Stop it this instant!"

Some of the children stopped, but some of them had no time for Mrs. Smith, and with one eye on Alice, they skipped a bit and rushed to the climax, when they got to have a shootout and die in flames.

Mrs. Smith's shoes were anvils, twenty pounds apiece. She walked onstage like the Industrial Revolution. Even the patriots were cowed. Silently, the starving habitants stood up, and the seigneur, who had been watching through the murky glass in the door, re-entered and stood uncertainly with the rest.

"What year is it?" snapped Mrs. Smith.

"1837!" cried half the class. And the other half cried out, "1914!"

"Of course it's 1914! Put down that potato!" The potato hit the floor and rolled a little; fifty-nine children watched it in misery. "And now . . . Sing!"

She might just as well have demanded they laugh. They looked at her. "You are going to sing a goodbye song to Mrs. McCormack. Mrs. McCormack has decided she will not teach here any more."

They looked at my mother in panic. Alice stuck her tongue in one cheek and rolled her eyes. The relief was instant. "Sing!" said Mrs. Smith. "It is your duty to the king!"

The children began to sing "England, My England" with all their ironic hearts and a trace of an accent. French, was it? German? Maybe Strasbourg, a bit of both.

Alice went to the closet and put on her cape and red muffler and red hat. The children were singing. She stood and listened a moment, and then she walked out, closing the door behind her. The song came to an end. The kids stood stunned, sentenced to compulsory boredom. In less than ten seconds, they learned the prisoner's fake submission. A sheet of ice mixed with manure hardened their hearts. And just when they were nearly lost, Alice stuck her head with its red tam through the door and said, "See you around, darlings."

CHAPTER THIRTEEN
GOODBYE, RICHARD. WRITE

RICHARD JOINED THE NAVY. His mother, Mrs. John Anderson, got out of the bath and organized a luncheon in his honour. So unhinged was she, I was ordered to invite "Helen's grandparents," Alice and Peter. Grandmother Alice brought with her the few students remaining in her school—seven children in all, the only kids permitted to associate with the agitator Mrs. McCormack and her School for Historical Drama (or as my mother herself liked to call it, the School for Histrionics). Alice wanted them to see the capitalists' domicile up close. And she thought they might like the food.

Everyone at the luncheon seemed to be very old, but the oldest person of all was Richard's great-aunt, Mrs. Crumb. Mrs. Crumb was deaf, but she did have an ear for the voices of children. She was a Victorian dowager right out of Dickens, a black lace doily who was always awarded the best seat by the fireplace, but not too close because she believed that the flush from the heat made her "as red as an Indian." My dad bent over to shout into the horn, "Or like an honest working man!"

Mrs. Crumb's teeth shifted in her mouth when she smiled. She smelled of phosphate of lime. "Eh what? Say again?"

Dad's back hurt. Reluctantly, he leaned over again and said, "The labourer is our only friend!"

"You haven't any friends?" Mrs. Crumb patted his hand. "I can't believe that." She sucked on her dentures and looked expectantly at the children, awaiting some real conversation.

My mother's smallest students ducked under the white tablecloth and reappeared with a piece of cake, a corner piece, thick with pink icing. Mrs. Crumb's fireside chair sat directly beyond. She saw them and smiled flirtatiously. They approached, a scalloped dessert plate proffered to the crispy lady who looked like a stale piece of blueberry pie. "May we play with your horn?" they asked, standing three feet away. Mrs. Crumb heard them perfectly. "Of course, dears," she said and handed it to them. They spoke to her in confidential tones through the horn. "Are you a suffragette?" asked one.

"What d'ye think I'd be? Stupid?"

"Have you ever been kissed?"

"A hundred thousand times," said Mrs. Crumb. "I was married to Mr. Crumb, don't you know? He was terribly handsome."

"Is he dead then?"

"Dead as dead." She sighed.

"Do you miss him a lot?"

"Oh." It was all Mrs. Crumb could say. Her tiny skull, with its sparse grey pincurls, bobbed up and down, and tears filled her eyes and her face grew tender. The children saw this and handed over the cake. She sniffed and tilted the plate towards herself and began to eat the icing first, all the while nodding, oh yes.

A lovely going-to-war party for Richard. He and Helen came in from a walk in the garden. Richard held Helen's hand. Everyone said how handsome Richard looked in his naval uniform. And then they remarked, Helen . . . well, isn't she always

. . . perhaps more so than ever before. Her dark wavy hair, a rather simple dress, they found it elegant on no one else; clothes could not compete with that kind of beauty. Though she doesn't say much, does she? And they sipped tea and hoped she could make Richard happy. A wartime wedding? My word, as young as that! Well, that won't do. I'd no idea! She seems much older. What a strange girl. But then, Richard . . . well, without a father's hand to guide him . . . Sipping tea. Prohibition. A rare sunny day, the end of April. Warm. The sun rubbed fragrances from the dried old earth yet again; what astonishing resilience.

Richard did not release her hand. They looked like they were playing at the maypole when they walked around the dining-room table. Richard avoided a conversation with his mother, who fluttered at him helplessly from behind the butler's wagon. He backed into the kitchen, pulled Helen with him.

Into my domain. I was surprised to see her. We looked warily at each other, yanked out of our normal roles. The war had created a special brand of sentimentality, a potpourri in the great under-wear drawers of the nation, infecting us all with the strain of being awfully nice, chipper and enthusiastic for our diet of horror.

The fight over Ypres had been going on for nearly a week. Germany had introduced us to chlorine gas. When we first heard about the yellow clouds of poison released into the wind, we stopped for just a moment; it takes only a moment for human beings to accept greater evil. A quick trip from a jagged blade, machine guns in Saskatchewan in 1885, smallpox on a blanket and exploding bullets to chlorine gas, mustard gas, napalm and Agent Orange. Within another three weeks, ninety-five thousand soldiers, Allied and German, would be rotting at

Ypres. Sir Robert Borden, the anxious and earnest prime minister, was sending boatloads of boys to the front. Without a doubt, we'd become a nation. We all suffered from neuralgia, even the prime minister. Real grown-up lumbago.

In those bad times, the kitchen became the only room where it was possible to breathe, blow a little smoke through the barrier between lump-in-your-throat cute and slash-and-burn despair. Sugar and strychnine mix better in the kitchen, as long as everybody has enough to drink, and if we still can't exactly tell the truth, we can at least respect its absence.

We were growing up. Helen, who came in with her soldier-lover, looked me square in the eye; the barricade crumbled, and we met each other warmly, if not safely, in the no man's land of womanhood. She even let me kiss her. I gave her a small glass of port. We talked about the war.

Richard lit a cigarette and leaned against the kitchen counter, Helen's round white arm reaching to take it from his lips. She was just about to puff on it when she caught my eye. I said, "Let's not push it." She puffed anyway, and I was gratified to see her turn green.

The talk was of the army. You could feel Richard's silence, as if he'd been cut out of the picture with scissors. In the lull, I brought it round to him. "So! The navy!"

He was too smart for that. Nodded.

"You don't like walking?"

He winced.

We were in the company of two seasoned fellows, a newspaper man and somebody in insurance, very bright and not too nice. They each had a son in Belgium. They hadn't yet heard if their children were safe. The two fathers looked closely at Richard. The kitchen faced north, and had a tiny porthole of a window buttoned up with flowery curtains. In the overhead light, we all looked ill.

"Where have they got you stationed, son?" asked the journalist, gruff voice, kind and resentful.

Richard raised his eyes, as if from under a helmet. He knew he was being treated with respect. "St. John's," he said.

Everyone mumbled, oh, yes, uh-huh, yup, nodding. We'd heard about the German submarines off the East Coast.

"Lot of ships in those waters from what I hear." The journalist sounded tired. It was hard to focus on anything those days, needled by anxiety, hard to finish a sentence.

The insurance man piped up. "St. John's, Newfoundland." Paused. "Yup."

Helen took a sip of port. A flush from the wine, but her face was utterly sober, as I'd never seen it before. As if she didn't need anything, neither flattery nor comfort. She'd let go of that doe-like apprehension.

The journalist pushed off. "Well," he said, putting down his glass and winking at me. "Thanks." He walked slowly, as if arthritic, though he was only about forty-five.

"I'll be going too." The insurance guy placed his glass, tidy, beside his friend's. "Nice party," he said to me, as if I were the hostess rather than the cook. "Thanks." Going out he stopped, remembering something. To Richard: "Newfoundland," he said. Looked at him. Then, noncommittal, uneasy, "Going back there, are you?"

Richard's jaw tightened.

The insurance man's eyes darted to Helen. "Going to have another look?" He noticed a cupboard door ajar and pushed it shut. "I'm sure your dad would've been relieved. Home turf and all. Nice to stay in Canada."

Richard said, "I hope I'll see my share of danger."

The insurance man looked at him sharply. "Oh, don't wish that." He shook his head sadly. "Never wish for that."

Richard stepped forward and aimed for a dainty, took one, looked at it as if it were roadkill. "I'm not afraid," he said.

The insurance man nodded. "No, I'm sure you're not."

"I'm not."

"We're pretty well convinced of that, Richard," said I.

Helen was attentive.

The insurance man asked Richard, "What kind of ship will you be on?"

"A minesweeper." Richard with his dry mouth, his defensive eyes.

"Good God," said the insurance man. "Do you have to?"

"Yes. Of course I do."

"It's a terrible war," said the insurance man.

I piped up. "What does a mine look like?"

Richard looked at me like someone remembering an opponent on his flank. "It's a . . . the size of . . . like a dinner table, only maybe smaller. It's round, you see, and it has horns."

"A sea monster," I said. "God, you'd think we were making all this up."

Richard's slight, nervous smile. "It does sound rather bizarre."

Mrs. Anderson plummeted into the room like a bird down the chimney. "Oh, my boy!" she said. "Don't hide yourself! Come!" She moored at his arm and drew him out of the room with her unsteady willpower, a tug drawing a ship to sea.

Helen sighed, eminently visible. The insurance man wouldn't look at Helen. His eyes strafed her, fast and away. For all his decency, he treated my daughter as something forbidden. It gave her peculiar power. She knew this well.

"Thanks for dropping by," I said to him.

He blushed and said, "I'm sorry." I felt sorry for us all then. We suddenly seemed to remember our places. "Goodbye, then," he said, and walked out slowly.

"Damn!" I said.

At the door he turned, brightened. "What's that?" He smiled. "Yes! Damn it all! Goodbye, then. Bye-bye."

When he'd gone, Helen looked at me dryly. "Richard wants me to get engaged when he gets back."

"What did you tell him?"

"I said I would."

"Do you love him?"

She gave me a sharp look. "Yes," she said. I was horrified to hear a new quality of obedience in Helen's confession. "He says he'll make me happy."

"You young people talk funny."

She lifted her right arm. "He gave me this."

She wore a delicate watch, a feminine timepiece with a tiny face. I squinted at it. "Hard to read, isn't it? Or is it just for show?"

"He says I'm supposed to—" Helen began to laugh.

"No!" I said. "*Watch* for him?"

"A little bit sickening."

"Well, he hasn't much education. We mustn't be snobs."

"He looks nice in his uniform," she said, and she put her head on my shoulder. I felt like somebody was filling my mouth with pretty buttons. My head hurt. I was trying to look out on acres of land, across an ocean, and somebody was putting a miniature cameo close before my eyes, so they ached. We had no name for brainwashing in those days. I looked into my daughter's eyes. She was almost engaged in this role. But somewhere behind the sentimental misery, I thought I could detect a latent restlessness.

"What made him go so late to war?" I asked lightly.

"He wanted the navy. Only there were hardly any boats before."

"His father wanted him in the navy," I said. I'd only then remembered.

"Richard wants to go back." Helen stood upright. The strings and harps faded away.

"Go back where?"

"Where it happened." She loosened the belt of her dress, an actress backstage. "Near where the boat sank."

"The boat. Oh."

"He has to go back there, he says."

To the scene of his loss, to the site, which itself was lost, which continues to shift. To drag the sea with his strange plough. Bring the bombs up to the surface.

<hr />

RICHARD CRUISED THE COAST of Newfoundland in a minesweeper, sailed a loop two hundred miles offshore, thrown to sea like a stone on a lariat. Traces of his father in the fight between salt and ice, in bodies they lifted from the sea. He furthered his studies in navigation and learned the ocean through its correspondence with the sky, the true fiction of celestial bearings.

For three years, he wrote Helen letters free of the effacement of the censors because he'd done that for himself. He never told her about the claustrophobia, the flaccid boredom spiked with fear, the maggoty food; he never mentioned the sleepless mines, how they float up like eyeballs. He never mentioned fire or explosions, or the German sailor they found floating without arms or legs and how they stuffed the torso into a bottle of vinegar and put him up with the pickled eggs behind the seaman's bar at the harbour at St. John's. He never told her about the man who burst into flames when a torpedo struck his ship; how the oil on deck rose up to clothe the man in flames as he ran, even as he leapt into the ocean; how he burned in the water, high yellow flames on the surface of the sea.

He never wrote about these things. His experiences went into his private vault, where they failed to pay him compound interest. He behaved bravely. He did. Yet nothing he did would ever recover the moment when he left his father on that ship and escaped with the women. With the women.

With an elegant hand, he wrote pleasantly brave missives, euphemistic, as if protective, always stylish. We read his letters for the metallic taste they gave us. But Helen was fixated. She hung heavily about the house, in her hand his most recent letter, compelled by his manly absence, his seeming austerity. She sat in a garden chair watching a shadow of a leafless tree on the wall as it eventually brought about the motion of blossoms and bees.

CHAPTER FOURTEEN

THE GOLDEN FIELDS WAVED at us from the farthest edges of land. Sepia sky from the bleeding of yellow light. Seeds hidden within the whiskers of barley. A border of sunflowers with heavy heads and strange pitted faces turned to the east, away from us, so we had to walk up from behind, tap them shyly on the shoulder and take a knife to their thick stalks, carrying back home the thick brown plates of seed. The sunflowers framed a field of rape. Birds jumped through the air when we walked among the yellow flowers, and on every petal was a spider, a wasp, a black-and-yellow beetle, a fly, a honeybee on every ripe spike and bloom.

I walked down Lord Selkirk Road to bring Eli some water. Beside me many white butterflies flew inches above the road. The crop kept Eli at home. Most young men in the vicinity had signed up all in a rush to escape the farm, so we were short-handed. We heard a rumour of some workers coming from Quebec, where the wages were lower and the young men didn't know the words to "Rule Britannia."

That fall, Prime Minister Borden sent 250,000 Canadian bipeds overseas. He'd gone to England and sat right beside Prime Minister Asquith at a meeting of the British Cabinet while they talked about whether cotton should be contraband—very alarming stuff—and Asquith told our leader that the tradition forbade the taking of notes in Cabinet, so this was never even supposed to be history, very hush-hush, very big stuff for Canada. Send men, you dreary colonial upstarts, not presumptuous small-time politicians. It was all going straight to Dada. Overseas, they got Dada. In St. Norbert, we got gas-burning tractors pulling three-bottom ploughs.

The tractor was terrific, vibrating under my bum, unhousing my kidneys. Goodbye horses. I thought it would grieve Eli, moving farther away from his boyhood, but he just said I was sentimental, which was a lot of dung. Eli could never keep up with Peter's philosophy, the built-in shiftiness of Impossibilism. Rebellious, yes, but I think he obeyed some innate discipline in change, in all the inherent loss. Eli, poor man, believed in progress at the time.

When the machine broke down, Peter would hobble out (my father had become as transparent and beautiful as a water spider in his ancient, agile motion, with the white butterflies fluttering beside him at shin-level, my impossible dad). Peter could fix anything. He'd been made famous for the deep-tilling McCormack blade, an improvement on old MacDonald's blade, or so we thought. The logic of the machine was the logic of speed which was the logic of the future which led Peter to the source of the problem every time.

Eli was on the tractor. I walked over the swaths and waved my arms above the din of the machine. He stopped and cut the engine, and I sailed over the mud waves and bit his dusty pant leg at the wrinkled groin, where it was sunwarm and smelled of geraniums, while the engine hiccuped a few times as it submerged beneath the hot sun. Perfect weather, air cool as a lake, geese yelling.

Onion sandwiches—Eli's favourite and something I'd grown to count on over the years. When Eli eats an onion sandwich, I know where he is. He once ate one out on the rodeo road, mid-summer, somewhere near Tyndal, where the bitter soil yields the hottest, juiciest onions, after he'd been away for seven weeks—and seven celibate weeks of warm weather is not the same as seven celibate weeks of cold weather—and that onion's juices aroused me all the way to St. Norbert while I was weeding the garden wearing nothing but a strategic kerchief, hoeing the radishes, and this set off a triadic sympathy, onion to radish to my optimistic glands, and it would have taken all my strength to keep my hands off myself. Women did that sort of thing back then too, you know. Not all our labour went to the making of post-war babies. Eggs slipped out of the basket, soup slipped off the spoon, and sometimes, when the garden was as warmly scented as the inside of a wicker basket and crickets zigzagged on freshly hoed soil and monarchs hovered over milkweed and the ash trees rustled like bedsheets and the heat made a bell jar, we might kneel a moment, overcome beside the sugar-peas, some white-blossomed, some fruiting, some emptied of fruit by birds or raccoons, and there in the privacy of our own field spill a little juice, just so the cup isn't overflowing while we wait for our Elis to come home.

But this day of autumnal plenitude, of booming wheat prices, of Eli's actual ripe-onion material presence, with the muddy flavour of Eli's pants in my mouth and him climbing down and all he had to do was loosen his belt and the wide waist of his trousers freed his warm, sweet . . . let me say his warm, sweet hard-is-welcome, so we buckled gracefully down upon a bed of shining wheat straw and then we heard, far from the quarter section at the railway tracks, the excursion train loaded with harvest workers hooting at us like a bunch of French grackles flocking in to stand the sheaves up in stooks for the final ripening.

CHAPTER FIFTEEN
THE MAGNA CARTA!

"SO WHAT! SO BLESSED DAMN WHAT!" But nobody heard the eti-
olated protests of a fallen Methodist beneath the desk-thumping
and the cheers and the applause of gloved hands in the gallery.
My mother alone, a scarecrow in her black cape and red tam,
surrounded by glowing women who had just that moment heard
the passing of the Bill for the Enfranchisement of Women.

God save the king. All the women stood and sang "For
They Are Jolly Good Fellows," and all the good fellows stood
and sang it right back. Alice rolled her eyes and sighed to the
vaulted ceiling of the chamber. "God blessed so what? So
blessed damn!" She was a dyslexic blasphemer. And then, when
the cheering reached its sober, self-congratulatory, gee-it's-a-
relief-to-get-that-off-my-chest bonhomie, and bonnefemme
too—of course they can vote; they have soldier-babies, they can
vote; they make munitions, they can vote; they vote Liberal, they
can vote!—bundled-up-in-good-wool-and-furs climax, Alice
said, "Hell it all to damn!"

But she was excited. She was, after all, a founding member of the Political Equality League, and had attended meetings
faithfully, especially after she'd quit and erased her name from
their records. But ever since the "enemy alien" midwife had
been run out of St. Norbert by the mothers of soldiers in

France, Alice had an inkling, like pepper in the salt, that women could be just as mean-spirited as men. But hush, it was time for the ladies to sit, nestling their velvet bums into comfy chairs, to listen with wifely charity to the men speak from the chamber below.

It was a love-in. Women who vote, it was testified, make good life partners. Why, we can all vote together! Ha ha ha! Only a coward would argue that the women's vote will threaten the family! Foolish bigots! Women's vote the cause of divorce? Ha ha ha ha ha ha. Give 'em their rein, I say. Eve might have caused a whole lot of trouble, but (with a gallant nod to the gallery) I'll bet Adam preferred a helpmate to a doormat. But seriously, if a mother will send her son to fight Kaiserism, she deserves the vote. And if that mother loses her son in the bloody fields of France, she deserves our protection and our undying gratitude. A-men!

And then the new premier rose; he rose and rose with his powder white skin and his way of inhaling all the time so his head seemed suspended by his nose, and his chest and neck remained full of air which he spent through a reedy, well-bred voice, a chivalrous milking of every milky election issue, and he said exactly this:

"If the women of the civilized countries had enjoyed the franchise ten years ago, then Mr. Kaiser Bill of Germany would not be doing what he is today, for he would have the privilege of being counselled and influenced by women as well as men. We hope the war will come soon to an end, but we must express our admiration of what the ladies of the Dominion are doing in this great crisis."

Prophecy? A Cassandra in a suit? How obvious it is to us today, with countless millions dead, when we may refer to Mrs. Einstein, Mrs. Bohr, Mrs. Goebbels, Mrs. Truman, Mrs. Eisenhower, to the silky legs and comely lisp of Mrs. Kennedy, in whose immortal words we find the sentiment that won the women of the twentieth century a frost-free fridge and a second car: "I go where Jack needs me and I try to stay out of the way." How stunningly obvious it is if we rerun the entire history of the human race, ride that movie backwards past January 28, 1916, past August 1914, back through Victoria's widowing war against the Boers, backwards down time's road to the hanging court sentencing Riel, to the moment in the courtyard when a blood-thirsty and pregnant woman dressed in a buffalo robe aimed her rifle at the chest of a blindfolded man; how blatantly obvious it is that if women were in the driver's seat, there'd be no war, there'd be no poverty, there'd be no injustice.

It was obvious to Alice, anyway, in the chambers of the Manitoba Legislative Building in the winter of 1916, and she turned to the healthy apple face of the matron beside her, who smiled kindly, excited, and pinched my mother's arm and said, "It's the beginning of a brave new future full of peace!" And Alice uttered the only articulate curse of her lifetime: "Bullshit!" And looking past the crestfallen matron, Alice saw the barely discernible trace of a skinny rounder with wet shoes and before she fainted she saw that the sky had opened and through the gaping hole in the ceiling there descended a cloud of white feathers, falling falling falling falling.

CHAPTER SIXTEEN

OUR SUMMERS OF WAR SEEMED to occur in every shade of brown. Green ferns, you see, or geraniums, succumbed. All, all was the colour of war.

It was as Alice had predicted. We got really good at killing on a large scale. The musket that Alice had so proudly pointed at Thomas Scott could fire maybe three times in a minute. Now, a machine gun could fire six hundred rounds in sixty seconds, or ten shots a second.

We get dressed up for efficient killing. The most stylish thing about the twentieth century is the uniform. The next most stylish thing is Helen in a three-quarter length wraparound with a mink collar and a greyhound on a leash. But that would come later; it was as yet a gleam in Richard's eye.

※

PETER AND ALICE intensified the last years of their long marriage with a torrid love affair with one another. Their passion was perhaps not fully apparent to the naked eye. Both my parents had become the colour and texture of fine sand, their eyes bleached by long looking and their bones so luminous you could see them at night. Walking by the woods in the dark, they glowed like a pair of old and skinny arctic wolves.

During the war years, my mother began regularly to faint. There are goats that suffer from similar symptoms, in Australia, I think, a kind of sensitive goat that will fall down in a dead faint if you talk too loud. They don't die, though; they just pass out. Alice would live many years like that. With a dry clicking sound she was always falling down, her sandstone bones as light as kindling. Once or twice, Peter would pass out too. But they didn't die. That's the good part.

After the vote at the Legislative Building, Alice kept her eye out for Thomas Scott, but he hadn't reappeared. She told us this during one of our nocturnal jaunts, Alice and Peter, Eli and Helen and me. On this occasion, it so happened that Mum fainted. We were accustomed to it by then, and we simply talked quietly in the night, waiting for her to wake up and continue our journey. I did, however, contribute a small shock to perk her. Mum, on waking, pushed away my hands and stood peevishly and said, "He's deader than a doornail."

My dad pressed a lingering kiss to the bare white shell of her temple and said, "He croaked long ago, my loved one." And then he let out a horse laugh. "Didn't stop him, did it! He's still croaking."

Mum was serious. "No, no, he'll croak no more." The tears in her eyes shone with phosphorous. "I think he might truly be gone."

We all sobered, stood silently, taking this in. The trees squealed, a crooked sound. We stood rigid, fearing the final absence of Thomas Scott. It takes more than mortality to make somebody dead. Since Scott's brief appearance at the legislature, the rest of us hadn't even given him a thought. We were becoming positive and absolute in our ways at home, and no one had considered our martyr of bigotry, our patron saint of Error. His final departure was a double strike against us, a second and perhaps more terrible murder. It could mean an end of a world.

Helen laid her cheek against her grandmother's hand. In the dark wooded night, the glow from Alice's hand cast Helen's beauty in silver.

"Grandma?" asked Helen. "Why did he not kiss me? When I was a baby. Why didn't I get the mark?"

"Oh, you don't want that devil's kiss on you," I said. Eli touched my shoulder, *Shhhhhhh, Blondie.*

"It's a defect you'll just have to live with," said her grandmother Alice, somewhat impatiently. Then, softening, she studied Helen's glaucous features. "Never forget, darling, what's right is also wrong. Don't let that scoundrel's death be in vain."

"I think we should go home," I said. It was exceedingly creepy out there if we were no longer haunted. The woods were stark and vivid.

Chastened, we began once more to walk. "Maybe we can get new ghosts," Helen said.

"Ghosts are not shoes," said I, the unnecessary mother.

Just then, we heard a cry. With what hope we turned back towards the forest. And listened. Then the owl's hoot. The night, stiff and real.

<hr>

ALICE THREW HERSELF into materialism. By 1918, her School for Histrionics had gained such momentum that she had to develop a semi-professional arm, which she called the Histrionic Theatre Company. The company thrived. She was so busy that she was forced to move a cot into the green room, and there she stayed for the duration of the war and the duration of her life. Her lover, otherwise known as Peter, visited her every day, bringing breads and dainties from various delicatessens and bakeries around town.

Every day a different dainty from a different country. When he ran out of countries, he began to research the tribal origins of dainties at the library on William Street, arriving daily in a brand new Model T and wearing a beautiful hat, which he removed at the door as he entered the tortoiseshell shadows. This coda in his relationship with Alice was a formal affair, and he began to dress in modest but handsome brown suits, set off by his luminous white hair.

The Model T was mine. It cost me $725. I'd earned every second cent of it. John Anderson (bless him) had taught me to invest in the stock market, and I was without a doubt the most skilled investor in town, though I declined to flaunt it. I went by the name of B. McCormack and it was assumed that the B. stood for William, and so somebody in a big law firm sent me a letter inviting me to join the eminent Manitoba Club and the eminent St. Charles Country Club, but I just wrote them right back saying, "Shalom! Love to!" I never heard from them again.

Peter was researching food, a fitting subject during the war. His specialty was grains, of course, with subsidiary interests in breads and pastries. He wasn't a cook, or much of an eater, but

he did adore recipes, and he tunnelled through the bulgur con-
nections between pilafs and tabbouleh like a diviner seeking
Mesopotamian streams beneath the Canadian Shield. It was perhaps one of his greatest thrills when he traced an unleavened kin-
ship between bannock and pita. In his eighties, he developed a
subtle sensitivity. The young librarians were all in love with him,
leaning close to whisper their perceptive questions, showing him
their pure complexions, their shining hair, all to no avail.

It might seem as if the Impossibilist had opted out. A war
on, and here he was chasing Chinese dumplings, honeyed
baklava, courting Alice with small boxes of cake. But it was more
than an old man's distraction, much more than a doddering
hobby. He sat very straight at a wooden reading table at the
William Street library, with a book set on its spine and the laugh
lines like sun dogs around his radiant eyes. He was reading
about cooking practices in Palestine, but he was thinking about
Marquis wheat, about No. I Northern. As he read of stone pestles,
cornmeal, rice flour (occasionally speaking aloud in his old
man's tenor; "barley," he would say, or "legumes"), as he read
about the ancient hands of women pounding grains and knead-
ing dough, there dawned in another part of his soul a terrible
regret, a chilling guilt. "Wheat," said Peter. "We planted wheat
and only wheat. My God. And the deep-tilling McCormack
blade. What have I done?" The wind answered with a handful of
overworked topsoil thrown against the tall windows of the
library. One of the pretty librarians looked up and smiled
hopefully at him.

Alice was his taste tester. He arrived at her office-boudoir,
where she was schooling her company of performers. She

shooed them away. He sat upon a plain oak chair and offered her a bit of seed cake. Alice nibbled, then nodded and said, "Yes. I see exactly what you mean."

She responded by developing a type of theatre theretofore, and pretty well thereafter, unknown to Winnipeg audiences.

Her friend Mr. Kolchella had resurfaced from the internment camp at Portage la Prairie. His wife had died of heart failure soon after they'd been imprisoned. The authorities had then let him go *on compassionate grounds.* I was saddened to see the hopeful part of him gone. I think he'd lost much of his love for the world. Still, he joined us, with a sharper, mordant wit, and with a certain disobedience that seemed somewhat dangerous despite his dancer's stature.

He brought with him several athletic German friends who went by the name of Smith, their European sensibilities rejuvenated by the yeasty nutrition of avant-garde prison aesthetics. The Ukrainian midwife found her way back to Alice too. She had lost a lot of weight in the camps, and her experiences had altered her from a good-natured chubby woman to a gristly skinny woman, not the same thing at all. Along with her body fat, she'd lost her songful speech; she became nasal and intellectual, and she began to talk about the future and the past in the same breathless gesture, an evacuation, a horrified refusal. The Histrionic Theatre Company made use of her revised physiognomy by writing new peasant roles for her—the kerchief, the apron, the fist.

And Helen. Helen played the Beauty in such a way as almost to save her own life. It would be her last parodic moment for many years to come.

After they got the vote, the ladies' clubs went crazy for Greek drama, so Alice knew she could fill the house if she put Helen into a cream chiffon dress with a loose gold belt and loosened her black hair and set her upon a wine red chaise. One of the Smiths painted Helen's portrait in this pose, and the company made up posters vaguely in the style of Toulouse-Lautrec. Gashes of red paint, Helen's raven hair and "*Helen of Troy* by Euripides" scrawled thickly, freehand, in white. Helen sat dutifully for the portrait, and when it was done, she stood up and laughed, a horse laugh.

Helen played Helen with the fierce intuition only a very young actress can achieve. Helen's (that is, the other Helen's) infidelity, the treacherous selfishness of her desire for Paris (or was it simply the necessity of freedom?) and the inexplicable justice of scandal, all of this came naturally to our Helen. She was a choreographic actress and worked very well with the freshly impassioned Mr. Kolchella. Generally, our theatre troupe worked with humorous sorrow; under our camaraderie ran the information, unbidden, ineluctable, that among men, war truly *is* an expression of beauty. My daughter *played* this, and I think she was so successful in her role because she didn't let this insane fact grab her ankles and drown her.

The stage was lit by floodlights, the sets exposed, the flooring harsh and loud, and the scenes were announced in big printed placards. Despite my mother's extraordinary direction, nothing could deter the audience from coming again and again.

The Greeks were the company's bread and butter, the commercial side of things. But Mum hadn't forgotten her original mandate: to produce histrionic history. She felt bad about taking all that money from war widows. She had to give something back. On waking up from one of her fainting fits, she walked dizzily to her desk and composed the following:

"The first battle of Ypres. 36,000 dead Germans. Get kids; they'll like the uniforms. Smoke, agony, blood. Everybody dies. Except one. An Austrian. No, he's German. Need A LOT OF SMOKE.

"One weird German, falls, gets up, walks away."

Alice stopped. One German. One weird German walking away. She stood. She went to Peter. He was seated in the oak chair. Alice held her scene out to him and he read it. "What's this character's name?" he asked.

Alice listened to the muses a moment and then she said, "Hitler."

"That's good." Peter handed the scene back to Alice. "Good name. I like the 'hit' part. It's going to be huge success. How are you going to do the thirty-six thousand dead Germans?"

"Oh," said Alice. "The usual. Placards and circus music. We'll improvise."

CHAPTER SEVENTEEN

IT WOULD BE MY MOTHER'S LAST and greatest and least popular production.

Everybody got involved, including the police magistrate, who would arrive to shut the place down. We worked at it for six weeks. We all took turns playing Prime Minister Borden. We made big puppets on sticks. It was messy and the midwife played the accordion and my dad, Peter, once again took up the fiddle. We called it *Massacre of the Innocents.* There was a lot of singing and fighting. Something for everyone. The audience might have liked it, but the timing was all wrong.

The world premiere was November 10. A Sunday. Maybe we went too far, opening on a Sunday. It was an innocent mistake that we made on purpose, because that was our theme. We were my mother's disciples. "Histrionics, Hyperbole, and How!" was our motto. "Push!" yelled Alice. "Push it till it falls over!" Each gesture and idea, pushed so hard, to such a crazy extreme, it became—if we were successful—its opposite.

The press gave us a glowing preview and a nice photograph of the entire cast in costume. Alice kept telling the reporters we were putting on a play of social realism. They smiled and nodded and pretended they knew what she was talking about. It was true, though—social realism through a meat grinder, just like real life in 1918.

We rented the Walker Theatre because it could accommodate the animals. We had a cast of two hundred people, one
white horse and a dog of little consequence, a bald thing from
Egypt. When the rioting began, somebody stepped on the dog
and killed it. Alice wept openly. "Another dog! Why me and
dogs?" One of the cast members, a wonderful little girl of
eleven who understood everything, said, "It's how it goes, Mrs.
McCormack. You have to go the mile to win the inch."

November 10 came all too soon. The place was packed.
The first act went okay because everybody thought we'd settle
down and give them some nice *Ben Hur.* Another innocent
mistake: the tickets said *Ben Hur.* The stage manager saw the
white horse and thought that's what we were putting on, so he
printed tickets saying *Ben Hur,* and that's what everybody
thought they were seeing, so they enjoyed the first act, I think
they did, I think we had them in our pocket. The chariot race
came as a complete surprise to everyone. The stage manager
took it on himself to hitch the horse to the chariot, and he took
off his overalls and rode on stage in his undershirt.

Dad knocked together a kind of tank out of an old boiler.
A Smith played this fellow Hitler, but he was afraid to say anything with his strong German accent. I was Woodrow Wilson,
and Eli was a German general, which was upsetting because we
were acting with an obsessive energy that transformed the world
into a battlefield, which in some ways wasn't at all what Alice
wanted from us, but we just got lost inside that play.

Woodrow Wilson was a nice enough character, saying things
like "We will fashion world order based on self-determination
without force or aggression!" Pleasant concepts, lousy theatre,

and it took a lot of courage to get up and declaim them, like shouting Newtonian formulas, so I played him with a strong subtext that I discovered in an ambivalent relationship with his mother, though God knows I wouldn't say this if Alice were still alive. She'd kill me.

Eli was stunning, distressing, a tragic ironic character, and even now, when I think back on his terrible moment at the end of Act IV when he stood, ghastly in a German helmet, and removed his red mask and revealed his white painted face and struck his head and said, "They fought for ideas! I didn't know! God help me! I didn't know there were ideas in this war! I thought we were fighting for land!" Well, it still stops my heart and my hands grow numb. Eli. How much of the world lives in the soul of one man.

Our audience was not possessed of a well-developed sense of irony. The German helmets upset them. The horse stepped on a Smith's foot, and in pain he shouted, "*Tante Gretchen, meine Knie!*" It was part of Alice's Freedom through Contradiction to have Helen dressed in sackcloth carrying the placards late in Act V, by which time people were throwing things on stage, their Histrionic program notes obviously unread, and later their own shoes. Backstage, the stage manager grabbed my arm and said, "They want Helen! Everybody's dressed ugly! Please, can't you give them something beautiful!" I was sorry for him, but this was my mother's most important production ever and I would not interfere.

Helen walked on stage into chaos. All two hundred cast members were ready for the final number. The horse was loose and the dog was dead. Helen's job was to parade four placards

downstage before the footlights, left to right, right to left.
"600,000 YOUNG MEN!" "CANADA SACRIFICED HER
YOUTH FOR NATIONHOOD!" "THE BRITS THINK
WE'RE SERVANTS!" And the last one: "PEACE THROUGH
FEAR!"

A groan went through the audience, half because of the
placards and half because Helen was wearing the hooded sackcloth instead of the chiffon gown. The police arrived just as
Helen entered with "PEACE THROUGH FEAR!" and they
rushed the stage and the audience ran after them and general
mayhem is what followed. Strangely, Alice did not faint. Peter
retired to the stage manager's office during the riot, then joined
us all for the ride in the paddy wagon.

By the time they got us to Stony Mountain, a good two
hours later, the Armistice had been proclaimed. Bells were
ringing everywhere, and lights from the city thrown to the
clouds brightened our way to the penitentiary. I was happy. I
imagined that I was following the footsteps of Big Bear, waiting
in *his* cell, sitting on *his* toilet, looking through the same bars
through which he had looked. All around us across the countryside, people were rising from their beds to celebrate peace. One
of the Smiths was locked up with us. We whispered to him not to
speak. We hugged each other and wept for joy.

The guards looked tired and relieved. No charges had been
laid, so they treated us gently, and one of them said, "Funny
kind of justice, putting you in here without charge." And Alice
said, "It's imaginary justice. Because we are imaginary." The
guard looked at my mother closely, with one of those sudden
penetrating stares. She was seated in a dark corner of the cell,

and my dad sat beside her. They were holding hands. The cell glowed, chiaroscuro.

At breakfast, the formal charges still had not arrived from Winnipeg. The day broached and boiled and dried up and failed to a snowless dusk. Still we remained in prison without charge. I was bored. I tried to imagine Big Bear's boredom, but stale waiting is simply not romantic. We did get let out for a short walk in the late afternoon, but I was somewhat taken aback to see that the place was mostly inhabited by Indians. In some ways, Big Bear never did get out of jail. It was actually very depressing.

I sat with my daughter. Helen looked flushed, excited. "What's got you stirred up?" I asked her.

Just then, she stiffened like a greyhound, listening to a dull vibration through the stone floor. The sound of marching grew louder. In our corridor, an overhead bulb went on and swung a little, and everything quivered to the rhythm of boots.

Eight pairs of boots in sync and the jingle of keys. The first to appear was the magistrate who had stormed Alice's Histrionic production, a mild man with amber eyes and a reluctant ruddy face, carrying a sheathed sword before him, blinking at us like a kindly beagle. His police officers arranged themselves around him.

One more set of footsteps, clipped, brisk, eloquent. Richard walked down the grey stone hallway into the light. He was in his naval uniform. He weighed about ninety pounds. "Well, damned I'll be," said Alice. Richard smiled slightly. He bore the air of a man who did not believe in the power of confession. "We've come to let you out," he said.

"Yes," said the magistrate. "No harm done." He motioned to his man to unlock the door. We stood on the threshold of the open cell, hesitant as budgies.

"It's all right," Richard said. "Come." He took Helen's arm and led us all away, folk following the golden egg. "There was a mistake. Quite an innocent mistake." He glanced at the magistrate. "Sir John did not know that you are my friends."

We were bundled into several waiting cars. Richard and Helen went alone in Richard's fancy Packard. I liked this much less than illegal imprisonment. Half an hour earlier, I had lived in a world of small-town bigotry and small-scale corruption. The police were driving fast. Everybody seemed to be under secret orders.

I realized it was dark in the silent car. I looked at my mother and father. They were sitting with their eyes closed. I leaned towards them, put my hands on them, emitting a mild jolt. No effect. "Are you all right?" I asked, the way a child asks her mother if she is sleeping.

"Take us to the Histrionic Theatre," said Alice. That was all she could say.

❦

WE ENTERED THE SILENT THEATRE. Alice fainted twice walking from the police car to the green room, which is where she asked us to take her. Peter was calmly attentive. When we reached our destination and laid Alice upon the horsehair couch, he sat and put her feet on his lap and closed his eyes.

"Is it all right if I stay?" I asked.

My parents nodded. I sat on the floor before them. Then my mother looked down and smiled at me. She patted my head and said, "Go get the moon, Blondie." I stupidly told her I would, thinking she was speaking metaphorically, forgetting that she'd given up metaphor at least a year earlier. She smiled again, forgiving me, and said, "The electric moon, dear. It's backstage."

I rushed out and couldn't find any lights and crashed about till I found it: the electric moon we'd used in *Antigone*. I could barely lift it. I stumbled back to the green room and tried to lay it gently on the floor. "Plug it in," said Alice. I leaned the moon against one wall and plugged it in. It was a full moon. The glass was ribbed in the art deco style, kind of jagged. It looked like an electric moon. "Hold it up," said my mother. I was about to protest. But I looked at her. Peter seemed to be sleeping, his head resting on the back of the couch. Alice was lying on her side now. She pulled her knees up and lay curled like that, and I saw how small she'd become, small as a thimble. I lifted the electric moon high over my head. It cast a warm urban glow over us, unnatural and strangely humane. Alice murmured something. She stretched one hand down to Peter, but she couldn't reach him. My father was still, his lovely white hair in the light, his face bone china. They were not touching when they died. Their bodies lay abandoned. I held up the moon as long as I could, until my arms went numb and my back burned and the edge of glass had cut my hands.

CHAPTER EIGHTEEN

Dear Lord, may my joy not leave me. —J. S. Bach, in his diary

NEWS OF THE RUSSIAN REVOLUTION reached "our property" like the first smoke of a prairie fire. Eli was inhaling Russia. When I woke him, he'd turn on his side and try to comfort me with stories of a Bolshevik revolution. Everyone will have enough to eat, he told me, and no one will be a slave to the factory or the machine. Men and women will be equal, Blondie, and children will be raised into freedom. People can become whatever they want: a fisherman, a farmer, a poet. I could hunt buffalo and write songs. And you could be a . . . be a . . . what would you want to be, Blondie? Eli whispered to me, lying on his side with our heads on the pillow, looking at each other. You could be what you like, he whispered. And that made it worse, because I was all willpower with no idea how to use it, other than for destruction.

Winter, blue as an egg, brought duty and exhaustion. Out of bed in the dark to prepare food, my skeleton was scrap metal, hunger and work clicking metal on metal. In sorrow I became a worm wintering in the red bark of the spruce. Click of beak in the bark of a tree; time a flicker's beak digging me out, an insect meal. Grief is dry. Thirst in every pore; even the molecules that make me, dry as pellets. My brain was crushed glass. My rash returned and my skin peeled off in painful scabs under the awful beak of daily duty.

I was untouchable, given my rash and the dry electrical field around me. Eli housed his grief for Peter and Alice as his adoptive mother had taught him. He didn't really believe in death. He lost a bit of weight, and gave up butter and coffee. His eyes were less green, more like ripe grain, but otherwise he looked purified and grateful for his life. He pulled back the curtains to let the white winter sun show a bit of coloured glass on the sill. Part of Eli always lived outside, the part of him that would almost outlive him. Calm, breathing deeply while his lungs got used to a world without the breath of Peter and Alice in it.

Sometimes in bed at night, when the air became too dry to breathe, I touched Eli and sparks lit the room with fast white light. Eli made a sound like a crow, or if my voltage was low, a cat.

Eli buried Alice and Peter beneath the strange black spruce trees, near the spot where we'd buried the crane long ago. The marshy profile of the trees, their despondent branches. The earth was frozen, but he said the frost wasn't deep; he said it got soft just a foot under. It was too cold. Their bodies rattled in their icy graves like dried beans in a bone whistle.

I outlived my parents after all. And when the grass began to grow on their graves, I hobbled down to plant lily of the valley where their bodies lay. It was too dark in the woods for many flowers. But when other things won't grow, lilies will.

CHAPTER NINETEEN

It was our avowed purpose to have the working class intelligent,
so that when the natural or revolutionary change came in society
they could intelligently take control.

—Robert Russell, at his trial for seditious conspiracy,

in Winnipeg, 1919

RETURNED SOLDIERS ROAMED the streets of Winnipeg like
injured birds dragging a wing, permanently dislocated. There
wasn't any work. Much of the North End of Winnipeg was a
slum. It made them mad. And very patriotic.

A great time for rhetoric. Robert, or Bobby, Russell and
his friend Dick Johns had gone off to Calgary in the late winter
of 1919 to the Western Labour Conference, where they
endorsed "the principle of Proletarian Dictatorship," which
would lead to "the transformation of capitalist private property
to communal wealth." My dad must have shuddered in his grave
at the word "dictatorship."

The rich were scared in the spring of 1919. The revolution
in Russia made it seem that the future was up for grabs.
Winnipeg's local elite ignored the fact that the labour leaders
were British-born, and they fostered the loving concept of the
"enemy alien"—presumably anyone fewer than two generations
removed from Europe. The federal government, as in 1870 and

1885, moved in with the army to extinguish the "revolt." And the lumbago-stricken prime minister, Robert Borden, banned publication in eighteen languages. No more Russian, no Ukrainian, no Yiddish, just English, English, English, only one kind of English bird to sing at the grave of Peter and Alice. Thereafter, our citizens would be saved from differing opinions. Borden had no lines on his face. He would preserve us from the wrinkles of dissent.

Winnipeg moved towards a general strike. The construction trades and the metal workers had been on strike for nearly two weeks when Helen got invited to a luncheon at the home of Mr. Richard Anderson. Another thing the war did: it gave Richard his last name. Mr. Anderson it was, no more Richard. When Helen said it now, *Richard,* I turned away, so intimate was the sound of his Christian name on her lips. I refused to call him Richard. I called him Dick.

"Say hi to Dick," I told Helen as she climbed out of the back seat of my Ford. She wore blue flimsy stuff that fell around her hips, and she smelled, flagrantly, of lilac. Hot day in May. "Hey!" I called out to her as she veered past Dick's baby blue Packard and up his stone stairway, swanky, on her slender leather shoes. "You match his car!" She daggered me, high upon her mountain of beauty.

It was my birthday. If I'd felt any older, I'd have been immortal. My daughter and I were electric eels. We did not speak, we zapped. I left the speaking up to Eli. She blew him a kiss. The flapper had not yet been invented. Helen was inventing her. "Bye, Daddy!" she called. Breathy voice. Eli was driving. He looked at her sadly. Shook his head and said goodbye. Helen, with that slight hesitation, taking on the limestone steps. Eli listened for the sound of the outer door being opened before driving away, not too fast. I turned in my seat and watched Richard answer the door. He reached out his hand and pulled our daughter into his house.

We went downtown. Eli and I had a cup of tea with Bobby Russell, at his office in the Labor Temple. I love the name Bobby. I love being In, especially with the Out crowd. And I'll always be soft for a Scot. Bobby Russell was the most decent man, moderate in his appetites (no sugar) and self-disciplined. But Eli was so distracted by his unease over leaving Helen at Richard Anderson's lair that Bobby finally put his hands together over his cup, stuck out his chubby lower lip, blinked curiously and with such shy sympathy that Eli finally smiled, shook his head and said, "It's a friend of our daughter Helen's got me in a knot. I guess I'm just an old-fashioned dad."

Bobby Russell clicked his tongue. "The lass has a beau?"

"Richard?" Eli sat back. "Good Lord, I guess that's what he is. What's to become of her? Richard Anderson, her beau."

Bobby's jaw dropped. "Richard Anderson?"

"You know him?"

Bobby forgot his own interdiction, added sugar, busily stirring. I poked his arm. "You'd better tell us what you know, Bobby. We won't shoot the messenger."

He glanced up sheepishly. "Well, I'll not be interfering with a family's business. And I don't imply any judgment upon your young girl."

Eli moaned.

Bobby hurried, "Nothing so much illegal, not at all. The rules of capitalism put him square with the law. He's a determined young fellow. An aggressive pup. We've been in negotiations since the construction trades went out, beginning of the month. That's his territory. He's put off. Seems he's been buying a lot of land for development and finds himself out of pocket and unable to get on with putting up houses." And here, Bobby's political blood pressure rose, and he smiled. "Square with the law, he is. And all that about to change. He'll be out. His kind. It's just a matter of time. And a revolution."

We three laughed, Bobby in earnest.

A few days later, the whole city was shut down by the general strike. About thirty thousand people (nearly the same number as the Allied soldiers killed at Ypres) refused to work. Winnipeg was always split in two. North End meant poor; South End meant rich. Poor often meant European immigrants, those scary "Huns" and "Bolsheviks." And rich meant Anglo-Saxon Protestant. At about that time, the birthmark beneath my left breast, the blister kiss of Thomas Scott, began to burn and itch and keep me awake at night. Richard Anderson, who was now openly courting our daughter, was working with his business associates to create a citizen's committee—funny who becomes a "citizen" when the underpinnings of power are under attack. So the general strike, which might have provoked a celebration in our home, spawned strife instead, and so much tension between us that I saw in Eli's soul, in that private space that belonged only to him, a vehemence too powerful to fit inside a cowboy ballad.

The Citizen's Committee was a crew of grain men, hardware merchants, real-estate brokers scared by the Russian

Revolution. They saw Bolsheviks in the foreign shadows of the North End. Despite their paranoia, or because of it, they considered themselves inviolably reasonable. They wanted the strike leaders deported; simple solutions carry the most weight, a signal of good management. They met at the Manitoba Club (Richard, at last, had been accepted), where they reassured one another with the beauty of their dinner jackets. The white collars on men are political forces never to be underestimated. Richard was in his element. Everybody was his father, and if his rhetoric was at times somewhat inflated, damn it, somebody's got to say it loud and clear! No to the enemy alien! God save the king!

They said Richard was a bit of a war hero, and they put him in charge of a unit of Specials—a private police force, like the good old Montreal Cavalry in the 1837 Rebellion; young men whose hatred was masked by good clothes, who had learned how to ride on fox hunts at the club. The regular police officers had been fired because they were sympathetic to the strike. It was all left up to the Mounties and the Specials.

The federal government ordered the arrest of twelve men— eight British-born strike leaders (Bobby Russell among them) and (for a dash of that exotic flavour of "Hun") four European Canadians. Four days later, the strike sympathizers organized a peaceful protest against the arrests.

It was June 21, 1919. Richard was on somebody else's horse, a bitchy mare with a stiff-legged sideways gait. He lifted in his saddle and handled the mare with his left hand, neck-reined, raising himself with his knees and his strong thighs. He leaned forward and pointed his pistol at three men standing in the doorway of a hotel near city hall: a farmer from Boissevain visiting his sick sister, my mother's old friend Mr. Kolchella, and Eli. They'd retired to the stairwell to avoid the Specials and their wooden clubs. Mr. Kolchella's eloquent face showed the strain of the past six weeks, for he'd been working hard for the Strike Committee, having made a name for himself with his fearless oratory on the subject of the imminent demise of capitalism. Richard, riding, focused on the lapel of Mr. Kolchella's worn jacket, to which Mr. Kolchella had pinned a Russian flag. Richard's horse bobbed across the streams of military, its stiff prance perfectly controlled by Richard's knees. He took aim. And fired.

Eli happened to look up. He saw Richard's gun. He pushed both men down to the sidewalk, but Mr. Kolchella instinctively fought back; Eli lunged over him, all of this seeming to take many minutes, and the bullet travelled slowly through the air. It struck the wattle of Eli's earlobe, the left ear, the deaf ear, went right through it and ricocheted off the building and back out to the crowd without doing further damage.

Eli fell in a dead heap.

He woke up in a pool of his own blood. His earlobe lay beside him. The chewy cartilage looked like a finger.

A nerve in his left cheek was paralyzed, but it would only make him more handsome because that side of his face suffered a sort of amnesia, became young and smooth, and hair never grew there again, so he had, like a mountainous continent with a single cultivated province, a new republic on that portion of his bushy head.

"NOT MUCH OF ME LEFT." Eli stood in the kitchen by the sink while I changed the bandages. He held up his paw, and then examined himself in the mirror. His remaining ear had gained in stature, taking all responsibility for ear-ness, increased in magnitude.

"Nobody will notice," I told him.

"No, I know." He pulled his undershirt gingerly over the bandage. "When the hair grows back, I'll look roughed up like always."

"You're perfect. This"—I touched his wound—"just gets rid of anything that might've distracted us from your perfection."

That nod again. The more Eli disagreed, the more he nodded.

He was resting when Richard came to call. The glamorous car looked like government itself in our yard. I met him at the door. He'd put on weight, strong weight. I could barely remember the slender boy, and I'm sure that Richard, in his self-assured, wilful clarity, had forgotten the origins of his own brokenness. When he came into our house, Marie set up a woeful, clattering ululation, so loud that Richard paused and looked about, and I shrugged, saying, "Those blessed frogs are mating again. Listen to all that lust. But come in, Dick. I'm sure Eli would like to have a word with you."

And Richard said, "I'd like to have a word with him too." I followed him into our bedroom, where Eli lay. Helen was in her room; Marie's keening and the clatter of the loom had prevented her from hearing Richard's arrival.

Eli had heard him, though, and he watched Richard enter our bedroom through narrow lids. Richard stopped a few feet from the bed. "I've come to apologize," he said.

Eli gave a short grunt of laughter, wincing but truly amused.

Richard looked down at his hands, one hand holding its other, and smiled that particular smile, at the real joke beyond our understanding. "You should be more careful," he said. And when Eli rose to protest, he added, "I don't underestimate the necessity of my apology, nor do I wish to suggest less than my utmost sincerity in offering it to you."

"You've been reading, Dick!" I said.

I saw the change to one of his eyes, a single black crescent in the otherwise perfectly blue iris, a tiny scar on his vision. A black sickle, there for good; it would always distract me when I looked at him.

"I do apologize," he said. His voice was lighter, purified. "And I do wish for your health and safety."

"You fucking little hypocrite." Eli sat up in bed.

It stunned Richard. His body let go of its stiff propriety. He rallied. "I am the hypocrite? I took action against something I felt was wrong. We can either protect what's ours, or we can help destroy it. I took a stand."

"You almost murdered a man."

"Yes." Richard thought about this with solemnity. "I felt I had to. He's dangerous. Perhaps I was wrong. The damn strike has been almost a war. Perhaps I did get carried away. But he's not dead. Thanks to you. He's not even been charged with any crime, not yet. But I know what he is. Disaffected. Dissatisfied

with his lot in life. But you're right. That's what I came here to
say. I shouldn't have shot at him. And I'm sorry."

"Oh, for Christ's sake," said Eli wearily. "I hope I like you
better when you're older."

"It's like having our very own Orangeman," I added.

At that moment, Marie stopped her clatter and Helen,
hearing our voices, came out of her room. She had taken to
favouring shades of yellow and gold, deepening at times to burgundy, even cherry red. When she was weaving, she fell into a
lazy physical aggression, much like someone riding a horse. And
yes, her beauty brought with it its own tendencies, its change of
direction. When she appeared, Richard forgot even the weight
of his guilt. I was somewhat relieved to see in him a measure of
affection for Helen, aside from his customary approbation. It
suddenly occurred to me that he loved her.

In her renewed association with Richard, since his father's
death, Helen seemed to have chosen to trust him, which of
course is a decision few of us can make. She thought that since
she had seen him broken, that night when his tuxedo didn't fit
him any more, then she must really know him. She had seen
him at his worst. Surely, she thought, that must make this bond
trustworthy. She came into the room with her lazy confidence
and joined Richard, unsurprised; she lay her head against his
chest just long enough to be reassured of his heartbeat.

CHAPTER TWENTY

IN THE FALL, HELEN BECAME ENGAGED to Richard Anderson as a kite becomes engaged to the hand holding the string. Eggshell lacquer and Chinese silk. November, and the land as ugly as a frozen rat. Yet Helen soared above us in ether, the sun queen.

I immersed myself in the strike trials. Helen sewed her own wedding dress. One night, I came home late from an evening session in court in the city. The Crown prosecutor had been going after Bobby Russell for days, wearing Bobby down. Enter the age of advertising. The prosecutor *identified* Bobby Russell; he named him nearly to death. He held up before him, in the eyes of the court, images of a revolutionary Marxist, a grinning, unshaved, dark-featured crazy man with an appetite for small children. An *incendiary*. The more he identified, the more Bobby took on the features of a traitor, perhaps a disaffection of his own. A family man, a gentle man, gradually R. B. Russell became an acolyte of a great international conspiracy to overthrow the world. This was not a time for subtlety. Helen sewed her wedding dress. Bobby Russell became more radical than Karl Marx.

I came home very tired. I missed my mother and father. It was a cold night. Bare fields. No shroud of snow. I drove as fast as my Ford would carry me, singing, "I'm so tired, I'm so tired. Oh, Lord, I am so tired." Pulled up with my auto's lamps shining on the house, and through the window saw the black hair of my daughter bent over the treadle machine. Her determined back. Her humility to the task.

I entered with some trepidation. I was embarrassed at how crabby I'd been with her. For a blissful moment, Richard was forgotten. I found her surrounded by frothy waves of white brocade. She didn't look up but remained intent, with her own tired dignity. On the kitchen table there were fragments of wedding dress. I found the sleeves and sat down to baste the inside seam. We worked in silence like that, and gradually the air softened between us. Helen had become a statuesque woman, taller than I was, bigger boned, muscled as a trout. She relaxed. We worked like that for many hours without speaking. I could offer her only my presence. That was all that remained.

<hr />

BOBBY RUSSELL WENT to the penitentiary for two years (from where he was soon elected to the legislature).

And Helen married Richard Anderson. In early March, three days after her eighteenth birthday.

Three hundred guests in the pink of health and witty as balloons. Much gin, much gin and much champagne, and then much brandy and eloquence. There was love; it was in the air. A very cold day. Our breath escaped like thin white snakes. He placed the diamond on her finger. The white cake was a castle. Everyone applauded. The wedding guests drew away from her; they protected themselves from her beauty, which filled the rooms with the richness of strings and woodwinds. Helen's white dress swayed around her, and when she moved quickly, it followed her, rustling. She kissed us goodbye, clear-eyed and regal. They left in the new yellow Packard, her crinolines filling the car and overflowing the pale cream leather seats. She smiled and waved and flew away.

And on that day, nothing happened to anyone else in all the world.

PART FIVE

1921

CHAPTER ONE

IN STORIES WHERE THE WOLF dwells with the lamb, and the leopard lies down with the kid, the calf with the young lion, the cow with the bear, and their young ones all lie down with one another, and together they are led by a little child round and round on a gold chain thinner than a strand of hair, a lot depends on water. Or wisdom. Water being the wisdom of the earth.

Ours would be a marine utopia, an ocean of air, which in its turn is occupied by our aging bodies, like sacs of ocean water, all of us muttering about love and pain as we swim here and there. In the realm of peace, as the weird old prophet Isaiah would tell us, *the waters will cover the sea.* This is pretty redundant, like rain becoming showers. And behind it, as in any utopia, lies an agreement that the large will also be the small (though the small will not necessarily be the large). It's an arrangement of totality.

A utopia is somebody's idea of a good time, that total agreement, the extreme familiarity, intimacy; the loss of distinction between wolf, lamb, leopard; the loss of distinction between the kid, the calf, the lion, cow, bear, child. The loss of distinction between the child and the utopia.

Into this utopia, this intimacy, we lost Helen. Marriage with Richard could only be a totality, and of course, it could only be bliss.

Bereft is a suitable word. It slides into place. Yes. We were
bereft.

⚜

RICHARD WEATHERED THE POST-WAR recession without a shudder. In those first years of their marriage, he proved to Helen
that the *Titanic* had never sunk in the Atlantic Ocean. He did
this by shopping for her. Richard knew the size of her gloves and
how tightly the buttons will close at the wrist. He knew the shoes
that would fit the high instep, the left heel that was slightly
askew. He bought her backless evening dresses; they fell from
narrow shoulder straps and clung to her hips, draped at her
famous white ankles. He knew the shape of his wife. She was his.
He did not suffer very badly from desperation at the beginning.

In 1923, in Thebes, Howard Carter and Lord Carnarvon
opened up King Tutankhamen's tomb and discovered the
mummified boy-king with all his beaten gold. It had a huge
effect on Helen. She promptly ripped out the red velvet interior
of John Anderson's house (an exhumation that excluded Mrs.
John Anderson's porcelain bathtub, which remains to this day,
a white-and-green tiled crypt occupied by Mrs. John Anderson
herself, an old lump of butter, soaking).

Helen made strange changes to the home of John
Anderson, bless him. From pompous early prairie merchant to
aggressive futurist supranational chic. The house seemed like a
box of lozenges. The Persian carpet was replaced with a pastel
floral, up the grand stairs, to the left of the mezzanine, a door,
closed. Now and then, when I visited my daughter in the quiet

of the afternoon, I heard the taps turn and the water flow, and I knew that Mrs. Anderson was adding hot. I wondered if she had anyone to help her. In addition to the remodelling, Helen had initiated a number of more practical changes in the Anderson mansion, copper wires and iron water pipes among the first innovations. Now her mother-in-law could add hot all by herself.

I once asked Helen if Mrs. John Anderson had anyone to look after her, to keep the bathroom steamy and replace the face cloth when it got mouldy. Helen regarded me, imperious, and then nodded. She had thrown herself into marriage. It was a management position.

She threw out the antimacassars, the red glass lamps with crystal teardrops, the photographs of bishops from Toronto. The new furniture would come from the catalogues of ateliers in Germany and France, with Morris's pretty cyclamen wallpaper from London. The dining-room walls were painted a Delphic blue with gold trim, a cosmic vista that Helen ornamented with her sketchings of ospreys and monkeys, fawns and dachshunds, the plumage of pheasant, a hare, and combinatory creatures with squirrels' feet, the body of a tiny horse with the tail of a fox. Stylized, libidinous cartoons. Even the birds looked like women.

The oak and mahogany were replaced by low tables in the Chinese fashion. Pewter, beechwood, plate glass with metal hinges. Helen filled the bookshelves in her sitting room with books bound solely in yellow chamois. They entertained their wickedly funny friends, freed from Victorian restraint. Helen designed a kidney-shaped swimming pool with a glass roof. Their guests displayed a tendency to swim in their evening clothes. When the guests got wet, they stripped down in glass-and-marble change rooms where a maid would provide them with silk bathrobes that they could take home with them, compliments of the house.

She felt herself married to the mummified boy; she would wrap the house in gold-plated weeds. Helen too seemed gold-plated, especially the liver, for she remained flawlessly beautiful, even after a night of cocktails and laughter.

And with all this, Richard was well pleased. The cat had swallowed the canary.

Helen abandoned the young flapper and became dangerous. The prolonged economy of the bride, her enforced uselessness, made her errant, distracted, impetuous. She began to attract suitors. Edward Pennyfeather for one. Harold Burnside for two. T. K. Giles (commonly, "the King") for three. Her black hair cut blunt, a sharp chevron, the inevitable bandeaux, her eyes blackened with kohl, as Egyptian as any wife on Millionaire Row. Of course she was bored. It was her duty to be bored. The suitors bored her. Richard did not bore her because he wasn't importunate; in fact, he slept in his own bedroom and rarely bothered her. She remained easily virtuous; she was *married,* and not the least interested in love.

Helen and Richard were friends, especially when they drank champagne. They didn't even *need* to talk. Helen's beauty compelled Richard much more than champagne. He didn't like addictions. He liked control. So he didn't like his addiction to his wife.

How did Richard love her?

Desperately.

At what temperature?

Forty below. So cold it feels hot.

Then the marriage was a success?

RICHARD'S ROOMS WERE adjoined to Helen's by a door that she wished she could lock. Not that she didn't trust her husband, and she was not yet afraid of him, but she didn't like surprises, at least not that kind of surprise. She needed to be assured that when she was alone, she was truly alone. Increasingly, she did not *feel* alone. She grew sensitive to the sound of the door opening from her husband's bedroom, a sound more rare than a cat's sneeze, interrupting the sound of the shuttle travelling the loom, for she continued to weave; she had become very skilled, very refined. She wore a gold velvet robe with a turquoise sash and she'd risen before daybreak, having been restless in her big bed upon its elevated dais beneath a short canopy of brocade. She had risen and lit the fire in the grate and turned on the fluted lamp beside her loom and worked with her thread till the sun rose and overcame the yellow lamplight and filled the room with thin windy shadows. She was a woman who would never grow old. That's another form of *ancient.*

Richard didn't come. Solitude is a state of readiness, a small island prepared for war. The sunlight inched across the bedroom wall.

THEY HAD DINNER TOGETHER EVERY NIGHT, the governance of "a good marriage." "How are things with Richard?" I might ask, as if I truly had a mother's claim to Helen. "We had dinner together last night," she'd say. "Veal. The vegetables are always overdone. I must speak to Cook."

"Does Cook have a name?"

"I don't know," said Helen, distracted.

I laughed. She didn't. She looked out the window. A little girl was walking down the street. "There you are," I said. Helen stared at the child, a pretty thing wearing boots trimmed with rabbit fur. She was her own Orpheus, looking back at herself. Turning herself to stone.

But that night he didn't come. Helen worked at her loom all day long and dressed only when night had fallen and dinner was served. They always dined at eight when they weren't entertaining. The house was in darkness. Through the upper windows on the landing, iron black branches, plainly unhaunted. Helen walked down the broad, dark staircase from the mezzanine, and she heard the croon of the water pipes. Mrs. John Anderson was adding hot.

Richard always came home for dinner if he wasn't in New York or at the club, and he always called if he was going to be late. As Helen assumed her place at the dining-room table and looked down its expanse with the candlelight reflecting like lights from a dock at the lake, as the butler shook the linen napkin and placed it across her lap, she looked down the telescope of her husband's dining room at her husband's empty chair, the place setting that always included his crystal ashtray and lighter, and she asked for white wine. She took a drink and set the glass down and ran her hand along its stem. She drank again. Nerves, she thought, and straightened her back. Nerves.

She had to acknowledge that she was not anxious for Richard's safety. She thought hard about this. Her dinner was placed before her.

No, she felt no wifely concern on Richard's behalf, none at all; nothing so friendly or intimate as that. She drank off several glasses of the French Sauternes without feeling any effect at all. When she tried to consider some danger to Richard—ill health, a car accident, an assassination—she came up cold. Surely this is intuition: she simply knows he's fine. She's just irritated that she's been stood up; she's in a snit to find herself on stage without her leading man, living this drawing-room farce alone.

But really, what a posturing ass Richard is. A cold, tedious man with trivial interests, self-indulgent, always looking out for number one. How greedy, really; decadent, profligate! (She heard her grandfather's voice, as haunting as the water pipes.) A dissolute, bloodsucking parasite, a goddamn son of a bitch, a useless leech upon the honest souls of the working class. She rang the butler's bell. Where *was* that man, what *was* his name, when *would* he come!

Helen was fixated on the revolution taking place within her and did not hear the butler's polite inquiry, Madame has not enjoyed the veal? She slouched, draped one leg over the arm of her chair and took a cigarette from her sequined bag. The man rushed to fetch Richard's lighter; Madame never smoked in the dining room. Helen held up her face with its cigarette and waited for a light. The butler was thin; he did not have a butler's hands, but the fingers of a musician or something. He snapped closed the lighter. He didn't even look like a butler.

A terrible longing had opened in Helen. She had swallowed a leopard, so fierce was the thing caged inside her. She groaned and then waved the man away before he could utter his paid-for solicitations. "I'm fine," she said, and waved her cigarette, go away. All around her, the impossible animals peaked out from art-deco foliage, wagging their smooth tails. The charm of the room curdled in her stomach.

Then Richard arrived. He pulled back his chair, took his place and looked at her.

"Hello, Hansel," said Helen, and she realized that her voice was drunk, whereas she was perfectly, icily, sober.

Richard seemed strangely innocent, in his elegant clothes, at the head of his big table. He looked surprised, as if he'd been injured out of the blue. He was all shiny and clear, like a tuning fork. He lit a cigarette and told the butler-person to bring him a Scotch and soda. Only then, inhaling, did he say hello.

He watched her stand and swing down to his end of the table. She wore a light shawl loosely around her bare shoulders. It accentuated her height. "You look very beautiful tonight," he said. A cool statement, somehow resenting.

She stood beside his chair. "I've reached a conclusion," she said.

Richard leaned back to look at her. "I believe that is a first."

She thought about it. "It happens," she said, "especially when you're not here." She touched his shoulder. And remembered that he inhabited a large space within her. So if he was a bloodsucking parasite, then she was a bloodsucking parasite's wife. "I need to work," she said.

"Was your mother here today?" he asked.

She tried to remember. "I don't know," she said. "Maybe."

"Won't you sit down while I have my dinner?" he asked. He rose to pull out her chair so that she might sit. Then he kissed her once upon her throat before resuming his seat. "I'm sorry I'm late."

"It's not just that."

"Some things have come up."

"Wall Street?"

"Wall Street. Yes."

"It's worse than before?"

"It will get much worse. But we'll be all right. We've still got the local property."

She shrugged. "I don't care."

"You'll always be looked after," he said.

Oliver-Jenkins-Higgins brought him the veal. "Oh," said Richard. "Veal."

"I will have wine," said Helen. "A fresh glass." Then, to Richard: "What does your broker say, your man in New York?"

Richard stopped, his glass at his lips. He said, "Walkins died today." Then he sipped.

"Well, that's a bit sudden."

"He jumped."

"Oh. He jumped. From Wall Street. Because of the big crash."

"It's more of a leak than a crash. Like a boat hitting . . . something."

"In New York. He killed himself in New York."

"And here. It's the same."

"Only smaller."

"Not the way we've been playing it."

"I'm sorry about Walker."

"Walkins. His name was Walkins."

"Yes. A nice man. His poor wife." Then she remembered that she'd never met Walkins. The name was so familiar, one of Richard's dramatis personae. "Or," she said, "everyone."

"I've no doubt he was a *very* nice man. They *are* down there. Yes, he was. We met at meetings. Of course, then he was all business. A fast-thinking man. As they tend to be, you know, more than here. Quite different."

He began to cut his meat precisely. He said, "Prices are going to fall very fast. You may want to warn your mother. I'll telephone her tomorrow if you like."

Helen gripped the wine glass in her fingers. Her hands were strong from weaving. The three broken fingers had healed, crooked. "I can't bear this," she said. She squeezed the glass until it broke in her hand. The blood was a glaze upon the cherrywood table, a crimson edge on Richard's linen placemat.

Richard's fork hesitated midway to his mouth. He put it down with the same measured composure. He kneeled beside her and wiped her fingers with his napkin. It was a small cut, but when he pulled aside the skin to see how deep it went, he saw the pink bone. Beneath the small flap of flesh was a sliver of glass, which he removed, for his hands were small, womanly. The cook brought out a bowl of ice water, and without moving her from the dining room, Richard bandaged Helen's hand and taped it closed. When he resumed his seat, she was as pale as ivory and his dinner was still warm. He made a polite show of eating, and then put down his cutlery and sat back with his arms extended to the table.

So it was, between them. If there were no guests, it was always just the two of them, Hansel and Gretel. Childless. Helen had not yet used that word. Perhaps because a child cannot be childless, and there seemed to be a moratorium on her maturity, though indeed Hansel was thirty-five years old and Gretel was twenty-seven. They sat in the dining room for a long time, among the palm trees and ferns, monkey, possibly antelope, lemur, greens and yellows, that peacock in the lilac tree. Helen leaned forward and with her good hand she stroked Richard's hair.

He told her which stocks had failed, who had become insolvent, who hung on, who let go. Pulp and paper, gold, railway stocks, Winnipeg Electric, International Nickel. The man who jumped, jumped again and again. Walkins, she tried to remember; Walkins was his name. It surely matters. They were served coffee, and she asked him the questions she knew he could answer. She showed no judgment, and received his information as if it were written on her. When they left the dining room, everything would be different. But she would never fall out of love with Richard.

They took each other's hands (Richard holding her injury; Helen thinking of her father, how Eli played open chords on the guitar, the music of the lost thumb). They held hands, how gently Helen was held by Richard, and how elegant she was, wounded, pleasantly subdued. Together they climbed the stairs, and Richard entered Helen's rooms and waited while she went to wash. Alone, she peeled away the bandage to see the white tear in her skin, the damp ridges of fingerprint; tomorrow it would be drier and then it would fall away, and under the lid of skin the blood vessels were throbbing.

When she emerged from her washing room, he was standing before the loom. He'd removed his jacket and now he stood in his white shirt, the collar removed, his gold hair curling at the nape. He studied the screen she'd placed before the loom, the sketching from which she would copy her weaving. The sketch was full-scale cliché, a replica of the old Flemish tapestries: "The Lady and her Lover," the unicorn, birds, laurel, the inscription "To my only desire."

She came out wearing a starched white nightgown, her arms bare and round, her black hair brushed back so that she looked less like a wife of the twentieth century. Richard walked around the loom to where she worked the treadles and shuttle. It was hard to decipher the picture because the weaver always works from the wrong side. But even so, it was clear the weaving bore no relationship to her sketching; none at all. Richard slowly walked around and removed the screen.

"What have you done?" he asked in surprise.

It was unmistakably an elm tree, and that would be caragana under it, the small yellow flowers of the honeysuckle, cumulus clouds; you knew that it was a hot day, that the wind blew. That those were Richard's blond locks, that he'd turned his back to her, the Lady, whose face was obscured by a yellow fan. And a ship. And a sea in the sky. The sky becomes an ocean, and a red-tailed hawk with a string of pearls flies away.

Richard stopped breathing. He would not look at her. He stared at his image, at the pearls flying off, as if staring would alter it or, better, make it disappear. Then he ran his fingers over the inchoate part, the new space that would scroll into view as she worked from left to right.

She'd begun with green, the familiar bush from her childhood home. There were the first lines of a man's face; a square-faced man emerged on the surface, a stolid brown-eyed man with a peaceful smile. Richard seemed to hum with pain. "Who is this?" he asked softly.

She shook her head. "I don't know." It was the truth. It was not Edward Pennyfeather, who had bony cheeks, or Harold Burnside, with the saggy eyes, and it was not "the King" because he was not drinking. This was a man from the world beyond. They both looked at him, wondering when he would come true.

CHAPTER THREE

IT SO HAPPENED THAT ONE DAY IN 1933, a young Jewish composer of twelve-tone music was assigned to a boondoggle a few miles north of "our property," in the bush near rich farmland cultivated by Trappist monks. A boondoggle was a make-work project devised to get men to work for their relief during the Depression. On this occasion, the foreman marched his crew three hundred yards into the bush, tied a red flag to an aspen and told the men to start clearing. "The government wants a road toot sweet," the foreman said. Somebody asked, What for? The foreman raised his eyebrows sarcastically. "Oh, it's the chairman of the board wants to know." It was an imaginary road in the middle, it seemed then, of nowhere.

The composer was as thin as a cadaver, six and a half feet tall and big with brain, his head like a heavy flower on a long stem. He had supported his wife in a refined, if modest, way by giving piano lessons, a service that proved dispensable in the Depression. He had no income. He'd never done manual labour. He looked up at the tops of the trees. Overhead, the wind was gritty with topsoil, but in the woods the mosquitoes swarmed in a moist green haze.

They worked like dogs on that boondoggle, though that certainly wasn't the custom. The work made them obsessive and spiteful—they needed to hurt somebody, but they had access only to themselves. They used a Swedish saw and ropes to haul down the trees, and their own backs to carry the boulders. The composer suffered from rheumatism. The pain was bearable, but the sense of futility was not. Reality had broken faith with him, so he had no choice but to break it right back.

The road to nowhere was nightmared into shape, the most perfect road in Manitoba. On the last day, the composer helped roll the gravel and then he walked three miles in the wrong direction, south, directly through the brush, without noticing that his feet were bleeding. He was falling from the constellation of the boondoggle road.

Eli and I were at home listening to CKY radio. I was sitting on Eli's lap. Eli, at the time, was like an empty paper bag in the wind, and I sat on him often just to keep him from blowing away. The carcasses of grasshoppers made a clicking sound when they hit the house, and we turned up the cowboy songs on the radio to try to drown the noise, but it never worked. The afternoon was dark with dust, and we were sitting with the electric light on, all dressed up in our cowboy dancing clothes, me in my red dress with the white crinolines and Eli with his spurs and hat (and under the brim of his hat, his shadowed eyes). We still weren't accustomed to electric lights, I guess, because we didn't have them till we were already middle age, so we still had a vulgar relationship with them. The lights and the radio ran our lives. With the garden in ruins and the rodeo no longer a paying option for Eli, we became employees of the light bulb, and we didn't even figure out that we could turn the damn thing off and go back to candles. Anyway, there we were, dressed up for a circus in the ugly glare of the overhead lamp, when I thought I heard a knocking. "Did you hear that?" I asked Eli, who turned his good ear towards me and said, "Say again?"

I slid off Eli's knee and tentatively opened the door.

"Could I trouble you?" said the tall, skinny man, leaning into the wind. "I am in need of a piece of paper and a pencil."

His mouth was very black and empty. Wordlessly, I fetched the things he wanted. Eli followed me to the door. With the blare of the yodel and guitar behind us, we watched his trembling hand draw five parallel horizontal lines. He looked up at us and nodded, as if encouraged by the function of pencil on paper. They were notes he wrote, all in a row, like bits of broken fence, like nowhere roads in the bush. Completely silent music. We stood on the front steps, Eli and the man and I, for almost an hour, not saying anything at all while we watched the notes come from his hand, though of course I heard nothing other than the click of the grasshoppers tossed in the wind. Later, Eli (who could read a chord chart, his only form of literacy) said that it was the strangest music he'd ever seen; he said it made him anxious, like he was under attack. I asked him, whispering, "So it's not very good?" And Eli, startled, said, "No! It's genius! It's just not for people's bodies, you know. More for their brains." He sought the word. "Intellects." It sounded funny coming through his long teeth.

The composer stayed with us for nearly a week, hardly saying a word, though we learned that his name was Daniel Zimmerman, and that he normally lived on Agnes Street, near the library downtown. We gave him Helen's old room. He never seemed to sleep. It was nerve-racking having him around. He seemed unbearably vulnerable. I have never met a human being with less *animal* in him. He filled page after page with those notes, and when I asked him to sing it, he gave me a look of such despair that I left off, only asked him, "Please eat something, then. Please, just this one sandwich, why don't you?"

Saturday morning found him at the kitchen table as usual, still putting notes on paper, when through the window I saw a deer-like creature enter the yard, a diminutive young woman dressed in a shabby fur coat, despite the heat. She was sizing up our house, checking the yard for dogs, and then she stuck out her chin and approached. I opened the door to her. She saw the composer in our kitchen and cried out. The composer lifted his sunken eyes from his task. They looked at one another for several moments. I invited her in. She seemed surprised at my presence, and entered, her eyes on Daniel's, like she was entering his cage. A slight thing with brown eyes, straight brown hair, her apprehension not quite fearful. A clicking distance between the two of them. Daniel spoke. "This is my wife," he said. She leapt towards the word as if he'd tossed her a biscuit. *Wife.* Somehow the name didn't stick.

It seemed she gained a certain stature when she wasn't drained by her fascination with her objective husband. She offered her hand. She had that déclassé dignity you saw so often during the Depression. "Thank you for taking my husband into your home. I am Ida Zimmerman."

I said I'd make tea. Daniel at last stood up and went to take her coat, and he fumbled trying to hang it on the hook by the door and then absently flung it over the woodbox. When he pulled out her chair for her, her hand darted out to touch his and he smiled slightly at her, oddly paternal, though they were of the same age, in their twenties, and mawkishly serious. While Daniel was obviously not a mean man at all, his sadness was an *idea,* and as such, an exclusive part of him. Ida watched him admiringly, hungrily. She told us she'd taken the streetcar to the end of the line and then walked, walked for miles, each day going farther south, until she found our yard. While we talked, she leafed through the music, reading it apparently, because she looked up at him and murmured, "This would hurt the ears, Danny; so broken."

The house was too stuffy. I left them and went out to milk the cow. For the moment, there was no wind. It was overcast, the day as warm and smooth as the inside of a wood chest. I was returning with a pail of milk when I saw, with some surprise, Helen's yellow car drive up. A train drummed by, stirring the milk. The door to our cabin breezed open and Ida walked out. Without her bewildering coat, she looked very thin. Her dress was a dreary brown. She had a brave way of standing. Helen emerged from her Packard wearing a yellow crepe tea dress. She and Ida stared at each other, as if each presented to the other an entirely novel concept. Rich! thought Ida. Oh, thought Helen, Poor! It was an immediate bond, firm as plywood.

They were like two bristling young dogs in the kitchen. Helen was strangely covetous, watched Ida enviously. While we chatted, Ida stroked her husband's hand. Helen must have smoked ten cigarettes. Eli couldn't bear to look at her, so strained and artificial. She put another cigarette between her lips. Eli reached over and gently removed it. "There now," he said. "There now." Helen's eyes filled up at her father's reproach. She kept looking out the window. She was scared of something.

I tried to get her talking. "How 'bout that Royal Bastard

Bennett?" I said. R. B. Bennett had been elected prime minister three years earlier, and had proved to be a punitive overseer for the unemployed and the farmers blown off the land by drought.

Eli groaned and said, "Not worth the tanning fee."

We winced at each other. Great way to calm down our daughter. But Helen had brightened. She seemed to shuck off an invisible golden cloak. She clasped her hands together in some ancient grieving act of prayer. "Goddamn bugger!" she cried out. "Bloody capitalist!" It stopped us all cold. The whole house shook. The rising wind battered the locusts into the walls of our wood shack.

Helen's early education in the biographies of rich courtesans and wives had led us to believe that she had no interest in politics beyond an appetite for wealth. But in our recent visits to the Anderson house, Eli and I had been surprised to see in her rooms pamphlets and books of political theory, the old library we had foisted upon her in her youth—my favourite marital tract, Veblen's *Theory of the Leisure Class,* and her grandfather Peter's dog-eared copy of *Capital.* I wondered how Richard would swallow his wife's new interests. But more, I wondered what the salty winds of political criticism might do to the fractured soul of our beautiful daughter.

We were startled then by the sound of a car braking in the dust, and then Richard entered, quick as cold gin. Helen instinctively reached out to her father and touched his missing ear, her good luck charm. She was truant, defiant and uncertain.

Richard barely paused to register the existence of Ida and Daniel. He walked close to Helen, inches from her, and said hello as if it were a funny thing to say. Then he looked more carefully at our guests (Ida sliding her arm around Daniel's shoulder). Back at Helen: "You came here, did you?" Strangely, his statement did more to call Helen's presence into question than to confirm her, yes, here. The only one obviously *present* was Richard.

"Dick!" I said. He stuck his hands in his pockets. Every chair was taken. He was as nervous as a propeller, spinning in tight circles. I wanted to hug the fear out of him, a sort of shuddering kindness—what people feel while they hold a bag of kittens under water. "You need a chair!" And we all scrambled to provide him with a place to sit, an ashtray, a cup of coffee, a little milk for his coffee.

At last, enthroned, he looked around. Again, that look of amusement. "It's a shame what happened to you, Blondie," he said, turning upon me his blue eye with its strange black sickle.

"What?" I asked. Considered. I was over sixty, so turning fifty wasn't a big issue. Felt pretty good. Still had a cow. A sudden gust of wind blew dust under the door. I brightened. "Eli's got a plan to fix the grasshoppers!" I told Richard proudly. "Tell him, Eli."

The last thing Eli wanted to do was talk to Richard. But he was tempted. Since he'd had to give up the rodeo when the Depression hit, he'd fed his love for lyrics by reciting recipes, much like my dad once loved to do. And his recipe for grasshopper poison was a favourite. Still, he couldn't bring himself to talk directly to his son-in-law. So he fixed his attention on Ida's acorn brown eyes, as if it was she that needed to know. "You don't know the green poison?" he asked. Ida smiled and looked at Daniel, hoping a story might interest him. "Well!" said Eli, "It's, I take no credit for it, it's God work." When Helen heard him say "God," she winced and said, "Oh, fuck," under her breath. Ida jumped. She and Helen exchanged a smile.

From his chair, Eli had a good view of the manure pile. He said, "In all of Creation, there is nothing as powerful as the attraction of locusts to horse manure."

We all looked out. There they were, the pile covered with insects so it looked like the scales of a fish or shingles on a roof; it glittered and moved.

"Laugh if you like," Eli said. "Laugh and say, 'Sure, old man; you've forgotten the birds and the bees, the power of pro-creation.' But decay! Waste! Guano, shit, forgive the French." He shook his head in wonder. "The sights we've seen, the sights we've seen."

Richard had seen the smile between Helen and Ida. It bore investigation. To Ida: "You live around here, do you?"

Eli, warming, also to Ida: "You wet it down. That's the tricky part. You've got to wet it down just right."

Ida, to Eli: "The guano." Then, to Richard, revealing childlike teeth: "The horse shit."

Eli felt a surge of love for Ida. He slapped her knee. "You've got it!" He began to list the ingredients on his paw. "You take your poison, Paris Green, one part. You take your two parts salt. Unless of course your horse shit's fresh. You take sixty parts horse shit." He laughed, his surprising teeth. "The banks might take the harness, the pasture, the buggy, but they hardly ever take the horse. And they *never* take the horse shit."

Ida laughed. "You've always got horse shit!" She nudged her husband with this evidence of bounty. Daniel smiled, per-haps at the joke.

Eli loved them both, a married couple! He warmly said to Daniel, a warning, "Ahhh, son, but here's the tricky part. You got to mix it. You got to mix it right. So you can spread it."

Richard said to Helen, "We have to be at the Allinghams' by four."

"You mean, like paint?" asked Ida.

Eli breathed happily through his nose. "You paint the whole damn field with it. Paris Green." Then, generously, to Richard: "Green."

"So, Richard," I said, "enough about us. Tell us your own tricks of survival. How've you managed? Still solvent?"

He smiled. "Oh, yes." His attention on Helen. "We'll always be fine."

Helen looked up sharply.

Richard continued. "But we mustn't think always of ourselves. At times like this, we have to consider the needs of others less fortunate."

I gather this was a form of seduction. Helen was rigid. I knew the signals: Richard was about to be dismissed. I put my hand on Richard's shoulder and said, "Don't do this for our sake, Dick. We're used to you."

He ignored this and blundered on. "Yes. I'm a man with a conscience. Especially when it comes to family." From his pocket he withdrew a chequebook and pen. "Listen Blondie, I know you and Eli lost everything."

"Not quite," I said, indicating the roof over our heads.

"There's no need to do without money. I feel slightly responsible. It was at my suggestion that you invested so heavily."

"Your dad's," I told him. "Mr. John Anderson, bless

him— Sorry." Richard winced so deeply that nothing showed on
the surface.

"I'm going to give you something to help you start over."

"No need," said Eli.

"You're poor!" said Richard.

"Lighten up!" I told him. "We're not *that* poor." I put my
hands in my pockets and tugged at my underwear, which was
falling around my hips. "We're not really poor."

"If you want to help, give it to . . . give it to . . . Good
Lord, I was going to say, 'Give it to the CCF,'" said Eli and put
his head in his hands. "So this is what it's like to get old."

Richard, looking hopefully at Helen: "I could contribute
to the CCF."

"Dick!" I knew then how badly he suffered. "To thine own
self be true!"

Helen had reached her saturation point. She stood like a
cobra prepared to strike. I moved to stand between them.

"Ask him how he feels about this Hitler!" she demanded.

Ida and Daniel sat upright. We all looked at Dick.

Richard, for the first and only time in his life, took my
advice: he chose that very moment to be true to himself. He
said, faltering, "I just feel the man should be given a chance."

Eli left the table and walked outside. Helen watched her
father go. Anger filled her up.

Richard pleaded, "He's got some ideas! Look at the
Volkswagen! I mean, he was in prison when he thought of that!"
He appealed to me, "Blondie! You usually like people who go to
prison!"

"Poor Dick," I said. "Oh, poor Dick." I reached out and

touched Richard's arm. His body was tight. "Not this Hitler," I said, and stopped. I couldn't look at Helen.

"You can't keep Germany in the dirt! Versailles was a stupid mistake!" he said.

It was Helen who handed Richard the gun and indicated which foot. "And who will keep Germany in the dirt, Richard?" she asked.

"The Jews. The Communists. The, the rabble," said Richard.

Ida slowly stood up, pushing back her chair. Richard looked at her, dry, keen. He was at last himself. "It's just the truth," he said. Then, to Helen: "We're leaving."

We heard a voice. It said, "I built a road." It was Daniel. He was talking to Richard. Again: "I built a road. In the middle of the bush."

Daniel did not look well. Richard could smell his illness. Daniel clearly knew this. His mind was clear. "They paid me vouchers, sixteen dollars a month."

A pause. Richard considered this. His chest always lifted when he was about to inflict *the truth*. "You mean the land in Fort Garry. It's not easy finding you fellows work. There will be houses there someday. You'll be able to look at them and think, I contributed to that."

A low-pitched growl started in somebody's throat. I thought it would be Daniel, but he had this sharp clarity then; somehow you knew that he wouldn't grieve for anything, that he'd let go. But Helen, the sound coming out her throat spoke of a long journey to come. Ida reached Helen just as she was digging her hands into Richard's mouth. Helen hated Richard, yes. And she hated that she had so far to go, so empty-handed.

CHAPTER FOUR

HELEN LEFT RICHARD IN THE AFTERNOON of a sunny day. The first warm day of 1934.

In her husband's navy backpack, she took whatever jewellery she could carry, the pearls and two wine goblets made of gold. The goblets were perhaps the only precious things she took that did not belong to her. Hand-crafted in the shape of her breasts, they were a gift that Richard had given to himself. She wrapped her gold breasts in a clean shirt and packed them beside her copy of Emma Goldman's *Anarchism and Other Essays.*

She left behind the yellow Packard, her dresses and shoes, furs and hats. She had waited six months to leave Richard. Over the winter, she'd quietly acquired a wardrobe of men's work clothes. She walked down the grand staircase in steel-toed boots, bought by stealth through Hudson's Bay mail order, the pack slung over her shoulder. She paused to look out her favourite window, the large one on the mezzanine. She heard the drone of the hot-water pipes. Helen walked out of the mansion and passed through the stone gate.

She didn't look back. Her rooms filled with light. The loom creaked, the way standing things do. Then the evening sun fell across her unfinished tapestry, its green bush and the face of a stranger staring out. A few hours later, Richard would come home to find her rooms unlit and the weaving left there like a forwarding address.

THAT WAS THE END of the larval stage of the most beautiful woman in the world. She took a streetcar for the first time in her life; it carried her a few blocks south of the Anderson mansion. Then she walked. She walked down the highway, all the way to the junction of the Red and the Rivière Sale, a distance of about twelve miles.

She and Ida had arranged to meet beside the trestles of the railway bridge. It was a mild evening and early spring, so the long daylight still came as a surprise and the aspen trees had barely begun to leaf, their hard brown buds exhaling a thin trace of green smoke. She walked over the bridge. It was another dry year. Marsh grass broke the water's surface, the sluggish river below seen through the slats of wood.

She rolled a cigarette. Back when she wore mink collars, she had smoked cheroots. As a kid, she'd watched farmers' affectionate handling of the gold leaves, stuffing the paper, bringing it up to a grizzled mouth for a lick. But Helen had studied for her new character downtown at the park by St. John's Church. She had told Richard she was going to church, but she went instead to the park to watch the loitering men. Her return to rollys had an urban flavour, and it was these men more than the old farmers of her youth that she mimicked now while she strolled and smoked; it was their dangerous futility she would emulate. As an actress, character came to her from the inside out, a reversal of her real life. She knew the heartbeat of a hobo.

There was a thin deer path. Aspen mixed with oak on the riverbank. She didn't see the swaying rope of the footbridge till she was under it. She flicked the flat yellow butt into the water and saw a reflection scrawled there, moving, a lanky construction of twisted hemp swaying in the windless air, recently vacated.

The footbridge gave all the security of a tightrope; it sagged and bounced. If she looked down, she'd fall in. On the other side, there was a cabin visible through the leafless trees. She passed through a miniature village of white wooden boxes, an apiary, currently a ghost town. Just then, the sun slid under a shelf of evening cloud and struck the trees at the horizon, lining each bud with light. Helen guided herself around the rough, tar-varnished logs. And saw the monk.

He stood several feet away. His arms crossed, his hands hidden in his sleeves. Helen held her breath.

He didn't see her. He was utterly calm. When breezes shifted, he turned his head towards the sound. He was *listening*. He disappeared into listening, devoted to the exchange between leaf and light. He was unlike anyone she'd ever seen. He didn't seem to *know* anything. He listened with his belly, with his feet. The motion of young leaves was infinitely eventful.

It occurred to Helen that her self-indulgence would be more difficult to abandon, that it had little to do with the things she'd left at Richard's house.

When he finally looked at her, she was part of the scenery, at first. But he did look; he looked at Helen for a fraction too long. She knew she had destroyed something, as the second breath necessarily destroys the first. He had, she noticed, a handsome square face with a buzz of blond-white hair. He stood still, his lips opened, his head back. He was framed by the gnarly branches of the caragana.

Helen approached him with delight. She always entered new scenes headlong, but now she tiptoed. She curtsied, or stumbled. His eyes focused on hers, curtaining off both her foolishness and her beauty. She touched his sleeve. With instant surging affection, she wanted to put her face to his, to speak as she would speak to a newly recognized brother. She wanted to put her head on his chest, to listen to his heartbeat. He had a mouth; I assume she found it charming, the parentheses on his face when he smiled. She told him too much, though entirely without detail, highly philosophical and not quite true. He enhanced the idealist in her, so it wasn't her fault she lied a little, rising to every expectation.

The subject was love. Of mankind. How it is expressed in a single stroke, a flash of the human spirit, the miracle of an individual.

And its manifestation in the structures of family, of the church.

Yes. Of course. The family. Love. Of man.

And God.

Him too. And the articulation of a leaf, budding, and the smell of spring this evening. "It's messy, this world," she said. "That's what I love about it." A shameless plagiarist, stealing lines from Grandmother Alice. But when he listened to her, it was like he was laying a blanket on the ground to wrap her inside.

It was getting dark. The trees were turning blue.

"I have to meet someone," she said, innocently touching his arm, a fraternal gesture. "You are from Our Lady of the Prairies, from Notre-Dame." The monastery, which she'd never seen but everyone knew; this was the property of the church. Then she drew her breath. "You are a Trappist." The monk was looking sadly at the yellow grass. "A Trappist monk. But you are not supposed to speak." There was a shade of anguish in her voice.

He let himself look at her face, travelled its contours, its frame of black hair, her mouth, her throat. Then he closed his eyes. "No," he said. "As a Trappist, I would not speak."

Helen could see nothing but his mouth; she could feel only the air slide open and pull her in. Her kiss was not fraternal. He had very soft lips. It was one kiss. On such things the world hinges.

———

SHE MET UP WITH IDA beside the train tracks in a dry field just as night was falling. The stubble smelled sweet, and the sky was a plate of blue glass with a hole for the moon. While they waited for a train, Ida cut off Helen's hair, a nest of black snakes on the ground. Then Helen cut Ida's hair into a short, thick pompadour that they brushed straight back. They appraised one another, circling, amazed. They had become, strangely, men. Helen rolled two cigarettes with one hand. Underfoot, they felt a train about a mile off.

"You look like a foreigner," said Helen to Ida.

"That's what I am, idiot." Ida lit a match with her thumb. "I'm a Jew."

"I'd like to be a Jew," said Helen. She didn't know what a Jew was. They didn't have any on Millionaire Row.

"Well, you can't," said Ida. She pointed at Helen with the hand that cupped the cigarette. "You're an anarchist."

Helen thought she said "adulteress." She panicked, thinking of the monk. The molten night was hammered by an approaching train. Its lantern strafed the bushes and then leapt out into the fog that rose over the river. It took every ounce of manliness to keep from running. Ida yelled something at her; there were red and yellow sparks, a light hit them, they flinched but stayed. The bullet of light coincided with Helen's full recognition of the man she'd just met, *he was the man in her tapestry*, and the train screeched and swayed past them. Ida was panting as if she had run after it. It left a red trail. They watched it go, coal wind in their faces.

Ida began to laugh. "Oh, fuck," she said. The curse would be their password. "We're fucking idiots! It was going south! At a million miles an hour!" Ida laughed. "What kind of Canadian hobos would go south?"

Helen asked, almost shyly, "Why not south?"

"We have to go west!" said Ida. She put her arm around Helen's shoulders, and they started to walk. "And when we've gone as far west as we can go, we have to turn around and go east. It's the *Canadian* way."

It was a long walk east to the railyards at Symington. They reached it at dawn. By then, they'd discussed the know-how of jumping freights. They were hungry, tired, dirty, thirsty; they hurt everywhere. By the time they jumped their first freight, they weren't even play-acting. They were hobos.

CHAPTER FIVE

FOR A WHOLE YEAR, THEY LIVED in the hobo jungles that had broken out like hives on a frayed nervous system. They lived on nothing. Helen was proving the unreality of money. It made her really skinny.

She was desperate to be homeless. It wasn't just the railyard bulls, the private patrols, they ran from. Richard had the police out looking for her. Helen ran away from her husband while Ida searched for hers. Daniel had put a pencil in a paper bag and walked out. Ida hoped that he was riding freight somewhere. It seemed he was on every passing train, that tall man who sat apart from the others, his arms on his knees, the solitary stranger moving in the opposite direction. When newcomers joined them, she searched their faces under their soft billed caps. This was not a romantic pursuit, and Ida was not abject; rather, she was exceedingly forthright, almost bureaucratic, as if she'd been hired by a magistrate to deliver a summons to the man. Once, Helen dared to ask Ida what she expected from Daniel if she found him. Ida carefully turned this over in her mind and then said, "I just have to see him one more time, to know if he's cruel, or if he's . . ." She paused. "Or if he's just beyond me."

Helen was watchful too. Anything in a uniform made her heart pound, anyone well dressed or driving an expensive car made her think of Richard. He came to be associated, in

Helen's mind, with the police. She was afraid of his blue eye with its black sickle. When he looked at her, he seemed to wipe her out. If she were to survive, she had to get away from his eyes.

In the summer heat, they rode on top of the cars. Their bodies hurt from holding on, their faces burned and chafed. Cinder got stuck under their eyelids, and they splurged on some goggles. But the cold weather nearly killed them, bedding down in a refrigerator car or in the bush by a fire, glad for the exhaustion that let them escape for a few hours. The trains were the bums' university. By starlight, on cold nights, flame from the boiler sprayed like red paint in the frosty air, the perpetual diagnosis of the world's sickness.

Sometimes Ida fell asleep while they talked and woke up screaming, with Helen's hand over her mouth in case she blew their cover. Ida said she saw people stripped and shaved, she saw wax and fire. In the dust, she drew stick figures laid in heaps. She felt ashamed of her dreams, but she couldn't stop them. The drone of the train tattooed itself on Ida's soul; she had to find protection, some religion. She questioned everyone, Had they seen a very tall, skinny man named Daniel? The men looked at her warily. And yes, of course, Daniel had been seen in Thunder Bay, Regina, Kapuskasing, Moose Jaw; Daniel was everywhere but here. She hadn't earned him. At last, she was infected with shame. Helen heard her muttering in German; she put her hand on Ida's forehead. "Shhhh," Helen said, "tell me."

They were riding on top. No moon, no light, clusters of men rolled up, sometimes three to a blanket, and one dog. Beside them lay a man so thin they could barely see his face, his eyes and cheeks reduced to shadow. His reedy voice drifted into their conversation as if it were something travelling in the air, like the smell of alfalfa mixed with burning garbage from the jungles they passed, and he said, or perhaps he said, "It's the Fascists." Ida turned to him. He was not Daniel. He looked at her through black sockets, eyeless, expressionless. Ida lay beside him with her face close to his. "Tell me about the Fascists," she asked him.

"*Gleichschaltung*. . . . They're joining . . . they're planning to take over Europe."

"*Gleichschaltung*," said Ida. She stared at the sky.

"What is it?" asked Helen. She was almost frozen with fear.

"It is an invitation to the end of the world. A command performance."

The train travelled quickly; it was night, and there were perhaps forty men with them. "But we're not alone," said Ida. And Helen thought, We are all alone, and this is our only hope, that we act alone. Helen had come to the trains through the leafy avenues of money, and she was frightened of what might happen if the rich joined with the rich, the poor with the poor, to fight for the government of each other. She would not be governed. She would fight like a cat against the restraints of government. She felt rage eating at her inside. It was worse than hunger.

CHAPTER SIX

WHEN IDA GAVE UP HOPE of finding her husband, it reduced her to ashes and finally forced her to reclaim herself as an entirely new woman. She lost her soft margin, her youthful faith in implicit goodness. She bounced back, tougher, sardonic. She and Helen laughed a lot, a slapstick sense of humour; life's one big kick in the butt.

Ida's speech was a hot pepper stuffed with quotations from Marx. She could be brutal and rude, but she got away with it because she was a walking satire and most people didn't want to be called bourgeois, whatever the hell that is when it's home. She needed a religion, something big and purposeful. So she became a Communist.

Three times during that year, they dropped off a freight car to see us for a short stay. They would casually walk into our yard, short and tall, gaunt men with purple shadows around their eyes, covered in bruises. Helen's long, thin hands descended from a beat-up jacket three sizes too small, and her pants stopped several inches short of her boot tops, so you could see her bony legs without socks. She sat down on the front steps and took off her boots, revealing her narrow feet, their finger-like toes blackened by dust and crooked from walking. Stretching happily, she'd smile at her dad and me, white teeth, a dirty face. The smell was so rank, she'd take her first bath outside in a tub in the yard, unabashed, desexed by starvation.

We fed them constantly. Our garden had a windbreak and was close enough to the river for irrigation, and we'd sold enough vegetables at the north-end market to keep the cow and a few chickens, so we weren't starving, though we didn't bother to seed wheat because prices hadn't come up much since hitting bottom in '32.

Richard would drop by often to see if we knew anything, had we heard. He'd look around carefully, casually. We were lucky for the first two visits; his timing was off. I was always edgy, though, and it felt ugly, hiding her from him. The more he looked for Helen, the more it became impossible for him to find her; the beam of light from his scrutiny was sending her farther and farther away. He was righteous and mad at first, though he affected more simple anxiety for her safety. I felt sorry for him and gave him coffee or a drink, and I could at least share his anxiety. He and I were talking so, one time, when he said, "She'd be better if she had a child."

He was getting into his car when he said this. We'd had a drink of Scotch.

"Oh," I said, "I don't know about that."

He nodded, convinced. "It would give her something. Other than herself."

"Well, that's a loving attitude, Dick."

"I'm a firm believer in family, Blondie." I'm sure I saw hatred in his face. "I'll never give up on her. I'm not that kind of man. Family is everything to me."

Third visit. Afternoon. Late summer, a drizzle, rain thin as radish seeds. Helen stood at the window, a slice of bread in one hand, a piece of cheese in the other, talking to Eli. Eli sat at the kitchen table watching her. He was somewhere past seventy years now, the old weathered barn of his body more ruined and more handsome than ever. He was still a big man, even if he did keel over a little and the parts of him missing were like holes in the barn roof. His beauty took your breath away. "If they can't speak English," he was saying, "if they're from all over, I can't picture how they can talk revolution, one to the other."

"Well, everybody talks about food mostly. Cake and soup and that. And sometimes their mothers. It's pretty easy to follow," she said, scratching her neck. We hadn't yet killed off all the fleas.

"Keep eating," I told her.

In this single thing, Helen was obedient. Chewing, she quietly added, "Gramma Alice would be happy as a pig in shit." She cheerfully swallowed the bread.

"Watch your language," said I, for old time's sake.

"A pig in goddamn shit. She would, eh, Mum? I think about her a lot. All the mess, everybody talking. She'd of loved it."

"Maybe. But she wouldn't want to be patron saint of a starvation train."

The fast approach of Richard's car, even the tires seemed high pitched and panicky. The three of us stiffened. Helen watched her husband slide out. He was very well dressed. She made a move as if to bolt, then stood frozen. Richard walked briskly towards the house. He saw her through the window. He stopped for a second and then kept coming at his quick pace. I let him in. He stood expectantly. "Well," he began, even now managing that half-smile. "You've cut your hair."

"I'm not going back with you," said Helen.

"You're very thin."

"I'll put it back on. See?" She indicated the cheese in her hand. She put it down on the table.

Richard looked nervously at Eli and me. I didn't want Richard nervous.

Helen said, "Go away, Richard."

Eli said, "Hush now, Helen. There's more to say than that. Have a seat, Richard."

He didn't take the chair, but entered farther into the room. Leaned against the kitchen cupboard and crossed his arms.

"There is nothing to say," said Helen.

"Calm down," said Richard. "You've got to calm down."

"No. I don't have to. I don't have to do anything."

"No one is making you do anything, Helen. I've always let you do whatever you like."

"You *let* me? Listen to me, Richard. I will do as I need to do."

"But now it's time you came home. It's not respectable. It's not right. You could get sick, if you're not sick already. You had an adventure. Now it's time to—what?—just grow up."

Helen looked so sad at that moment that Richard was encouraged. He went to her, took her hands between his. "I'm being loyal to you. Not many men would do that." He touched her face. "Where is *your* loyalty?"

It wasn't a question. It struck Helen. She avoided his eyes, but she said, "You would never understand. Please, leave me alone."

"I never thought you'd go that way," he said. "You're going nowhere. She's a little unbalanced these days, right, Blondie?" He looked at me for confirmation, which I declined to give him. I had so often had the same thought myself, but, damn it, in a different sense than Richard's. In many ways, Eli and I were proud of our daughter just then, scared but proud; it takes courage to lose your balance, to learn to fall. Richard continued, his confidence rising. "Get rested, come home. We'll make a few changes, if you're so unhappy."

"Just . . ." She broke away from him, backed away. "Just give me a few days. Then, maybe."

He shook his head. "You always expect too much." He sighed. "A few days. Blondie will look after you, will you?" He appealed to me. I gave my best poker face. He needed to leave on a high note. He did his best to walk out casually, the winner.

When he'd gone, we were quiet for some time. Eli looked upset, the way he used to, in the days when he couldn't look at Helen.

"Are you really going back to him?" I dared to ask.

She scratched, the tension easing out of her. "I'd rather be stuffed."

"He's not going to give up."

"Well," she said, "what can he do?"

We three thought about it, and though we couldn't come up with anything, Richard stuck with us like a bad debt.

CHAPTER SEVEN

"FELLA," SAID THE PRESBYTERIAN MINISTER to Ida while he scratched his hide (the fields they passed looked unseeded, straw-littered), "you're talkin' Moscow Excretio."

Ida squinted. "I hate money," she said. "That's not so hard to understand."

Helen, Ida, the minister named Ebenezer and a Spanish-looking kid, chronically impressed and speechless, sitting side by each atop a freight car.

"Ebenezer," said Helen, "can I ask you something personal?"

Ebenezer wriggled his bum like a warm scone in butter. He was among *the salt of the earth!*

"I've been sitting here listening to the way you talk," Helen said, "and I can't get a handle on who you are. I mean, you look like a Scot. You talk like a railway bull. But you act like, I don't know, you remind me of my grandmother Alice."

Ebenezer tipped his head, his eyes filled with tears. "Thank you, son," he said. He smiled, his teeth like pale church pews. "Is that where you got your wealth? Was it old money?"

Ida, who had had to pee for the past hour, blurted out, "Hell, no! It was her husband's—Oh . . ."

"My grandmother's husband's money, that's right. How'd you know?"

Ebenezer was satisfied. "You look like someone who could go home for dinner. Just say it's the cut of your jib. You're a strange piece of work. Why you'd throw away comfort to live a hard life is beyond my ken."

The rail line at that point ran close to the highway. Helen saw the yellow Packard, a sedate, purposeful car; she saw Richard's golden hair, his single-minded pursuit. The road was about a hundred yards away, but he sensed her, looked over at the train, looked right at her.

Ida said, "Are we going to slow down soon?" She crossed her legs, too *girl;* she really had to pee.

"Just go over the side," said the Spanish boy seated beside her. "Downwind," he said. His grin involved his whole neck and chest, a lopsided, quirky tension.

"Might. If I have to." Ida rolled a smoke, offered it to Helen. Helen was staring at her blue-eyed husband driving. Then the highway wound away behind some trees.

"I'll have one of those," said the boy. Accepted a light, said, "The name's Finito." Inhaled. That grin, white teeth, clear skin, black hair. "Know why?"

Ebenezer said, "You're of Spanish descent."

Finito burst into a laugh, slapped his knee, the overly demonstrative civility of very lonely people. "Everybody says that!"

Ida uncrossed, crossed, wondered if she'd hurt herself so she could never have any kids. Wondered if she'd ever *want* kids. Wondered if she'd be able to be a wife if she found Daniel now. Marriage is a feudal corruption. Finito smoked so fast he went pale. He'd left home in Portage la Prairie just a few days ago, was already so lonesome he didn't know if he could take it. "Yep," he said, "everybody thinks I'm Spanish."

Helen searched the bush for signs of highway, the yellow car. Ebenezer, again compelled by the refinement of Helen's face under the dirt, asked her, "You a Communist too?"

"Ukrainian!" cried Finito. "You never knew!"

"No," said Ida. "Never would've guessed."

"That's why they call me Finito," said Finito. "Someday I'm going to go there."

"I'm an anarchist," said Helen. It was the first time she'd ever said it. Was it the right name for the leopard that lived inside her?

"The Ukraine," said Ida. She found that when she talked, it relieved some of the pressure on her bladder.

"Spain!"

"Going to be a war there," said Ida.

"Good!" Then Finito aged a decade, the bitterness crabbing his handsome features. "At least I'd have a job."

"An anarchist," said Ebenezer. "Now that's a rare bird."

They were on their way to Regina to meet up with a huge bumming parade, about fourteen hundred men riding the rails to Ottawa to protest the conditions in the relief camps. The On to Ottawa Trek. Bums on strike. The rail line was suddenly littered with RCMP. They were coming into Regina when Helen spotted the yellow Packard. It was parked at the Exhibition Grounds. Ida was unbuttoning her fly even as she hit the ground running.

Helen and Ida had just dropped into a trap.

Regina was a central depot for the RCMP. The railyards were situated so they could be closed off. So Regina is where this strike, this On to Ottawa Trek was going to end.

The trek had been stalled in Regina for more than two weeks. Ida emerged from the bushes. They made their way to the town's Market Square. There was going be a big bum-rally with a lot of galvanic speeches about the right to decent work and pay. The police were on their way to Market Square too. The RCMP had just decided they had enough evidence to arrest seven of the trek's leaders, on what charges I don't know, but remembering what had happened to Bobby Russell in 1919, I assume they simply called these men subversives and that was that.

The RCMP charged out in the midst of the speeches, and everybody started running. Then the local police joined this mess, armed with baseball bats. Ida was one of the first to pick up a rock and chuck it at a cop.

Helen dragged Ida away. "Let go of my fucking arm." Hate poured out of Ida like electric light. She was less than five feet tall. Starving that year as a hobo had made Ida stocky, made her muscled and heavy of bone. She moved like Jack Dempsey. She pivoted out of Helen's grip and leapt in the air, coming down with a man's throat in her hands; she hung on, and you could see the holes in her boot soles when she kicked at the air while the guy spun circles in the dirt, trying to fling her off. Helen caught her wrist as she wound up to hit him with a brick. Ida let go, so the brick fell on his face. Helen held Ida under her arms, pulled her on top of herself, and Ida struggled against her till she could turn around. "You fucking bastard,"

Ida said, and punched Helen in the jaw with a fist like a small stone. Helen had slow anger, a pilot light; ignited, it never went out. She didn't forgive, ever.

One man died. Det. Charles Millar. He was hit from behind with a piece of wood. Smashed his skull. The rioters hit the cops who were trying to carry Millar to an ambulance. The cops got beaten with lead pipes, wood bats. Cops on horseback beat the strikers with clubs. This happened for about six hours. Trekkers hid behind streetcars, threw rocks at the police; it rained glass. The police shot at the rioters. Real bullets. This was a riot, mind you, not a civil war. Trekkers hit by a bullet in the foot, in the back, a bullet in the stomach, in the face. Ambulances pulled up and hauled away the injured men. Ida reclaimed Jerusalem; she proved herself a man of steel, and finally, exhausted, let herself be carried back to the Exhibition Grounds and fell asleep in the hay. Finito had watched. The riot was torture for him. He remained dead pale and quiet.

Finito misunderstood this country. He thought we knew what we were doing. Each side. He believed that we had a plan. Scared him half to death.

Helen thought she saw the war beneath the surface. She thought, Scratch the surface and a war bleeds out, and it's always there. Helen saw this, the civil war under the skin. It is safe only at the centre of the battle, where the danger is not hidden beneath the false surface of peace. She believed that, deep in her gut.

But the riot had all the reality of the boondoggle road. It was an occasion. There are so many innocent people. Almost everybody.

Just before dawn, in the hours after the riot, Helen strolled through the Exhibition Grounds, fingering an unlit cigarette, and watched the remaining Trekkers sleep, still dressed, wearing their boots. *War is chronic.* There is something deeply painful in the look of a man curled in the fetal position with his boots on, both hands tucked between his knees, the blood in his ear dried black, blood cupped between his praying palms.

Grandmother Alice had taught Helen to listen to languages she doesn't speak. Helen listened to the men breathing.

For the first time since she had left Richard, her own hands ached for her loom. It was a rare spasm of nostalgia. For reverie, for privacy, the luxury of soft surfaces, the illusion of depth. Part of her missed being kept. She even missed his jealousy. The riot left her with a hangover. The biggest building at the Exhibition Grounds had become a minimum-security jail. Ida, with a wealth of hatred that surprised Helen, had already tried to escape. The riot had triggered something in them both. Rage, pure and simple, ran like booze through their veins from the distillery of their hearts. Ida and Finito lay on their backs, hound muscles twitching. Helen inhaled the funk of hay and livestock, the stink of blood and meat, and then went outside to smoke.

Richard stood against the building; she saw his white collar. He barely moved, only his eyes followed her. Seemed he carried a shield, a field around him. "Are you satisfied?" he asked. His voice as soothing as gun oil. And something erotic, a suggestion of her promiscuity. As if her place in this mess could only be sexual. Her homesickness of a few minutes ago was irrelevant here. He kept her out.

"How are you going to live?" he asked.

A few days later, the authorities put them on a passenger train to Winnipeg. According to Ida's analysis, it was a Fascist coup. "Rotten Bastard" Bennett had outfoxed everybody. The Trekkers had vented in the wide, empty Liberal province of Saskatchewan. It was safe to send the boys home, or to whatever tree the hobo crows might land on next. Ida and Helen got two tickets to Winnipeg.

"Where are you going, Finito?" asked Ida.

Finito shrugged. "I don't give a shit," he said.

Ida squinted at him. The three of them stood there, scratched their head lice. After a bit, Ida went back to the long table where the commissioner of labour, fellow named Malloy and not a bad man at that, was handing out train tickets. Ida elbowed her way to the front of the line and said to Malloy, in a no-nonsense manner, "I need a ticket for my brother."

Malloy looked up from under his hat at Ida. Helen got the impression that Ida didn't fool him with her disguise. Malloy stared at her and at Finito, not unkindly with his brown eyes. Then he rubbed his jaw with one hand and, with the other, handed Ida a ticket. "Here's for your brother," he said.

"Thanks," said Ida, kind of softly.

"That's okay," said Malloy and nodded at her. Somehow that was the kindest transaction Helen had seen in years.

They had three tickets to Winnipeg. It was the summer of '35.

They walked back south from the railway yards, separated mid-town. Ida was taking Finito home with her. Helen grabbed Ida's arm, and nodding towards Finito, she asked, "You going to tell him?"

Ida didn't answer. She took off her cap. She tipped back her head. "That's what home smells like in summer." She smiled lazily at Finito. "It smells like fresh-cut grass." Finito looked. When Ida took her next step, it was as a woman. Finito's eyes slid sideways; he kept his cool, watched her for about a hundred yards. Her hips grew round, her breasts grew big. When she turned and called out to him, "Hey, Finito! There's a meeting at the Labor Temple!" Finito ran after her, slowed, shuffled, then ran again.

Helen stood alone awhile. It did smell of lawn clippings. The modesty of the yellow sunshine on the grass could only be the daylight of home.

CHAPTER EIGHT

SHE WALKED THE REST OF THE WAY BACK to the village at St. Norbert without rest. The pilot light burned inside her, a cool blue flame. At the bridge over the Rivière Sale, she stopped. She was only five miles from home, but she stopped.

To the west, the quiet greenery surrounding the Trappist monastery.

The land looked fat (an illusion). In full leaf, the elms resembled florets of broccoli. My daughter sat smoking on the high road looking down to the woods. Every time she looked at the spire of the cathedral, blond stone rising above the trees, a sanguine desire surged through her limbs. She sat at the road-side like a monarch on milkweed, feeding on the pleasure inspired by the forest and church spire, the haven of the monk. She thought, *He* is in there.

She'd kept him in mind. All year, every time somebody turned her down when she tried to bum a dime, the monk was there like a good promise. She knew damn well she'd messed with him. So be it. Treat desire with respect. She thought about Richard. His fidelity. His hatred.

Helen lifted her sweaty pack and began the last five miles, dying to see her mother. After a time, dizzy with hunger and heat, she saw the figure of a man a hundred yards beyond, and she knew him from the way the fields on either side rippled and folded. This would be the man who *listens.* His brown robe blew in the wind. He must be very hot inside it. The heat gave the illusion of his walking backwards; he approached her with the oddly distracted attitude of a man wholly focused.

Within hearing distance, the flagging of robes and the profoundly silent voice of a Trappist monk. Brother Bill (for that was his name) was completely transparent. When the wind blew, it blew *with* him. Like water. In his hands he carried a wooden box. It was large but appeared to be lightweight because he carried it before him like an offering. Helen put her hands out to receive it, otherwise he might not have stopped. Maybe he didn't recognize her. She'd had a fresh brush cut, and she must've lost twenty pounds since their first encounter. So there they were, chewing dust, roadblocking one another by accident. But when he looked into Helen's face, it was like his whole soul took a picture. The shock shook the ravens in the dead oak half a mile away. It was seriously portentous. He read her face, his own expression rippling with kind amusement. He had the most virile kindness.

She reached to take the box from his arms. "Thank you," she said. That's when something occurred that was either a miracle or simply a delight. Cabbage butterflies are common things. I've many times seen a half-dozen fly in a loose group. They keep to paths, maybe from growing up in a garden. Now, like a kite into the wind, a trail of them flew from behind the monk. There were a thousand white butterflies in clusters of four or five, so at first you might notice a small bunch and then, as your eyes tuned in, more and then more, until there was only a wave out of particles, a peaceful, wavering, dancing movement. Helen and the monk, joined by the wooden box, an edge of which each clasped, stood their ground and the butterflies flew over their heads, twenty feet in the air. Because there were a thousand and because they wavered unevenly, patches of several and then several more, this passage took half an hour or longer. The monk had patience. Helen, desire. Neither noticed the passage of time. Though Helen was aware of a marvellous prolongation.

When she thought they'd passed, she was again conscious of the heat bearing down on them, her thirst, the high-pitched exhaustion of land and body. The monk didn't move. He was a relaxed man. He could drop into a pocket of time as if it was a divine manhole. Standing face to face with the most beautiful woman in the world (derelict, rented out, but rub a little, see her shine), he listened for the last butterflies, which soon appeared and flitted overhead and away.

She thought to look at the box between them. One side of it was a sliding glass panel. Inside, three inches of soil and two jars filled with plants. Otherwise empty.

"What's that?" she asked.

He hesitated before answering. "Hibernating chrysalides." He balanced an edge upon his knee and laid his head upon his palm. "Sleeping butterflies." Something Oriental in his movements, a blond, brown-eyed, talcum-powder-complexioned Canadian with the soul of a Chinese ancient. Pied piper to cabbage butterflies. She wanted to join his congregation.

She returned the box to him. Backed away. Wiped the sweat out of her eyes with her sleeve. He looked at her, worried, and walked on towards the junction to the monastery. He half turned and nodded, indicating she should follow. By the time they made the footbridge, she was singing "Brother, Can You Spare a Dime?" Crooned like Bing Crosby, another tenor.

He could've approached the church through the back, but he chose instead to take her to the front gate, to make her arrival official. Lots of transients sought sanctuary with the Trappists in those days; they put a strain on the Cistercian solitude.

They bypassed the stone church, where even male visitors were not allowed, and went directly to the guest house, one of those white Catholic buildings with the green mansard roof, beautiful as a loaf of French bread. It was a building like the land around it, innocently exposed. Their shoes were loud on the wood floors, the doors shut firmly and sunlight poured through the tall windows, open and buzzing with flies. Five monks were having tea and reading in the guests' refectory. It was cool down there, with a mud floor and high stone-silled windows. Light like amber. There was a cookstove in one corner, but it was unlit. Several monks sitting; they smiled slightly and nodded hello. Brother Bill put the butterfly cage on one of the long, low tables, slid open the glass and searched the soil with the tips of his fingers. He removed a chrysalis, which is the jewel of burnt sugar we uncover with the early planting of peas. It lay on the palm he opened under Helen's nose. That repugnance and intrigue of embryonic forms, shocking for a woman who, while not a young debutante, was virginal to the glistening aspects of life. Her disgust was equalled by the acute desire to pop the thing into her mouth.

One of the monks cleared his throat and turned a page. The room was so quiet, this seemed as loud as laughter. A black cat leapt to the table and was idly petted by the reading monk, who poured a bit of his milky tea into his saucer without once looking up from his book. Brother Bill was on his hands and knees on the earth floor recovering yet another box, which when opened revealed a bed of sphagnum moss, that grey-green stuff, not a local fauna, into which he plunged his insect prize, returning the box to its spot in a cool corner of the cave-like room. He stood, sweeping his hands together with a decelerating motion and looking steadily at Helen. She began again to doubt that he recognized her. His white hands and head set off from his brown robes glowed in the shaded room. The sweeping slowed till his palms were pressed together before him. Still he looked at Helen.

She thought she might bolt if he said anything. But he put the fingers of his right hand to his lips, as if blowing a kiss. Somehow she knew it was a question: *Are you hungry? Yes,* she nodded. With his left hand, Brother Bill made some flying motions, and again Helen knew: *Do you like barley soup? Yes,* she nodded. *Very much.* Brother Bill smiled, pleased.

A rather large monk was sitting near by. A man at least six-foot-two, with a full frame and an untonsured, naturally balding head, he looked cultured, though he wore the brown robes of the lay brother rather than the white vestments of the Trappist fathers. This pleasantly authoritative man grew aware of their conversation and rose to indicate to Helen that she should be seated. Then he went to the cookstove and filled a bowl from a pot there and, returning, humbly offered it to her. With one hand he touched her shoulder, and with the other hand he said, *Enjoy!* The large monk went back to his book, one hand opening and closing quickly in a gesture that clearly expressed, *Peace be with you.*

It was the best soup ever made, thick, with firm slices of

carrot and herbs and tiny islands of fat. She felt a small bony body sit close, and glanced quickly at the monk who had taken the seat beside her before losing her way again in her meal. Little, a big French nose and an attractive, prominent mouth with thin lips, a bit of a gibbon monkey, he cocked his head and raised his neat eyebrows, indicating that the soup was of his making. *Did she like it?* Oh yes oh yes oh yes. He grinned, and with his hands, he said, *You should taste our cheese.* The bigger monk sensed this and looked up from his book with a gentle remonstrance: *You should not boast, but I must admit, our cheese is awfully good, especially the Tomme de Beaumont, that earthy, pungent stuff. Oh,* said the French monk's hands, *not at all! It is our Fleur d'Hermitage that is the best!* The big monk nodded at the little monk somewhat condescendingly, and with both hands, he said, *Ahh, you simpleton, I forgive you.*

Brother Bill sat down with an eloquent sigh. The big monk (but Helen, rejuvenated by the soup, dared to put her hand on his sleeve, a gesture that said, *Please tell me your name,* and the big monk's gentle smile said, *Brother Joe,* or something simple like that), Brother Joe, nodded in agreement. *Yes,* his hands said, *it is very sad.* And all the monks (even the two who had turned their backs to read) nodded with the silence that is the essence of compassion. *What is sad?* gestured Helen, the newly fed man. Everyone's eyes went to Brother Bill, and then they looked away guiltily because it is wrong to think of one man as one man. You could see that Brother Bill himself would not survive the delusion of singularity. He seemed to evaporate, to send his cells outwards till he was light, almost invisible. It is generous, Helen saw, and dexterous, to be so light of soul.

She fell in love as permanently as someone who looks directly at the sun, scars his retina.

A tiny cry escaped her. A womanly cry.

Five monks started half out of their seats. Thinking fast, Helen wiped her nose, horked eloquently. It took away a lot of the tension. But the authoritative Brother Joe and the small French gibbon—though they didn't stare—knew something was amiss at the monastery. They were discomfited. Helen held her breath. She overacted, scratched her armpit. It was almost too late.

Brother Bill came to the rescue. With uncharacteristic egoism, he told with his hands of the monastery's difficulties with the municipality, which was currently suing them for back taxes. *Protestants,* said the gibbon with his small, fine hands. Brother Joe chastised him with a glance, but you could tell he agreed. *Godless Protestants and their land swindles.* Outside, summer thunder began to roll and the approaching storm bruised the yellow light of the cellar refectory. *What will you do?* asked Helen's hands (she was getting the hang of it). A Gallic shrug. Brother Bill waved, *Give them the land.* And Brother Joe's hands, as if unwilling to say it, closed at his heart, and then his arms extended in a gesture that a father might make when his child is ripped from his grasp. *Give away our beautiful land that is our bread and our delight, over which we have toiled, where even when the crops failed and the animals got sick, we could listen to the aspens and the silence of the sun; they take away the land we listen to, so it is not only our bread they take from us, these Protestants from the suburbia of Fort Garry; they will make us deaf!*

Suburban Protestants? Richard! Helen raised her fist, the

salute of solidarity, and brought it down upon the table, jumping her spoon and bowl, and with all her might, she cried out, "No!"

The two discreetly reading monks quickly fled the room.

Brother Bill, Brother Joe and the gibbon looked at Helen with shy astonishment. The gibbon spoke first. "You are offended for our sake!" And Brother Joe said, "It is indeed very painful, but we'll survive!" And Brother Bill said, "Ahhhh, it is wonderful to complain!"

At last, they spoke, all the hurt and anxiety tumbled out: vilification, accusation, the purgative of blame. They rose into speech like fish breaking the surface of the river.

But their chorus brought into focus one unavoidable fact: their gracious visitor was beautiful. Inspired by pity, Helen took on her most dangerous, least fraudulent role: not only beautiful, but an anarchist, a tormented and tormenting Woman.

The gibbon was charmed, charmed and beguiled. He tipped his head and smiled. Brother Bill's skin was breathing in his new future. He had that newly born look of glad greeting, humbled by love. The thunder that had been rolling over like a piano on wheels suddenly crashed overhead. It started to rain. The stone refectory was as a bean composed of two hemispheres, North/South, East/West, I/You, Helen/Bill. The room swirled with weather and energy and the gibbon and Brother Joe looked at them and *they knew,* and the gibbon was happy even while he was scandalized, delighting in beauty and recognizing the imperatives of love.

But Brother Joe, tall and profound, grew solemn. Once he saw Helen's beauty, he would not look at her again. He stared gravely at the stone wall. It hurt Helen keenly. She wondered why she felt the need to please him. She tried to meet his eye (he had stopped speaking, his posture once again posed for listening, and his dignity filled Helen with yearning for his comradeship), but she was out of bounds, cut off.

The storm was upon them. A downpour that quickly flooded the window wells and streamed down the walls, and it smelled of electricity and growing grass. In thunder and lightning, they heard the sound of running footsteps, a whole army descending the stairs. Word had reached the prior, a woman was on the grounds. Helen stood, waiting for eviction. For some reason, she felt terribly afraid. The running monks were descending the stairs. Her heart pounded, her body shook; it was not that they would hurt her physically, but suddenly she knew why she was so scared: *They will turn me into a woman!* She gasped in terror.

The gibbon took her hand and put it into Bill's—*Go now! Run!*—urgently, ushering them to the east end of the room. Bewildered, they followed. It looked as if they were walking into a wall, but the gibbon placed his palm against it and shoved, and it swung on great hinges and he pushed them inside. *Go!* he indicated to Bill. *It will take you to that stone altar by the Rivière!* And with four kisses and a last fond look at Brother Bill, he closed the door behind them.

They emerged from the tunnel by the Virgin's altar and slipped past her blue statue and out into the pouring rain. They ran through darkness and stark white light, past the rotting woodshed (behind which a lone monk was dancing; a strong old man, he indicated, *Shhhhhh,* and then, *Joy be to lovers*), over the dangling footbridge, through the woods and away.

After many miles running to the east, they stumbled over a fallow field and got hopelessly stuck in the gumbo. Blue mud climbed up Brother Bill's robes, turning him into living pottery. They slogged on, overcome by shyness. At last, the monk could walk no longer. Encased in livid gumbo, his robes weighing at least two hundred pounds, feet of brick, bone weary, he came to a stop. Helen was a clay stick woman, gasping for breath, she said, "Let's . . . go . . . on. . . ." Bill shook his head. The rain had stopped, but heat swelled up between purple earth and purple sky, which sent ice-hot twigs of silent lightning, ominously silent, long shoots of electrical juice sending roots. He shook his head again. His breath came in sobs. She turned around to him. They were in a field that, in years before, had been sown with alfalfa and was now mixed with clover, white moons of dandelion, clutches of thistle. He shuddered.

She went to him and tugged at his robes; she thought they might pull him right into the earth. Her hands fumbled at his chest, seeking buttons, some way out. It didn't occur to her till much later that she was desperately trying to undress a monk. Somehow he slipped away from the rough fabric, and it opened like an acorn or the skin of the chrysalis. He emerged pale and streaked with mud.

The lightning flicked the ground, a near miss, no sound. His first sight of a woman's breast, white alabaster veined with blue, his first touch, as lake water moving in his hand, his first knowledge, bold, her thirsty kisses. She travelled all over, uttering her joy. His blond face, his body wrapped in rain. A sandpiper soared smoothly by, whistling its long, scared note. They were standing, a lightning rod, and just before it struck, they pulled back from a kiss and looked at each other closely, eye to eye, and then, with that leader stroke, leapt in the air still joined, straight up, united; they flew forty feet high, their nuptials in lily white light.

Their dreams that night were of baptisms, mud baths, mustard plaster, healing poultices. They slept as their ancestors before them, but much longer, forty-eight hours, waking once in the middle of their second night to feel themselves joined by love and by Manitoba gumbo, a casement of silky mud. They heard the sociable chittering of the otters near by and knew they must be near the river. The mosquitoes died entering the force field that surrounded them. Helen no longer had fleas. They slept in thistle as soft as a bed of down.

They were awakened by ten wild turkeys. Wild turkeys stand about two and a half feet tall. They have brown feathers and bright red wattles. Some say that they are the souls of dead monks. Whether this is true or not, no one knows. But it's obviously a great privilege to be woken up this way, by the stolid paunches of turkeys, standing there. Quietly. It was still raining, just a little.

CHAPTER NINE

FINITO JOINED THE UKRAINIAN LABOR TEMPLE, where his greatest difficulty was proving that he was indeed Ukrainian (a feat he
achieved with his stomach, his fondness for *stoudniak,* pickled
pigs' feet).

But it's strange that by the trick of his good looks, he would
develop a loyalty to a foreign country that would lead him to war
to fight for its freedom. He was a street kid who had gained a
political education from the misery of riding the rails. His idealism was a byproduct of youth, but Finito's particular brand of
naïveté was the accident of a handsome face. He was inspired by
his own Mediterranean charm, and he loved Spain as if he'd
been cross-pollinated with her. Ukrainian by blood, Spanish by
instinct. He dreamed in Spanish, though he didn't speak a word
of the language. Still, he retained a stomach-stubborn fidelity
to Ukrainian food.

Finito so believed in freedom that he gave it away, assum-
ing it would be returned to him in kind. He had absolute faith
in the success of the coming revolution. He misunderstood our
local rich; he thought they had a political ideology (which of
course they did, but not one that would stoop to *opposition,*
with all the necessary self-definitions; nothing other than the
dictates of *common sense*). In this, he was very European. He
was prepared to sacrifice his life for the proletariat. When Ida

took him to see Richard Anderson at his mansion, Finito thought that they were going there to assassinate him.

Ida took him along for the purpose of dunning Richard for money. Einstein was at Princeton by then, and she wanted to bring him to Winnipeg to tell everyone what was going on in Germany. She figured she could embarrass Richard into coughing up the costs. Hitler had reoccupied the Rhineland and was soon to turn his eye to Czechoslovakia. His army was getting big; he'd created an air force, and now there was the black-shirted *Schutzstaffel,* the SS. Richard was a bigot, sure, but he was also a WASP with colonial pretensions, so Ida thought that he'd be fretting over British security. On the way to his house, she daydreamed his apology, Richard looking sheepish, trying to make amends. He wouldn't know anything about Einstein's science, but like everybody, he would know he was a Jew. It was the perfect way for Richard to hide his bigotry, to appear generous and broad-minded.

Finito loved the Anderson house. He wondered what they would use it for—perhaps a convalescent home or a nursery school—after the revolution. Maybe the headquarters for the People's Army. He was so preoccupied with this when Richard answered the door (Richard had caught Higgins-James-whatever stealing from the liquor cabinet and had to let the man go) that Richard thought he was casing the place for theft.

Ida was polite. "This is Mr. Richard Anderson, Finito. Shake the man's hand."

Finito smiled at Ida indulgently and then shook Richard's hand with an air of such revolutionary fatalism that Richard thought he was pitying him for losing Helen and his cold dignity became absolutely Germanic. He invited them into the sunroom

at the back of the house. Ida had pictured this conversation taking place in Richard's office; they hadn't been home long, and she
still retained many male assumptions. She felt ashamed of Helen's
elaborate murals. She stiffened, remembering Daniel. Ida's husband had not come home, had not contacted her, and though she
had resigned herself to this, still she wished that she'd understood
his strange music, and she wished that he had given her another
chance. She was as uncomfortable as Richard was (seated on a
Louis XV chair that had somehow escaped Helen's modernist
redecorating), with all the mannerisms of a Female Visit. It felt
especially unhappy in this female-less house.

Richard assumed that Helen had sent Ida. He had not
grieved for Helen. He would not. It was likely neurasthenia, of
a sexual sort, enticing Helen to low life and dirt. Helen had
probably sent this Jew to get money from him. He was not so
much hurt as disappointed.

Only Finito was relaxed; as a revolutionary soldier, he had
to be calm and alert during a crisis. He was about to witness his
first political assassination. He felt only love; as the hunter loves
the hunted, so Finito loved Richard. He looked at Richard
gravely.

"You know—," Ida began.

"Of course," said Richard.

"—Einstein," said Ida.

"Oh," said Richard.

"He's in Princeton now, you know."

"Great rugby team. Wonderful school."

"The Nazis ran him out of Germany."

"Top-notch. You're close to New York."

"We'd like to bring him here."

"Einstein."

"And we need your help."

"Who is 'we'?" Richard looked at Finito. Finito was gazing at Richard passionately. "Is something the matter?" Richard asked.

Finito nodded slightly.

Ida said, "The professor is very busy. And some say he's very shy. We need to offer him . . . something."

Richard met Finito's eye. Finito's smile was sad and Spanish. God, I hate queers, thought Richard.

Ida stood up. Richard could feel Finito's eyes upon him, and he crossed his legs, took his silver cigarette case from his jacket pocket, removed a cigarette and tapped its end, put it in his mouth and, without looking, was reaching for the crystal lighter when his hand touched Finito's. Finito was thinking, This is the man's last cigarette! and he held out the lighter with great ceremony. Richard felt their electric touch. He turned his attention to Ida; she would be one of those women who turn into men when they age. "Tell her to go to hell," he said.

Ida knew immediately. "Tell her yourself." Then, "We're not getting along that well these days."

"Comrade Ida punched Comrade Helen in the jaw," Finito explained. "It is difficult for a Communist and an anarchist to remain friends. It is very difficult. They love each other, but Comrade Helen never forgives." His heart pounded after his long speech.

Ida said, "She's not involved with this. She's been . . . otherwise occupied."

"She is expecting a child with Bill, the ex-monk!" said Finito. It was wonderful to live at such a stratospheric level. His handsome nostrils flared. A publishing house! That's what we'll put in here!

Richard tweezered his cigarette; he slipped his fine Italian shoe from his heel, dangling it from his toe. The pain burned in his veins.

"I'm sorry," said Ida.

Smoking, Richard shook his head. Finito realized he'd made a mistake. He suddenly felt homesick for Spain. I don't like Canadians, he thought.

"We'll go," said Ida.

Richard rose automatically to usher them out. At the front door, she turned to him. "Will you give our cause some consideration?"

"No," said Richard. He was going to go to sleep. Finito was already down the front walk. It was a desperately ordinary day. Richard looked down into Ida's brown eyes. "You think I'm stupid, don't you. Einstein was run out of Germany because his so-called science is soft. He's iffy. Now is not the time for iffy. He'll upset people. The market doesn't need it. I don't need it. Now's the time for clear thinking and clear people."

"Richard." He flinched to hear his own name. Ida was too familiar. She stood close to him, looking up. "Something terrible is happening. This man . . ." Richard tugged at his ear, squinting, though it was overcast. "This man is evil!"

Richard did not believe in "evil." He stood coldly.

Ida, tone-deaf, persisted. "He's not going to stop with Czechoslovakia. He'll take it all. We've got to stop him."

"Envy makes people small," said Richard, sizing her up. "It's a tough world, Ida, I'm sure you agree. Not a place for weaklings. I'm not afraid of strong men. I like a success. Christ, Hitler's turned that country around. Three years ago, they couldn't borrow a dime. Now? They're the strongest in Europe. Three years. Now tell me you don't admire that."

Ida shrugged and turned to go, careless of herself, mumbling at her own feet, "Poland's next, then Denmark and Norway." She was talking all the way down his leafy driveway, all the way down to the street, where Finito joined her like a kid embarrassed by an eccentric mother (and only six months minus ten minutes ago, he thought she was sexy; subtract six months plus ten minutes, and he thought she was a man). "He'll make friends with the Soviets, the Italians, the Fascists in Spain. He'll take Holland, Belgium, France. You'll see. He wants Britain too." She was so mad she thought she'd faint. From the street, she shook her fist at him where he stood on his stone portico, wearing his smoking jacket and that half-smile. Ida yelled at him, "You fucking idiot! You arrogant lackey!" Richard's gardener heard the racket and came to peer at Ida. Ida saw the gardener. "And you!" she cried. "Slave!" She stopped. Finito was walking ahead a little ways. She followed him, grief-stricken, exhausted. The great houses were not listening. "Slaves," she muttered. "Even the rich. Slaves."

CHAPTER TEN

IN THIS COUNTRY WE HAVE TWO RELIGIONS: Winter and Summer. Our doctrine of Winter is stern and dutiful, an Old Testament faith in the laws of Cold Night. But Bill, an ex-monk now, was decidedly of the Summer faith. We could hear it in his laugh, we could see it in his wonderful feet. Then we would think, No wonder he became a monk, with a laugh like that, with his fat square feet, it's too delicious!

Helen wore a dress the colour of bluebells, her black hair grew fast and she was the most pregnant woman the world has known for many centuries. She did not divorce Richard or marry Bill. She would never be owned again. She often felt happy, brilliantly so.

She was deceptively tall and he was deceptively short. When they waltzed, and they did, enamoured, they were of equal stature, she in her Raphael dress and he in the white pyjamas that had replaced his brown monk's robe. He became famous in St. Norbert. Everyone trusted the man who—though he might have left the church—conducted his life with simplicity, in elegant poverty, a celebrant of modest things: a well-carved wooden spoon, a candlestick.

And the baby grew in her womb. But there was a darkness in Helen's light, like the moon's path across the sun. Her happiness was a camouflage. Now that she was in her mid-thirties, her beauty was at its height. The air surrounding her seemed to hesitate, withheld. Bill no doubt was capable of seeing ultraviolet rays; he recognized his love by this shine. So their union was the garden in a desert. But Helen never lived in only one place at one time.

April. Dirty snow remained in the willow shoots. It didn't flood at all that year. The riverbank was a torte of sand, clay and roots, and the sun was already hot. Ida and Finito appeared in the old beat-up Ford I'd given them, looking for Helen and Bill, so I directed them down to the riverside, where they'd gone off for one of their gently sporadic conversations.

Ida lumbered through the path to the "dock" (yet another construction of oil drums and pine), her face beaded with sweat. She had revived her shabby fur coat. She launched herself onto the platform, tipping icy water over Helen's and Bill's backsides, and she handed Helen yet another pamphlet on "The Tasks of the Revolutionary Trade Union Movement." Finito followed, careful to stay dry, a prairie boy after all.

Helen looked wearily at the pamphlet. She and Ida were at odds, partly because Helen felt that the Communists were only helping Hitler gain ever more power in Germany. Helen had a seething hatred of Fascism, which she shared best with Finito, because Finito was frankly obsessed by the prospect of war against the Fascists in Spain. Together they spent hours talking about Franco, their fearful fascination bringing them so close to the events in Europe that, sometimes overhearing them, I would imagine they were gossiping about nasty friends. Helen had an aversion to broad strokes; she insisted on details, the pennies that derail mass movements. The anarchists in Spain had not yet joined the coalition with the Communists; Spain was still the only place on earth where an anarchist army (a fission) could fight for liberation. And Helen was growing ever more uncomfortable almost anywhere on earth.

Ida insisted on being "reasonable." Helen's resentment (she could still feel the impact of Ida's blow) was not reasonable, so according to Ida, it did not exist. Helen was *extremely* forgiving, but her ideals were almost savage. She had to forgive all the time, just to get through the day. Ida was always showing up like this, with a book, to stare Helen down and talk about "the larger issues." Why the hell does larger mean truer? At any time, Helen could think about her own jaw and feel Ida's little fist there, like a cyst.

"I saw Richard," Ida announced, looking at them blandly.

Helen nervously checked the path.

Ida shook her head. "Don't worry. He'll leave you alone now. Poor bugger. Next thing you know, he'll be contributing editor of *Deutsche Zeitung.*" Finito laughed his quirky laugh. He adored foreign expressions. "Anyway," Ida said, sighing, "he knows about the baby now. Finito told him." Now Ida laughed while Finito looked anxiously at Helen. "So obviously you won't be bothered by him any more."

The heat pressed down on Helen. Bill pursed his lips, an extravagant show of displeasure.

"In fact," said Ida, "I imagine Richard thinks you're *cured*. He was always talking about getting you *with child.*"

"Why don't you ever shut up?" asked Helen.

Ida would not accept personal prejudice. "Oh, come on,

Helen. It is too funny. *Kirche und Kinder,* all that. You're the perfect wife now. Just not his. Don't you have any sense of humour any more? Or do you just—what?—produce milk." She nudged Helen's arm. She missed Helen really: she wanted her buddy back. "Come on," she said again, "there is a certain *divine* justice in it."

Bill softened, tipped his head. You can hear a river, even on a windless day.

Helen had been more or less holding her breath ever since Ida hit her. So. Richard would leave her alone. And go his way, into the New World, like all the happily prosperous burghers in Winnipeg.

"I got a letter from Daniel's uncle," said Ida. She found it increasingly difficult to speak of personal matters.

"Does he know where Daniel is?" Helen asked.

Ida shook her head. "No, no, nothing like that." She reached inside her coat for her tobacco. "He's from the German side. There's Zimmermans in Russia, Poland; this side stayed in Germany." She withdrew two cigarettes already rolled. Lit Helen's. "His son was killed by the Nazis. Some kind of street brawl. They said he was drunk."

"Oh," Helen breathed. "Ida."

"Well, we have to do something. Obviously. So I thought we could bring Einstein here. He could give a talk or something. People just don't know. Or they don't care. Richard sure doesn't give a shit. Pardon my German," she added, to Bill.

"I could talk to him," said Helen.

"You!" Ida laughed bitterly. She touched Helen's belly. "I think you lost that vote, Mama."

Helen took a deep drag of her cigarette. Ida was right. It was irrevocable. How he must hate her. Helen felt that old impulse to go towards the war zone. She nervously touched Bill, who sat quietly beside her. But she was pinned to her fear of Richard.

———

HELEN'S CHILD, MY GRANDDAUGHTER, was born in May 1936, just as Italy occupied Ethiopia. Conceived in July, the baby took a full ten months to be born (there was a wild turkey for each month of gestation), abiding in utero the contrary gospels of the two religions: the dance of Summer (as well as the poignant agnosticism of Fall) and the no-dancing of Winter. A little girl. Stalled till mid-May. It would turn out to be a typical move, a natal pattern in which she would persist all her life. An innately a-theological child, deeply irreligious, and fixed to the cusp. They named her Dianna.

She was born with her eyes wide open, solemn and atten-tive, as if what she was seeing for the first time was a confirma-tion of some earlier appraisal. One of those refined babies, slender and long of digit, her narrow face dominated by dis-cerning eyes. She almost never cried, but she rarely slept. Such a degree of consciousness filled her father with awe. She would lie for an hour in Bill's arms while they stared at one another, Bill stroking the space between her eyebrows. He began to carry her around in a sling he strung at his chest.

Helen walked beside them. She was thoroughly baptized in love for Dianna, immersed in the extremity of such love. She began to worry that the child wouldn't love her back. Dianna had such a noncommittal gaze. Helen decided that she favoured her father. She felt, with increasing panic, that she was essentially invalid. Despite the love that seared itself to her bones, Helen yearned for her pre-baby days, when she knew her own edge. She was melting into a sea of milk.

Anarchy meant for Helen an active and prolonged extinction of her own counterfeit character. She was always at war with herself, and she could ask no one for confirmation. Her love for Bill was profoundly imbued with respect for his solitude. She felt that she too had to be solo, to be entirely responsible for her own life. In her days as a man, the pain of hunger, the occasional fear she'd felt aboard the trains, all that confirmed her passionate need for acts of individual courage. She was rushing away from her marriage to Richard, as if from an embarrassing reflection in the mirror, reinventing herself as her own opposite; yet always she looked back, compelled, because she could not extinguish her other side, her conservative impulse to fulfill her marital obligations. But Helen so hated to be told what to do. And her impulse towards anarchy, her hatred of governance, her fear of and distaste for easy agreement, and her idealism (that restless rejection of the kiss between the perfect and the imperfect)—all of this became unbearably acute with the birth of Dianna.

Bad timing.

How she missed being a man. Not a receptacle, not a passive fountain of milk, not a mirror, not an ornament. A man! The very opposite of early motherhood. She fiercely kissed Dianna. And handed her to Bill.

They traded times of solitude. Sometimes Bill would silently apologize and take himself away to the sunny inland spot he'd cleared, where he transplanted a selection of weeds and wildflowers, milkweed and grasses, an erratic patch desirable to mourning cloaks, monarchs, swallowtails. The world was too sweet to be tolerable. He needed silence, his listening form of prayer.

He was there, at the edge of grass and aspen, standing as if he'd just landed on earth, when Helen walked out of the woods wearing her blue dress, hovering like a spring azure, with Dianna in her arms. She spotted him, his white pyjamas, and called out. Ida had phoned. She wanted them to meet her at a picnic in town. She said it was important. Would he come? Bill thought he didn't hear her right. He crossed the wild garden.

"It's Ida," Helen said, leading Bill to the car. "She was upset."

Bill looked at Helen curiously. He got in the car. And they drove away. Bill in his white pyjamas, their judicious baby and Helen in blue.

CHAPTER ELEVEN

THERE WAS A BIG CROWD. Tents set up, picnic tables, lawn chairs, the men swilling steins of beer, the women with sausage and sauerkraut and the kids in their lederhosen, the hot air rich with smoke. At River Park, at the end of the Osborne Street car line, a modest area north of our home, on the banks of the Red. Wrapped around the telephone poles and the trees, around brown shirt sleeves, a swastika, thousands of swastikas.

As soon as they arrived, a man with a kindly face spotted them as strangers and asked Bill his name. Bill never did get into the habit of speaking. Questions intrigued him, but it seldom occurred to him to answer. Someone was singing, a handsome young man who rose on the balls of his feet, lifting his Adam's apple to the air. Bill always preferred light rising things, in one way or another. The young man sensed him listening and stopped, and for a moment they listened to one another. The noise suddenly dropped away, and you could hear the mourning doves. Bill had the most pleasing blond head. His skin was as translucent as a slice of soap. He smiled. The singer went to Bill and embraced him. Everybody suddenly laughed, surprised; they slapped Bill on the back.

Women put plates of pickled beets in his hands, and he was offered beer with golden foam (he accepted). It was boisterous; there was loud singing, German folk songs, punchlines, teasing,

373

that hypersensitive aggression of successful people. The men drew Bill to a green bench. Helen stood uneasily between the kitchen and the beer keg, looking about for Ida. She and Dianna sweated against each other. Then Helen was subsumed by the crowd of women, who merrily pulled her to a circle of folding chairs littered with babies and little kids, where they cheerfully spoke a few words of English; she picked out "cute little undershirt" and "diarrhea" and "nap time."

When their hosts realized that they were English-speaking, their laughter grew mischievous, a whiff of malice like meat just off. Yet there was, drifting through, the camaraderie of immigrants, a sort of hypothetical nationalism. A man with a swastika wrapped around his arm grandly entered the women's area and asked Helen where she was from, her blood, originally, and she said Scotland-mother, father-not-too-sure, and he said, "That's okay! You're a pretty girl!" Then he looked at Dianna, solemn, grey-eyed, examining him coldly (even as an infant, my granddaughter could make people paranoid), and he said, "Not a big laugh, you Scots. Me! I am German! From Munich! The most beautiful city in the world!" He hooked his thumbs in his armpits. He waited for Helen to seduce him; it would hurt the feelings of his good wife, but "Yah," he said, nodding, "such a pretty girl." Then his face darkened. Helen looked back. Ida stood there.

Ida was wearing her fur coat. She had a bleeding nose. With one hand she held a bloody rag to her face, and with the other she thrust a bunch of pamphlets towards the man from Munich, who grabbed at them, intuitively offended. "PROTECT THE WORLD FROM FASCISM!" Photograph of Hitler, one of Goebbels. The German cocked his head, wounded.

"Tsk," he said, and crumpled the pamphlet as if it were a soiled diaper. "Get out. Stupid." He moved towards her.

The parade was a few blocks away. You could hear the tuba and the singing, sounds pushed out with heavy-heeled gaiety, with this kettledrum marking time for many choruses, because when they came into view, the crowd was organized into platoons, each with a flag and each with a different song, but always that big backswing: OOOM-pah, OOOM-pahpah. The parade ran for miles, overflowing the street and sidewalk, sweeping back and forth; there could have been ten thousand marchers, they just kept on coming. The picnickers ran from the park to wave at them, holding their kids up to see. The man shoved Ida, knocked the pamphlets all over the grass and pushed her ahead of him as if he were throwing a volleyball out into the street where the forward motion of the parade caught her up, a stick in the current, and swallowed her into its centre. Helen rushed after her, almost forgetting that she was holding Dianna. All three of them now moved with the crowd. With the baby in her arms, Helen was treated carefully, and she often felt someone's guiding hand at her elbow as she pressed forward, trying to keep Ida in sight, the orangey-red smeared across the face, Ida bobbing on the surface of the crowd like an awful petunia.

Helen saw somebody's elbow clip Ida's ear, and in her fear she called out to that guiding angel of polyglots, her grandmother Alice. "Please! Grandmother Alice! Give my tongue German!" And then Helen was singing German lieder. "Excuse me!" she sang in High German. "Thank you! Let me by! Excuse me, you plump duck!" She got ahead, bumped over the cushions of fat arms, knocked down a little boy and picked him up again; she lost sight of Ida and found her, called out, "Ida!" and at last Ida heard and turned to her, and then Helen saw that her rational, fearless, stubborn friend was scared, wild-eyed, her mouth opened in a gaping *O,* and Helen breathed out rancour and inhaled hatred.

She surged forward on a crest of hatred, pressing Dianna so firmly to her breast that to this day Dianna shows an addict's attachment to her mother's shade of blue. Helen pulled people roughly by the arm. "Out of the way!" she said in Low German. "Swine! Get out!" She clutched the baby with one arm and took hold of Ida, twice coming away with a handful of loose fur, and then, getting a good grip, she propelled them all on a traverse through the crowd, Helen singing in a weird baritone what could have been "The future belongs to me!" They popped out of that parade like empty whisky bottles at the river's edge, on Jubilee Street behind a lilac hedge. Dianna's second obsession would be the tight, grapey buds that occur on one afternoon in June. Helen held her baby over her shoulder and patted the baby bum till Dianna threw up all over her mother's back.

Everything Helen did then she did with one hand, finding her handkerchief, spitting on it, wiping the blood off Ida's face, spitting again (this time the sweet taste of blood). Ida pulled away. "Leave it!"

"Will you take off the goddamn coat!" yelled Helen. On the other side of the hedge, a brass band was marching past. People were laughing. Laughing not at them, but despite them, as if things would be *really* funny if *they* weren't there.

Ida pulled the collar of the ancient muskrat coat around her throat. "Finito's gone over," she said in a low, grieving voice.

Helen gasped. She thought Ida was speaking Jewish folklore; she saw Finito in the stern of a gondola crossing a foggy river. She would really miss him. "Oh, my God," she said. "Finito."

Ida nodded. "Lucky bastard. He ships out of New York. God, I'd give anything to go." Envy embarrassed her. She straightened her back. "Give me the baby."

Helen handed Dianna to Ida. "Go where?" She winced. Distracted as she was, she didn't like seeing her infant cling to muskrat fur. "Take off the damn coat or give her back."

"Spain. Idiot." Ida didn't remove the coat. She did hold the baby away from her, cupping Dianna's head in her hand, the two of them, baby and godmother (for such it would be), eyeing each other, solemn. "A boat to Le Havre." Ida said this to Dianna. "Then trains to Paris, trucks, over the Pyrenees, maybe they walk, I don't know. They go to Figueras, Albacete, Valencia." She whispered these names to Dianna. "Quinto, Ebro, Saragossa." She brought Dianna close to her and inhaled the warm, fat neck. "You smell like shit," she said, inhaling, "I love that."

"Barcelona," said Helen. "Madrid. To fight the Fascists."

Ida knew at once. She looked up sharply. "You can't go."

"Finito went."

"Finito is a boy."

"I'm a boy." Helen stood, scratching at the grassy sting on the palms of her hands. She looked over the lilac hedge. The parade had passed. The swastikas remained, tacked to the trees. She was filled with hate. "Why is your face smeared with blood?" she asked Ida.

"They came." Ida shrugged. "They wrecked the press. Broke the glass."

Helen spat at the ground. It was her grandmother's gesture but different, taller, elegant. As Ida watched, Helen became ever more statuesque, darker somehow. "Helen," said Ida, "these were local Nazis. You don't have to go on my account. We're talking Spain here. Franco."

"It is the same. They are one. Fascists," she hissed this word. "Fascists." Helen raised both fists. She was claustrophobic. And so lonely. She had to fight with those who shared her love of freedom, or her hatred of confinement.

She yearned to see Finito. Finito! Brother! How often they had talked of going to Spain. Of palm trees and yellow trams climbing pale green hills; of peasants fighting to overthrow their landowners, fighting in the streets and villages to rid themselves of priests. To fight for liberation.

Finito never questioned Helen's right to join the anarchist army. They had talked about it forever—during Helen's pregnancy, while they stoked the stove—Finito never even noticing that Helen could no longer get out of her chair. They practised saying, "*Confederación Nacional del Trabajo.*" They said, "*Federación Anarquista Ibérica.*" It appealed to the latent Impossibilist in Helen that the Canadian government had made it illegal to fight Fascism in Spain. Helen, anarchist, celebrated the advent of the absurd. Not since the days of the Histrionic Theatre had she been tempted by irony. She would join the republican army!

"Think of it!" Finito had said. "Madrid! Hand-to-hand against the Fascists!" Helen drank in the pure whites of Finito's eyes, fondly watched the muscles work in his taut neck. On the Spanish highways! With Italian warplanes zinging over our heads! A people's army, with rifles that were useless even in the First War! Badly equipped! Untrained! Against German machinery! It was Impossible!

She was looking for Bill. Maybe he was still at the picnic grounds. She started to walk across Jubilee. Her blue skirt swayed against her legs. Like petals, like wings. Her arms moved gracefully at her sides, her long black hair curled around her neck and her breasts moved beneath the fabric. She was a woman. Her breasts were full of milk. She loved being a woman. She loved it. The ache seized her belly and cramped her thighs. In the months to follow, the need to hold her baby would squeeze her lungs; she would become asthmatic with longing for Dianna and ruthless with desire for Bill. She looked over her shoulder. Ida, godmother, cradled the baby, stopped at the curb and stared, incredulous. "No, Helen," said Ida. "No."

Helen looked over her shoulder, but she kept walking. She met her daughter's gaze, the terrible clarity of Dianna's grey eyes. The baby did not cry. Perhaps it was Dianna's proximity to the violence of birth that caused her to maintain a sense of proportion, for she was not surprised. And maybe she retained the intimate knowledge of her mother's impossible body, for she was not accusing. But Helen looked into Dianna's eyes and was knifed by commonplace immeasurable mother-love. The pain it made her know led to the only promise Helen ever made (next to her wedding vow, and that was another Helen).

She promised to come back.

"I'll only be gone for a little while. A few weeks," she said.

"I promise I'll be back. Very soon. I have to do this. Please."

She sobbed and turned away. She was looking for Bill. She was going to say goodbye.

THE McCORMACK LAND is surrounded by the Red, on an oxbow. The lowest part, at the end of the oxbow, like the bottom of a cup, flooded too often and we left it wooded, oak and aspen mostly, dogwood, wild rose and the like. Marie's ancient house was near the bottom of the cup, in the stand of black spruce. We had fixed it up for Helen and Bill, and moved our things into the old house Peter had built. Helen had loved to be close to her grandmother Marie again. Both she and Bill had learned a lot about love from Marie's boggy voice.

When Helen left for Spain, Bill couldn't bear to go back. He chose instead to put up a modest cabin for the baby and himself a short distance away. It was still on "our property," the quarter-section "purchased" by my parents, Dianna's great-grandparents, back in 1869. Bill moved their few belongings while he finished the inside, just in case Helen was late getting back. She had gone away for one month, six weeks at the most. It was only a little while, and then Helen would be here and they could all be home. Marie mourned for them, her loud croaking in the night, but Bill was firm in his instinct for transformation, knowing when to accommodate the changing face of fortune.

Even within the circumference of our land, Bill and the child seemed nomadic, though when their yearning for Helen was most acute, such restlessness was more accurately fugitive.

Bill breathed in her temporary absence. He would never judge Helen's urgent flight towards war. It was something she needed to do, and such a passion must be honoured. Bill was definitively light. He was devoted to metamorphosis—hunter to running stag, bereaved lover to pool of water; it kept him looking ahead, sustained his abiding faith in the illusory shiver of things—loss, fear, doctrines, even faith itself. He survived Helen's departure. He was a deep breather. In his lungs, Helen's spirit would endure. Spirits do. Until our breath runs out.

As for Dianna, deprived of her mother, she grew as cold as perfection itself. The kind of cold that slows decay while it sustains life, a brave accuracy. As if she'd been born exactly suited to endure the uncanny, ideal, formal logic of Helen's fateful leave-taking.

So we all waited, listening for Helen's footstep, for the soldier's return from war.

PART SIX

CHAPTER ONE

I never could take any interest in the atomic bomb, I just couldn't any more than in everybody's secret weapon. That it has to be secret makes it dull and meaningless. Sure it will destroy a lot and kill a lot, but it's the living that are interesting not the way of killing them, because if there were not a lot left living how could there be any interest in destruction. Alright, that is the way I feel about it.

—Gertrude Stein, *Reflection on the Atomic Bomb*

BILL GOES BACK TO WATCHING THE WOOD NYMPHS patrolling the grass in the meadow. His bare legs have bright yellow hair. He shines. The stubble presses against little Dianna's back. The sky is not a blue bowl that shelters us from angels. It goes, she has just learned, straight up. Forever. If she goes up fast enough, faster than light, she'll get so young she'll disappear. This information will make her eventual understanding of the birds and the bees comparatively soothing. It is one thing to learn about babies. Quite another to think about *before*. *After* there is a carcass, lots of them, partial mice, bad meat in the woods, roadkill. Bodies. Being dead is one thing. But *before*. Dianna rubs her forehead. Where are we?

Missing.

It is 1941. Dianna is five. Her mother, Helen, is "missing" and her godmother, Ida, is "underground." Not dead. Hiding from the government. The wild blue flax has not yet bloomed, and skinny little aspen spawn out from the witch-fingered oak. With her muscles made of child fat, Dianna raises both legs straight up and forms a V framing the blank blue sky washed with sun. Actually, the sky is black. She turns to look at the grass, the fresh leaves. It only looks blue, it only looks green, because of the air.

Hitler attacked Russia last week. Godmother Ida isn't going to be "underground" much longer. She's coming *up*. Then they'll go to town together. Ida is a Communist. The government didn't like Communists in the winter or before. Now that Hitler is fighting in Russia, Communists can come *up*. And maybe, when the Russians beat Hitler, her mama will come home.

Her father, Bill, explains this to Dianna. Dianna gets so tired she lays her head on his lap. He strokes her hair and smiles. "It's so complicated, it's simple," he says.

She always has a dream. In her dream, her mother is home. Dianna can hear her fighting with Dad in the kitchen, both of them sad. It is her mother's voice. "Where can I go?" her mother is asking. "Everywhere on earth is the same, and I cannot go to heaven." Her mother cries, "I don't want to go to heaven." When Dianna has this dream, she wakes up crying.

She has been worried. Her mother doesn't want to go to heaven. So Bill tells Dianna about the sky, how it is really black. That it is not a blue bowl. That there are no angels behind it calling her mother's name.

Sometimes they imagine themselves healed. In the afternoon, when the soothsaying dreams are most forgotten. This is a happy land. Through the war and after, it will be increasingly, persistently, happy. Oh Canada. A big pie with a fly net over it sits on the kitchen counter in the mid-afternoon.

AND SUDDENLY MY GRANDDAUGHTER was nine years old. Ida hadn't been underground for a few years running. The Russians were winning the war for us, and everybody loved the recordings of the Soviet Army Chorus. Ida's background was Polish/German /Russian Jew. Close enough! She cheerfully joined a local chapter of the Canadian—Soviet Friendship League. It was the spring of 1944, and Soviet troops had broken a German Panzer attack. All the good war news was from the Russian front. To celebrate, Ida cooked up a big Bolshie picnic with Russian-style borscht, coleslaw, fruit soup, cheese blintzes, potato knishes, gefilte fish with horseradish. We ate outside in icy sleet, a grey slush thrown at us from the north. We were all bundled up in our smelly old buffalo robes, stamping our feet under the picnic table while Ida served us with blue fingers sticking out of her gloves. Ida sang in fake Russian—Irving Berlin songs backwards. "*Enil ni llaf ot emit eht si won.*" And the prophetic "*won snaciremA eb lla s'tel.*"

Dianna cradled in her grandfather Eli's lap. Her grey eyes examined the infinite lines on Eli's soft skin, the grainy old barn-wood face, while she played with his missing parts—the lost thumb, the smithereen of his ear. When the wind gusted, we all sighed together, Ahhhhh, Ahhhhh. And laughed like spies in the Arctic, irrelevant and naughty.

Bill was quiet, as usual, listening. He wore a sky blue toque with earflaps tied under his chin. He looked like Khrushchev. Dianna, with one hand caressing her grandfather's cheek, reached back to touch her father's arm, to make sure he was still there. She sensed his distraction right away, pulled herself up and stared at him anxiously. Bill cocked his head at the crevice of the picnic table, where a moth was tucked headfirst, sheltered from the weather, a big black moth with cape-like wings. Bill smiled a small smile, like someone who has passed away in a dream of peace. His eyes were full of empathy for the living. "Oh," he said to the black moth, "you have come very far."

Ida's singing faded. The wind blew a frozen blueberry out of the bowl, onto the table; I picked it up, cold and seedy. Dianna said nothing, read her father's face, as always noncommittal. The rest of us were uneasy. Bill's neat frame was eloquent with compassion; you would envy the object of such kindness. He looked up. "It is Helen," he said.

Dianna began to cry. So did I. Weeping came up from the earth into the glands under our ears, into our throats. Helen.

"Daddy . . ." Dianna tugged his sleeve.

Bill was startled; he never forgot Dianna's presence. Guiltily, he put his hands to her face and closed her eyes. "See?" he said. I closed my eyes. I could see her too. She had hidden her hair in a leather hat, wore a black flight jacket, and behind her was a sunny parade of men, their fists raised in the air. "*La Luna*," said Bill. "Helen."

Helen turned to look at us. We were leafy shadows on the grass at Fuentes de Ebro and somehow it made her ache for home. She raised her fist. In the Spanish wind, the red-and-black anarchist flag slapped us from our reverie. When I opened my eyes, Dianna was on the ground under the picnic table, barely breathing.

Bill was no ordinary Catholic seeing the devil in a blue-bottle fly, nothing so guilt-stricken. He saw Helen.

Helen became a black moth.

The first time Helen appeared to us, Dianna was inconsolable. She lost weight while she grew tall, a svelte exoskeleton, a hard handsome nut with coarse brown hair around a narrow face, X-ray eyes. All that sullen spring she suffered. Her vulnerability frightened us and enraged her. She would sleep for twelve or fourteen hours and then go out walking with her sketch pad, wearing a big green raincoat. She made a one-person tent out in the bush, sketching inside her coat. Her drawings from that period include the skull of a red fox. She drew a hand without skin, an amazing accomplishment since she'd never, to our knowledge, done any dissection. A squirrel's heart; the abdominal organs of birds, dogs, weasels. Reproductive organs; the wombs of a cat and a bear; eventually a woman's anatomy, a beautiful sketch in pen and ink with chalk, architectural, like the anatomy of a cathedral, a spherical womb suspended by strong ligaments, warmly shaded and symmetrical. If these drawings were not scientific, they were in another sense *true*.

Bill never tried to protect his child from his own imagination, which is a highly unusual parenting practice. Helen would appear to him and he would stop whatever he was doing and close his eyes. If Dianna saw this, she'd shut her eyes too. They called it "visiting Mama."

Helen had been missing for eight years when the Russians finally closed in on Berlin. From the McCormack perspective, the war had lasted nine years. (We were, according to the Canadian government, "premature anti-Fascists.") For the last year, Dianna had shared visions with her father that would surely have caused an aneurysm in the brain of the toughest general. They had spent a morning (outwardly, walking down the frozen river on a winter afternoon) with a British soldier who had been captured by Spanish Fascists after a bomb blew off the fingers of his left hand and his entire left leg. Bill and Dianna—thanks to a beckoning motion from Helen, something perhaps of a crow landing on the snow beside them, blue crow, steel grey light— were witness to the man's awakening in the Fascist hospital to find that his captors had removed his *right* hand and his *right* leg. They were there with him when he died of shock, their frozen fingers upon his dying pulse.

The war focused on the Eastern Front. January 1945. The young Russian soldiers raped the German woman and nailed her hands to the family cart. Her children huddled in the watery ditch beside the road.

War is about family, about mothers, Dianna thought. On the first of May, in the bunker at the Reich chancellery in Berlin, Mrs. Goebbels murdered all her six children. After that, neither Bill nor young Dianna said a word for many days. They just said they'd been visiting Helen. "Seeing Mama," Dianna would say.

Dianna sketched the bone structure of owls, raccoons, beavers. Formal. Classical. The premise of living without hunger, the remote premise. Please. When the bones stop wanting.

CHAPTER TWO

AFTER THE WAR, CANADA BECAME a tragedy-free zone. It was like watching puddles dry up on a parking lot after a hard rain. The vets migrated home. I read the *Canadian Forum* to Eli. The magazine was raising a fuss over low-cost housing and "the victory of capitalism." Eli sighed. He was sitting in the same spot where Peter, my own dad, had lectured him (that fake Socratic catechism) on the spacious logic of Impossibilism.

Yesterday, we had learned that Eli had developed diabetes. That was in the morning. In the afternoon, he'd had his last eight teeth removed. The old barn was caving in; his beauty was epic. He pointed at the open page with his good hand—his slightly livid hand; the diabetes was harming his circulation.

"Only 37,964 this time?" he said. He shook his shaggy head and smiled daintily, not wishing to impose upon me a view of his strawberry gums.

"When you get your new teeth, you're going to look younger than me."

"Last time, they killed . . ." He squinted, his memory trained by illiteracy. "62,817."

"Less this time."

"Less. But they sent more. A very efficient war."

"We never had it so good. Kiss me."

He did. With polite gallantry, with puckered lips, not letting me into that maw. This done, he sat back, opening and closing his fist.

"Hand bothering you?" I asked.

Eli shrugged. "The radicals want affordable housing."

"These are tempestuous times."

Eli's sadness had softened into a sweet and enduring depression. It was the lucky outcome of Impossibilism, a unified field theory: the world is not to be trusted any more than a dream. In a lesser man, this might have made a nasty cynic. Not Eli, past eighty now, calmly bemused, reassured by scepticism. He cradled Helen's absence in that place in his old heart where the world was infinitely possible and latent. His sorrow was of an eloquent pigment, a sort of violet hue. Though of course he was strong as an ox, and when he did get his teeth in, it was true, he looked younger than I did—damn all men for this—and he thought they were very funny, grinning for him, false as day.

And me, I dreamed of giving Helen gifts. Every day, through many nights, I gathered stones and flowers for her. The war ended when the supple fields of wheat turned from green to gold. I looked for my lost daughter, and found her everywhere.

⚜

IDA WAS FRESH FROM MOSCOW, where she'd spent a year and a half as a student in the Marx-Engels-Lenin Institute. Now she was an agent of the Comintern. She bustled secretively. She had the manners of a hammer; her soul was the foundry for the utopia. Like many people in this country, even those with more timid left-leanings, Ida was under the constant surveillance of the RCMP.

A deep cold calm covered the earth. That year's cold "snap" lasted five months. On the third of April, 1950, the wind rose and it started to snow, sticky stuff added to snowdrifts that were even then as high as the eaves of a house, drifts at least ten feet high, so we lived in choppy seas. It was already flooding down in Minnesota. I slept in the afternoon, full of dread.

Dianna, nearly fourteen years old, sensed approaching danger the way a dog knows its family is going to take a trip, becoming wary, clinging to the edges. Until that April snowfall, her father had steadily ignored the prospect of a flood, but that day Bill got on the phone, a rare event for a silent man, entering the real world as steady and alert as Eisenhower. Offended, Dianna stuffed her pencils into her drawing kit and stumbled off to their butterfly field, under six feet of snow. She was fascinated by the swellings on the branches of the rose bushes that pushed up like drowning hands. It was her intention to sketch the leaves' development; she approved of the slow motion of that spring.

She waded down the road and across the field, feeling for firm ground. The wind was from the northeast, so she figured the bush on the east side might be most revealing. A good spot, near the place where her father always put down salt and alfalfa for the surviving deer. By then, she had developed an economical way of sketching: quick, fluent lines that captured the essentials of the plant before her hands got numb.

She is looking, as she likes to do, at the foreground. She hears deer in the woods, snow falling on snow. She looks up. The wind had switched to the west at twenty-five miles an hour. She hears the silent sound of flight. She stares into a white sky. A glider, delicate as a maple seed, flies in circles above her head.

The glider spirals in diminishing rotations so close that she can see the amber glue that holds it together. Its bird-like wings are made of peeled willow wands and it is wrapped in waxed linen. The wind sighs as it sets its burden down before her, a big white snowbird. It settles. Then slowly, its left wing dips into a snowdrift. The pilot in his glass bubble removes his goggles and straps, then slides the lid off and looks about at the field of snow.

He spies Dianna before climbing out of his plane. A big, handsome man with black hair. Despite the cold, he wears only a black leather flight jacket with fleece-lined gloves, warm-looking boots, a white scarf about his neck. He gives a casual salute.

Dianna is waiting to see what language he'll speak. Maybe Russian.

He approaches her with some difficulty through the waist-high snow. He has dark shadows beneath his eyes and a blue chin. Not Russian. His jacket is nice. Dianna thinks that he must be a Fascist spy from Italy. She holds her ground, as her mother would. He comes right up to her, breathing heavily from the exertion of his walk. "Howdy," he says. "Take me to your field commander." Then he smiles. He has normal teeth.

Dianna brought with her the fresh scent of snow, stamping her feet at the door, snow peeling off her leggings onto the floor. She said nothing, but silently removed her wet things and went to her table beneath the south window and placed her sketches there. Black branches, the bare suggestion of buds, white page. Bill was pacing between phone calls, wildly out of character, but he stopped briefly, ran his finger above her drawings. A wintering rose bush, like a map of the Red River. Everything was becoming river. I thought, with a lurch in my nervous system (my nerves, my veins, Christ, even my bloodshot eyes, were maps of the Red River), We have to pack her drawings carefully. I looked at all our belongings. We have to get everything *up.* Our house became an ark. Around us, the white sea of the yard. We were already floating, scarcely moored.

Dianna kneeled on her chair and began to fill in the quick sketches she'd just made. "There's a man outside," she said. So distracted were we, no one paid much attention. Again, louder: "There's a man outside, and he wants to come in."

Bill had the phone in his hand; he was just about to make another call to try to get sandbags. He stopped and put down the receiver and opened the front door. The pilot stood there, his back to us, but he turned towards Bill then. He didn't smile. He looked Bill keenly in the eye. "Come in," said Bill, without surprise, with solemnity, overcoming his dread.

Dianna went to the bathroom, slamming the door behind her.

The man kicked the snow off his boots. He looked around the house, as if seeing a room that had already been described to him. "You can come all the way in," I said. "Come on. Have a seat."

"Thanks," he said.

"Are you from Toronto?" I asked him. I've always been good with accents.

"Why, yes!"

"You've got an Italian grandmother, though, am I right?"
I guess I was showing off.

"Amazing," he said. Stuck forth his hand. "The name's Jack."

Eli popped up. "Want some tea, Jack?" Eli had been sleeping under the afghan on the couch, despite the chaos. "*I'd* like some tea." He filled the kettle.

Jack took sugar in his tea. Dianna emerged from the bathroom and placed a kitchen chair where she could watch us at an oblique angle, staring through strands of hair. Her face was as white as bone, and her eyes had grown larger, almost purple.

"So, Jack. Where'd you come from?" I asked. He had a slight overbite. Broad mouth; high, windburned cheekbones; a messy, flannel way with clothes. He was strong, stocky, square-shaped despite his height.

"I was flying out of a club just east of here." He sipped his tea as if he'd given a full answer. He nodded, looking handsome and pleasant, the confidence of a popular man.

"This is nice land," he said to Bill. Bill had the habit of sitting cross-legged on top of the coffee table. It didn't occur to Bill to respond, but he was contemplating Jack's assertion and in his mind he'd travelled back to the meadow by his and Dianna's cabin. His house would soon be driftwood. Since Bill left the monastery, his innate generosity had found strange use, as if he was forever holding out the treasures of his heart to be swept away.

We sipped our tea. Blue-green sunset.

"Dark out," said Eli, and turned on a small yellow lamp.

"Stay for supper?" I asked Jack.

"Thanks. I'd like that." Then, "Can't really fly tonight anyway."

Eli peered out the window. It was snowing again. "You flew, did you?" he asked.

"His airplane's in our meadow," Dianna complained to her father.

"What kind of plane do you fly, Jack?" asked Eli.

"She's a glider," said Jack.

"A glider! Now *that's* a pretty thing," said Eli.

"Yes, she is."

"Pretty cold up there, I imagine."

"Yes, it sure was."

"Fly off course?"

"Had no course. The wind blew me. I lost altitude. Had to land."

"Where's Ida?" I asked. I felt a pang of anxiety. Ida wasn't entirely well. I hoped this visitor wouldn't upset her. "You're not with the RCMP, are you? No offence."

He smiled. His deep voice. "No. But I was with the RAF."

"Germany?" asked Eli.

"That's right," said Jack.

"You're older than I thought," I said.

"Old enough," he said.

We had a quiet dinner of steamed curiosity and fried frustration. Ida came in, late and tired, but revived herself by watching Jack eat. "You look so familiar," she told him.

Jack looked her straight in the eye. I grew more anxious.

"You're a pilot, are you?" Ida asked.

"Yup," said Jack. He picked up his spoon and tapped the edge of his plate. Over and over, till we all stopped eating and watched him. Tap-tap, tap-tap, a hypnotic rhythm; it went on a long time. When he stopped, we were all lulled and ready. He sought out each of us. His face was very sad.

Bill said, "Come here, little girl," and picked up Dianna, putting her in his lap.

Dianna settled herself into her father's arms. She looked at Jack with purple eyes. "Why aren't you frozen?" she asked him.

Jack didn't answer.

"Are you a friend of my mama's?" Dianna asked.

Jack nodded his head, up, down.

"Then you know where she is," she said flatly.

Jack tipped his head, looked to the side.

Dianna sat forward. Bill could feel her bony joints dig into his thighs. "When is she coming back?"

Jack suddenly straightened and brought his gaze to Dianna, without any mollification for the child.

"Stop it!" It was Bill. It was the first time he'd ever raised his voice.

Jack looked at Bill. Dianna was cradled in Bill's arms. "I can't say," Jack said. "She was captured at the Ebro River."

"Then the Fascists have her," Dianna said.

Bill stood, and he set Dianna on her feet. "It's time you went to bed. You stay with your grandmother Blondie tonight." Then, to Jack: "We'll go get your plane now."

Pitch black, a wind with snow. "Okay," said Jack.

The door closed behind the two men. Dianna gave me one of her botanist's stares. "That man knows my mother," she said.

I could feel the tendrils of my attachment to Helen dig into my palms like copper wiring. Where light fell, from lamp or fire, it seared my eyes, and white light filled the veins in my arms, gave me that force I needed to get Dianna washed and settled. I was old. Too old. Still, I was connected to my daughter, Helen. She had been captured. Captured is not dead. Maybe she was safe. Tired as I was, I gave this love to Dianna. Pulled the blankets up around her; she of the purple eyes dryly stated, "The Fascists must have let her go when the Russians beat them."

"Yes," I said, "I think so."

"She's trying to come home." There was hope in the back of my granddaughter's eyes.

I kissed her bony forehead. And then I fell asleep in my chair.

CHAPTER THREE

THE PHONE RANG, WAKING ME. Morning. It was Jack. His deep, confident voice was already familiar.

"Howdy," said Jack. "Did you sleep okay?"

"Where's Bill?"

"Well, that's why I called. We're going to try to haul a couple of loads of water for the cisterns today. Bill's out clearing your drive so's we can get through with the truck."

I looked out. Bill astride the tractor pushing the snow-plough. There was something angry in Bill's movements.

"See him?" asked Jack.

"Thanks for calling, Jack."

"We'd best get what supplies you'll need. Before the junction goes under."

"The junction's not going under, Jack."

Pause. "Lot of snow," said Jack. "Gotta melt."

"There's time." This was *our* flood. But we needed the help. "We could use some milk and bread, if you're going to the station."

"You'll need more than that," said Jack.

The junction went under two days later. The river that had been so far away, dimes shining on the other side of the trees, came near, underfoot. There was no tomorrow. We'd say, "Tomorrow we'll have time to truck in more sand." But there was no such thing as time. We witnessed the water with a sense of rightness, a sort of decency. That's prairie spirit in the nutshell; we felt the justice of our doom. The river became a lake, a huge inland ocean. Growing, always. The lake had been there before us—let it resume. It started to rain.

It was wonderful to let go of cleanliness, sleep, routine. In the absence of cleanliness we were immaculate, purged of habit, speaking to one another in special terms, our good manners a dike protecting us from fear. People kept arriving from nowhere, driven by the need to work, by doing without words for each other. Generosity is one of the simplest instincts of crazy old humankind.

We built a dike with sweet-smelling burlap bags. It soon got too dangerous to get helpers out to our place. Our crew dwindled. We formed a small commune, which made Ida very happy. We were generally ecstatic; even Bill was strangely out of his skin. *The waters covered the sea.* It was simple. Everything was water. And in my ecstasy, I grieved, knowing that Marie's grotto and Peter and Alice's graves were now under water, with the first bruise of knowledge, the intimation that my daughter had suffered. I waited for a chance to question Jack. But the temperature rose suddenly, and we were going flat out to fight the flood.

Jack was tireless. Anticipated what we'd need next. A very muscled chest and nice forearms. He never seemed to need any sleep, was running off heroism, I guess. Late at night, I fetched a couple of glasses and the bottle of whisky. I'd soon be eighty, and I'd developed a fondness for Scotch in the evening, like my mother before me. Jack and I sat at the kitchen table.

"Tell me about Helen," I asked him.

"She was with the Mackenzie-Papineau Battalion," he said.

"Well, we know that."

"She was dressed as a man." We both smiled fondly. "The last time I saw her," he said, "she was in a line of men."

"A line?"

"At the end. It was almost dark. She was like a shadow. She raised her fist, like so—" and here, Jack raised his right arm, fist forward—"that was very brave."

"And she was all right?"

A trace of bitterness crossed his face.

"Tell me what you know," I told him. Then, I remember thinking, This man doesn't like his life.

"She was taken prisoner," he said. "She was at the end of the line." Again, Jack raised his fist. "That's how she faced the firing squad."

"She was . . . what?"

Jack drank off his glass, poured more, added to mine.

I caught sight of Dianna standing straight and thin near by. "Go to bed!" I barked at her.

She faced Jack fiercely. "Where is my mother?"

"Now!" I cried. "This instant!"

Dianna walked close to Jack, put her face inches from his. "You tell me where she is or you'll die in your sleep."

I caught her, roughly turned her away from him, with little control over the strength of my own hands. Jack slouched in his chair, avoiding Dianna's eyes. I pushed her to the cot we'd placed in our bedroom. Eli was already asleep. All my will went into putting Dianna into bed, forcing her to lie down; I think I forced her into sleep.

I went back to the kitchen. Jack was as I'd left him, fingering his glass. I sat down. We didn't say anything for a long time. Sometimes I'd look up at him, hoping for mitigation. There should have been more. A second part of the story, the escape. Jack was quiet as night.

"Where is her body?"

"They buried them there."

"Does Bill know?" I asked.

Jack nodded, yes.

"We're not going to tell anyone else about this," I said finally. "Not now." Jack said nothing. "I have to be alone," I told him.

He stood up to go back to Bill's cabin. As he left, he put his hand on my shoulder. His hand was ice cold, I could feel it through my dress. I waited till the latch closed.

CHAPTER FOUR

WE LIVED WITH THE INTENSITY OF FERAL CATS. The river seeped through the ground beneath the dike, and as they became sodden, the bags were like pulpy fruit oozing sour juice. We took turns minding the pumps. We became an island. The fields of wheat or snow surrounding treed islands, at night the lights of our cottages blinking. More recent were the windbreaks, planted since the Depression, breakwaters of maple or willow in single rows, bending south. Eli took up his guitar, partly to entertain himself through flood-inspired insomnia, partly to insure its safety. We discovered that Jack liked to sing. The bitterness I'd seen that night did not resurface.

I hadn't yet told Eli. He was working so hard against the flood that I was afraid he too would die. My own pain entered a place bordered by a sort of untested hypothesis. I relived the moment before the firing squad over and over. I would just stay there, could go no further. I didn't sleep, but under the circumstances no one noticed. I relived my daughter's life. She was vivid. I experienced every moment of my time with her.

We stuffed everything we could into the rafters: furniture, food, bedding. We tied Jack's white glider to the roof. All else stood on the sandy floor, cleansed of value. Dianna occupied a couch balanced precariously in the beams above the kitchen, the warmest spot on our island. I brought her beetles and white worms, moles and voles from the sump pits, lifting them up to her perch as if I were feeding a barn owl. She preferred drawing flora, but fauna must do on the ark. She watched our proceedings with disapproval. And she never questioned Jack again.

The phones were still working. During this time, Bill seemed released from the tension of listening for Helen's return, and he spoke more that month than at any time before or since. "Something's clicking the line," he said and looked accusingly at Ida. Ida's muskrat coat, soaked with sand and river, weighed two hundred pounds. Proudly, she puffed up her chest, nodded and smiled. Her right incisor had died and turned grey, but her face was fatted, so age flattered her and she had become one of those handsome pigeon-women. At that moment, we all were thinking, It isn't just Ida who's brought the RCMP into our lives. Anyone who had gone to fight for the republicans in Spain was considered a subversive. Our eyes flitted to the window to look at the trench warfare of our yard, searching for Helen. There was only water, liver grey. When the Mounties asked for Helen, we told them, "Off with the Mac-Paps. Off with the anti-Fascists. Is there a problem?" They looked at us strangely. One officer blinked in disbelief and said, "Since 1936?" Still, we had harboured her; she was a gate left open, a light left on. I didn't change that; I couldn't extinguish the light.

We had one cow at the time—thank God only one—a good milker, so we were getting loaded up with milk. Steel canisters lined up as clean as bombs on top of the potting table on the porch. It was on a Wednesday, near the end of April, that Jack took my arm. "Time to go," he said. "The road's wiped out, and we can't put Bossy on the wagon."

He was right. And as always in the flood, it was too late. We had to grit the sand in our teeth and wade through a cold current that boiled the gravel off the road. I tied the cow to my wagon, which was loaded with several of the milk canisters, and tried to walk west, to the railway tracks. Jack gave the cow a thwack on the butt. No time, ever. Water came over my boots, rode up my pants, made walking painful. The kind of cold that amputates.

Eli's hand was frozen in mine. "She's dead, isn't she," he said.

We slid on the broken road. I didn't look at his face. I looked at the ice and branches in our path, so it's that face, the face of the river, I see when I remember Eli's voice that day, when I hear his reckoning. In the rain on the day the road went under, we came to our loss as if it were a presence, a constant. Our daughter's death had always been so, and would be evermore. That was the utopia of the flood. The singular means of Helen's death would strike at us later.

We put Ida in the wagon and pinned her down with luggage. Eli and I held on to each other. We didn't know where Bill and Dianna were. We reached the tracks and boarded Bossy, milk, Eli, Ida, myself. And Jack.

Jack was cheered by the walk out. He went off to talk to the conductor. It was the first I would see of Jack's explorations. Jack travels. Then I remembered that he'd literally *dropped in.* Jack had simply become part of the broken machinery of our lives. All around the rail line lay the vengeful old lake. Resuming. Bill would've stayed behind with Dianna. Fugitives have to stay near the source of their innocence.

Bill and Dianna were having an argument. Dianna was refusing to leave the house. She could only picture her mother coming back through all that water to reclaim her. And find Dianna gone.

When the dike broke, they watched the oil-like patch enter the front door and cross the floor till it reached all the walls, where it climbed up. The windows exploded, now one, then another. The smell of mud was rich and exclusive. The river entered our home with an animal persistence, sliding up steadily. Then it stopped a couple of feet below their perch. Bill looked at Dianna with the mildest reproach. "Here we are," he said.

Dianna crawled over to look out the small porthole under the eaves. Her mother would need a boat.

The sky cleared in May. The prairie was an open sea except for the giveaway windbreaks, just the fingertips of the drowned. It warmed up. There was much to observe. Things reduced to a minimum give a slow, ample yield. Every day, Dianna measured the river's erratic ebb with charcoal, dangling from the rafters with Bill holding her upside down by her feet. Only the two of them, waiting for Mama, who would come in a boat. They'd be like two boats on the sea. They would give her all their attention. There is time here. Everything changes into the next thing, but slowly. So you're ready. So you know, you can draw it. They lived on raw potatoes, carrots, wrinkled rutabagas we'd hauled up from the root cellar. She refused to eat her parsnips but was otherwise uncomplaining. Through all the discomfort, Dianna never grumbled. She was afraid that her dad would make her leave.

Marie was at large, hovering over the sallow sea. Helen's return was imminent, especially now that there was only water.

Dianna listened. She could not keep her eyes focused when the bullfrogs droned. Even in the sun, while her father was reading and water slapped against the house, she heard the footstep, felt the caress, and she slept.

CHAPTER FIVE

I WAS ALWAYS SWIMMING THEN, when I walked down our road. Even in our living room, when we built it new, waltzing with Eli was wading with Eli, an effect not improved by our wonky sense of rhythm. The branches of trees were webbed with flax straw that floated up from septic fields, Gothic and hairy. Houses were turned inside out, swollen, distended couches and rugs, the colour of chicken fat, hauled out to the front yards. Our house had turned as black as a wet box of tissue. The old house, built by Peter and Alice. And Marie's place, who knows how old it was.

We hauled everything out in buckets. Jack came back with us. He said he needed to get his plane. Richard showed up wearing tailored chest waders with railway gloves and a hunting cap. The trees were full of shredded sandbags that masked Richard's approach, for he'd parked at the junction and walked down through the muck, like a landlord come to reclaim his castle after a peasants' revolt.

It was Jack who greeted Richard. He walked up to meet him like a sentry. I watched from the doorway while the two men talked. Jack turned around and pointed at the roof. His glider, strapped down, its wings disengaged and laced to its sides, a trussed white goose.

Richard nodded and brushed by. He had an unfortunate blindness to whatever disturbed his consuming scheme of things. Richard approved of the flood. It cleansed us of a lot of old junk. He worked with us for about nine hours. We tore down plaster and shovelled the mess into a dump truck. The smell was vegetable but sweet as blood, and it would sit in the back of your throat.

Richard worked non-stop, wordless, as hard as a man could work, though he was past fifty then. But he took one break, when Dianna purposefully, meaningfully, stood in his way. The two of them went for a short walk down the driveway. He appeared to be asking her the standard questions about school and hobbies and she giving him the standard answers. But the two of them were romancing. Dianna lisped beside him, toe in, tucking her straight brown hair behind her ear. She was feeling beautiful; I think she imagined that Richard admired her for her resemblance to her mother. Dianna didn't look at all like her mother. She always watched the foreign map of Richard's profile, but he never looked at her, though he was tuned to her presence. Richard soaked her up like she was a bandage on his wounded pride. And when Bill stumbled by with his buckets of rot, Richard lifted his head (age had lightened Richard's hair from blond to an excessive eight-karat white gold, thick and wavy, very sensual), with a victorious and thoroughly covetous gleam in his eye.

At fourteen, Dianna appeared to be acquiring fathers. It was an era that demanded of women a gaggle of fathers, a parliament of dads. She twitched her skinny hips. The two fathers each, differently, nodded their paternal heads: Bill with his unspeakable compassion; Richard, a monarch with his subject.

Richard took up his shovel once again. I knew him to be

quickly bored and felt uneasy about his long stay with us that day. I wondered what he was after. Soon after, I discovered him out back, hiding behind the remains of the woodshed, being sick to his stomach.

"Can I get you something?" I asked him.

He shook his head. "Funny smell," he said, wincing and spitting phlegm.

"It is. You should quit. You've been a brick. A real Samaritan. I like your pants too."

Richard, covered in the white cheese of waterlogged plaster, nodded; he never refused a compliment. I took his arm, and we walked towards his car.

"Richard!" I said. "A Cadillac!"

Richard retched again. He put his head down, looking at his putrid boots. "The Americans are miles ahead," he said, and gagged. "That smell. It reminds me."

We stood at his car. Shakily, he put the key in the lock and stood there, too sick to move. Then he said, "It was like that in the war. When we'd find a body. That's how they smell coming out of the water. Very similar—consistency. Drownings." Pause. "Now I'm talking like a real vet."

I leaned up to pat his shoulder.

After a short while, he said, "Of course, my father stayed in the water. He would have been cleaned."

"Richard," I said, "the graves are everywhere."

Something in my voice alerted him. "You never heard from her."

"No." Damn him. I hadn't told anyone but Eli and Ida. Ida had looked at me with gently frustrated pity. "I know," she had said. "It was obvious. Finito died too. At the Ebro. Helen had false papers, so we never got told properly."

Richard scanned the yard. Jack was washing down a chair for Eli to sit in. "Who is that fellow?" Richard asked.

"He . . . dropped in."

"Is he foreign?"

"Aren't we all?"

Richard shook his head with distaste. "What are you going to do?" he asked mildly.

He meant, how would we rebuild. Richard, as our private banker, knew very well we hadn't any money. I'd had to borrow from him already the year before when we fell behind in our property taxes, and I hadn't paid him back yet. I was light-headed, so I sat down on a dead tree fallen by the drive. I looked at my filthy old kilt, my skinny legs blotched with eczema, stuck in rubber boots.

Richard stood over me. "You're going to need a loan to rebuild," he said. "Almost no interest, just to cover my costs."

I nodded. "Thank you," I said. He had been good to us. I suppose I was being perverse, but I decided then that I'd never tell him how Helen died. It was our private property, and I felt we needed something of our own just then.

With watery eyes, Richard sought Dianna. Dianna snapped to attention, as if he'd called her.

CHAPTER SIX

"DON'T WORRY," HELEN SAYS. "The wind does not soothe, but the idea of wind soothes." Helen's hand strokes our hair. "Don't worry any more."

The memorials to the flood were a lot of new houses with plywood walls and teak veneer. But Bill (with Jack's help and Richard's money) built a graceful wood structure at the edge of their butterfly field. Marie's grotto was nothing but four corner posts and an iron stove. But that is where Jack wanted to be, and he rebuilt the cabin much as Marie's old place had been, following the logic of the stone base and the trees. Soon after, Marie returned. I saw her shadow walking in the woods. She looked content. Jack thought she was content too. "She keeps an eye on me," he said.

Elsewhere on "our property," because of Ida's political affiliations, we were subject to a different kind of surveillance. The clicking phone, the occasional gleam of a camera lens. It was nutty, but the Canadian government saw Russian spies under every bush, and Ida was a sure candidate. While Ida and Bill, Eli and I protected ourselves with a level of duplicity thin as eggshell, Dianna was open to surveillance. She couldn't possibly understand solitude, having never experienced it. She understood the world as a diagram or a formal plan upon which our mad relationships ricocheted between points of observation. I guess she was a physicist. She saw the world as lines connected by force.

Her childhood was constructed out of wartime propaganda, but she was drawn into pubescence with the news of the Holocaust, its mechanisms conveyed to her by her godmother, Ida, who offered this information with heroic discretion. It was an era so sordid that everyone, even Stalin, wore pyjamas. My clear-sighted granddaughter told her best school friend and the RCMP that her periods had finally started. She was the true Canadian girl.

I never did tell Dianna about her mother's death. Not in so many words. She saw it in the change of light, in the way time passed without mercy. But one day when I was cleaning her room, minding my own business, I came across a photograph of the Mackenzie-Papineau Battalion, those rare birds, the discrete collection of Canadian lefties newly arrived in Spain back in '36. The photo lay at the bottom of her drawer, hidden beneath her socks. My heart seized up, and I pulled it out. There were some handsome faces, but no one with Helen's beauty. Then, one. A figure at the end of the line, must have been in some shadow thrown by a nearby building. A black cutout figure. Fist raised, palm forward. The optimistic, convivial group of men. And then this singular figure in the shade. I turned it over. On the back was written, "For Dianna, whose mother was brave. Jack."

Dianna knew that her mother was dead. But that didn't stop her from waiting, listening for the return. It spiked her resolve, and this is maybe peculiar to daughters; the errant mother becomes a daughter's burden, and a burden will make one hell of a loyal woman. Dianna's loyalty would be to "our property," the site of Helen's abandonment and the scene of her eventual, infinitely deferred, return.

BY THE TIME DIANNA WAS TWENTY, in 1956, her virginity was nuclear. She stayed as far away as possible from Jack, clinging to the opposite end of his lazy attraction. Jack would disappear "up North" to work for a month or two, and then come back to live in Marie's grotto. We gave him the bottom cup of the oxbow. We couldn't see why not. We had more than enough space, and he paid his own expenses. He wore red flannel shirts in the summertime. He drank quite a bit and he smoked pot, which didn't help our relationship with the Mounties. But he was free of the forthright, obvious, alert egoism of the 1950s.

Richard provided the money for Dianna to go to law school. Now her drawings were limited to the margins of law books. Buttercups bloomed over case law, the Bank Act, superior ovary, trust, sepals of calyx, inheritance tax, pistil. She wore sweater sets. She had lunch with Richard three times a week. I don't know what they talked about, but knowing Richard, it would be free of substance and stuffed with bone-building bigotry against Indians, Jews, Communists and women. Subtle as fluoride, Richard distributed hatred as if it were in the best interests of those he hated. He was a most canny man, Richard, increasingly so with age. But Dianna, inured to speculation by her National Character, seemed unaware of Richard's power over her. She liked his *style*.

It was on a Wednesday after lunch that Dianna entered our house, humming. "Gramma," she said, and kissed my cheek. "Where's Ida?" Seeing Eli: "Hey, Grandpa." She put her cheek against his scarred head.

Eli, at ninety-something, had not lost his hand to diabetes, but his left leg was gone just under the knee. He was illegally blind, so he could still drive a car. His miraculous muscle tone was actually improved by these impairments. When Dianna came in, he was restitching the pommel of his Spanish saddle with a needle a sixteenth of an inch in diameter, pushing it through the leather with the knob of his lost thumb. I occupied a footstool beside Eli's rocking chair. Above us, like stalactites, swung five small microphones. We looked up at Dianna. She hadn't seen them. "What are you two smiling about?" she asked. And looked up. "Oh, my God."

"We were cleaning the attic," I said.

She walked between the mikes, waving her hand, making them sway, and started to speak but thought better of it. There was a dome of silence suspended from the rafters. For several moments, the three of us blinked at one another. The latch lifted. Bill walked in. He had dropped by when we found the first bug and was obviously surprised now to find so many. He came silently into the middle of the room and stood, his fingers pressed together in a sad sort of prayer, a spider doing push-ups on a mirror. He was so seldom compelled to speak, but this new reticence was a terrible satire.

When Dianna suddenly spoke, I thought I'd have a heart attack. "Jurisprudence," she said, "coterminous with fiduciary care." With her sweater set she wore a pleated skirt.

"Confidentiality," she spoke into one mike, then another, "is intended to convey that extra quality in the relevant confidence that is implicit in the phrase 'confidential relationship.'" She stopped and smiled at us, and then resumed. "Undue influence is commonly regarded as occasions when the will of one person has become so dominated by that of another that the person acts as the mere puppet of the dominator. Cf *Tate v Williams, Allard v Skinner* and *Morley v Lough.*" She made her way to the backroom—the room occupied by Ida ever since the death of Stalin and the marriage of JFK to Jacqueline Bouvier in 1953. Something in the concurrence of those two events had left Ida unhinged.

Years of police surveillance had made Ida intensely lonely. She was shadowed. We didn't know how thin she had become until the muskrat coat finally fell apart, revealing a body ravaged by exegesis. We put her to bed, spooned honeyed milk between her lips. She whispered, "How kind," and looked away, deliberating all possible interpretations of her words. The RCMP had decided a priori that she was a spy; their phone taps and observation were for the purposes of proving themselves right. Guilty till proven guilty, she became furtive and fraudulent. The police destroyed the integrity of her every action—brushing her teeth, mailing a letter—leaving her with chronic indecision.

The bugs must have been put in our rafters when we were rebuilding after the flood, when we'd had to hire out some of the work. Ida's depression grew more severe. We knew it might be terminal. The mikes were the idols of her spooky governance. She was one of those rare people who will fall in love with mankind. Communism had reached her on a beam of light. But now she shrivelled, dry as stone.

Even in her darkest depression, Ida never stopped reading the newspapers. Bedridden and emaciated, she renewed her subscriptions to *Vochenblatt, The New Republic, The New York Times.* Since Stalin's death, information had been dribbling out about the purges. Khrushchev's famous denunciation of Stalin, his "Secret Speech," had reached her last summer—his long exposition of mass arrests, torture, false confessions, the purposes of terror. She had had to accept the fact that the Great Terror began not long after the time that she and Helen had ridden the rails, when Communism was still a campfire. Stalin had exterminated "Fascist" minorities, the Chechens, the Ingushes, the Karachins, the Balkars, the Tartars of the Crimea, the Kalmuks and the Germans of the Volga. Ida tried desperately to remember what she was doing on the twenty-third of February, 1944—the day the entire population of the Chechen-Ingush Republic, almost a million people, were arrested and removed to an unknown destination. Stalin turned his radiant eye upon the Lithuanians, Latvians, Estonians, Greeks and Jews. Ida gave herself the task of experiencing every death. It was torture tailor-made for an imaginative social democrat.

On the very same day we discovered the bugs in the rafters, Ida had learned that more than a hundred thousand people were fleeing the Soviets in Hungary. She understood that she had taken part in the biggest sting operation in human history.

Grief is lonely and often full of self-hatred. Ida sat in the tablet of sunlight by the window and stared down at the buttons of her dress, her sagging breasts, stockings the colour of Band-Aids. She took a Kleenex from her pocket, blew her nose, returned it, like someone forced to care for an unpleasant relative. But she caught me looking at her from the doorway and beckoned to me. "Come in."

Dianna joined us, chatting, leaving gaps in the dialogue that Ida would normally occupy. When Ida finally began to speak, the objects in the room flinched ever so slightly, no more than the shiver made in objects by our sudden perception, an almost invisible standing-to. "Do you see the days get a little longer?" she asked.

"The days are very long now!"

"Yes! And the snow is melting!"

"You don't have to go overboard on my account," said Ida. "A few minutes every day, a bit of colour in the dawn and a sunset bigger than a mackerel's eye, that's all I ask."

Life magazine saved IDA'S LIFE. Dianna brought the magazine to her to show her an ad for a movie called *I Married a Communist.* The Communist in question was a "Nameless, Shameless Woman! Trained in an art as old as time!" It starred Laraine Day. "Obviously," said Ida, "I'm a blonde. With very big breasts." She was really ill by then; perhaps she'd had a mild heart attack, I don't know, but she was weakening. She laughed for Dianna's benefit, and then began to cough. Dianna opened the window and the wind blew the pages of the magazine where it lay on the bed. It was the special VE day issue, full of wartime photographs. Ida stopped coughing. She went quiet. She didn't touch the page but drew herself up till she was hovering over the magazine. The smoke from Churchill's cigar hung in the air. Roosevelt sat in the middle and Stalin on the right. Roosevelt wore a cape over a suit, looking long of limb, capable of dance, like an artist stuck between two generals, their chubby necks squeezed by wool collars. "The Big Three at Yalta, 1945," the caption read, "where the shape of post-war Eastern and Central Europe was decided." Just the three of them. Doing all that.

"The gods," whispered Ida under her breath.

Churchill, Roosevelt, even Stalin, took the sickness from Ida's body and gave her back a marvellous sense of personal futility. She was a pawn. From the disease of indiscriminate social responsibility, the lion that had nearly torn her limb from limb, Ida had been saved. She felt herself shrink-wrapped, a garlic sausage, a single item on the great shelf of history, just one irregular heartbeat.

CHAPTER SEVEN
1962

I see no end of it, but the turning upside down of the entire world. —Erasmus

Only the gumbo is immortal. —Blondie McCormack

IDA STARTED TO COLLECT PHOTOGRAPHS of duets and trios caught in a moment, very particular, as moments are. Sometimes, but not necessarily, *deciding the shape of post-war Europe.* Sometimes just hanging around.

She was fond of one that was particularly offhand: Winston Churchill standing beside a fireplace with Canada's secretary of state, Lester B. Pearson. Pearson, whom everybody called Mike, is smiling that toothy, wholesome smile, whereas Churchill looks dyspeptic and embarrassed. Maybe what's embarrassing Churchill is the fact that Mike Pearson is wearing the exact same clothes as he is. Exact: The bow tie, the deep blue pinstripe suit, the watch chain; they're doing the same thing with their hands, left hand in trouser pocket, right hand holding a cigar in front of a paunch in a vest. Ida loved that picture. They looked liked such nice men, just standing around after dinner. It helped her to start getting dressed in the morning.

She got out of bed mostly for Dianna's benefit. Dianna

watched Ida like a baby hawk. If Ida hadn't made it, she would
have proved to Dianna that her mother had been afraid when
she died. That may not be reasonable, but it's true. So Ida rallied and tried her best to become reacquainted with the world.

Here we were, with the Second World War vets all grown up
and running the show less than twenty years after yet another
armistice, and it seemed *natural* to consider the circumstances in
which we were about to experience an atomic war. It must have
been all that war-jism. Dianna accepted the threat of nuclear war
as if it were a birthmark on the face of reality. Bill, Ida, Eli and I
were stumped. We wanted to protect Dianna from fear, but we
didn't know how to do that, short of giving her an anaesthetic,
and we did think she should be awake, aware. It was a dilemma. I
had to work a miracle. So—I made a casserole and set the table.

Soft food was just the thing. Here we were, trying to provide Dianna with a sense of terra firma in Canada, with nothing
better to offer than a lunatic prime minister named John
Diefenbaker, an overwrought prairie lawyer forced to play monkey
in the middle between Russia and the States, two superpowers at
high noon. Yes, I thought, in a pinch, make a shepherd's pie.
I sat Ida at the head of the table and passed her a quart of the
casserole on a paper plate. "Worcester sauce?" I offered.

She took it reluctantly, saying, "Why are we doing this
gravy stuff?" She added grumpily, "I don't know if I can eat."
The pressure had been building up intensely with the Cuban
Missile Crisis. Ida spread the shepherd's pie miserably about
her soggy plate and put down her fork, bursting out, "Let's face
it. Diefenbaker's nuts. We're looking at a nuclear holocaust,
and we've got a complete nutcase as our prime minister."

A pause. Bill, tired, seated cross-legged on his dining-room chair and wearing his white cotton pyjamas, said, "It *is* a bit tricky." We all stared into our mashed potatoes.

"We've got to keep things in, um, perspective," I said brightly. "Diefenbaker makes this country seem . . . *small*."

"Small," said Bill.

I passed the creamed corn. "Eat what's put before you." And went on. "Our prime minister is a Saskatchewan man. He may be paranoid, yes. But he's paranoid in such a *Canadian* way."

"Paranoid about his Eaton's card," said Eli. I plucked his paw from his lap and kissed it.

"Paranoid about the air-defence agreement with the States," I said, waving the margarine before Ida's nose.

"Paranoid about being a nuclear ballboy," said Eli.

"I'm proud of that," I said. "I really am."

Eli's blood sugar took a sudden surge. "Diefenbaker hates being a serf to the Americans."

"He hates it!" chimed Bill.

"For sure!" said Eli.

Ida peered at Eli and Bill, *through a glass darkly*. Suddenly she figured it out, turned to Dianna and chirped, "What a guy!" and bit into a slice of Wonder Bread.

Dianna watched Ida chew. "Paranoid about Kennedy," she said, as if in her sleep.

Bill moved over to crouch at his daughter's side. "Khrushchev's not paranoid about Kennedy," he said softly. "Khrushchev's *worried* about Kennedy." Bill ran his hand over Dianna's forehead. "Nobody's going to be paranoid any more, Dianna. The war is over. We're at peace." His lie sat on the table. Ida cleared her throat, embarrassed.

"President Kennedy thinks Prime Minister Diefenbaker is an idiot," said Dianna. "That's what Richard says." She yawned.

"Shhhhh," said Bill.

"Dief doesn't care," I lullabied. "He's *used* to that kind of thing. He's a Western Canadian."

We had strawberry cheesecake with whipped cream in the living room, with the TV on but the sound off. Ida kept shaking her head, saying, "What *is* this stuff?" I followed it up with a nice cup of Ovaltine, turning down the lights, speaking softly, "Diefenbaker wants *the North*, like a *frontier*. Imagine. An enormous landscape with a tiny ecosystem, huge and fragile as an obese little girl." Ida yawned. Dianna laid her head upon her godmother's shoulder. I removed their plates, softly, softly. "One sneeze with DDT and every gull's egg falls to pieces."

"That was rather *good*," said Ida. She couldn't keep her eyes open.

We were stuffed into obeisance. Outside caromed the moonless night. The sky was a bulletproof ceiling, remote-controlled, ready to fall on our heads. Ida had come *up*. And the governments had bunkers *underground,* and the missiles were hidden in submarines in the surrounding seas and in thick lead silos buried deep in the deserts. Ida said she could hear the missiles whistling down under the earth. She always did have good hearing.

⟨━━⟩

RICHARD FOUND DIANNA a position in Winnipeg's most limestone law firm—what he called "the old firm," which meant no

Ukrainians or Jews. It made her an instant "spinster," or what they'd soon call "a women's libber." She dressed the part, but you could see the heat build up in her, especially when Jack was around. Though she was only twenty-six, Dianna considered herself dry around the ears. She sustained a lonely life. She saw a lot of Richard.

Richard was the most static man. He absolutely would not let anything happen. Nervous people have a hard time with change.

Dianna was determined to remain lucid. Her mother had been a romantic. So Dianna was anti-romantic. She didn't realize that Richard was a romantic too. A nervous romantic is a dangerous thing. Richard was especially nervous about Jack.

Among her many dads, Dianna's real father, Bill of the butterfly garden was neither romantic nor entirely rational. Bill walked beneath the shattered sky as transitive as a new leaf. In his white pyjamas, he walked so much that he remained lithe and light. Somehow my dark daughter had given us this bright man full of grace.

With Helen gone, poor Dianna had no mother to kill. I did try to offer up myself; I criticized, drew inaccurate analogies from my own life, read her diary, felt hurt and anxious. I did what I could, but she didn't take the bait. And she misunderstood her father's scepticism. In her hungry mouth, his indifference tasted of bile. She might have avoided romanticism, but she sure got trapped by rage.

In the era of "mega-deaths," of intercontinental ballistic missiles and all that bogus sanity, it was easy to mistake scepticism for cynicism. The poor kid started to believe in some kind of anxiety she liked to call Man's Freedom. (At the time, I guess she was a man.) Despite her position at the old firm, Dianna began to talk about "taking action against American imperialism."

"What are you staring at?" I asked her. She was transfixed by the blank television set.

"Things as they are," said she.

"Darling," I said, and handed her an old sketch pad from her girlhood, "if I fetch you a dead squirrel, won't you draw us a nice picture?"

She kissed my withered cheek. "Peace, Gramma. I'm going to kick butt." Then she rubbed her lip. I'd discovered the energy to deliver a small jolt.

She rode off to deface an *American* flag at the Legislative Building. She was, she said, politically *involved*. Dianna was mad. So was the Hungarian refugee who took the placard reading "PIGS GET OUT OF CUBA" out of Dianna's hands and broke it over her head. When she came to, she was in the back seat of my car, wrapped in the Stars and Stripes, bleeding all over my leather seats, being driven home by the same Hungarian (weeping) who had rifled through her wallet till he found her address, who drove her all the way to St. Norbert, who backed out of the car apologizing, I think, in Hungarian, I guess, who was last seen walking north back to Winnipeg in a most abject state, of whom we have not heard since.

<hr />

RICHARD'S CADILLAC ROLLING PAST our house and down the drive. I assumed he'd be going to Bill and Dianna's cabin by the butterfly field, and hobbled out after him. But he drove on, down to the cup of the oxbow, to Marie's grotto, and parked. By the time I got there, he and Jack were talking at the screen door. In fact, the interview was over. Richard, about to get back into his car, pointed his finger at Jack. "He told you he was from Toronto," he said to me.

"What does it matter?" I asked.

"I don't like being lied to. I've had enough for one lifetime."

"Helen never lied to you."

He stopped. "I was talking about this fellow Jack." Paused. "Besides, she lied to all of us."

I marvelled at the black sickle in his blue eye, wanting to poke my finger into it.

Jack turned his back on us, the door squeezed shut behind him. Wasn't like Jack not to call out one of his flirtatious insults.

Richard bristled. "I've spent a small fortune tracking him down. Listen, Blondie. Nobody knows who he is. Not my detective. Not the RCMP. Not even the tax department."

"That's a very wide net you're throwing." The sun darted through the branches of pine and the despondent shadow of spruce, and hit me on the head.

"He's hiding something."

"Yes. I like that about him." Black splotches in my vision. Richard's gold head seemed to consume all the light.

"He shouldn't be allowed to stay here under false pretenses."

"That's not for you to say."

"Actually, Blondie, I've got enough of a stake in this property to feel I do have a say."

"If I weren't ninety-two years of age, Richard, I would punch you in the nose."

He stepped back. And smiled. "Falling behind in the taxes again. I don't mind for myself. I can carry you. But this land—" he looked around; the black spruce sank deeper into the bog— "it could go for a song at auction, if the municipality decides to call your debt."

"You always were a pain in the ass, Richard, but I never thought I'd consider you an enemy."

"I'm not your enemy. I'm your benefactor." He touched my elbow. Then he looked up sharply. Dianna crossed by the car, angling sideways. She had a black eye and her hair was still matted with blood. She smiled blandly at us and nodded hopefully, and then backed her way into Jack's place, entered without knocking and closed the door firmly behind her.

CHAPTER EIGHT

1 9 6 4

JACK WAS A MAN WHO NEVER EXPLAINED or apologized, nor asked for permission. He knew, perhaps better than any person I'd ever met, the extent of himself, and he rode out into the wild blue yonder of his own frontier. Always pushing himself. He needed to be out of his element.

He began to fly again. And he cooked for us all, mung beans and sweet curries and God knows what but it was wonderful, the scent of peanut oil, the glow of saffron. We'd congregate at one house or the other, and eat from wooden bowls and drink warm wine and get drunk in such joyful sorrow I laughed with tears leaking from my eyes. Didn't eat meat, didn't even drink Scotch that winter.

Dianna grew brittle. She gave all her intensity to "our property," as if it was a formula for the entire world. She quit the old firm. It seemed to be a minor decision; she barely acknowledged the change in her life. And began to draw botanical illustrations of rare and subtle honesty. At night, she lay on paisley pillows in the rafters with a book of Ginsberg's poems to *enjoy her space.* She was elaborately *cool,* didn't want to be *crowded* and didn't believe in *monogamous relationships.* Jack, oh, Jack, he's cool, right, but I don't believe in . . . And oh, the erotic fraudulence of speech.

On such nights, Bill reconstructed his butterfly boxes, pine wood burning, candles lit, the multifarious wings and her drawings; the stained-glass pre-Raphaelite hues belied an ache, a melancholic tension increased by three feet of snow on the roof. I wondered how Bill could stand it. He was oiling wood. He smiled at me. There was something of the rogue in him, a bemused wayfarer on the side of the road. I opened the door and fled to the glitter of moon in snow, to the bland comfort of our post-flood drywall. Crawling into bed beside Eli, the old bear in our cave, I said, "Remind me, my love, we are mortal, please, yes?" He was asleep. In sleep, he raised his paw and touched my face.

TV made us too sceptical to go out. It was just too obvious. Now everybody knew what I'd always known: we are irrelevant. Ida found breath enough to inhale the spirit of irrelevance. It lifted her up as it set her down.

"Flying weather," said Jack to Ida, and he snuggled up beside her on Bill's horsehair couch. "Come up, you sexy mama. Lemme take you flying in my willow plane."

Ida smiled at Jack and laid her head on his shoulder for just a fraction, till she caught herself and then tsked and complained of the cold wind, all the while dimpling at him and barely breathing, but not from her heart condition, or rather, from a condition of the heart. We never knew how old Jack was—he was ageless, rugged and handsome as a whisky barrel—but the illness made Ida look much older than her years. That's how much she loved Jack; she let him make her silly.

"You're a bad boy, Jack," she said.

Jack and Ida were easy together. By now, he knew all about

everybody. He was a gamekeeper, a hunter; he hooked his nets to the trees and we just flew in. Ida held up her face to him as if she were receiving a wafer. With most people, Jack kept up a tough laissez-faire front. He never talked about himself. But he was different with Ida. Whatever had led Jack to fly into "our property"—perhaps he had the heart of a hawk—whatever divisible, discontinuous, stray characteristics had brought him our way, it was clear and welcome to Ida, who understood words very well, very well, the way you get to know someone who has betrayed you.

"C'mon." He hauled her up. "If you won't fly, come out and sit in my teepee."

Jack's tent was an Indian-looking contraption made of deerskins he'd bought from a Native friend of his on a reserve to the northeast of "our property." And Indians weren't even trendy at the time. He sought out all kinds of people, had a habit of hitchhiking.

He hurried her outside, held the flap open and seated her on robes he'd gathered—new robes, maybe not buffalo, but muskrat—Ida touching the fresh fur with a whimper of delight, "Where did you find these?" while Jack grinned and scratched his nose. Ida curled her skinny legs under her old hams, leaning on one hand while she waited. Outside the tent, the grass scratched and blew. It smelled of tanned skin, the sweat on your lover's sunburned shoulder. Ida's skin was yellow. The pouches under her eyes were fruit sacs. She felt gorgeous even though she knew she wasn't. At long last, Ida was willing to *believe*, in short bursts. Gradually, Jack was coaxing her into subjunctives. "What's the story?" he'd ask, a question that once would have

driven Ida to bed in Stalinist misery. Now she'd respond,
"Today? You mean, like, today anyway?"

Jack never waited for "appropriate moments." He wanted
to smoke a marijuana cigarette, so that's what he did. Ida knew
he liked the stuff, and was familiar with the scent on his clothes,
but she was surprised nonetheless. Lanky Jack leaned against a
canvas duffle bag with his thin blue "reefer," inhaling, offering
it to Ida, who barely hesitated and voted yes. Was a matter of minutes before we heard them hooting. Then Ida's cough. Out of
control. "He's going to kill her at last," Eli said in consternation.
Then he shrugged. "Oh, well." Eli was close to a hundred. He
was being freeze-dried without anaesthetic and wouldn't wish
longevity on anyone.

Dianna blew out of the house. She wore three skirts and
earrings as big as muskie lures, beads and feathers dangling
under her long, limp hair. In her hand, Ida's recent issue of
The New York Times. On her feet a pair of Eli's old cowboy
boots. She met Jack at the flap, backed off shyly as he elbowed
Ida out as if he were escorting her to a state dinner. They were
laughing crazily. Dianna smiled, wanting to be helpful but not
too helpful. She gave Jack lots of "space."

Dianna held out the newspaper. "Look! It's them!" Ida's
eyes were squeezed nearly shut she was laughing so hard; she
nodded, friendly, put her nose to Dianna's and looked at her
cross-eyed, wheezing, "Will *you* take us up?"

Dianna indicated the newspaper. "This came," she said,
"and there's a picture."

"Yeah?" asked Ida. "Maybe later. I'm going up in the
plane now."

We hitched the glider to my Chrysler. Dianna drove, and I went along for the ride. A bumpy ride over new alfalfa helped me to forget myself. Into a wind from the west we released the plane, and up she flew. Ida was crammed into a little spot behind Jack. She looked oddly passive, being carried away. The car rolled to a stop. *The Times* was between us, opened at the photograph Dianna had wanted to show her godmother. The glider climbed in broad circles. Creamy white, it looked like a cabbage butterfly, its shadow scrawled across the stubble. I looked at the picture: Khrushchev and Fidel Castro in the Caucasus. Sun lights upon Castro's knee. He is in fatigues, his pants tucked into heavy boots, an army jacket, though it looks as if it's about 70 degrees there in the Russian mountains; he wears a hat, and with his beard his flesh is hidden, like a woolly monk. Dianna gets out of the car and stumbles across the harrow trails, staring up. Khrushchev looks very happy. His pants ride over his belly, his white shirt glows in the sun; he has a nimbus. A shiny thug in the company of a poet. Dianna turns circles in the dry mud, looking up. Castro is happy and well, his big eyes young and hopeful. His hand is raised, a double gesture: the revolutionary fist and a wave, *Salut! Okay! I love you!* His forefinger points at heaven, the hand of Man seeks the hand of God. And behind—the sweep of treed mountain, ancient evergreens rise in the sun. Dianna spins, the face she raises to the sky is etched with dread. Jack's glider climbs down the corkscrew in the air. The sky is full of such invisible thumbprints. He makes a beautiful landing, and the plane settles fifty feet away. Dianna runs towards it. I shuffle across the seat and lean on the steering wheel. Even from this distance, I can see that Ida's head has fallen to one side. She is *unnaturally* still. Dianna slowly reaches to touch Ida's shoulder. In death Ida was round. In a dark red dress with a brown collar. She had given over. At the end it was simple; she'd been delighted. Jack didn't move. He looked from his hands to the field, from his hands and up to the long deer-coloured hedge, aspens still more grey than green.

CHAPTER NINE

WE BURIED IDA NEAR A STOCK DAM on the oxbow, not far from Bill's meadow. The geese were passing through on their way north. But no whooping crane nested in the reeds. No swift fox, no bear or bison, no trillium, no orchid, no lady's slipper. But Richard arrived, in a summer suit.

We tucked her into clay and marked her place with a big granite fieldstone engraved with her name and the words "Reality is not to be trusted any more than a dream."

On both sides of us, the river glided by. There were clamshells in the mud they dug for her grave. We tucked her in and stood helpless in the alluvial field, and a big flock of seagulls tipped up past an abandoned harrow red with rust.

My granddaughter stared at mice stirring the grass, at whitefish snapping at water spiders. Dry, keen, stiff as brick, her mouth like a tiny aperture in stone. When we had covered Ida's coffin, Dianna eyed it sceptically. It was a decoy. She refused to be sentimental.

Richard stood at the gravesite, hat in his hands before him. Dianna had surprised me by greeting him protectively, and she stood beside him now. She happened to look at Richard just as he bowed his head in private prayer. Richard liked funerals. In the background, moving like a gangly black harlequin, Jack, smoking a cigarette. Jack wandered restlessly through our casual service. He and Bill had dug her grave together, a gruelling task. It was Jack who had built her coffin. And laid her down. When he shovelled the clay over her casket, he had a cigarette in his mouth and tears on his face, though he didn't appear to weep, and his attitude, strangely, did not lack respect.

Richard turned to Dianna, his bright blue eye scanning her for pain. He guided her away from the grave. In the background, Jack grunted under the weight of gumbo. Dianna kept looking his way.

"No class," said Richard, nodding towards Jack. He smirked at Dianna. Then that old haunted look of fear skimming the youth from his face.

Dianna was going to stay loyal to Richard; she was going to prove that she was at least as strong as her mother. She'd already let Richard assume that the old firm was just too much for her. She knew to choose her battles, and she was learning the ancient art of feigned diminution. "Tough business, law," Richard had said. And Dianna had grazed him once with her purple eyes and then agreed. "Oh, boy, really tough."

Richard put his hands in his pockets and leaned back on his heels. "Well, the old girl's finally gone."

Dianna blinked.

He considered. "She was—hard to say—but a real old-fashioned character. Out of the Old World. *Communist*." He smiled fondly. Then, back to business: "How about you?" he asked Dianna. "What are you going to do, if you don't like law?"

"Draw," Dianna said, surprised. She opened her hands. "I want to draw every plant, every blade of grass on this land. And in season too, see? Through all the changes. Some of it's quite rare, you know, and it needs to be—what?—marked. Kept on paper. I might even try to draw the things that used to be here, that went extinct." She looked down shyly. "It's . . . I know it's a big job, but I'm . . . well, obviously—as Ida would say—*obviously,* I'm pretty excited about it. I think it's going to be . . . big."

Richard's small, distracted smile. "Well, that's great. Great. But, Dianna"—and he faced her closely—"supposing, just supposing you don't marry anybody and—how are you going to *live?*"

"Here," she said.

"I didn't ask where. I asked how. How."

"I'll get by. I don't mean to be ungrateful. I am."

"No, but—That doesn't matter. What I'm getting at is, this place won't be here forever. It doesn't take a rocket scientist to figure out there's not enough money in this family to . . . to seed weeds. They're losing the land, Dianna. That's just a fact."

She stood back to get a better view of Richard. Having delivered the obvious, he was as if without guile; he felt purged of a long-held deceit, and waited for the world to begin again. He stood expectantly, though even in his still posture she detected an innate tremor.

And a word came to mind, as if Ida had whispered from her grave. *Fascist.* It was a word from Dianna's girlhood. She had come to know it as the word that took her mother. Now, here, with her godmother buried beside her, Dianna thought, It's not out there, it's standing right in front of me and it is completely banal. Maybe it's not quite the right word, she was thinking, and Richard was studying her face, and Richard was thinking, Ahhh, I've struck something! and Dianna thought,

Maybe it's not right to call it Fascist, but what shall I call it? And then she jolted awake.

She would simply call it Richard. *Richard.* Because Richard will never let anything happen other than Richard.

She touched his shiny summer suit. "You're going to call our debt, aren't you?"

He shrugged pityingly. "I'll do what I can," he said.

CHAPTER TEN
1970

WE KEPT OUR DEBT TO RICHARD at a low simmer for another five
or six years. I'm not the daughter of farmers for nothing. About
that time it was fashionable to return to nature, get back to the
land and all that invention. So Dianna's becoming a radical
fawn was normal and *hip*. I knew she and Jack were growing
marijuana stinkweed down by the river.

Eli and I tried it once, and I can see why it's against the
law. I saw many things: that green leaves have a pulse, for one;
that Eli's thoughts are honeycombs, for two. I can't remember
what was three.

The young were as messy as us. If it weren't for Bill, who
refined our collective, we'd have looked like hippies. Eli was
ancient and I was close behind and getting really tired of washing. I was busy. I watched the passing river. So the years covered
us in sweet decay.

My granddaughter's volcanic soul produced illustrations
that were never merely decorative. The way Dianna painted
meadow rue, even blue flag, was uneasy, the very atoms had been
destroyed so they could be reassembled on the page, where they
shivered with certainty. Exposed ovaries, stamens, fruit, in the
perfect restraint of scale, utterly sexual yet without the flagrant
exaggerations associated with lust. This made them all the more

potent and bold. I tried to speak of it once with her. "They are so . . . reproductive." Dianna looked at me, as formal as her art. "You know," I added, "you look like a purple coneflower." She let me brush her long hair from her shoulder.

Jack wandered, women followed. They often showed up at the front gate, traipsing down the road to find Jack, who was likely cutting firewood or tilling his vegetable garden. He poured these ghoulish blondes tea and chatted with them about music, and eventually they left by the same route, blandly disappointed. The Americans had been exfoliating the North Vietnamese jungle. We watched it on TV. The ground troops seemed like Peace Corps workers while the air force was burning people alive.

Jack sat silently with us to watch "jungle." He was drinking a lot by then, tumblers of Irish whiskey, as if it were apple juice. A prize drinker, he never appeared drunk or hungover. Dianna accompanied Jack only as far as the brink of his travels, which turned into binges. We came to understand that he was different when he was out. Young men, as well as women, followed him home, and it appeared they were disappointed to discover a flannel homesteader, apparently sober.

Eli and I sat on the verandah bundled up against a chill. We had long since celebrated Eli's more-or-less hundredth birthday (a happy-faced occasion that made Eli cough the phlegm from his throat and spit into his handkerchief). He was melding with his blankets; you could hardly make him out. The only thing that kept us going was a good jog on the Rototiller. The garden was what we shared (besides an evening nip) with Jack. With his help, we grew enough to take to market as we had in the old days.

We were shuffling with the tomato plants one day when three young hobos suddenly presented themselves at the garden's edge. They looked hungry. I suspect they were suburban brats in disguise. Their camouflage, a sort of Halloween get-up, was vaguely something, and when I asked where they'd come from—thinking, outskirts of Regina—one sallow pup replied, "Shangri-La," while the girls tittered, and I said, "They must be devastated by your absence." This kid had a habit of nodding his head like he was *grooving* to implanted music. Nodding, he intoned, "Everywhere is Shangri-La, man; you just have to tune it in." Eli looked up from his weeding, a great smile splashed across his face, and he laughed appreciatively, saying, "Tune it in." He pivoted on his wooden leg and resumed his husbandry, mimicking the child perfectly: "Everywhere is Shangri-La, man . . ." Noddy, well, nodded.

We let them camp on "our property." They were perfectly nice, if limp and wilted. Jack was the high priest of their vagrant religion. The two girls were obviously in love with him, but Jack seemed to have lost the coitus impulse, perhaps from drink, and they were too young besides. They went by the names of Aquarius and Pisces.

Eli tried to engage them in political discussions. They'd made camp by the firepit, where I recall Eli bedding me in his days as a cowboy, and there remained a kitchen chair of chipped teal where he would sit, seeking conversation. He thought they were disenfranchised radicals, and in his confusion, he believed that he caught a whiff of brine. Noddy was in Cubs when Kennedy was assassinated. They all knew that Pierre Trudeau was prime minister, and they agreed, he used to be an okay French dude but he'd turned Fascist like that CIA pig Nixon since he let the U.S. do that atom bomb *thing*. This was news to Eli, and he innocently asked, "What *thing?*" But the kids were tired out by all this political rap; you know, man, that shit de*presses* me.

For comfort, Eli went to Bill. Bill had built up the butter-fly garden to enormous proportions. The entire meadow was wildly cultivated with asters and black-eyed Susan, catmint, milkweed and little bluestem. At the centre of the meadow, surrounded by marigold, coreopsis, globe thistle, he'd built a small square room with a canvas roof and mosquito-net walls, and he'd installed a desk and several chairs. He was composing a book, "a manual of the butterflies," with his own sketches and photographs. "The wings are clothed in a dust-like substance, which is in reality a flattened scale," Bill was scribbling when Eli rather shyly lumbered up and banged on the fragile screen door. "Beautifully ribbed with a series of projected teeth at one end"—Bill smiled at Eli and indicated a low canvas deck chair, into which Eli descended for perhaps the rest of his life, while Bill finished—"and single pedicel at the other. These scales are arranged in regular, overlapping rows, like the scales on a fish." Eli sighed peacefully; the soft whistle of Bill's writing, like wings against a screen. "The scales are the butterfly's orna-mental armour." "Armour," said Bill aloud, and he put down his pen.

Right off the hop: "Why do they eat rice?" asked Eli of Bill. "What's the matter with potatoes?"

Bill tipped his head and placed his fingertips together, as he liked to do. "It upsets you?" he asked.

"Well, yes!" Disconsolate, Eli looked out at the yellow blooms. "Christamighty, I sound like Richard," he said, truly miserable.

"It's not the rice," said Bill.

"Sure it is. The entire contraption, all the bare feet, and honest to Pete, I hate myself. Why should I hate myself? I'm so damn *mad* at them I could spit."

"I'll ask them to go."

"No, don't do that."

They sat quietly for several moments. Seagulls strayed over the meadow. Fighting the need for a doze, Eli recalled the scent of the sea. He struggled against the deck chair and asked, "What is it they see in Jack? I mean, I *like* Jack, even respect the man despite his . . . his inclinations. But what is it they *want* from him?"

Bill brightened. Now he understood the question. "Jack will jump without hitting the ground," he said. "At night, he destroys himself. In the morning, he rises."

"But that's just a strong constitution. That's what they want? A strong gut for drink?"

"Counterfeit," said Bill. "They need counterfeit. They think it is the way to stay . . . light. Everything is *too heavy, man.*" Paused. "The children are very sentimental. They don't see that Jack plays for keeps."

Eli sat back. After some time: "What about Dianna? I worry about her."

Bill was sketching the venetian of a butterfly wing. He hesitated. "Yes."

"She sure knows how to draw flowers."

Bill brightened. "She has talent."

Eli nodded. The two men savoured their pride awhile. Then Eli said, "Yup. Beautiful paintings. Though—they're not a big laugh."

Bill grew sad. Then: "Dianna is a war artist. It is a noble tradition. Only, the war has become more subtle and dangerous." He sifted through his papers till he found one of Dianna's sketchings, a prairie fringed orchid, extinct, at least on "our property."

Eli, gratefully, breathed. "Ahhh," he said sadly, and shook his head, mystified. All the same, bad news is all right as long as it's interesting. His blood began once again to circulate, prickling in his purple hand.

CHAPTER ELEVEN

I STOPPED OPENING THE MAIL when we got so far behind in the property taxes, when what we owed the municipality got so far ahead of us we couldn't even make out its dust. We owed Richard plenty too, and I was paying what I could towards the interest on his loans.

Richard was sympathetic, even offered to write off the interest and let us start paying the principal, but I was so mad at him, I refused his offer. I guess if I'd been following the paper trail building up like a muskeg road between "our property" and the municipal offices, I'd have known about the auction. It wouldn't have made a damn bit of difference to our fiscal circumstances, but I might have been able to protect my granddaughter, somehow. If we can do such a thing, protect one another.

As it was, Dianna saw Richard's latest Cadillac (pink, I'm afraid; he too was showing signs of age) drive right past the garden, slow down as it passed Noddy and the girls snoozing in their sleeping bags, and then speed too fast past Bill's butterfly meadow and bump on down to Marie's grotto. Dianna ran to the oxbow in her boat-shaped cowboy boots.

Richard got out and stretched. Dianna, breathless, had a weird image of herself holding a clamshell like a shield. He smiled at her with more indifference than he'd ever shown before. "Well," he said, "I think I just saved your collective butts." He used the occasional colloquialism now; generally, the world was bound to get more liberal. "Come." He took her arm. "Take me on a tour."

Dianna shook her arm free. She was mute. Nearby, the graves of Peter and Alice and Ida's pink fieldstone, and from the bush, through the stifling summer heat, an insect drone that might have been Marie's refrain.

Dianna thought it was Marie, a shadow come up from the river through the black spruce, but when it came into the sunlight, she saw it was Jack. He stopped at his screen door.

Richard stuck out his chin. "You know, I never impose myself on you, Dianna. I let you do as you please. And bear the costs. I don't mind. I'm doing it because someone has to." Then, softly, "And because I loved your mother."

Without a word, Jack went into his cabin.

Richard, more stiffly, "But *he's* got to go." He held up his small hands. "That's my one condition. The rest of you can stay as you are. Except those—What are you people doing? Kick the bums out. Don't slide into the mud, Dianna. Buck up. Jack goes. And the—what?—the *hippies,* they go too."

Dianna refused to speak. She turned him her anatomist's stare. It spooked Richard, but he made himself get back into his car casually. "Come out for lunch with me sometime. I'll buy you something to wear. This is a new role for me too, you know, Dianna. Help me out a little. I've turned lots of properties in my time, but this is the first time I've been a landlord. Landlord. Not sure I like the sound of that. I'd rather be your godfather." He laughed. "Or patron, better. Let's not go overboard." Turned the ignition. Through the car window, his tanned, sun-lined face. "Lunch. Promise." Pointed his finger at the cabin. "But he goes. Hear me? He goes, or I let the land go up for sale."

It was then that Dianna began to incorporate insects into her drawings, spiders and wasps and the like. Not only the leaf and bloom of wild geranium, but the entire roadside, the dust, the neighbouring plantain and the beetle. These were her most ter-rifying paintings. They invoked themselves, over and over; this is this is this is this.

That very night around the campfire, guitars and wine and stinkweed, Noddy begged Dianna to "stop looking at him with those eyes." Dianna turned away for his sake.

Noddy and the girls liked us, even though we were *straight.* We had finally been out-squatted. They had no mirrors in their hippie camp. But they looked into the mirror all the time; all they saw, or would see, was themselves. In the lotus position. "East," Noddy said, "has met West."

CHAPTER TWELVE

Jack, in a red wool shirt with that long, loping stride, walks from the potato patch down the slope of lawn to the willow mess at the riverside. Drink has not diminished his physical strength. He lopes down the gangway to the floating dock, which he himself has repaired. The green river curdles, but when you look straight down, the water shows red-grey. It's the same water we used to swim in, and of course it's not.

Dianna has seen him cross the lawn; she sees his shoulders and the handsome neck, the blue shadow of his jaw. But by the time she reaches the dock, she has been joined by Noddy and the girls. Suddenly everybody is on the dock, which keels and gurgles foolishly.

"Man, it's hot," says Noddy.

Pisces touches Jack's arm. "Aren't you dying in that thing?"

And Aquarius teases, "Why don't you take it off?"

Jack's eyes dart to Dianna, surprising her.

Noddy is taking off his shirt and pants. "I don't care if that water's *nuclear,* man, I'm going in."

Noddy and the girls strip naked and leap into the river, up to their knees in gumbo. A medallion dangles on Noddy's breastbone. Dianna is shocked to see how skinny he is, his dark hair and remarkably long penis hung from hip bones like dinner plates. The mud here is almost quicksand. She calls to them to be careful. They are splashing each other; they are "free spirits." Pisces says, "Okay, Mum." Pisces has nipples like rosehips. When they climb out of the water, they smell of fish and excrement. Aquarius is already scratching, though perhaps it's psychological.

Dianna helps Jack hose them off. They use all the water in the rain barrels and everything left in the cistern. The children still smell sour. Jack smiles, but he is always disinterested. He holds a hose against Aquarius's blue flanks.

Dianna turns off the pump. Jack lays the hose on the grass. The smell of mud is intimate. Jack teases them while they move to dry ground, lie down and lean back on their tanned arms and flick water from their hair. A drop of water remains in the cup of bone beneath the throat. Behind their closed eyes, the light is red. Small smiles upon their faces illustrate that happiness is simple.

Dianna decides to give that sentiment its full expression.

She walks away, then breaks into a run. Jack lifts his head, twitches the air. The hot day has turned a strange yellow. Thunder travels through the oak trees and under their feet.

Eli and I felt the storm like a cold glass placed over the yard. There could be hail. Eli grunted while he plucked green tomatoes off the vine. The colours were excitable and strained. I heard Eli, and the flesh of tomatoes and beans hit the woodbox, and the children giggle in the clapping maples, elfish voices entwined with a cold wind cutting into the heat. My back was in knots, but I kept going. Under the brim of my hat, I saw the hem of Dianna's skirt as she ran by. Hail for sure, and this our best garden in years.

Down at the end of the oxbow, five tall pines emerged from the stand of black spruce near my parents' graves. Separated by an expanse of clover, alfalfa, dogwood shrub were the cattail and rushes of the slough, and then Ida's grave with its pink fieldstone marker. Jack followed Dianna. The blue leaves of locoweed lit the path to where the grotto was almost buried in the trees. Dianna, teeth clenched, sucking air. Behind her (she didn't dare to look), Jack would be coming. The scattered rain hit so cold she gasped, yet the heat was stifling. Dodging rolls of thunder as if they were missiles, she made it to the pine stand in that horrified glare of sheet lightning. At last she was unnerved, unlucid. She stroked her breasts; the smell of dye from her skirts rose like alcohol; where rain hit, it steamed upon her. She had almost won, she had nearly proven the simplicity of happiness. It would cure the world. Jack was the aperture through which she would invent her own life. If only he'd hurry.

At last he found her under the pine trees, his red shirt like a lit match. His face was suddenly haggard, he seemed almost frightening when the irony was stripped away. She drew him into Marie's grotto. His clothes hung from his bed frame. The room was the inside of a bomb. He touched her, committing himself to that touch.

When the lightning hit the pine, it passed to the black spruce and over to the cabin like a hammer on a nail. It drove the lovers down through the earth, which gave way upon the ruins of Marie's grotto, the scarce touch of stone beneath Jack's restoration. Sap exploded, pine cones burst, needles roared into flame. He entered her and lifted her up like a burning flag. The roof blew away and they clung together through a snowstorm of seeds, an explosion of gunpowder, a cluster of hot stars kindled between them.

Then they were running. Jack ran behind her. Through the path towards the meadow under a tower of burning trees. Dianna held a branch of black spruce. She looked back, then stopped. Jack slowed down and stood close to her. He touched her face. He was utterly foreign to her. And then he turned and ran. His red shirt disappeared down the path.

Dianna retraced the path, back to the burning trees. The roof was gone and the black walls of Marie's cabin were like worm-eaten leaves. The fire smouldered, but it seemed it might die. She searched till she found the deadest pine, and there she laid her kindling, on the dry grass beneath the dead tree. She watched it burst into flames.

The wind, which had been light and from the west, suddenly gusted and veered to the east. Fire ran up and leapt across the tops of the trees; it travelled much faster than Dianna could run. She was surrounded by fire. The heat hit her as hard as a baseball bat and threw her out towards the river. She was standing in the mud at the riverbank. She saw the flames travel from the tip of the oxbow, through the spruce grove, over the stock dam, through the butterfly field, the mosquito netting an orange membrane; it consumed the cottage with its carved wood and travelled up the road to our house, where it devoured even the box that held the tomatoes.

The two girls fled east. It was Noddy who carried Eli out on his back, and we ran with the flames till we found the road. The wind dropped, but the fire made its own gale. Noddy went back in. He found Jack at the shed, fighting to get the glider free.

The boy got into my car. He and Jack hauled the plane out of its shed and towed it to the west and then angled towards the fire, Noddy speeding nearly into the burning ash trees at our drive, braking fiercely, but the glider was already in the air. It lifted on heat, in the firestorm, a thermal that carried Jack high. The glider's pearly underbelly turned orange, gold, black, and its wings blushed and as it flew higher it became a pale pink bird, paler and paler, and soon it flew so high it was a new moon, a pure white spur with Mars in its hook.

EPILOGUE

IN THE UNFOCUSED AFTERNOON OF FIRST THAW, especially after a hard winter, the quiet is unruffled by a loose muffler on a pickup driven ineptly, gears grinding. Black mud is very black, and snow as it melts turns the bluest shade of white. The road is lined with puddles, and as the old red pickup splashes through them, the sound is softened by the mists of melting snow.

The truck is equipped with brackets for carrying glass, huge sheets of glass that reflect the feathered sky and crisp black twigs, charred claws of burned trees. Occasionally, Bill jumps out, a halo-headed man as calm as morning, and he hauls the corpse of a spruce off the driveway, jumps back in, drives on. He drives to the end of the road, stopping often to clear the way, and when he comes to its conclusion, he continues. He has to dodge the field-stones, but otherwise it's clear sailing for about twenty yards, when the truck becomes mired in mud up to its axles.

This is a man who does not curse. In a sense, that's what makes him happy. He jumps out of the truck and gingerly, one by one, removes the two-by-sixes he's salvaged from somewhere, and he makes a sidewalk over the mud to a spot beside the slough, a ring of cataract-coloured ice with lashes of burnt cattails. Here is where he will build his daughter a house and studio.

He builds a Dutch frame in the shape of two hands with their fingers pressed together, its southwest and northeast sides made of glass. When Dianna arrives six weeks later, she holds her skirts above the mud and ash and enters a cedar-smelling prism. The light, bright and austere, falls from a sky that was long accustomed to branches, arrives like an immigrant pleased to have shed an exhausted past.

These are our ruins: the standing trees like black tooth-picks, the stone floor and the remains of an iron chimney, a green copper box that once held Seneca root. Bits of pottery, scorched clamshells. And Ida's granite headstone. Gone are the deer paths in the woods, the trails between the houses. And of course, there is no trace of the lilies that marked the graves of Alice and Peter.

There's not much left of our houses at all. The land has changed shape. The river comes close. All summer long it will circle her, flow east on one side, west on the other. The seagulls come back, but they're almost outnumbered by owls and hawks because the mice and snakes are plentiful.

The first thing to grow is fungus. She draws the mush-rooms at the base of burnt trees. Then the June grass, arrow grass, thistle, and slowly, poplar, birch, willow sprout up from underground roots. It is Dianna's ideal environment, at the cusp between the dead and the living. Saplings, moist green against black ash. Paradise.

When it rains, paradise turns into Hades. The mice drown in new streams flowing where there once were paths. Dianna will be housebound for as long as the ground lies saturated, for a very long time, because the big roots are dead. The rain just runs off.

Dianna's baby arrives on one such night, in a downpour. She'd felt birth pains for three days. I'm not clairvoyant, but

I'm old and I can count, so I know, when Bill's truck stops at the last firm ground, we're not a minute too soon. To the whumping sound of the windshield wipers, gazing ahead into the rainy night, we see the ghosts scatter from the headlights. "Well," I say to Bill, "we'll walk from here. And we'd better be quick."

Some of my father's old fencing still stands, marking nowhere from elsewhere. We hurry as best we can, Eli's wooden leg causing us some slowdown. Dianna's house is lit up, a glass palace, and when we climb the stairs, we find the door wide open and the mice leaping about on the floor and in the rafters.

Dianna is in the loft, like a whelping box. Bill heaves me up, and I find her sweating, soaking wet. She's taller than I remember, and the hands that grip the bedpost are powerful, sinewy, with veins of blue twine. The baby is already half-born. So I only have to open my hand and she's out. Dianna falls back onto the pillows. And sees her daughter's face for the first time. Dark hair, black eyes. Born with her eyes open.

We're busy for a while, cleaning them up, and only when I've wrapped the infant and returned her to her mother do I really see her. She's infinitely familiar. And infinitely new. We light the candles. The mice play, and rain runs down the glass and the ghosts sit in the shadows. Alice and Peter are there, and Marie, and even the damp Orangeman, Thomas Scott, his clothes ill-fitting, his shoes wet. I long to speak with my mother and father. They don't glance my way but sit in silence, they on their side, we on ours. I search for Helen, but she's not there. My heart gapes open. I do get tired of the raw part of living. Morning has not been thought of when the shades grow remote and fade. Receding in the dark, they travel past Dianna and her infant. Dianna has removed the swaddling blankets so as to stroke and admire the beautiful girl. As our guests pass by, a mark appears upon the baby's chest, a tiny plum, a burnt kiss. Dianna cries out and touches the mark with her lips, as if to keep it there. In the gaunt light of dawn, we make our beds and soon we are asleep. In our brief sleep, Helen wanders through our dreams, and when Dianna awakes she feels the greatest happiness it is possible to feel. She names her daughter Helen.

When the sun dries the mud, we begin again to pace out the place where the garden will be. Bill, with some hired help, builds us a brand-new shack near by. Jack doesn't come, and I begin to think he's among the crows who have taken up residence in the single remaining oak tree, but I don't say a word to anyone, not even to Eli. When you are my age, you can't afford to seem flaky and it's best to appear matter-of-fact.

We live there in peace for many years. Dianna has the stubborn, rather frightened dignity of one who has chucked everything and gained everything in the same grand gesture. She always wears three skirts. She continues to draw: marshland, growth under the weight of decay. We search the oxbow for signs of Helen. And everywhere, there are signs.

We plant an orchard where the pines once grew. In their fourth summer, they blossom. That is the summer Eli passes on. My hands reach for him. I continue to talk to him, and his silence, obdurate, relentless, wears away at my happiness. Death never does become less shocking. For a long time I consider following him, but I do grow curious to see the fruitfulness of the apple trees. And besides, my great-granddaughter has the blackest hair, the reddest lips and the most insolent habits ever known to womankind. She's running across my garden, the sun soaking into her long hair. We're overrun with wild cucumber. She has become a high and mighty young woman, and she's absolutely no help at all with the weeding. I'm tempted to chase her out of here before she tramples my delicate nest of meadowlarks hidden, there, doesn't she see it? Among the blue-eyed grass.

ACKNOWLEDGMENTS

In the course of writing this novel, I have consulted many books, and owe a debt to all of them. I am particularly grateful for the following:

Maggie Siggins, *Riel: A Life of Revolution* (Toronto: HarperCollins, 1994); Blair Stonechild and Bill Waiser, *Loyal till Death: Indians and the North-West Rebellion* (Calgary: Fifth House, 1997); Mary Weekes (as told to her by Norbert Welsh), *The Last Buffalo Hunter* (Saskatoon: Fifth House, 1994); A. Ross McCormack, *Reformers, Rebels, and Revolutionaries: The Western Canadian Radical Movement, 1899–1919* (Toronto: University of Toronto Press, 1977); Victor Howard, *"We Were the Salt of the Earth!": A Narrative of the On-to-Ottawa Trek and the Regina Riot* (Regina: Canadian Plains Research Center, University of Regina, 1985); Victor Howard and J. M. Reynolds, *The MacKenzie-Papineau Battalion: The Canadian Contingent in the Spanish Civil War* (Ottawa: Carleton University Press, 1986); Len Scher, *The Un-Canadians: True Stories of the Blacklist Era* (Toronto: Lester Publishing Ltd., 1992); and John Henry Comstock and Anna Botsford Comstock, *How to Know the Butterflies* (New York: D. Appleton and Co., 1915).

I wish to thank the Manitoba Arts Council and the Canada Council for the Arts for their generous assistance. And to Janice Weaver, Victoria Marchand, Lorraine Sweatman, Alan Sweatman, Dawne McCance, Linda Stecheson, Elizabeth Sweatman, Connie MacDonald, Sally Sweatman, Peter C. Newman, Lindy Clubb and Barbara Schott, many thanks.

Diane Martin at Knopf Canada has helped me countless times with her canny, witty editorial talent. And it is a delight and a privilege to work with my agent, Anne McDermid.

At last, at the end of Blondie's journey, I am able to thank my husband, Glenn Buhr. Without his humorous wisdom, his clarity and courage, this book and I would have long since lost heart.

MARGARET SWEATMAN began *When Alice Lay Down With Peter* in St. Norbert, Manitoba, where her studio overlooked the Red River. During the writing, her house flooded twice and was eventually lost to the river. "Everything about the book is located there," she says, "in a much-loved place." A playwright and lyricist, she is the author of two previous novels, *Sam and Angie*, and *Fox*. Margaret Sweatman lives in Winnipeg.